a SPELL for
HEARTSICKNESS

a SPELL for HEARTSICKNESS

THE RUNE TITHE ♦ BOOK ONE

ALISTAIR REEVES

Podium

Cover design by Alistair Reeves

ISBN: 978-1-0394-7589-2

Published in 2024 by Podium Publishing
www.podiumaudio.com

For Cait,
who taught me the meaning of cwtch
and the correct ingredients for fish pie.

CONTENT WARNING

When I wrote this story, I knew I wanted it to feel cozy and comforting. For me, that meant it needed tense and uncomfortable moments that the characters could find respite from. I think this book's stakes are intense for a cozy fantasy, and I want my readers to feel safe and informed going into it. I've done my best to list any potential triggers below. If you don't need content warnings or would consider these spoilers, feel free to skip them.

Much of this story centers on Briar's curse, which is terminal and affects both his magical ability and physical health. I wrote this relating to my experiences with extreme burnout and illness during and after college, but I think it could easily be read as an allegory for disability or chronic illness in general. Many stories centering "a cure" can have ableist connotations. In Briar's case, the cure in question won't make him non-disabled, but it will render the curse non-fatal. I hope I've managed to approach this side of the story with empathy and sensitivity, but I want readers to be able to decide for themselves if they have the spoons for that kind of content.

Other content warnings include: the death of a parent, one incident of domestic violence (which is not between the main character and main love interest), and mentions of past homophobia.

I believe, at the right time and for the right person, a book can be a powerful source of catharsis, but sometimes we need to prepare or protect ourselves first. I hope this gives you the context to make an informed choice.

a SPELL for
HEARTSICKNESS

CHAPTER 1

It was the eve of the Witch's Rede, and Briar Wyngrave had run out of time to break up with his boyfriend.

"Boyfriend" was a generous term. Hardly anyone knew about Briar and Celyn's relationship, as it was a strictly casual arrangement. If the secret theater of sneaking off at parties and trysts in potion pantries hadn't been so appealing, it might not have lasted. Yet it had—for their last two years in Wishbrooke, no less—so a bittersweet goodbye was in order. Tomorrow, their paths would split.

The difficulty was Celyn had been avoiding him.

Music and the chorus of voices floated in from the street below Briar's flat, barely muted by the single-glazed windows. Every pub in Wishbrooke heaved with witches celebrating their final day as apprentices. Glass shattered and beer splashed to a chorus of "Eyyyy!"

Eager to join the party, Briar tied the last stitches on his outfit. The fabric shimmered midnight blue, gold embroidery forming swirls of shooting stars. He'd fashioned it from scraps of velvet found in the bin behind a textiles shop. It had taken a lot of magic to heal the seams so the cloak didn't look like a scarred patchwork of misbegotten trash.

His familiar, Vatii, clacked along the windowsill, peering sideways at Briar's clothes.

The magpie croaked, "You look like a harlot."

"An expensive one, though." The sheer top wasn't the most conservative of choices, but no one ever described Briar as shy. With the new cloak he'd made, his ensemble would look tasteful enough.

Briar's television crackled as the news switched segments. It was an ancient, boxy thing—static scored the screen unless Briar touched a very precise spot on the top. Outfit procrastination aside, he'd waited to join the festivities so he wouldn't miss the unveiling of Linden Fairchild's autumn fashion line. With his hand on the warm spot, the television's picture came into sharp relief, and he watched a journalist interview Linden. The designer's raven-black hair had been plaited into a patterned scarf over his shoulder. He smiled, blushingly nervous despite how often he'd made public appearances.

"This line marks the end of a very successful apprenticeship," said the journalist. "Fans and viewers are all dying to know: What's next for Linden Fairchild?"

"I'm afraid I don't know the answer yet," Linden said. "I have ideas, but nothing set in stone. For now, I'm just enjoying this moment."

Linden had clear blue eyes, fringed with lashes pretty as a girl's. The journalist sounded dazzled as she asked about the fashion line. The camera cut to models strutting the runway in thick, woollen fabric. Neutral colors with splashes of terra-cotta, mustard yellow, hunter green. The garments looked austere and expensive while recalling the coziness of drinking hot chocolate in an indie café. Linden recounted his time spent in the countryside, the haunted beauty of the wild. His voice was mellow as red wine.

Briar sighed. "He is so dreamy."

"Sounds like a posh wanker," Vatii argued. "For autumn, those models have a lot of skin on show."

"He's a savant, Vatii. You're just a prude."

"And you're late for the party. We'll miss the food."

"*You'll* miss the food. Go now, if you're so eager."

Briar slid the window open for her. Music and the pop of firecrackers drifted on the spring breeze, along with the honeyed smell of lilacs and cinnamon buns, roasted pork and Bramley apples. Briar's flat, with its groaning taps and cracked plaster, smelled perpetually of raw meat due to its dubious convenience of being located above a butcher's. The party smells were a welcome substitute.

Cuffing Briar with her wing as she flapped into the night, Vatii screeched, "Hurry up, and don't forget your potion!"

Briar groaned, but he rooted through his bedside drawer for a full vial of the viscous scarlet liquid. His last dose. He'd have to refill his prescription tomorrow.

He downed the acrid brew and got dressed, donning his cloak and swooping about in front of the mirror. The way it billowed satisfied his affinity for the dramatic. Even by Briar's picky standards, he looked quite good.

In the streets, the party spilled out of pubs with reckless enthusiasm. Charmed fairy lights winked from ivy-covered eaves and pots of blooming larkspur. Non-magical folk joined the witches. Any excuse to party was a good one, but they'd also befriended many of the potion masters, tarot readers, and witches apprenticing with their local apothecaries over the past four years. Some witches would stay on as permanent staff. Others would find job placements elsewhere.

Briar prayed for the latter—had been praying for four years—but he wouldn't know until the Witch's Rede.

He headed for the city square. One of the main benefits of apprenticing in Wishbrooke was proximity to everything that mattered. Built upon a slim finger of a peninsula on the southern sea, the city could not sprawl outward, so it stretched upward, everything built upon the old foundations in a game of architectural Jenga.

He set out to find Celyn but found Vatii stealing finger sandwiches from an outdoor buffet instead. "You should try the cucumber ones," she said from a lamppost. "Crunchy."

"Have you seen Celyn?"

"Why would I be looking for him?"

"You're my familiar. You're meant to help me."

"That stuck-up friend was knocking around drinking home-brewed philter. Purple dress. Philter has something extra, so be quick. She'll be away with the fairies soon."

That sounded like Sybine.

Briar found her whirling around the fountain, half-empty glass in hand. They rarely spoke, as her aura gave him a toothache like he'd been chewing tinfoil. With the number of people milling around, the auras all blended together, muting Briar's perception of them. Up close, the protection of the masses lifted, and the bruise-colored malaise of Sybine's collided with him just as she did. Bodily.

He caught her. "Have you seen Celyn?"

"Briar! Hello!" She had never before looked so delighted to see him.

"Yeah, hello, where's Celyn?"

"Callum?" she shouted. "Callum Holt? He's fit, isn't he?"

"No, Celyn. Kell-in."

"Oh, Celyn!" Said as though her best friend's name was an epiphany. "No. Hm, maybe I did? Hard to remember. I think he had a stupid scarf on. It's nearly summer, I told him."

"Whereabouts, can you remember?"

Sybine lurched, catching herself on Briar's shoulder. "Mmm, Greenheath Park, maybe? No, wait! The Raven's Brew! You know, pub up that-away, nice part of town?"

Briar knew of it. "Are you all right?" This close, her aura made him feel like he hadn't brushed his teeth in weeks. He couldn't leave her like this. It was early in the night to be so pickled. She surged upright and waved him off.

Briar took the near-empty glass before she dropped it. "Where did you get this?"

"Made it myself. Why? D'you want any? I have a flask. You'll never guess where I've hidden it." She procured the flask from between her ample bosom, like pulling a rabbit from a hat—no secrecy charms required. At Briar's furrowed brow, she laughed. "Don't worry. I know you don't team for my bat. Pitch for my team. Swing my way!"

Triumphant, she unscrewed the flask. Briar sniffed it and barely avoided retching. The vile decoction reeked of magic. Enchanted liquors weren't unheard of or particularly frowned upon in the right doses, but this would do more than let your hair down. Get the balance of liquor and spellcraft wrong, and the resulting potion could render a person impotent, poison their magic well so their spells were all cursed, or make them forget who they were.

Briar loved a party as much as the next person, but too much of this would be dangerous. He'd have scolded Vatii for not intervening sooner, but familiars could only communicate with their particular witch.

"Have a sip, babes!" Sybine slid sideways. Briar caught her and lowered her onto the edge before she fell in the fountain. She put her head between her knees.

He checked around them. Most of the people nearby were drunk or distracted. He slipped a stick of charcoal out of his pocket and pulled up his sleeve. Inky scars covered his arm in a litany of runes, sigils, and magical symbols from mid-forearm to above the elbow. He only lifted the sleeve enough that most remained hidden. Just in case anyone noticed.

Magic didn't require words or wands—though some witches found they helped. What magic did require was a tithe. The sort of tithe depended on the spell. A crushed berry to dry your clothes, a feather to make a heavy load lighter, or a buried tooth to help a garden grow. The rarer the tithe, the more powerful the spell.

If you didn't have the ingredients, there were alternatives.

On his wrist, he drew a rune.

Stuffing the charcoal back in his pocket, he covered the mouth of the flask with his hand, focusing until his well of magic responded like water to the tidal pull of the moon, but sluggishly. More like molasses than water. Electric light fizzled between his fingers. His skin burned under the rune as the magic took a tithe of flesh from him, but he was so used to it he hardly flinched. The magic left behind another midnight-colored scar to join the rest. With a flick of his wrist, his sleeve covered them. Spell finished, he brought the purified flask to his nose and sniffed. The toxic odor had dissipated completely, but the magic had tired him.

He put out a hand to steady himself on a lamppost. The dizziness passed quickly enough, but it was becoming more common with each spell he cast.

Sybine looked up at him quizzically, and he put it out of his mind. He couldn't tell whether she'd seen him use the flesh tithe, or whether she was only waiting for him to take a drink.

He drank. The alcohol still burned going down, but with a balmy after-taste of soothing aloe. A counter spell to heal whatever damage the drink had done.

He handed back the flask. "It's good!"

Sybine beamed and, to his relief, took a swig. The pride in her face flickered. The drink didn't taste the same, but she was too drunk to place what he'd done. He briefly worried she'd think he'd spiked the drink for nefarious purposes, but she she went on chatting nostalgically about their final days in Wishbrooke.

Briar lingered long enough to ensure she was all right before politely extricating himself. "I'll see you around!"

He headed for the Raven's Brew. He'd never been inside before. The floor didn't stick to the soles of his shoes, nor did the music pump through his blood. Celyn was there, drinking from a novelty horn, telling a gaggle of friends tall tales about a prank he'd played on a new apprentice. He looked at ease, lounging in a leather armchair. In his smooth smile and affable posture, Briar understood why they'd wasted so much time together, and it made him a little sad to think that this party might be the last they would see of one another.

Celyn caught sight of Briar, and his smile faltered. Some of Briar's fondness faltered too. That confirmed it: Celyn really had been avoiding him.

While one of the girls elbowed her friend and jibed that it had been she who cleaned up after the prank, Briar sidled up behind Celyn's armchair.

"Hey."

"Hey?" Spoken like a question. Celyn's frostiness didn't go unnoticed amongst his friends. Some paused to greet Briar with mirrored looks of curiosity. At most, Celyn's friends knew him as a casual acquaintance. The only one aware of their relationship was Sybine. But sod it, if Celyn wanted discretion, he shouldn't have left their goodbye so long.

"Enjoying the party?" Briar said.

Celyn unwound a fraction. "Enjoying it more with this cider. My parents sent it from their trip to South Orillia. Famed for their apple orchards, you know. But I gave it an extra kick." He held up the horn with a wink.

"Can I try?"

Celyn glanced toward his friends. None outright stared, but some looked inquisitive. All the same, Celyn held out the horn, and Briar took a sip, giving him the excuse to lewdly lick his lips.

There was no reason they couldn't make this goodbye a memorable one, and no mistaking the way Celyn's eyes stuck to Briar's mouth. Celyn lived only a couple blocks away.

Briar seized his moment. "Can we talk?"

Celyn shifted uneasily. "Uh, sure."

He led Briar to a private alcove. Enchanted lights flitted like fireflies, and in their faint glow, Celyn's expression hardened.

"What is it?"

If Briar hadn't rehearsed this moment a thousand times in his mind, Celyn's callousness might have thrown him off. Their relationship hadn't been serious. For witches, casual sex was fine, even encouraged, but it was kept private. Serious courtship was a more public affair, with announcements to the family and marriage intentions in the cards. Briar and Celyn never had any illusions about the fact that they were solidly in the former camp. But it had still been companionship through a . . . rough period of Briar's life. A cold, isolated time in which his only solace was Celyn's bed.

They could pretend all they liked that the relationship meant nothing, but two years was two years. They'd shared spell-casting textbooks, the squished bed of Briar's gray flat, kisses in deserted aisles of the library. Celyn had been the one to console him when Briar's mother . . .

They'd shared a lot of *time*. That had to matter.

"I just wanted to say that it's been wonderful knowing you," Briar said, "and I've appreciated our time together. Even if we were never serious, we had a lot of fun. So I wanted to say goodbye. Officially break up, I suppose."

"Break up?"

"Yeah. And I wanted to wish you luck in the Witch's Rede tomorrow."

"Oh. Uh, okay."

"Okay?"

"Yeah. Thanks? Good luck to you too."

The brusque delivery undercut Briar's confidence. Why did it feel as though he had to justify the need for a goodbye? "That's all?"

"I mean, it's not like we were *together* together," Celyn said. "You don't have to make a big deal of it."

"A big deal of—I'm not. You'd rather I just never spoke to you again?"

As Briar's voice rose in volume, Celyn cast a furtive look toward the bar, to the milling people who might overhear. "It's not like that. Only, it's obvious, isn't it? We knew it would end by the Rede."

"But we could still say *goodbye*. Besides, it'd be awkward if we both ended up in Pentawynn after spending these last few weeks ignoring one another."

Celyn's face did something very unattractive that Briar hadn't seen before. He sneered. "Come on, Briar. I know you love your flights of fancy, but be serious."

"I *am* serious."

"Yeah, but Pentawynn? You don't really believe—" Celyn cut himself short. It struck Briar like a physical blow.

"You don't think I'm good enough."

"No, Briar, come now," Celyn said. "You're very talented, it's just that it's Pentawynn, isn't it? It's a touch out of reach for someone—"

"Someone . . . ?"

Celyn cringed as he tried to finish as delicately as possible. "Someone of limited means, I meant."

Briar choked on his outrage. He'd worked hard, shared his lofty aspirations with Celyn, and all the while Celyn thought he'd been blowing smoke? Watching Celyn glance toward the pubgoers, another realization dawned. The secrecy of their relationship was traditional—no need to raise the expectations of friends and family that he and Celyn might marry by making their dalliance public—but it had also served to conveniently separate Briar from Celyn's network of wealthier, more influential personalities. The reality settled over Briar like a lead shroud.

"You're ashamed of me." He could see the truth of it in Celyn's face.

"Hey, now. It's not like that."

"It is!" Briar's voice rose in pitch. "I thought you'd been avoiding me because we weren't serious, but actually you were just, what? Embarrassed to have wasted so much time with a *peasant* like me?"

At the increase in volume, Celyn's head snapped around to the bar again. He raised a quelling hand. Briar sidestepped it, moving out of the alcove into full view of the patrons. His blood boiled. The marks on his skin itched. He remembered Celyn tracing his scars with a finger, telling Briar they were a mark of bravery, to practice a taboo magic that many found disgraceful. The warm memory turned fallow with the seed of doubt that any of it had been honest.

Briar's hurt curdled into anger. If Celyn feared their conversation would draw attention, he had insulted the wrong man. Briar lived for attention, and he was immune to embarrassment.

Louder than before, he said, "So all of this? All the nights we shared? They meant nothing to you?"

"Wait, no, that's not it."

Celyn made to grab his arm. Briar danced away, backing out of the alcove and into the full light of the pub. Conversations hushed to listen. The witches watching rugby on the television turned to look. Their audience captivated, Briar let loose.

"You said I was your honeybee!" He flung the saccharine pet names like missiles. "Your pretty little secret! Your sweet candy peach! And all along you just wanted me for my *body*?"

He heard someone snort into their cocktail.

"Briar, stop it! You wanted to talk? Let's talk. Come here?"

Ignoring his pleas, Briar puffed up to his not-insubstantial height and threw up his hands as theatrically as he could. "Well, I am not some trifle!"

"Briar, please—"

"Some toy to be played with and discarded when you've grown bored!"

"Please, I will pay you to shut up!"

"And now you treat me like some strumpet who can be bought with your big, fat—"

"Briar!"

"—bank balance!" Turning on his heel with a swirl of his cloak, Briar delivered the final verse of his punishment over his shoulder. "Goodbye, Celyn. I *curse* you. May all your socks lose their matching pair."

This parting shot gave him infinite satisfaction. Amongst witches, flinging curses at enemies ranged from harmless pranks to generations of grave misfortune. Briar's curse was somewhere in between, neither friendly nor grave enough to befit a rival or nemesis. It was an inconvenience. A condemnation of Celyn as too unimportant for something grander.

That Briar hadn't used actual magic was irrelevant. Celyn might still have matching socks tomorrow, but he'd have a harder time locating his dignity.

CHAPTER 2

Briar woke to Vatii squawking in time with his phone. It snarled across his bedside cabinet, vibrating to his alarm. It took several flailing attempts to untangle from the blankets and grope the phone off his bedside. He caught it before it plummeted to the floor.

With magic at their disposal, human technology might not have been strictly necessary, but some inventions performed better than ravens and soothsaying in ponds. His old flip phone had a penchant for amassing messages, notifying him of them all at once. But he couldn't afford a new one, and snapping it shut appealed to his sense of drama. Plus, it was purple and had lots of dangly star charms.

He flipped it open to dismiss the alarm. Several texts from Celyn awaited him.

>>*what the hell Briar?*
>>*everyone's asking what happened with us now*
>>*the whole night is ruined*
>>*u know i didn't mean it the way u took it. did u have to go that far?*
>>*srsly ur just going to ghost me? no apology?*
>>*fuck u I'm not drunk enough for this*

Scowling, Briar typed out a solitary reply.

>>*Should I post the fancy underwear through your letterbox, or was the thong you left behind a bit of charity for the lowly pleb who sucked your dick for two years?*

He snapped the phone shut, ignoring the barrage of angry vibrations that followed. Vatii's claws tickled his head as she landed in his messy hair.

"No time to mope. You should be getting ready," Vatii said.

Briar shot up. "The Rede!"

With less than an hour to get dressed and go, Vatii flapped about his wardrobe, tugging fresh clothes off their hooks, while Briar went to shower.

Upon his return, the voicemail light on his phone blinked violet.

"Here's your monthly reminder that you're due a refill on Briar Wyngrave's prescription for milk thistle elixir from Odell's Alchemical Solutions. Thank you for shopping Odell's and have a pleasant day!"

Briar groaned. The apothecary closed at noon. If he wanted to pick up his prescription, he had to go now.

He jumped into the clothes and cloak from the night before, grabbed his broom, and pelted out the door. Vatii winged after him as he hurtled into Wishbrooke's streets, heading for the apothecary as quickly as his broom could take him.

Unfortunately, that wasn't very quickly. According to his mother, the branch of elmwood had once been nippy, switching direction with the acuity of a bat on the wing. But it had been years since the branch bore the tiniest sprig of a leaf, and it sagged through the air, requiring a good kick and more prayers to get to Odell's. Vatii's talons dug into Briar's shoulder in her efforts to keep balance.

It started raining.

Not a drizzle, but a downpour that soaked him through in seconds. Walking into Odell's, he looked as though he'd swum there.

A bell tinkled to announce his arrival. The apothecary's shelves of desiccated herbs and mummified animal bits made a grisly quilt of the walls. Common tithes, like clover and snake skins, filled jars in the aisles. Rare tithes were displayed behind the counter—powdered bat bones, claws from a nearly extinct hare. Briar had never liked the shop's atmosphere, not only because it served as a reminder of his condition, but because everything here felt like taxidermy, toeing the line between alive and dead.

"Briar," Odell said. "Wait outside, you're dripping everywhere. Oh, never mind."

With a long-suffering sigh, Odell crushed a holly berry in his fist. The spell wicked moisture out of Briar's clothes and off the floor in shiny pearls, which turned to mist then vanished altogether. Odell's badger familiar, curled up in a cat bed on the counter, opened a single eye to watch.

"You're here for your milk thistle elixir," Odell said.

"Yes, sir, and if you could—"

"How are you faring? Hopefully better, now the weather's warmer."

Briar never knew how to answer this question. Honesty made people uncomfortable; the polite response was a lie.

Briar was cursed.

A wasting illness had killed his mother before passing to him. It had spent the last two years devouring his magic, his health, and his future. He avoided speaking of it because it changed the way people behaved with him, acting as if he'd already died and they were communing with a ghost.

He said, "I'm well."

Odell's fingers walked the drawers where he kept each prescription. He stopped at N. "Hmm, isn't the Witch's Rede today?"

"Yes," Briar said. "I've got a date with destiny, so I'm in a bit of a rush."

"Which were your top picks, then? Bellgrave? Bit of a serious place for a boy like you, but it's superb if you're ambitious."

"Pentawynn," Briar said. "It's been Pentawynn since I was five. Can we please hurry? If I don't get back soon, I won't have time to get ready, and I'd like to look fabulous on the first day of the rest of my life."

Odell had the audacity to tut. "With such dramatics, you'd fit in well there, though it wouldn't be my first choice."

Briar refrained from telling Odell what he thought of Bellgrave. He'd heard a necromancer had accidentally raised up all the rats that had ever died there. Given Bellgrave had suffered a bout of plague in the fourteenth century, the place was overrun. Rumor had it they were still exorcising spectral vermin to this day.

At twenty-one, witches who wished to become certified tradesmen of their chosen discipline had to serve a four-year apprenticeship under a master. Cities like Wishbrooke were central to such apprenticeships, with many masters offering tutelage while unpaid apprentices got hands-on experience in their shops. Afterward, they were rewarded at the Witch's Rede. A witch's services were highly sought after, so cities offered newly Reded witches free lodging for a year while they started their business or joined an established one. City councils requested witches based on their talents or recommendations from their masters.

Four years of magical training, then they were thrown in the deep end with nary a class on filing taxes. Nevertheless, Briar had looked forward to it since his magical talents first appeared—an alarming moment for his mother, who'd had to peel Briar off the ceiling. He'd never replicated the trick and needed a broom to fly now, but that moment set the stage for all his hopes and sky's-the-limit dreams.

Those dreams centered on Pentawynn, the glittering metropolis of modern witchcraft.

Odell placed a box of potion vials on the counter. "That will be one hundred and fifty copper."

Briar's heart sank. "That's ten more than last time."

"The way with inflation, I'm afraid."

Briar counted out coins from the velvet pouch at his waist. Vatii shuffled closer to nibble his blond plait. Briar brushed her away, though she only tried to comfort him. He came up short, his pouch empty. "I can bring more tomorrow."

"Hmm. You could leave me that pendant." Odell pointed at the blue teardrop hanging from Briar's earring.

"Pillock," said Vatii. To Odell, the magpie's language was only a croaking caw, but other familiars could understand. Odell's badger cut her a dark look.

"It's my mother's," Briar argued.

"Then your broom."

"It's also hers." Nearly all of Briar's possessions once were. "And a broom is worth a lot more."

"I'm not running a charity. What about your cloak, then?"

He hesitated. His fingers still ached from all the stitching. Though fashioned for the party, he'd wanted to wear it daily in place of a casual one. He'd worked too hard to only wear it on special occasions.

But he had nothing else of value on his person.

He untied the laces. Vatii hopped onto his head to avoid being pulled off with it. Odell took the cloak and coins, then handed Briar the box of potion vials. It weighed significantly less than the copper.

"I'll come back for the cloak later, with the money."

"Yes, good. Why don't you wait until the rain stops before you—"

"I'm going to be late."

With less than half an hour until the Witch's Rede, they had just enough time to get back to his flat to dry off. Briar took off on his broom. The rain poured in sheets, now accompanied by blistering wind. Vatii sheltered under his bowed torso, clinging to the broom handle. The thought of dry clothes and a warm cup of tea pushed him on, and he urged his broom with a few kicks.

They were about halfway home when the broom kicked back. Briar nearly fell face first into the handle. As he scrambled to regain his balance, the broom gave another dangerous buck. Vatii took wing in alarm.

"What'd you do that for?"

"It's not me!" Briar protested.

The broom juddered and banked while Briar fought to get it under control. With a coughing motion, it listed sideways and descended steeply, heading for the street below. Gravity reclaimed him. He fell, picking up speed, his insides twisting like taffy. Vatii clutched a clawful of his shirt and flapped in a frantic attempt to slow their descent.

Briar reached for a piece of charcoal, only to recall he'd left it in the pocket of his cloak. Panic seized him. All spells required a tithe, but he had nothing with him to sacrifice. He only realized he'd clamped his eyes shut when he felt talons against his neck. Vatii's beak appeared in his periphery, clutching one ebony feather. With a burst of desperation, Briar took it and pressed magic through it.

He stopped abruptly in midair. Vatii clawed up his sleeve, flapping and swearing. The spell stopped him from falling, but not his broom. It sailed down and splintered against the cobblestones, scattering the people milling below. They all looked up. Briar looked down. A little girl pointed and laughed. A wave of dizziness broke over him, but he couldn't tell if that was from the curse exacting a toll for the spell or from beholding his mother's snapped broom tumbling along the street.

It felt as though his heart tumbled with it.

By the time a passing witch cast the spell to bring Briar down to earth, he was late.

He picked up the two halves of his broom with a pang and sprinted the rest of the way. On foot, the trip took longer. He had no tithes for speed. Vatii's feather had been a stroke of luck, but it wouldn't make him faster.

The Rede took place on Gallows Hill at an old hanging tree. It stood at a crossroads on a grassy knoll, surrounded by the shopfronts of Wishbrooke high street. The twisting boughs of the old beech looked incongruous, haunted, a piece of grim history preserved amongst the traffic of modern society. Someone had erected a barrier to protect against the rain. Briar arrived to find the crowds of witches and their family members dispersing. His legs shook too much to get up the hill at more than a jog. At the outpouring of people, his hopes gave out before his legs.

He'd missed it.

The implications didn't register. Inexplicably, he hoped Celyn wasn't near to see him soaked in sweat and rain and dismay.

He staggered through the crowd. He had to catch the head seer—she announced everyone's placement. He'd wallow in disappointment that he missed this rite of passage later.

Under the hanging tree, which was bedecked in emerald banners traditional for the Rede, stood the council of master witches. Briar couldn't spot the pointed green hat of the head seer. Fighting hopelessness, he raced the rest of the way and skidded to a stop before the council.

"Where has the head seer gone?"

The masters startled, looking at him, perplexed.

"I beg your pardon?"

The words came tumbling out. "I missed the Rede. I'm sorry, but it was an emergency. I had to get a prescription, and the apothecary closes early Sundays, and my broom broke on the way back, so I missed it, and I don't know where I've been placed."

The witches all looked at one another like chickens, clucking and bobbing their heads in confusion. Perhaps no witch had ever missed such an important rite before.

Derringer, Master of Enchantments, cleared his throat.

Briar's encounters with Derringer were numerous and unpleasant. Numerous because, given Briar's aptitude for spellcraft, he'd worked under Derringer more than any other master. Unpleasant because Derringer had an aura like a funeral dirge. Briar had first met him on initiation day, when all apprentices were paired with masters. Despite Briar's talent, Derringer always found fault in his achievements. When Derringer caught him doing work on behalf of the other apprentices for quick cash, he'd threatened to drop Briar as an apprentice if he was caught again.

It narrowed his dwindling earning potential. Living in Wishbrooke wasn't free, and his apprenticeship ate the hours he could work a paid job, so he needed the money however he could come by it. Every encounter with Derringer felt like a misstep, and this was no different.

"Seer Niamh left on pilgrimage to recover her strength after the Rede," Derringer said.

Briar persisted. "Then did any of you hear where my placement is?"

"Unfortunately, Niamh divined a placement for you. A special circumstance. We weren't privy to the details."

Though the word "special" sparked Briar's hopes, Derringer's obstinacy chafed. "What's the use in that? Why are we deciding my future by divine tea leaves and loose teeth? What was the point of working hard as an apprentice if my destiny is chosen by a doddering old—"

"That's enough, Mr. Wyngrave!"

"—woman who can't be bothered to ensure I get my placement before she portals off?"

Derringer bristled with all the unprofessional things he'd likely say if his colleagues weren't watching. Briar didn't care. He'd put every penny he earned into this. He'd missed social events, holidays, and plenty of meals in order to fit his work in between magical study and the odd job to keep him afloat. He'd paid for it in debt and stress and sleepless nights.

His mother's dying wish had been that he follow his dreams.

He *needed* this placement.

The master of potions raised a placating hand. Briar had worked under her only briefly, and though he had no special talent for potions, she'd always been kind to him. "It's possible you could get in touch with Seer Niamh personally."

"What's her number?" he asked.

She looked pitying. "Niamh does not have a phone. You'll have to reach her by SoothSight."

"I don't have any—"

"I have ghost orchid pollen I can lend you. If the other masters approve?"

Most nodded their agreement, but Derringer took his time answering. Briar had met his ilk before. From shop managers to teachers, there was a sort of person who enjoyed lording their power over those from whom they stood to lose nothing by helping.

At length, he said, "Fine."

The master of potions led Briar to her shop down the street. Pinching a measured portion of ghost orchid pollen into Briar's cupped hands, she instructed him to take it straight to any stagnant water. Despite his anger and earlier outburst, he felt selfish. The tiny teaspoon of powder cost a great deal. If he'd been at the Rede on time, there'd be no need. It grated against his independence, but he had little alternative.

He thanked her and carefully carried the pinch of pollen back to his smelly flat.

He sat on a stool in his bathroom, filling the sink and washing every grain from the creases in his palms. It turned the water a metallic blue, rippling as if struck by sound waves. His reflection stared back from it. Still dripping wet, his hair a tangled mess. He'd looked better.

Vatii shuffled along the rim of the sink. "Call her."

Briar pictured Niamh's face. She'd visited apprentices to check on their progress plenty of times and had encouraged him to build upon his aura-reading ability. He didn't often tell people about it, but she'd known.

"A rare gift," she'd said. "Fortune smiles on you."

"If it were a gift that could make me a fortune, I'd have more to smile about," he'd said.

Niamh's aura smelled like tobacco smoke in an old pub but pricked like the torn edge on an aluminum tin. She had dropped the facade of a wise seer and spoke plainly with him, which had been a blessing and a curse. At least twice, she'd called him an idiot.

Briar waited with his feet pulled up on the stool, cheek resting against his knees, looking out the door at his flat. It was so small that the kitchen, living room, and bedroom were all one and the same. He'd covered a crack in the wall with his vision board, filled with garment sketches and magazine clippings of Linden's face. Despite the disappointing day, his heart managed an excited plonk at the sight of his postcards depicting Pentawynn's glass spires. Though he'd never been there himself, his friends had brought him souvenirs.

This wasn't as exciting as sharing the Witch's Rede with his peers, but he'd still discover whether he'd be traveling to the city of his dreams. He could plan his future.

Vatii sensed his excitement. "I know you've got your hopes set on Pentawynn, but if you get a different placement, you'll still be a great witch."

"It's Pentawynn or death for me, Vatii."

A flash of refracted light off the mirror drew his attention back to the sink. The water's ripples moved faster, until droplets vibrated on its surface. Niamh's scratchy voice came through in fits and starts.

"Who's—connection's dog shite. Hello?"

Her image shone through as the ripples vanished, leaving the water's surface glassy and smooth. Niamh's countenance peered at him. She wore black and the same expression most professors did when dealing with Briar—a pinched look of long-suffering patience, frayed to the point of breaking.

"Briar, the state of you. Why weren't you at the Rede?"

He leaned forward, nearly tipping his stool over. He spoke fast, the words all blurring together, recounting in unnecessary detail the catastrophe of his day.

Until Niamh appeared to look away from him at something or someone in her environment. "Hmm? No, no bother. One of my apprentices missed the Rede. He's called me through my pint."

Briar ignored the implication that he was talking to Niamh from the surface of her beer. "Are you even listening?"

A woman with gray-streaked hair appeared next to Niamh and spoke with the same musical accent. "Who's that?"

"Wind your neck in, Maebh."

Maebh rolled her eyes and vanished out of view.

Niamh said, "I suppose you'll be wanting to know where you're being sent, then?"

"Yes!"

"An unusual circumstance, yours. A vision came to me. It gave the impression a specific placement is of supreme importance."

"Where?" he prompted.

Niamh paused to answer. The prospect of finally knowing clattered around in his chest like a spool on a sewing machine. He'd awaited this day for years. He hadn't expected to find out while crouched, gargoyle-like, over his bathroom sink, but that no longer mattered.

His desire for Pentawynn was tied deeply to the curse eroding his health. If his mother's decline was a measure of the norm, he had six to eight years to live.

It wasn't long. He wanted, more than anything, to leave a mark upon the world with whatever time he had. To leave it better than he'd found it. To be beloved and remembered. He wanted to tell the world who he was, and that he owed it all to the brilliant woman who raised him. Perhaps it wasn't the immortality imagined by alchemists, but it was the only hope Briar had that he and his mother's time on earth, however brief, had not been meaningless.

Witches with dreams like that, they all found their fame in Pentawynn.

"The fate I saw for you," Niamh said, "brings you to Coill Darragh."

Briar froze.

He waited for her to laugh. Tell him it was a joke. She didn't. Instead, she brought the pint to her lips, giving Briar an inelegant view of her nostrils. When she set the pint down again, it sank in. She'd meant what she'd said.

"Where?"

"Coill Darragh."

"Where's that?"

"Island, up north and west across the channel, like."

"You're joking. I've never heard of it."

"Lovely place," she said with a sly look that made Briar suspicious. "Full of history."

He tapped frantically at his phone to pull up a search on the name. He misspelled it, getting the "did you mean Coill Darragh?" option. "You're sending me to a tiny town of a few hundred people in the middle of the ocean five hundred miles away from here?"

"Yes."

"In the middle of nowhere, with no one?"

"There'll be another witch. There are two every year."

"Niamh. You're ruining my life."

"You'll be grand."

"There must be some mistake."

"No mistake." She nodded sagely. "I've seen your destiny in Coill Darragh."

"Tell me what you saw, then," he said. "Am I rich? Do men and women fawn over me in the streets? Do I eventually go to Pentawynn, where I meet Linden, and we fall madly in love and become the two most popular people on the planet?" Though he'd adopted a sarcastic tone, he hoped even a portion of that was true.

Seer Niamh rubbed her temples. "Do you know the price of a prophecy?"

A chill ran down the length of Briar's spine.

In his eagerness to hear the details of his fate, he'd forgotten the price, though he knew it well. He'd had one prophetic reading before, at a traveling fairground in the tent of a young seer. Only a teenager, barely older than Briar at fourteen. With a belly full of soft-serve ice cream, he'd gone in hoping to hear about his high school crush. Instead, she'd flipped over the Tower from her tarot and foretold the slow, agonizing death of his mother.

He'd never told his mum why the news of her curse hadn't surprised him.

A tithe old as time: you could learn your future, but you could never speak of it.

"The price is my silence," he said.

"You do know, then."

"I want to hear it."

"You understand the price? You're sure?"

A pang of grief reverberated through him. Vatii would know because she was a part of him. He wouldn't be able to tell anyone else. But apart from her, who else could he tell?

"Yes."

Niamh stood and took her pint somewhere private. The noises of the pub fell away. As she folded her bony hands, knobbed like tree branches, under her chin, Briar felt magic creep like ivy up his throat, binding his tongue so he couldn't repeat what he was about to hear.

"I saw," she began, "a man with a hole in his chest."

"Gross," said Briar.

Niamh's voice took on a quality where the lilt in her accent and the rhythm of her words became poetry. "Everyone could see this man's heart beat slow when he was calm, fast when he was scared, and skip when he was in love. He tried to build over the hole in his chest, but his heart was too full of feeling, and every material he used melted."

Briar nodded along. Yes, that did sound like him. Passionate. Sensitive. Vulnerable.

"So," Seer Niamh continued, "he fashioned a mask so terrible that no one noticed his bare heart. That worked for a time. People were too frightened to get close. But in the absence of love, his heart turned to stone. Known to all but known by none, he became a deified pillar of the people, stripped of humanity in the eyes of those who loved him from afar."

Briar frowned. He supposed his gregarious nature *could* be seen as intimidating, but—

Niamh's tone shifted. "Until an idiot showed up and was too stupid to be scared of the mask. With much time and patience, the man took off his mask and gave his heart to the stupid one—"

"Wait," said Briar.

"To keep safe whenever he needed to take off the mask and breathe."

"Just a sec—"

"And the stone heart will turn golden in the idiot's hands. Together with his lover, he will leave a mark on every life he touches, reaching beyond the borders of his humble beginnings, finding prosperity and longevity beyond his own mortality. *That* is how you'll meet your destiny," Seer Niamh finished. Just as Briar demanded with all the weight of righteous indignation,

"Am *I* the stupid one?"

* * *

After speeding through the seven stages of grief, Briar realized two things.

The first, Niamh would not change her mind. (She claimed to be "a servant of Fate, not its master." *Bollocks*, thought Briar.) The second, his congenial relationship with Niamh was clearly a lie, and she must loathe him.

Once she said goodbye and the liquid in his sink turned clear, he searched for information on Coill Darragh. The Magical Travel Bureau mentioned needing special permission to visit because the town was protected by powerful wards. A few sources touted the village as the site of a magical hotbed, the details of which were obfuscated. Otherwise, there was little information he could find.

Somewhere between bargaining and begging, Briar considered refusing the prophetic summons and going to Pentawynn anyway. An empty threat—he couldn't afford lodging for one week, let alone a year.

He consoled himself by looking through Alakagram on his phone. There were plenty of photos of apprentices getting their placements at the Rede. One post recorded all the Reded witches alongside their placements, with congratulations. Briar's name was omitted, which hurt far worse than the news he'd be going to Coill Darragh. It was like he'd ceased to exist already.

Still, Celyn was being sent to Bellgrave. Hopefully he liked exorcising rats. Briar took some comfort that his dreams weren't the only ones broken today.

As if summoned by Briar's thoughts, Celyn knocked on his door.

"Oh. You," Briar said upon opening it. "What are you doing here?"

"I didn't see you at the Rede."

"I was late."

"Oh. So you don't know where you're going?"

Celyn was the last person Briar wanted to talk to. With a sting of grief, he realized the only person he would've shared his disappointment with was his mother. She'd have known exactly what to say to comfort him. Instead, he had Celyn. His aura of spring rain and ice cream melting over fingers no longer appealed. Looking at him across his flat, Briar wished the conversation at the Raven's Brew had gone any other way. It galled him to think he'd spent so much time with someone who thought of him as unimportant and shameful by association.

"Did you speak to the head seer—"

"What do you want, Celyn?" Briar said. "Aren't you afraid someone might have seen you coming here? What will all your posh friends think?"

"Oh, don't be like that. Really, where's your placement, Briar? Is it in Pentawynn?"

Asked directly, Briar couldn't avoid the truth. "No," he said bitterly. "A place called Coill Darragh."

"Well, that's a shame." Something in his tone rankled. Not bristling and eager for a fight, but calm. Smug.

"I heard you've been sent to Bellgrave," Briar said.

"Yes, but my family's pulled a few strings."

"And you're going to Pentawynn," Briar concluded. Celyn hadn't come to make amends. He'd come to gloat.

From his pocket, Celyn produced a train ticket with gold-embossed letters. The destination, in a curling font, was Pentawynn.

Briar willed his locked jaw to open. "The accommodation won't be covered—" He cut himself short. "But I suppose your parents can help you there as well. Must be nice."

It was a cheap shot to throw his mother's death in Celyn's face. They'd started sleeping together not long after she'd passed away. Celyn had known, but Briar didn't speak about her often, nor about the curse that took her. He didn't want to be bedded or befriended out of pity. Looking back, his desperate loneliness was obvious.

Celyn said, "It's not as if I didn't work hard to earn it."

And just like that, Briar's blood pounded. Sure, Celyn had worked hard. But while Briar filled his every hour in Wishbrooke working odd jobs to pay for rent, books, and tithes, Celyn went on beachside holidays. Even if Briar's mother *had* been alive, she'd never have been able to rearrange Briar's future to suit their whim. There was such indignity in his toil. Time wasted. He could have spent that time with his mother while she was alive. He'd lost her, the only one who'd believed in him. He'd fitted apprentice work and jobs in between outpourings of grief that threatened to drown him, in between missing her so bitterly that loneliness pushed him into the arms of a man who disdained him, though he'd been too blind and desperate to see it.

He pointed at the door. "Get out."

"What? Why are you so angry? I only came to—"

"You came to lord it over me, and now you have. Well done. It must be so *satisfying* to have the power to bend everything to your will with some money and a few phone calls."

"That's hardly—"

Briar was shoving him toward the door. "Some of us don't have that luxury. But do you know what? Sod it. I don't need it. I don't *want* it."

Blustering, Celyn said, "Christ, you're such a diva lately."

"I'll see you in Pentawynn, Celyn, but I'll get there with actual hard work. I'll *earn* it. And I'll do it *on my own*."

He slammed the door in Celyn's face.

CHAPTER 3

That summer, Briar worked three jobs. One at a clothing chain, the second stocking shelves at a tithe shop, the third at an ice cream parlor—his favorite. They charmed each flavor with the sort of mundane magic he liked. Pistachio helped you tell funny jokes. Chocolate gave you the fuzzy feeling of a hug.

It was enough to pay his rent in Wishbrooke and buy back his cloak from Odell. In his meager spare time, Briar scribbled ideas for his shop in Coill Darragh. With his remaining money, he squirrelled away tithes and materials.

After work one September evening, Briar returned to his cramped, smelly flat and found an envelope on the floor. Inside was a letter and a folded paper plane with runes inked on the wings. A waxy coating prevented it from dissolving in the rain.

They were from the Coill Darragh alderman. The letter read:

Briar Wyngrave,
The paper plane is charmed to lead you to Coill Darragh. Tell it "show me the way" when it's time to go. Be sure to wait at the border, where I'll meet you at noon. Don't pass through the wards.
Signed, Rowan O'Shea

Briar checked on his broom. It stood in a pot of growth elixir—he had fished frogspawn out of a stream for the brew. The fractures he'd healed with bandages and salve. It took all summer, but the branch had grown a few buds on the twiggy end. It would be strong enough to fly.

Brooms were fashioned from the branch of a hanged man's tree. Since hangings were outlawed, the trees still standing were protected and pruned judiciously. This elm broom had been passed through generations of his family, even to ancestors who'd been non-magical. In spite of hard times, they'd always resisted the urge to sell it.

It had served his mother well, and now it would carry him to his destiny. Much as he dreaded going to Coill Darragh, bittersweet as it would be to leave Wishbrooke behind, he would have to make the best of it.

The sun shone clear on the cool September morning as Briar prepared for his journey. He stood outside his flat with three pieces of luggage containing everything he owned. Ropes bound the luggage together. Vatii perched atop it all, flicking her tail.

"I still think we should have bought badger fangs to fit everything in one suitcase," she said.

"Too expensive. Your feathers will do." Briar kept them whenever she molted. He had enough to last the journey to Coill Darragh. Lots of floating luggage was better than one item that weighed a ton and broke his broom. He took several feathers from his belt of tithes and pressed them against the luggage, dredging magic up from the churning well within him. One by one, the cases rose and hovered above the pavement.

He unfolded the wings of the paper plane from the Coill Darragh alderman.

"Show me the way," he whispered.

The plane glowed from within like a paper lantern, floated in front of him, then shot toward the sky.

He whispered a plea to his broom as he hopped on. It shivered before obeying his call. The chain of luggage swung below, aided by the charms of Vatii's feathers. He lolled through the air, guiding the broom into a cautious ascent. He'd only gone for a couple test flights, preferring to give the broom as much time as possible in its healing elixir. It had paid off. Aside from a couple twitches and hiccups, the broom sailed more smoothly than before the break.

They reached the coast to the chorus of gulls and the smell of salt and brine. The sea sprawled, vast and fathomless. Vatii perched on the front of his broom like the proud statue on the stern of a ship, the glowing light of the paper plane leading the way.

Two hours into their journey, a sliver of their destination appeared on the horizon. Slate cliffs plummeted into the sea, lacy foam spraying the rocky bottom. The island was hilly and bearded with forest like a sleeping giant. Briar could make out a port where a ferry had docked. Before long, the sea was at their backs, and nothing but green hills below and before them.

Their paper plane banked into a steep dive. Briar had to pull up short, but he'd been flying too fast and overshot. As he prepared to reel around, he struck something non-corporeal. It glided over them like a second skin, thick as whale blubber. Briar's broom slowed to a crawl. His luggage froze in its ceaseless sway. A sensation like jaws preparing to snap shut scraped against the back of his neck. Then, before he could grow accustomed to the way this strange magic clung to him, it spat him back out.

Briar, Vatii, his broom, and the string of luggage flew backward in an arc. He let out a yell, spinning top over tail, the sky and earth swooping past like on a sickening fairground ride. He had the most ludicrous thought that he didn't know if his broom could handle another fall rather than appreciating the delicacy of his own bones, but then the magic ensnaring him peeled away like shucked corn. He righted his broom, wobbling and precarious but enough to slow his alarming descent. They fluttered to the ground, Vatii screeching angrily.

"The wards," Briar gasped. He stepped off his broom with shaky legs. "We must have hit them. Eugh, I can still feel that slimy magic. I think it wanted to eat me, Vatii."

"Rude!" Vatii grasped the paper plane off the ground in her talons. "Useless thing could have given us some warning!"

"Don't wreck it, I want to keep it!"

"It nearly killed us."

"Probably the wards mess with the charm a bit." He smoothed out the wrinkles and fussed at the holes from Vatii's claws. "It's still my first keepsake from my placement."

"You're so sentimental. I thought you were dreading coming here."

"I'm making the best of it."

They'd landed on a dirt road. Hills dipped and swelled to their right. In the valley between were the shadowy rooftops of a small settlement. Coill Darragh. With the sun low in the sky, detail fell away, but the forest for which the town was named hugged the border like a crescent moon. Or a hungry mouth.

Moss stuffed the cracks of a stone obelisk on the side of the road. The engraving, which might have once been the town's name, was weathered to illegibility.

"We wait for the alderman." Briar flipped open his phone to check the time. "We're on schedule, at least." He took a seat on the dry stone wall framing the lane.

Vatii landed beside him. "This would be a good place to take up hiking."

"Absolutely not," Briar said. "I'm delicate and not too proud to admit it."

"Coward. These aren't even mountains, they're steep hills."

Though absent of the bright lights and bustling streets of Pentawynn, the countryside exuded its own charms. The air carried an autumnal scent of bonfire, and the tree leaves were gilded with gold. The quiet seemed to sing with growing, breathing things. He might have enjoyed it if Vatii hadn't pecked some foul insect out from the cracks in the stone wall.

"Ew, Vatii!" Briar shot up and away from the wall, dancing into the road and brushing off his backside.

Vatii cackled. "It's only a centipede."

Briar turned away as she tossed back the wriggling thing and ate it, snapping her beak.

The crunch of nearby footsteps drew their attention. A figure came around the bend in the road, tall and broad. His countenance struck a strange resemblance to the dry stone walls and the obelisk and the craggy hillsides. Square-jawed and bearded, he looked carved of rock and softened by moss. The closer he got, the larger he seemed.

"Now that's a mountain I would climb," Briar whispered to Vatii.

"And you call me disgusting."

"Briar?" said the mountain man.

He crossed through the wards, and his aura washed over Briar. It was the taste of hot stew on a rainy night; it was soft like hand-knit mittens. Carved through it was a magical scar with a signature all its own. Like a shadow in a dark room when you couldn't quite place what made it. From within the collar of his wool cloak, a visible scar—the source of the one that marred his aura—crawled up his throat, over his face, and branched up into his hairline. The hair it touched was threaded with white.

Briar put on his most charming smile. "That's me. What's your name?"

"Rowan. Here." He held something out in his hand. A bracelet of leather cord and copper wire, woven through a wardstone with a rune engraved on it. It would grant Briar passage through the wards.

He took it with a coquettish tilt to his head. "For me? You could ask me out to dinner first." At Rowan's confused look, he elaborated, "A gift of jewelry is very forward."

"It's for the wards."

"I know. I'm teasing you."

Vatii nipped his earlobe. "You're incorrigible! Stop flirting, you're making him uncomfortable."

Briar didn't think so. "Could you help me put it on?" He held out his wrist. Rowan tied the bracelet on with surprising dexterity for his big hands. "And now the wards won't try to eat me?"

"No."

"And this bracelet won't fall off?"

"Charmed not to."

"So you're the alderman?"

"Mm."

"You seem young to be. How old are you? Twenty-five? Twenty-six?"

"Twenty-nine."

"How did you become alderman?"

"Long story."

Briar remained undeterred by the monosyllabic responses. They provided brief tastes of a lilting accent like Niamh's, with syllables that pitched upward and downward.

He looked back at his broom and the pile of luggage strewn across the road. "Is it far, the rest of the way to town?"

"No," Rowan said. He passed Briar to heft each case, using the ropes as handles.

Briar stared. "Oh, all of them." Even Vatii's chirp sounded impressed.

"This way."

Briar followed, pausing briefly at the space where he could feel the wards prickling against his skin. He stepped through one foot at a time, marveling at the way the magic that once clung to him now slid off like oil separating from water. He'd paused long enough that Rowan stopped, a question in his arched brow.

Briar flexed his fingers. "The wards feel weird. Juicy."

Rowan said, "This way."

"Are you sure you don't want me to carry at least one of those?"

"You're grand."

They set off into town. Built into the hills, the thatched cottages stumbled into one another haphazardly. The streets twisted such that you could never see all the way down a lane. There was something nostalgic about the place. Old and yearning, stretched across time. Few cars parked along the lanes, and even fewer neon lights lit the storefronts. People walked at an amble, unlike the brisk, purposeful strides of city-goers.

Rowan and Briar reached the square, with a fountain and a statue of a man holding a potion bottle in the center. A church stood tall and proud behind it, a bas-relief of elaborate knotwork over its lintel. Magical scars pocked and streaked its stone walls. Briar could make out gouges in the stone and bloody purple magic coiling through them. Their auras coiled through Briar too, coarse like steel wool. All living things had auras, but sometimes significant moments in time left signatures of their own. Briar could read them too. These ones set his teeth on edge, made his heart ache. Though he wanted to, he didn't ask how the town came to bear the marks. They resembled Rowan's scar, which made it feel like too personal a question.

Rowan stopped outside two empty shops, their glass displays vacant. Both had doors painted with the universal sign of a Reded witch—an acorn. Setting the luggage down, Rowan fished in his pockets for the key.

"Here you are." He unlocked the door to one, gesturing Briar inside.

A naked light bulb illuminated the bare interior. The space was empty except for a dusty rug. A rusty cash register perched on an island counter, the noises it would make a spectral echo in the vacant room. Built-in shelves begged to be filled with curios, potion bottles, and pretty rocks in velvet pouches. Only a dusty bottle, containing something coagulated and the color of infection, sat there now.

Briar opened a back door to a staircase.

"Is the flat upstairs?"

Rowan nodded. Inside, he seemed larger, like the world wasn't built for him. Briar offered to take a case, but Rowan shrugged him off.

The stairway felt like a funhouse or a death trap for drunks. Narrow, steep, each step slanted, the wood sagging from wear. Briar would be going up them on all fours when company wasn't around. He paused at the top to see if Rowan needed help. Though the alderman and the luggage filled every inch of space in the stairway, he managed with an undue amount of grace.

Briar explored the flat. A wood-burning stove in the kitchenette gave the room a smoky smell. The bed, with its sunken imprint in the mattress, told the story of how many witches had served out their placements before him. As he stepped into the room, something crunched underfoot. A sprinkling of white granules across the floor. Sugar or salt, perhaps.

Though modest and old, it was his, and it didn't smell like meat. Despite his reservations, Briar's mind swam with ideas of how he might decorate. Candles were a must.

Rowan set Briar's luggage at the end of his bed. He brushed his hands on his pants and turned to Briar, but seemed to lack anything to say, and just watched Briar investigate the contents of each kitchen cabinet.

"What do you think about a rug there, where you're standing?" Briar asked. "Autumn tones? Or maybe faux fur to go with all the rough wood?"

"Ehm . . ."

"Is there a store in town that does rugs?"

Rowan sounded uncertain. "There's a fabric shop."

"Even better!"

Briar didn't know why he asked. He couldn't afford luxuries and would make do with what he'd brought from home or could scrounge together. Still, inspiration felt good.

"I'll let you settle in," Rowan said. He shuffled past.

Feeling like it was only courteous to see him out, Briar followed.

"Thanks for coming to get me. And leading the way. And for the ward charm. And for carrying all my luggage."

At the door, Rowan turned to him and held out the keys to the shop.

"And thank you for the shop! I'll make it homey. Light some candles."

Rowan nodded. "Good."

"So, I'll see you around? You could come visit and tell me how I'm doing. Oh, wait!" Briar reached into his pocket to pull out his phone, flipping it open to his contacts. "Can I get your number? Just in case I have any questions about the town, settling in."

"Ah, sure."

"Great!" He handed over his phone, watching Rowan painstakingly tap each number in with his overlarge fingers. "How many times a day can I call you before it's too much? Five? Fifty?"

"Ehm . . ."

"I need limits. Boundaries. I'm a lot, so just name a figure. I won't be offended."

Rowan's gaze turned inward, perhaps performing the mental maths of how much time he had to spare for an enthusiastic-but-utterly-out-of-his-depth witch.

He said, "As many times as you like."

Briar thought, *You'll rue this day.* But he found himself too captivated by the softening of Rowan's stern face to say so out loud as he accepted his phone back, and Rowan ducked out the door.

With the place to himself, Briar returned to rummaging. In the shop drawers, he found scraps of paper, faded inventory notes. Vatii landed on the counter but quickly sprang up in a flurry of feathers at Briar's howl when a spider the size of his palm skittered out of a drawer, across the floor, and halfway up a wall. Briar looked at it. It was large enough he could see it looking back. It only occurred to him then to look up at the ceiling too, where cobwebs, gray with dust and thick with insect bodies, still clung.

"It's only a spider," Vatii scolded, but Briar had already run for the door. He hadn't locked up, so it was a straight shot out into the open air of the street.

"Kill them, Vatii!" he shouted behind him, nearly tripping over the cobblestones in his haste.

"I am your familiar, not a harbinger of death. And I'm not hungry."

Breathing hard and whirling on his heel, Briar considered the shop in a different light. His first instinct was to cleanse it with fire. His second was to find some useful spells that required dead spiders.

His third was to look to his left, where he felt eyes on him.

Rowan hadn't gotten far. He stood in the middle of the street, brows reaching for his hairline.

"Spiders," Briar said by way of explanation. "Just, so many spiders."

Rowan tilted his head, stoic and considering. He padded back toward the shop, though, and without explanation, went inside. A moment later, he returned with something cupped in his enormous hands.

To Briar's horror, he knelt to put the spider in the flowerbed just outside the shop.

"No, no, uh, farther away? Maybe? How about the flowerbed across the street?"

Rowan met his eyes. He didn't quite smile, but his mouth tilted as he passed Briar to put the spider where instructed.

Then he went back inside, where he caught and gently relocated all the squatters from Briar's residence one by one.

CHAPTER 4

Once Rowan finished evicting the spiders, Briar set upon his luggage to unpack. Equipped with cleaning essentials and gripping them like weapons, he got to work. From the detritus, he suspected the previous witch had very low standards of hygiene; the least pleasant but most useful discovery was the mousetrap still containing a skeleton of its victim under the kitchen sink. Bones were useful tithes, but Briar still wore gloves while scraping them into a jar. Most peculiar was the salt scattered across the floor, plentiful as the dust. Vatii identified it by taste for him.

Only once every surface was clean enough to eat from did he venture out to search for food. He returned with a bag of bargain bits. Beans on toast for breakfast, cucumber sandwiches for lunch, fish pie for dinner.

Stirring the pie filling together in a pan, he asked Vatii, "How do you think Rowan got that scar?"

"I think it's none of your business."

"The whole town has scars like it. Something definitely happened here."

"I don't see how that's going to help you start a business."

"He could be the man from Niamh's vision." Briar cast Vatii a questioning look. "He could be my destiny, Vatii! Niamh said a man with a mask and a heart of stone. He's a bit mysterious. Quiet. Could be him."

Vatii said, "Have you thought about what you're going to make and sell?"

"Since I don't have any capital for materials, I figured I would offer my services for any old magical tasks the good people of Coill Darragh need doing. Then, with that money, I'll buy some fabric and make some clothes and—"

"That was a terrible idea when you first told me."

"Well, I don't know what you expect me to do!"

"Be more creative."

Briar returned to his fish-pie filling, which smelled awful, frankly. Or burnt. As he ladled a spoonful into the instant mashed potatoes, something flashed brightly in his periphery at the same time Vatii screamed, "Get down!"

A cleaver slid out of the knife block and hurled toward Briar of its own volition.

He flattened himself to the floor. The air above his head rippled as the knife sliced past and sank into the wooden cabinet with a meaty thunk. He looked up to see two more knives—the paring and carving ones—slide from the wood block like the last.

Vatii abandoned him, hopping under the bed as fast as her skinny legs could carry her. Running out of the kitchenette, Briar did the only thing he could think to and knocked over the small wooden dining table. One knife went skittering across the floor behind him. The second hit the table with less force than the first. It bounced off and clattered to the floor.

Peeking over the table edge, Briar watched the cupboard blow open and a slew of weighty cast-iron pots and pans clang onto the floorboards. They didn't make it far, scraping along a few inches before stopping. Another cabinet flew open, but nothing streamed out. Then the washing-up tray twitched, and it was over.

"Poltergeist!" Vatii said. "I knew there was a reason for all the salt on the floor."

"If you knew, why didn't you say so? And I can't live in squalor! Rowan didn't tell me this place is haunted."

"Probably didn't know. He didn't strike me as too bright."

"He's quiet, not thick."

"You only think so because you fancy him."

Briar rose from his hiding spot and assessed the disaster made of his flat. "What a mess."

With a scrabble of claws, Vatii emerged from under the bed and flew to the counter. "What are you going to do about it?"

Briar picked up one of the cast-iron pans. "I have a plan."

It took effort to find enough iron items to contain a ghost, but between the pots, pans, and filings packed into his tithe belt, he had enough. He arranged the items in a wonky circle. In charcoal, he sketched a sigil on the floor, then dug a few candles out of his trunk and lit them for good measure.

"You're going to summon it? Are you insensible?" Vatii said.

"I just want to talk with them. Have you got a better idea?"

"Yep. Ask Rowan for the shop next door."

"Then the second witch who moves here will have to deal with it. Might as well find out why this ghost is so agitated. Anyway, you're the one harping on me to find a talent to capitalize on. This'll be great practice for exorcism."

Vatii croaked sourly. "Not the talent I had in mind."

Briar finished lighting candles and sat facing the circle in a dining chair. He focused on the circle, but not intensely. It felt rude to drag the ghost out of hiding without permission.

It took time. Briar wasn't patient, so he started to hum a naughty verse from a sea shanty he'd learned as a teenager while living above a pub in Port Haven. He hadn't understood the words at the time. His mother had laughed and explained, kindly and factually, what was really happening with the barmaid's tongue in the third verse. Briar had been equal parts horrified and delighted.

He didn't make it far into the song. The candles flickered then guttered out in a violent draft. Light danced mirage-like in the circle. One pan gave an alarming judder, and Briar toed it back into place to keep the circle closed. The mirage shifted, purple and undulating, before resolving into a human.

The ghost had sleek black hair worn in a messy bun. She wore an oversized jumper, leggings with holes in the knees, and enormous boots with scuffed toes. She carried a miasma of gloom about her, shoulders slouched and hands stuffed in her jumper.

In a drawling voice, she said, "Well, this is inconvenient."

Briar tried to sound friendly, but it was difficult when addressing a near-death experience. "It would have been more inconvenient if I'd lost my head just now. I wanted to ask you not to throw knives at me."

The ghost looked at him as if she'd only just noticed he was there. "Oh. You." She looked down at the iron pots and pans, nose wrinkling. "You know ghosts are allergic to iron, right?"

"That was the point."

"It's pretty uncool. Like if you were allergic to peanuts, and I trapped you in a creepy circle of them."

"I'm not allergic to peanuts. And again, knives."

"That was, like, ten minutes ago. Get over it. You'd be peeved too if someone came into your house and made it smell like a chum bucket."

Briar sat back in his chair, affronted. Vatii cackled so hard she nearly took flight.

"Okay, my cooking needs improvement, but it wasn't worth killing me over."

"Ugh, the living. So obsessed with not dying. It's really no big deal." She somehow managed to sound aggravated and disinterested at the same time. "What do you want?"

"I'd like to not be haunted. But you're not striking me as very agreeable, so maybe we can sort something out? What do *you* want?"

"I want you to leave me alone, obviously. And let me out of this dumb trap."

"The second one I can do, but I sort of live here. Don't you want to cross over? Be at peace?"

"Look at me. I was a witch your age. Just finished my apprenticeship when I got murdered. Would you be feeling peaceful?"

"Oh." Now Briar felt awkward for asking. Her words plucked an uncomfortable chord, a flat note in a trilling rhapsody. It left his skin prickly and cold.

Her life had been cut short, just as his would be.

"To top it off, I'm stuck here. Spirit's tied to the house 'cause I died here. I can't leave."

Briar perked up at that. "What if I found your murderer?"

"Fat chance. I don't remember anything about them. I was kind of dead right after."

"Well, what about leaving here? If I found a way to let you out so you could explore and live a little, or as much as you can, would that help?"

The thought seemed never to have occurred to her. "I don't know if that's possible."

"I'll find a way. Just promise you won't try to kill me even if my cooking is bad."

"And you'll let me out of this trap?"

"Of course."

Vatii chirruped uneasily, but Briar ignored her. Sometimes placing trust in people was the best means to convince them to behave in a manner worthy of that trust.

"Fine," said the ghost. "I guess you should tell me your name."

"I'm Briar."

"Gretchen. I'd shake your hand, but I exhausted my ability to affect the real world by chucking the whole kitchen at you."

Briar stood and nudged the frying pan again. The moment the circle broke, Gretchen's transparent figure flickered before vanishing in ephemeral wisps of violet smoke.

She didn't return for the remainder of the evening. Briar's fish pie turned out barely edible.

He got into bed and lit a candle to dispel the lingering fumes of his supper. Sitting with his phone propped on his knee, he checked messages and status updates from his friends on Alakagram. He took a photo of Vatii with her head tucked beneath her wing to post with the caption, *Settling into our new home sweet home.* It took ages to upload. Likewise, the live video of Linden Fairchild hinting about his "super-secret exciting news" spent longer on the whirling loading screen than on his speech. The WitchiCom internet seemed dodgy as anything. He wondered if the wards affected it, or if everything here was ancient and dragging its technological heels.

Settled, he took his potion, as usual.

Before his journey, he'd had a checkup with his doctor. He'd had blood drawn and dripped into a beaker of water and honeysuckle pollen, which turned carmine. It had been scarlet when he was first diagnosed, and the slow darkening of the color was an indication of the curse's progression. If he was on death's door, it would be nearly black.

"That's a bit darker than I would have liked," his doctor had said.

Briar didn't see the point in these annual tests. The curse would wreck him regardless. The potions he took mitigated symptoms, slowed it down, but that was all. They'd guessed that his mother had the curse for four years before her diagnosis, and she lived four more. If their estimates were correct, Briar still had six years to make a name for himself.

Where normal curses were cast by witches, Bowen's Wane was like a small plague that had struck a couple thousand people eight or so years ago. None of the victims appeared to have any connection to one another, and no one knew who cast it. Where a witch's curse could condemn a victim to never finding true love or forever having an unexpected item in their bagging area, Bowen's Wane had no such template.

Only when it claimed its first victim, an elderly man by the name of Hubert Bowen, did the aim become clear. It was a wasting curse. A simple thing. It drained you, and then you died.

His mother's had begun with chronic fatigue. A sense that no amount of sleep would ever be enough. Helplessly, Briar had watched as his fat, rosy-cheeked mother, who gave bone-popping hugs, was reduced to a shade of herself. Her aura—once as vibrant as basking in the first sunlight after a long winter—became a threadbare blanket that couldn't combat a whispering draft. Her hugs were bony, her arms light as Vatii's wings. She'd had seizures.

He still had nightmares about those.

The days to come would be critical in preparing his shop for opening, and he balked at the thought of making the vacuum of space below into a welcoming place for customers. He needed fabric, sewing supplies, ingredients for spells, and he honestly didn't know where to begin. Wishbrooke had given him the skills but none of the tools and resources. They'd taught him how to fish and then thrust him into the world without tackle, bait, or even a boat.

He would have to muddle through. He didn't have much time to figure it out.

In the morning, Briar searched the flat for anything that was tethering Gretchen's ghost to the house. According to his textbooks, poltergeists had often suffered violent deaths. Trapped spirits could be tethered to a place by an object of importance or even a ward spell. Searching every cupboard and under loose floorboards, he found no such tether. Luckily, he had an idea to temporarily circumvent her imprisonment.

He'd simply have to take part of the house with him.

While making toast and boiling the kettle, Briar took stock of the flat's available fabric. He had limited options between the floral curtains and the wool blanket but opted for the curtains. He tore out the lining. Between sips of tea, he pinned the rough edge into a hem and ran it through his sewing machine, stitches gliding into place.

Once complete, he performed a maneuver he'd used with his bedsheets as a child. He hung the newly stitched hem over his head like a hood, then pulled the corners under his arms and tied them in a knot. Putting the knot over his head, he managed to make a fairly stylish cloak.

"The flowers," said Vatii.

"There's nothing wrong with flowers."

"*Those* flowers."

"It's not ideal, but I haven't got time for something elaborate right now. I want to look around town, get to know people, ask what jobs need doing."

As if summoned by the prospect of leaving, Gretchen materialized, baggy-eyed and sleepless as the day she died. She sat on the kitchen table. "If this works, does that make me your tour guide?"

Despite how unenthusiastic she sounded, Briar said, "I'd appreciate it!"

He strode out the front door and awaited Gretchen. She hovered at the threshold the way cattle did before a bit of broken fence.

"Don't watch. It's embarrassing."

Briar turned around while passersby stared. He waited, rocking on his heels, admiring the job he'd done on the hem of his cloak. He almost called to ask for a status update, but then Gretchen's sour voice issued in his ear.

"Don't take this as a compliment or anything, but it worked."

It wasn't a permanent solution, but Briar allowed himself a moment of pride anyway.

His first port of call was the local pub. It was past noon, so seniors and regulars would likely be arriving for lunch and a light beer. Briar could acquaint himself with the townsfolk and see if anybody had work for him. Gretchen said the best pub was the Swan and Cygnet, an old barn conversion on the west end of the village, so they set off.

Only magically gifted people could see Gretchen, which would normally make Briar's integration with the locals awkward, as it appeared he was talking to himself. Thankfully, with Vatii perched on his shoulder, most townsfolk assumed he was speaking with her and not a poltergeist.

As they walked past shops and through the town square, he wondered at how few recognizable storefronts he saw. Not a single Fabian's Favours or Calysto's Café in sight. The signs and doorways, handmade and painted in bright colors, had weathered a lot of rain and faded. Untouched by feverish modernity, Coill Darragh was as slow and meandering as its winding streets.

One particular shop stole Briar's attention. The colors and glint of jewelry had him backstepping to take a closer look.

The hanging sign read *Sorcha's Textiles and Treasures*. In the window display, custom jewelry lay on plush velvet and in carved wooden boxes. Decorative silver knots of promise rings, necklaces on chains light as lace. A bolt of rich red cloth draped onto the display, showing off the way it caught the light. Though enchanting to look at, none bore magical charms.

Briar longed to go inside, but the lightness of his coin purse made him carry on.

Gretchen floated to a halt in front of the Swan and Cygnet, attempting to tap its stone foundation with a toe but only phasing through it. Briar went inside. A few people, most of them wearing wellies, sat at the bar and tables. They chatted animatedly with easy familiarity, casting curious looks at Briar. He sat at the bar and studied the bottles lining the shelves behind it. Several looked like standard liquor; others had suspiciously viscous, bubbling contents. One, a tall, twisting vial of liquid steel, caught his attention.

Liquid courage. An apt addition to a pub's menu.

Following his gaze, the barkeep said, "That one's not for sale. I'd normally say you don't need bravery here, but *you* just might." Tall and broad-faced, the barkeep had an aura that rumbled like thunder and smelled of fresh-cut grass.

Briar recognized her. She was the woman he'd seen speaking to Head Seer Niamh in his bathroom sink.

Racking his brain to shake loose the memory of her name, Briar cringed upon recalling some of the unfavorable things he'd said about Coill Darragh. "You're Maebh, aren't you?"

"And you're Briar. One of Niamh's apprentices."

He mustered his confidence. "I hope I didn't offend you with my, er, disappointment?"

"You offended yourself," she said. "No better place to practice magic than here."

"Are you a witch too, then? A potion maker?" He pointed to the bottles.

"No, not a bit of magic in me, like. My husband was. Have you an order for me, or shall I go?"

"Oh." Really, he ought to save what little he had for materials in case he got a job. "No, thank you." Despite Maebh's raised eyebrow and the sense he'd caused further offense, he forged ahead. "I actually wondered whether there's any particular jobs for a witch in town?"

A muscle in Maebh's jaw ticked. "Bold. Won't order a thing, but you're asking for work?"

Briar winced. "I'm really sorry, I didn't mean any—"

"Offense. Yes, you said as much. Look, sure, we invite witches each year so as they can practice their magic in the real world, give you free accommodation 'n that so's you can help the folk here. Ask around town. Plenty of people desperate like for the odd potion or enchantment, but I'll not help more than that after the slight. Apologize proper with your actions, then we'll see."

Thoroughly chastised, Briar nodded in understanding. He hadn't meant to insult Maebh. His disappointment would have been of equal measure had Niamh named any city but Pentawynn. That was the pinnacle. Everything else fell short. It didn't excuse his attitude, though, and a mortified part of him wished he could turn back time, take back what he'd said.

But there was no such magic. He would have to make up for the insult, as Maebh said, with his actions. "I will," he told her, and she left to converse with her regulars.

Briar exited the pub with Maebh's words and all his future fears nipping at his heels. Gretchen, who'd remained silent throughout the exchange, whistled as if impressed.

"You really pissed in her cornflakes."

"Yes, I gathered. Why don't you get out the stocks and throw rotten fruit?"

She seemed to admire the idea.

They made their way back by another route. Gretchen pointed out landmarks—the weeping religious statue, the bell tower—but Briar only paid half a mind. He felt terrible and didn't know who he could ask, beyond every stranger on the street, about a job.

His anxious inner monologue quieted as the smell of fresh bread wafted down the lane. A bakery with window decals of croissants and pies exuded delicious smells. He wasn't the only one drawn in—people crammed inside, queuing to order.

Vatii said, "Something small wouldn't hurt."

"You just want me to share."

"It's your first day, and things haven't gone well. Just a treat."

Briar chewed his lip. "Oh, twist my arm, why don't you?"

They joined the throng. Gretchen, grumbling about how she didn't appreciate when people stood on—or in—her, decided her tour was complete and ventured off to see how much range Briar's curtain-cloak gave her.

Briar waxed philosophical about which treat would be the best use of his money until Vatii pulled on his plait and pointed with her beak behind them. A familiar figure loomed in the bakery's doorway.

Rowan should never have fit inside, with the crowds of people thick as they were, but they parted like a wake around him. He wore boots caked with mud, and when he spotted Briar waving at him, he waved mildly in return.

None of the other patrons said hello to him, even though he was the alderman. Briar gave up his place in the queue to join him.

"Morning," Rowan said.

"Morning," Briar returned, smiling. "Got any recommendations? I'm flirting with the cinnamon buns and the pain au chocolat, but I'd rather flirt with you, so tell me what you're getting."

Rowan cleared his throat, looking askance. Whether because of the flirting or the townsfolk staring, Briar didn't know. "Ehm, can't go wrong with a cherry bakewell."

Briar tilted his head to the side. "If it's disappointing, on your head be it."

At the tills, Briar let Rowan go ahead of him.

"I think the townsfolk are scared of him, you know," Vatii whispered. "They look at him like he might bite. I know the look. I get the same one plenty."

Briar couldn't mistake the way the other patrons stared. "But you do bite."

"My point exactly."

Rowan turned around holding two paper bags. Briar stepped forward to order but was met with one of Rowan's fists holding him back by the chest. In his hand was one of the paper bags.

Briar looked at it, perplexed. "For me?"

Rowan nodded. Briar opened the bag to find the cherry bakewell, alongside a pain au chocolat and a cinnamon bun. In shock, he allowed Rowan to corral him out of the shop.

"Thank you, but you didn't have to—"

"Not a bother," said Rowan.

"I didn't mean to make you feel like you had to get them all for me in case I didn't like your recommendation—"

"You're grand."

Briar watched him go, the buns warming his hand through the paper bag, and a not dissimilar feeling welling in his chest. It was the sort of kindness he itched to repay, and the kind of generosity he struggled to mirror. Not for lack of wanting.

Pastries aside, his trip into town had borne nothing. He asked the baker and a few people waiting outside about work, and they looked at him as if he'd asked where he could buy poison for humans. It was not that they were unfriendly—they engaged him in conversation with eager curiosity—but at the mention of working with him, grew leery. He didn't understand how he was meant to make a livelihood in Coill Darragh when the townsfolk mistrusted outsiders, and with so little to his name that he could barely afford a pastry. A snarl of varied emotions tangled in his head. He'd worked hard through his apprenticeship, but even now that felt like only a tiny step on a ladder upon which others who had been born to higher rungs already stood.

Everything always cost more when you had less.

The injustice of it stung in older, more grievous wounds. If his mother had been alive . . . She'd been the sort to send care packages, to make him a cup of tea when he was disheartened. Vatii could advise him, but she couldn't pick him up when he fell.

He had to help himself.

He'd wandered far without taking note of where. The houses weren't packed so closely together, giving way to farmers' fields and dirt lanes. Preferring the fresh air over returning to his empty flat with nothing, Briar walked and looked out at the green fields, dotted white with sheep and glazed with fog. Beyond that, the canopy of the Coill Darragh woods seeped into overcast skies. Though nowhere near the forest's edge, its aura throbbed like a heartbeat in the soil beneath his feet.

Vatii said, "Maybe we should go home. Have some tea. See if we can come up with something."

Reluctantly, he agreed. Back toward town, he spotted a figure bent near a fence. An elderly man, wearing a tweed cap and grass-stained dungarees, stooped to examine a broken gate. His legs quaked, and he only bent halfway before having to stand again, rubbing his lower back.

The farmer's stilted movement reminded Briar of his mother precariously climbing stools to fetch things from the top cupboards.

Quickening his pace, he called out to the farmer, who surveyed his approach with a crinkled expression. "Need a hand?"

"Might just be a lost cause," said the old man. "I'll be hiring a carpenter by day's end, make no mistake."

Ivy covered the gate like a spider's web. The weight of it, or perhaps the wind, had torn the gate down and rent a great hole in the sod where the support posts once stood.

Briar tried hefting it upright. It was a lot heavier than it appeared, but the difficulty lay in the vines. They bound the gate to the soil. As Briar's fingers brushed a leaf, magic tickled like pins and needles up his arm. He couldn't free the gate.

"It's banjaxed, I'd say. Don't bother yourself, boy." The man said this last word in an intonation that had none of the chastising implications of

Briar's teachers saying it. Instead, it sounded familiar, friendly. And more like "bye."

Vatii whistled and flitted from Briar's shoulder to the stone wall bordering the collapsed gate. "A flesh tithe would do it, I think," she said.

Maebh *had* told Briar to help people around the village. Determined, he said, "Give me a second."

He turned his back and pulled charcoal from his pocket. Rolling up a sleeve, he drew a quick rune on his wrist. The powdery scrape of charcoal was comforting, familiar, but he didn't want this stranger to see. Perhaps he imagined it, but he felt as though the woods watched him work.

He let his sleeve down to obscure the rune and bent to draw a second symbol on the stone wall. An anchor. That done, he straightened and put his hands on the beam of the gate. The magic coursed through him, a pulse beating its way to the surface. He recalled how it had once been like water barely restrained beyond a dam. Now, it trickled out of him and into the wood, securing loose nails, mending torn earth. The ivy crept back, loosening its hold, until he could raise the gate into place. His magic packed the soil around the post. When Briar lifted his hands, they shook, but the gate stood as sturdy as the dry stone flanking it.

"Ah sure, that'll do it!" The farmer gave the gate an experimental wiggle. "You must be that new witch in town. What's your name, boy?"

Extending his hand, Briar introduced himself, the farmer's grip stronger than his own after the spell. The man gave Briar's elbow a slap, his aura overwhelming with a smell like ripened figs.

"Briar? I'm Diarmuid. And what's your particular talent?"

"Ehm," Briar hedged. "A jack-of-all-trades? I specialize in enchanted clothing, but—"

"We had a witch here several years past," Diarmuid interrupted. "She made the best potions. My joints haven't known peace since she passed, they haven't."

Though the rune tithe had sapped Briar's strength and left his mind foggy, he knew an opportunity when he saw one. "I could try my hand at an elixir, if you like."

Diarmuid fixed him with an assessing look. Briar wondered if he'd toed some invisible line, asking for paid work from a stranger. He needed this opportunity badly. Something, anything to make some money.

"Ah, sure!" said Diarmuid. "If you can make my bones sturdy as this here gate, that'd be grand."

CHAPTER 5

Upon returning to his flat, Briar was intent upon setting himself up for success.

He unpacked loose paint swatch cards he'd collected from hardware stores and arranged them on his desk in an appealing palette. Periwinkle blue, lavender, and dusky pink. With a calligraphy pen, he inked his to-do list on one of them in exquisite, curling lines.

Derringer had always told him, *If you spent half as much time practicing spells as you did the calligraphy of your notes, you'd perhaps make a half-decent enchanter.*

This wasn't encouraging. *Half-decent* had always been the superlative prediction of his peers and masters, but Briar would not settle for less than fame and the undiluted adoration of the masses. Thus, he labelled the pink card *Dreams and Aspirations*. Below, he detailed those far-flung fantasies.

1. *Make clothes.*
2. *Make clothes that make people happy.*
3. *Make lots of people happy so they remember me when I x_x*

It brought him a measure of accomplishment to pin these to his corkboard and mount it on a rusty nail above his desk.

"Is that really necessary?" Vatii griped.

"It helps me organize my thoughts."

"It's procrastinating, but in a fancy way." Vatii plucked up the card he'd yet to pin—the one with his immediate to-do list. "This is most important."

The list, he'd thought, was simple, but looking at it now, a knot of worry formed in his throat.

1. *Brew Diarmuid's potion.*
2. *Find fabric?*
3. *Sew something nice for the shop.*
4. *Make amends with Maebh.*
5. *Gift for Rowan.*

As the only thing guaranteed to bring in money, the first was highest priority.

Briar gathered ingredients and instruments and lit a candle for ambience. Cracking open a tome of elixirs, he flicked to the recipes for arthritis and joint pain. He had no clue which would be best for Diarmuid. Online research yielded inconsistent results, with some claiming any would do, others touting home brews and non-magical alternatives, and still more advertisements for patented market varieties with glowing reviews, which helped him not at all.

He wasn't terrible with potions, but his master had always chosen the recipe for him. He'd had one project geared toward creating a recipe from scratch; the final test was to imbibe the potion yourself and see if it worked. Healers were on hand, but all the same, Briar had chosen to create a potion that made his hair turn pink.

That would not help him. Or Diarmuid.

Since Briar was the sort of person who required plenty of walks and sunshine to maintain equilibrium, and this task took him past midnight, candle burning low and no affordable solution in sight, he spiraled into histrionics.

"I'm a failure."

Vatii peeked out from under her wing where she'd been napping.

"I'll never find the perfect elixir, and then I'll never find more work, and I'll go bankrupt. I'll fail to get my business up and running, and no one will ever love me."

Gretchen chose this moment to reappear, floating around the kitchen counter. She'd vanished the moment Briar got home and the curtain-cloak pulled her back into the house.

"What's wrong with him?" she said, perching cross-legged in her usual spot on the kitchen table.

Well used to his moods, Vatii said, "Nothing. He's a drama queen."

Briar whined, "What do I do, Vatii?"

"I don't know."

"You're the worst familiar." He pressed his forehead into the wood table. "You're supposed to advise me. How do I make money?"

"I'm meant to advise you on magical matters and give you guidance of a spiritual nature. Not that you listen when I do."

Gretchen lurked over Briar's shoulder and regarded the tome of potions spread on his desk. "I was quite good at potions, you know."

Briar perked up. "See, Vatii? Gretchen didn't even want to be my flatmate, and already she's more helpful than you."

Gretchen folded her arms. "I didn't say I'd tell you for free."

"What would you like in return? More walkies around town?"

She looked annoyed by the term "walkies" but chose not to argue semantics. "I'd like more control of them. Coming and going. It's inconvenient, how I'm beholden to whichever times you're home or not."

Briar didn't particularly want to wear a curtain everywhere either. "What if I left something from the house outside so you could come and go as you pleased?"

"Will that work?"

"We can try and find out."

Gretchen considered that, floating three feet off the ground, her messy bun wobbling from side to side as she tilted her head. "A pint of water, two sprigs of chamomile, a tablespoon of turmeric, crushed blackberry, a wishbone, and a half cup of golden-eye lichen."

Briar scrambled to grab his pen and parchment, scribbling as she spoke. "This isn't any of the recipes I've found."

"It's my own blend," she said. "Who's it for? Diarmuid?"

Briar gaped at her. "Were you the witch he raved about?"

She beamed, the first smile he'd ever seen her wear. "When I was alive."

Briar's to-do list expanded to include: *gather the ingredients for Diarmuid's elixir* and *figure out a means to give Gretchen free rein of the town.*

He cut a square of fabric from the curtain-cloak to bury somewhere and test the limits of Gretchen's imprisonment. It meant he could wear his Rede cloak instead, which he honestly preferred. Floral curtains weren't the statement he wanted to make as a budding fashion designer. ,

At lunch, he set out into the breezy air, ablaze with the campfire smell of autumn. The local apothecary was a mom-and-pop business, Gretchen explained. Though it had a similar smell to Odell's, Briar found its low rows of individual troughs, full of different dried herbs, more tactile and welcoming than the sterile archive he'd grown used to. He shoveled ingredients into brown paper bags, but one gave him pause. Searching through the moss and fungi section, he couldn't find any golden-eye lichen.

"It's rare," Gretchen said. "You might need to ask if it's behind the counter."

He had no better luck there. The shopkeeper said they hadn't gotten any shipments of golden-eye in a few years, as its increasing rarity meant it wasn't purchased enough to warrant restocks. She offered to custom-order it, but Briar couldn't afford it in bulk, and a small order wasn't cost-effective. If he were to continue making this elixir for Diarmuid, it would be catastrophic to Briar's long-term finances. He left with the majority of what he needed, but the lichen presented a big problem. Gretchen said it was the most vital ingredient of the lot—no alternative would achieve the same results.

It needled Briar. This was meant to be a simple task. The money he'd saved over the summer wouldn't begin to cover ingredients for even a rudimentary potion service at this rate.

He wandered, feet itching to move and stomach growling at him. He'd packed a cucumber sandwich for lunch, but it tasted of disappointment, given the smells wafting through the high street. He sat on the lip of the fountain in the town square to eat, chewing sullenly while townsfolk streamed by. He studied the statue pouring its potion into the pool below, a man with a severe set to his brow and a jutting chin. If he'd been flesh and blood, Briar imagined he would still seem carved of stone. A plaque at his feet read:

Éibhear O'Shea
For his magic, which protects us still, and for the ones he left behind.

A group of teenagers in school uniforms chatted over their packed lunches. They discussed, loudly and in tones of self-import, the party they'd had that weekend, who kissed whom, who got blind langered, which of the popular lot failed to show. The conversation veered into recollections of a game of truth or dare where one boy was dared to go into the woods at the stroke of midnight. They guffawed at the notion, but in an odd way, danced around the subject of the forest as though it was benign and perilous. Malignant and silly. As if there was nothing to fear in it, but no one sensible would ever go in.

Local superstition prevailed, Briar thought, as the girls ran back to school at the toll of the church bell. Their conversation planted an idea in his mind, though. He looked down the lane leading out of the square. The forest crowned the houses, its canopy aflame in fall colors.

Feeding the crusts of his sandwich to Vatii, he walked until he reached the edge of the village, where the houses fell away to fields and the forest beyond. Perhaps it was all that superstitious talk, but looking at the woods, he felt as though they stared back.

"Vatii, lichen grows in forests, doesn't it?"

She gave an affirmative caw. Beside them, Gretchen's flickering outline solidified with a spasm of emotion, her face frozen in a mask of terror.

"You're not that dim," she said. "You can't be thinking of going into the woods for some stupid lichen."

"Why not? You insisted it's important to the recipe."

The purple haze of her swirled. Her moods swung between ambivalent and mildly grumpy, but now she struggled to articulate her meaning.

"It's just—they're not—" She growled in frustration. "Look, I can't remember why, but no one goes into the woods. You heard those girls, yeah? It just isn't done. You respect the woods. You look at them from afar like, oh, how pretty. In the abstract *I would never set foot in there* sense. Not without its Keeper." She stopped. Frowned. Shaking her head, she added, "But you don't go in."

"What do you mean, its Keeper?"

"Nothing. I don't know. I can't remember."

"I don't like nature either, but it's just a forest," Briar said with a tone of sarcasm that riled her further.

"It's *not* just a forest," Gretchen said. "It's old. It's alive. Not in the normal sense, either. Those trees are all part of each other—pretty sure they've all got the same underground root system or something. Whatever, they can *communicate*."

"So?"

"So it's powerful. Can't you feel it?"

Briar looked at the dark depths of the forest, listened to the way the wind whistled past like a rattling voice. He understood what she meant, and it made him shiver, but he didn't have any other options. "How do you know all this anyway?" he asked.

Gretchen folded her arms. "I do remember *some* things."

"Maybe we shouldn't go," Vatii put in. "That place could be full of wild magic—untamed and unpredictable. We should be cautious."

"It's the best shot I have of finding lichen. Witches used to forage for tithes from their back gardens all the time."

Gretchen's face contorted. "Fine! Go if you like, but take my curtain off. I'm not going in there with you."

"I won't make you. Either of you." Briar fished in his pocket for the scrap of fabric he'd cut from the curtain cloak that morning. He found a soft place to dig a hole in the soil. The forest's magic had sunk into the dirt and stung like nettles under his nails. Despite his bravado, the sensation and Gretchen's warnings unnerved him. He wanted to get this over with.

He buried the fabric scrap and stood. "There. We'll see if the piece in the ground is enough to let you roam freely once I get home."

"You're making a mistake," Gretchen said.

"Vatii?"

"I think you're a fool, but I'm coming with you."

They parted ways, Briar heading up the dirt path as Gretchen faded away behind him until she wasn't there at all.

From a distance, the forest was an abstract concept, but close up, Briar understood Gretchen's aversion to it. All living things carried auras. Every plant, animal, and person. Each tree had a signature, and yet the forest as a whole exuded something utterly its own. Coill Darragh was a curious invitation in an unmarked envelope. It was the sting of a papercut as you slit the letter open.

The path ended. It didn't snake between the trees—the grass swallowed it. No sign proclaimed this a dead end or warned him not to go in.

He exchanged a look with Vatii. With breath held, they entered.

Passing under the sprawling canopy, an immutable quiet enveloped them. Sunlight dappled the ground and danced over shrubs and fallen logs in defiance of physics. One step, dead leaves crunched underfoot. The next, moss squelched and sank. Leaves hissed, trees groaned, the earth rose and fell like something huge breathed beneath it. On some level, Briar understood these were natural phenomena. Moss and earth stretched tight over tree roots could rise and fall as the trunks leaned in the wind. The forest was alive, as all plant things were, and it changed and transformed with the world around it.

But on an instinctual level that went beyond Gretchen's warnings, he sensed the forest wasn't alive the way plants were. The forest watched. The forest knew things. And it yearned.

The thought crawled like spider legs across skin. Briar pushed farther in. He made note of landmarks to find his way back. Two cracked trees that formed the letter "M" with the peaks of their broken trunks. An irregular red-leafed bush amongst the green. A moss-covered stone speckled with flowers. The density of growth and lack of footpath made the search slow, but Briar eventually came to a landmark that stopped him dead.

An enormous tree riddled with bumpy sores rose up, tall and twisting. Around it, the forest shrank away. No toadstools or shrubs grew. No ivy climbed its boughs. He noticed even the surrounding canopy refused to touch it, creating a halo of sky around this tree's leaves.

A scar—like the ones on the buildings in town, like Rowan's—marred the trunk, but here it seemed fresh. Veins of magic twisted through the injury like barbed wire. They smelled of rotten meat.

"This is cursed magic," Vatii said. "Wild magic. We should leave."

Briar agreed, but he was incomprehensibly drawn to this tree. This fetid, stinking thing that was neither alive nor dead.

Briar wondered, If the forest could look back at him, perhaps it could talk to him too. "You wouldn't happen to know where I can find some lichen?"

The wind picked up, and the trees around them moaned, braced against the gale. All but the twisted tree, which remained steadfast. Briar watched in silent terror as a fingering branch sprouted from the trunk. It grew in a zigzagging coil, coming close enough to touch. At its tip, a tangerine-colored lichen grew with spidery gold-green lashes framing each polyp. It grew prolifically, covering the bough, until the branch snapped and fell to the ground.

Briar hesitated. Stepping closer to the tree felt dangerous. He approached the severed branch and, after a pause, lifted it, examining the lichen. There was enough to make a hundred elixirs.

"Um. Thank you." He felt he had to offer something back. But searching his pockets, he had nothing. Only his charcoal for flesh tithes.

As if reading his thoughts, the tree hissed in anticipatory revelry. It liked the idea.

Fear wound around Briar's throat. It seemed foolish to offer the tree something of himself, equally so to give it nothing. He couldn't ask Vatii for a feather—it felt treacherous to offer up his familiar. Much as they bickered, she'd come to him, chosen him.

Taking the charcoal from his pocket, Briar pulled up his sleeve and prepared to draw a rune. As he did, something intangible climbed up through the earth, through his feet, thickening his blood, loosening his muscles. The tree piloted his body as if possessed. The first scratch of dark ash across his skin was rough and shaky. His heart pounded. Why were all his childhood warnings about accepting candy from strangers, not bargains with trees?

The tree's intent fled his body, leaving behind a spiral mark with rays around it and a series of arrows beneath. He didn't recognize it. Swallowing hard, he approached the tree. The rotting smell made bile rise in his throat, but he pressed a hand to the gnarled bark. His flesh burned where it was marked. He bit down on his lip and watched the magic leak out of him in veins of bright light that bruised violet. The tree, no, the whole forest breathed a sigh. The magic fizzled out, leaving the symbol as a permanent addition to the rest on his arm.

He pulled his sleeve down. Tried not to shiver. It seemed disrespectful. This was a dangerous dance, and now he wanted to go home. "Thank you," he said again.

A susurration of sound went through the leaves. The tree tugged at Briar's heart like a question.

When will you return?

He shuddered. Had this bargain opened him up to communication with the forest? "I don't know?"

Ours.

"What's yours?"

You, soon. Your mother.

A bolt of real fear went through him then. His veins were vines, and they curled around something poisonous and sharp lodged in his chest. He understood with petrifying certainty what it was.

"*You?* You cursed us?"

Curse. Yes.

"Why?" Briar's voice rose. "We've never even *been* here. We never did *anything* to you!"

The wind hissed ferociously, and the voice chorused in his head. *Thieves. Killers! It was owed.*

"But we never—"

He didn't finish. The whole forest quaked, a shriek of wind in the boughs, and he realized suddenly that he was surrounded by things that had killed his mother, that would kill him, too.

The forest screamed, *There is no you!*

Vatii said, "Just *go*, Briar!"

He ran. Out of the clearing and into the woods, searching for the landmarks to lead him home.

But they weren't there.

Not the fallen trees, the rock with the flowers, or the crimson bush. Everything had shifted, as if the trees had gotten up and walked off. He knew himself to be emotional, hyperbolic, given to flights of fancy, but he also knew the forest was warping his sense of direction. He could feel branch-like fingers in his hair, in his head.

He went faster, nearly tripping over roots and sinking pits of moss.

Come back.

Please let us go, he thought. *I gave you what you wanted.*

In answer, the woods said, *More*.

The forest floor was treacherous. He slipped on stones, caught himself on trees, then shrank away from them. The canopy above merged and closed, blocking out the sunlight. In desperation, Briar pulled out a lock of his own hair and scrunched it in his fist until the golden strands burned away and formed a floating torch above his palm. It only lit so far, though, and he couldn't tell which direction led out and which farther in.

It was only a matter of time before he fell.

Soft tissue crunched as his ankle rolled off a smooth stone. Vatii took off, screeching wildly. Briar crashed to his knees, the lichen branch bouncing away from him. His magic light went out. Grit bit into his palms and broke skin. A scream tore at his throat as he felt the forest drinking blood out of the scrapes.

Let me go, he thought. He scrambled to right himself.

Ours. Cursed, said the Coill Darragh woods.

Briar tried to get up, but something coiled around his ankle. It swept his feet out from under him. Ivy twined around his arms and legs, the sibilant sound of it like a snake's oily body gliding through dead leaves. Vatii snapped at the ivy, trying to sever it, but she couldn't land for more than a second before the forest tried to claim her, too.

Briar's eyes fell on the bracelet around his wrist, the stone that kept him safe from Coill Darragh's wards. The sight filled him with dread as the ivy tangled around it in tight coils.

And began to tug.

"No!" Briar shouted. If the forest severed that bracelet, he was done for. He could sense the wards pressing in, their teeth at his throat, waiting to bite. He tried to unwind the ivy. The magic charm keeping the bracelet from falling off his wrist dissipated. A bit of leather twine broke like a violin string.

"Vatii, get help!"

"I can't leave you!"

"Please, Vatii." One of the wires on his bracelet melted at the ivy's touch. The wardstone vibrated. "Get—" He shouted the first name that came to mind. "Get Rowan!"

"He won't get here in time!"

"Then get my charcoal."

He didn't know what spells he could use. Wishbrooke hadn't taught him how to combat a malevolent forest intent on devouring him. Vatii danced around the swiping vines and pecked a stub of charcoal from his pockets. She deposited it in his hand. He clutched it fiercely but could hardly move. Flat on his belly, ivy crawling over him, it took colossal effort to bring his arm close enough to draw on. His hand shook with the strain.

The first mark went down in a shivering scrawl. Then his bracelet gave an audible whine of tearing leather, and the last piece snapped apart.

The wards clamped shut around him. His vision went black, the forest obliterating the sunlight. Vatii called to him, desperation in her voice. He could feel her plucking at him. Then hovering over him, wings spread protectively.

He must have passed out and dreamed.

He dreamed one of the trees pulled up its roots and slashed away the vines. He dreamed it picked him up, cradled him to its trunk, and bore him away.

Then he truly blacked out.

CHAPTER 6

Briar awoke in a room he didn't recognize.

Judging by the chaotic collage of toys that made up the floor and the rabbit painted on the wall, it was a child's room. He sat up in a bed with fairies on the covers and groaned as pain lanced through his ankle, which was bandaged. Vatii landed in his lap, clucking about him like a mother hen.

"Whoa, there," said a woman's voice. "Take it easy, like. Or I'll get it in the neck from my husband for letting you ruin his handiwork."

Briar's gaze settled on a woman sitting in an rocking chair next to him. She was a couple years older than him, her auburn hair in a plait, her square features oddly familiar.

His experience in the woods washed over him in a wave of nausea. The forest. Its grisly confession about the curse. And—he grasped his wrist. Scratches from the ivy remained, but the wardstone bracelet was gone.

"What happened? How'd I get here?" he asked.

"My brother brought you in looking sick as a small hospital, all scraped up. Said he found you in the forest, your familiar hollering over you, and the ward bracelet broken." She crossed her arms, looking formidable and stormy. "He didn't tell me why he was in the woods, so I've a mind to give him a bollocking. It's lucky he found you. Connor—my husband, he's a physician—said there was nothing wrong with you besides a sprained ankle, but to keep an eye, so we brought you here."

Briar's head spun. "How am I even alive? The wards—"

"Should have torn you to pieces."

"Why didn't they?" Rubbing his wrist absently, he allowed Vatii to climb onto his shoulder and preen the twigs out of his hair.

"I'm no witch, but if I had to guess, whatever happened to you in that forest made you immune to the wards." She frowned like this explanation dissatisfied her. "I'm Sorcha, by the way."

"Briar."

"Well, Briar, I said I'd give my brother a bollocking, but he isn't here, so you'll have to do. What the feck were you doing in those woods?"

The answer made Briar shock fully upright and startle Vatii off his shoulder. "The lichen!"

"The what?"

"I had a branch of lichen. Mossy fungus-y plant stuff? It was for a potion."

"Ah, that. You were cradling it like a baby. It's downstairs with your clothes."

Briar blew a relieved sigh up into his fringe. At least the trip hadn't been wasted. The horror of his escape from the wood and what it had said haunted him—if he closed his eyes, he could still feel the forest trying to consume him. Vines around his chest, soil slurping at his wounds. Vatii landed on his knee, and he stroked her feathers with a finger.

"Thank you for helping me."

"Not a bother. Stay as long as you need."

"I won't impose anymore, really. I should get back to my flat."

He stood, relieved to feel floorboards underfoot, not moss. Favoring his sprained ankle, he followed Sorcha downstairs through a modest kitchen. It smelled of pumpkin and had open shelves crowded with mason jars of spices and foraged herbs. Pages of crayon art were stuck to the fridge with heart-shaped magnets. A television blared in an adjoining room, some sort of children's program singing a song. Sorcha led Briar through a locked door into—

A shop. Like Briar's, the flat Sorcha lived in was attached to a small shop. He recognized the glint of jewels, the shape of many bolts of cloth leaning against walls. This was the shop that had so enamored him during Gretchen's tour.

Sorcha turned the lights on. "Normally, I'd let you out the side door, but the lamp's broken, and I don't want you tripping through our alley. I'll let you out the front."

"This is your store?" Briar asked.

"Yeah. Not much, but—" She cut herself short, eyeing Briar as he turned, taking in the store's materials with hungry eyes. She went to the counter and pulled Briar's cloak and lichen branch from behind it. She held them out to him.

"It's a nice cloak."

"Thanks." Briar pulled it on. "I made it for my Rede party. Seemed a shame not to wear it more often."

"You know—" Sorcha started to say.

Keys jingled in the door. Bells chimed as it opened to reveal the familiar source of Sorcha's facial features. Rowan squeezed inside, shaking rain from his hair. When he saw Briar, he froze.

"Rowan?" Sorcha said. "What are you doing back?"

"You're siblings," Briar blurted. "So *you* saved me from the evil forest and carried me all the way to the clinic?" His grin faltered. "Shame I don't remember it."

His flirting left both of them stunned.

Eventually, Rowan said, "Good to see you're all right."

"Right as rain." Briar didn't want to recall his time in the forest, so he pointed at the container in Rowan's hands. "What's that?"

"Oh." Rowan avoided Sorcha's eye as he set the container on the counter next to Briar. "Just soup. To help you feel better."

Briar picked up the container. It warmed his hands, a hearty mix of vegetables and pasta sloshing inside. He just caught the thunderstruck look Sorcha cast Rowan before she recovered herself to say, "None for me, though!"

"You hate soup," said Rowan defensively. He was saved from further explanation when a creaking door announced the presence of an eavesdropper.

A ginger-haired girl in footie pajamas stood in the door to the kitchen, staring at Briar wide-eyed.

"Ciara," Sorcha said. "Go see your da."

"Mammy, is he a witch?" said the little girl.

Sorcha made an impatient noise, but Briar didn't mind the question. "Yes, I'm a witch."

The little girl's eyes lit up. She ran into the shop, clutching at the front of her pajamas with tiny fists. Giving up, Sorcha introduced her. "This is my daughter, Ciara. Who should be watching television with her da, but here we are."

Ciara said, "Are you a prince witch?"

"Yes," Briar said. "Very famous."

"I like your bird. And your cape."

"Cloak," Sorcha corrected.

"Cloak. Can I have it?"

Sorcha flushed with embarrassment. "All right, that's enough, you beast."

"I could make you one like it," Briar offered. Sorcha opened her mouth to protest, but he interrupted. "It would be no trouble. If you have any off-cuts of blue fabric, I could do it."

"Yay!" Ciara bellowed at a decibel only children could achieve. "Princess witch Ciara! Fly me, Uncle Rowan!"

This made no sense to Briar until Rowan bent to pick Ciara up and flew her around the shop like an airplane. A feat most impressive due to his size, the lack of space, and the general impression from the townsfolk that Rowan was terrifying, not the type children took well to. His niece, apparently, was an exception.

Sorcha slapped him lightly on the shoulder. "Don't wind her up; it's her bedtime."

"Bye, prince witch!" Ciara called. They both disappeared into the kitchen.

Sorcha turned to Briar, hands on her hips. "What I wanted to say before that creature interrupted me is that it seems we have compatible trades."

Briar gaped at her. If he understood her meaning . . .

"Have you ever considered making clothes, maybe enchanting them?" Sorcha said. "Or enchanting jewelry?"

"You want to go into business together?"

"Sure. We could trial it. I could sell you fabrics at a discount. Let you enchant my jewelry, give you a cut of the profits. Seems a mutually beneficial relationship to me."

For a moment, he just stared at her, imagining all the dream garments he could create. The beautiful displays he could put in his shop window. He could hardly believe his luck.

Rowan returned before Briar could answer. Sorcha pounced. "Rowan. You think it'd be a fantastic idea if Briar and I went into business together, don't you?"

Rowan froze, confusion written across his face.

"I don't need convincing." Briar grinned, fit to burst. "You have a deal."

He left brimming with ideas. Though he wanted nothing more than to go home and start planning, he had one thing left to do.

The path wending between houses toward the forest was more foreboding at night. The darkness swallowed all the surrounding fields, narrowing visibility to the fencing and the dirt path before him. He could just make out the signpost where he'd buried Gretchen's curtain. He jogged up to check on it but froze as he got closer.

Something twisted, like a bolt of lightning, rose out of the earth next to the signpost. He hadn't noticed at first because its shape blended in with the dark. Only when he moved could he see it silhouetted against a patch of navy sky.

On the spot where he'd buried a square of curtain, vines had grown. They coiled around one another, lethally tipped corkscrews rising as tall as Briar. Taller.

Ensnared within the cage, speared through in places, were the bleeding remains of a hare.

At the very top, impaled on a single point, was the scorched scrap of floral curtain.

CHAPTER 7

A commotion of voices babbled outside Briar's window.

Coill Darragh wasn't usually bustling early in the morning. In the street, a thick knot of people crowded in front of the shop. Some held cameras aloft, flashing with the same frenetic energy as the people. All faces pointed at the front of the shop neighboring Briar's.

Some buoyant combination of hope and intuition coalesced in Briar's heart, sending him careering around his room in search of clothes. He recalled a teasing Alakagram video.

The other witch coming to Coill Darragh couldn't possibly be . . .

Dressed so quickly that both socks were inside out, Briar flung himself down the stairs and out the door. The street heaved. No sooner had he joined the throng than he had an elbow in his ribs, the press of auras smothering him like overbearing cologne. Though the crowd was filled with all sorts, one thing every person had in common was the wardstone bracelet fastened about their wrists. Tourists, all. Briar squeezed between two men with cameras to peer on tiptoes over the heads of a number of teens. Through the vibrating crowd, he glimpsed a head of sable hair, flicked over a shoulder adorned with a feathered epaulette.

It was only a passing glance, but Briar would know the face anywhere.

Disbelief, feverish excitement, and a little trepidation all warred within him, but the excitement reigned triumphant.

It was unmistakably Linden Fairchild.

Briar had seen him once before, though in a crowd several fathoms larger.

The Fairchilds were famous for their healing potions. After a bout of illness had killed most of their family, they'd dedicated themselves to medicine. Yet, even compared to his parents, who were world-renowned for their elixirs, Linden was the jewel in the family crown.

Like Briar with aura reading, Linden had a unique talent for healing. The Fairchilds had once run a traveling miracle tour. Briar had been fifteen on the sunny day he and his mother went into Port Haven to watch Linden cure a young girl of cancer and a man of multiple sclerosis. Briar had insisted on bringing his mum. Though she'd protested she wasn't ill, he knew different, or thought he did. Linden had asked what ailed her, and she'd looked to Briar. He'd said, "Please just check." Linden had laid his hands on her shoulders. Briar remembered how they had looked. Long fingered and gentle. He'd admired Linden distantly before, through the barrier of a screen, but this encounter, up close, had birthed a different sort of fascination. A yearning to be as bright and world-changing.

Linden had closed his eyes. His magic quested like a tuning fork searching for discordant notes. But he'd opened his eyes and proclaimed there were none.

She wasn't sick. Not yet. The Seer's fortune hadn't come to pass. Briar hoped she'd been wrong. A quack. But a year later, his mum was tired all the time. A couple years later, she had a diagnosis of Bowen's Wane. By then, Linden's Miracle Tour ended with a public announcement. Years of being on the road and overusing his magic without breaks had taken its toll. He'd exhausted his abilities.

Try as he might, he could never heal anyone again.

It struck Briar as criminally unfair that the one person who might have saved her had been robbed of his talent to do so.

It wasn't unheard of. Witches could burn out their abilities, sometimes permanently, and Linden had been young—a teenager—during that tour. Linden took up fashion design afterward. For Briar, it had been a lifeline. Much of what he'd learned to sew, he'd done through Linden's online tutorials. It allowed Briar to dress himself for success even when he couldn't afford the flashy brands his peers wore.

Now, Linden was everything Briar remembered. He didn't strut or gleam or preen in front of the cameras but carried himself with a quiet charisma. Effortlessly beautiful, from every angle a composition made for painting. He stopped at the stoop to the shop, emerald half cape swirling around him, the cupid's bow of his mouth quirked in a smile. A white cat prowled at Linden's heels—his familiar, Atticus—while an assistant tailed them, filming their arrival for Alakagram.

Briar couldn't get a sense of Linden's aura. It looked like he'd cast a spell to keep the crowd at a distance, but he hadn't needed to. Rowan cut a path through the crowd, which shied from him like a murmuration of starlings around a bird of prey. He carried a single suitcase, white with gold fastenings. Too tall and blocking the view of many cameras, Rowan set the suitcase at Linden's feet. It hit the cobblestones like a dropped anvil, spelled to contain multitudes. Rowan departed quickly.

Linden waited as the crowd held an anticipatory breath. When he spoke, it was in the crisp, clean vowels Briar had often fallen asleep to while watching live videos from his phone.

"Hello, everyone. I know you must be excited to hear what I have planned for my modest shop in Coill Darragh. Though I'm equally excited to share, I regret that now's not the time."

He allowed a moment for the mutters of disappointment. Many of the crowd were reporters and paparazzi raring to tell the story first.

"I won't leave you without even a clue, of course," Linden continued. "There's been a lot of speculation that I might make this my first brick-and-mortar store outside Pentawynn, or that I'm about to announce a new fashion line for winter, but I can let you in on a secret. None of those rumors are true. This store will be a return to something I've always held a deep passion for."

A second pause, this one peppered with feverish whispers. Briar's stomach flipped. *A return to something I've always held a deep passion for.* Linden was prodigal, talented beyond the norm for witches. Perhaps his powers had returned. Perhaps . . .

Briar didn't want to give in to the hope Linden could cure him of his curse, but seeing him here, it felt like—

Fate.

"Which brings me to the next important detail: a date," Linden continued. "Coill Darragh holds an annual festival on the twenty-first of October. At six that evening, I'll hold a grand opening to my shop, here on this doorstep."

To the cheers and claps of the crowd, he said, "I'll be getting started now. I hope to see you all very soon."

He opened the door and swept inside. Bright banners unfurled in the interior windows, flashing the opening date and Linden's logo of a cat in a witch's hat in enchanted lights. The crowd's checked enthusiasm during Linden's speech crashed through the streets of Coill Darragh. People took photos outside the shop in front of the new banners. Many more dragged their luggage to check in to their lodgings.

The magnitude of Linden's fame only sank in for Briar as he watched the town transform. A fanatical pulse replaced the quiet thrum of locals going about their daily lives.

Briar found it infectious. He returned to his shop. Very little daylight penetrated the pack of bodies outside his window, so he had to put lights on, but he didn't mind. The knowledge of who lived and breathed just on the other side of his wall left him effervescent.

"His shop will make for stiff competition," Vatii warned.

This failed to temper his enthusiasm. "Could do the opposite," Briar said. "Maybe people will go to Linden's and come here because they're curious. And besides, I'll be able to *talk to him*."

There was always the risk Linden would outshine him, but he refused to entertain the notion. He skipped over it and straight to the most attractive possibility, the one that tickled at the back of his mind the moment he'd woken up to the crowds buzzing outside:

Last night, starved from his adventure in the woods, Briar had heated up Rowan's soup and basked in the warm smells filling his small flat. He'd wondered about the man with an odd scar and an odder habit of feeding him at any given opportunity. When he'd first arrived in Coill Darragh, he'd thought perhaps Rowan was the "man in a mask" from Niamh's vision.

Now, he doubted it.

Rowan was quiet, and he had an odd effect on the people of the town, but nothing about him seemed masked or stone-hearted. He was kind, playful with his niece, generous with a complete stranger. He'd probably saved Briar's life. Moreover, Niamh had described a "deified pillar of the people." Who else but a celebrity fit that description? Rowan couldn't be the cold man of Niamh's vision—if anything, Briar associated him with warmth.

He'd been disappointed. Now, he considered the alternative. What if this man of destiny was Linden? Getting even more carried away, Briar thought of how this man was meant to have a heart of stone that turned golden for Briar. Perhaps it was a metaphor. Perhaps Briar could unlock Linden's blocked talent, and Linden could cure him of the curse, and—

"We are definitely going to fall in love," Briar said. "It's destiny. Niamh said so."

Vatii clicked her beak. "You're a pillock if you believe that."

"What else besides destiny would bring someone like Linden some-place like this?"

"You *should* be focusing on how you're going to make anything that can compete with a world-famous witch."

She was right, but Briar would have to wait until Sorcha brought his fabric. For now, he had to brew Diarmuid's elixir.

He prodded a fire to life in the wood-burning stove, setting his cauldron atop it with water to boil. As he arrayed the ingredients and scribbled the recipe on the counter, Gretchen appeared at his elbow in a waft of creeping cold, finger tapping her lower lip. She hadn't been pleased when Briar's return to the shop last night dragged her back, the buried fabric rejected. They still hadn't come up with an alternative, but her inquisitive look implied she'd gotten over it for now. She'd been insufferably smug after his trip into the woods. The spectral embodiment of *I told you so*. Briar hesitated while crushing blackberries with his mortar and pestle, eyebrows raised.

"Do you want to help?" he asked.

"Well, you'll mess it up without me."

But he could tell she was pleased. Whether because she missed making potions or because she enjoyed bossing Briar around, he didn't care. He followed her instructions, dropping in the wishbone only when the bub-bling froth nearly boiled over, mixing the turmeric into the crushed berries until it made a paste, stirring the brew whenever she reminded him. The liquid in the cauldron looked gray-green and unappetizing at first, but Gretchen said it needed time to simmer.

As he retrieved a bottle to contain the potion, his arm gave a sudden jerk. His fingers seized too, dropping the bottle, glass shattering underfoot.

Vatii said, "Clumsy!"

"It wasn't me. It was—" Briar cut himself short. Gretchen watched, eyebrows raised. He looked at his arm, at the tithe he'd made to the tree yesterday, and that sharp thing lodged in his chest hurt like he was breathing around it.

His curse had never given him muscle spasms before.

"Is there something the matter with you?" Gretchen asked.

Briar couldn't help bristling a little. He barely spoke of his curse. Not out of any sense of shame, but because most people didn't want to know and regretted bringing it up. The notion that he was already experiencing muscle spasms frightened him.

"I'm fine. It's nothing."

Gretchen didn't press him for answers.

Briar poured the cauldron's contents into a round bottle and wrote a label for it in curling script. He took it downstairs, setting it on the barren shelf behind the counter. It looked lonely.

He sketched garment designs, cut out patterns, preparing what he could for Sorcha's delivery. She came mid-afternoon with a bolt of blue fabric for Ciara's cloak and a binder full of sample inventory. An hour flashed by as they nailed down the particulars of their joint venture. Briar went through page after page of fabric squares, touching each, imagining what kind of garments he could create. Assessing the prices was less pleasant, but Sorcha made it easier by scratching twenty percent off the retail price and presenting him with a bag of scraps for free.

He placed his first order with his heart in his throat. It took most of his meager savings, but he needed to fill the store. There were things he couldn't yet afford. Clothing racks, a dressmaker's mannequin to make fittings and different sizes easier, hangers and frames for the shop. That didn't even factor in tithes for enchantments. The fabric was the tip of the iceberg.

It was a start.

Briar spent the following week crouched over his sewing machine, stitching garments. Even before he enchanted them, there was a certain magic to the rhythm of the needle stamping its stitches, the glide of scissors through cloth. He loved embroidery, but his fingers ached from the press of the needle by the time he set his work aside to sleep. His drafty flat couldn't keep out autumn's chill, so he warmed himself with many cups of tea and lit fires in the potbelly stove.

Of Ciara's cloak, he was particularly fond. It matched his own, except tiny. He'd enchanted the embroidered stars to animate and twinkle, and he hoped fervently she'd like it.

He charmed a few of the jewelry pieces Sorcha left with him, too. One necklace would help dispel a person's shyness at parties. The engagement rings would prolong the emotional heights brought on by a proposal. Though subtle magic, it was the sort Briar liked best. It did not so much change the wearer as make their lives a little happier. His mother had made him smile, and that left its mark on him. He hoped his clothes could make the wearer smile, too, and leave their own marks.

He precariously balanced hangers against the edges of structural beams in the shop walls to display what he'd managed to make. A wool jacket for winter, lined with indigo silk and hand embroidered with enchanted thread to keep the wind from slipping under sleeves and down collars. A boatneck silver dress enchanted to sit just perfectly without need for fidgety adjustments.

None of this fixed a growing issue: nobody came inside his shop.

Closing time neared in the beginning of his second week, and not a solitary customer ventured inside. His eagerness to get a display together became unbearable. He'd lost hope that anyone would come through today, but at ten minutes to closing, the door chime jingled.

Rowan towered in the doorway. Briar shot up. Though he should have felt disappointed it wasn't a potential customer, a pit of warmth opened in him instead.

Vatii said uncharitably, "Dammit, we need business!"

Briar ignored her. "Busy week?"

Rowan nodded on a huffed breath. As Coill Darragh flooded with tourists, Briar could only assume he spent a good deal of time doling out wardstone bracelets. He looked around at the few things Briar had on display and approached the jacket. If he'd wanted to buy anything, the only thing that would fit was the scarf Briar hadn't finished. Though normally quiet, Rowan's silence was particularly poignant today. He kept half turning to Briar then looking away.

Briar suddenly remembered. "The soup!" He sprinted upstairs and returned moments later with the empty, cleaned container to return. "Thank you again. It was really good. Really, really good. Did you make it yourself?"

"Mm." Rowan looked at the clothes hanging up on the wall.

"You'd look ravishing in the silver one," Briar joked, pointing at the dress.

With a rumbling chuckle, Rowan reached out to touch the fabric. Unsurprisingly, the hanger teetered off the edge it clung to and fell to the ground in a glittering puddle.

"Sorry." He picked it up and tried to put it back but couldn't work out how Briar had balanced it.

"It was inevitable. Don't worry, let me." Briar took the hanger and began the circus act of balancing it again. "Just haven't had the chance to get the stuff together for charms, but I'll have them on floating, invisible mannequins soon."

"They look good."

Briar smiled. "Thanks. Sorry there's nothing in your size off the hanger, but I can make anything you like to measure. I've got a scarf on the go too. Not sure it's your color, but . . ."

He trailed off. It wasn't often he was lost for words, but Rowan's quiet was stuffed full of something unsaid. He hadn't stepped out of Briar's space, still close enough that his aura brushed up like a cat arching under Briar's chin. It beckoned him closer. He couldn't understand how Rowan had the opposite effect on everyone else.

Rowan's Adam's apple bobbed, and he nodded towards something behind Briar. "Is that the one for Ciara?"

Briar didn't have to look back. He held Rowan's gaze for the second it took before Rowan lowered his. "Did you come to tell me something?"

"Ehm." Rowan's aura fizzled like a carbonated drink shaken too vigorously. The words burst out of him. "It's Saor ó Eagla in a week's time."

"What's that?"

"A festival."

Briar's mouth formed around an "oh" of understanding. This was the festival around which Linden would launch his store, later in October.

It then occurred to him that Rowan was trying to ask him on a date.

At least, it seemed that way until Rowan cleared his throat and took several steps away from Briar. "Just thought to tell you. In case you wanted to go."

"Will you be there?" Briar prompted.

Rowan nodded stiffly. "Probably."

"Then I'll see you there."

Rowan muttered something unintelligible, perhaps a "see you" or "okay goodbye," then turned and ducked out the door. Briar found it left his heart hammering. If Rowan had just asked him on a date, he hadn't said whether he'd come by to pick him up, meet him there, or what time. Had he mistaken Rowan's intent altogether?

"He," Vatii declared, looking pompous from her spot puffed up on the cash register, "is a very strange man."

Briar shook it off and went to lock the door, turning the sign to "closed," but a young man appeared from the gloom to knock on the glass. Briar opened it to the frantic words: "Sorry to bother you, mate! I know you're closing, but you wouldn't happen to have any engagement rings, would you?"

Stepping out of the doorway to let him in, Briar said, "Er, yes, a couple."

Ten minutes later, Briar made his first sale.

CHAPTER 8

Coill Darragh metamorphosed with the arrival of Saor ó Eagla and Linden both. The streets thronged with tourists. Bonfires burned, carrying woodsy smells through thoroughfares. Strings of bunting, wreaths of pinecones, and autumnal leaves decorated all the eaves and doors. It was cozy and convivial, unlike the drunks puking in the streets of Wishbrooke, and Briar pondered how parties in Pentawynn might compare.

Over the past week, Briar had scrounged for tithes to make three garments float, as though on invisible models, in the window display. They spun in slow circles and won him a few potential customers, but the sheer emptiness of his shop was daunting. He really needed a sale, but nothing had moved since the engagement ring. It didn't discourage him, his mood buoyed by the promise of celebration. The chance to meet Linden gave the night of Saor ó Eagla even more promise than most.

And if Briar's mind strayed to the thought of bumping into Rowan, it was not an unpleasant thought.

Since Briar still hadn't discovered a means to let Gretchen roam freely, his work ethic kept her cooped up. At his promise that on the night of Saor ó Eagla, she could roam all she liked, she chucked a spatula at his head.

"That's the anniversary of my death, you pillock!"

Briar ducked, the spatula flying just shy of a potion vial on his desk. "I didn't know that!"

"Well, you never asked!"

"I'm sorry, but it seemed a bit personal, and anyway, a walk about could be good. Think of it like a birthday present. A deathday present."

She tried to hurl a whisk at him that time but had exhausted her ability to affect the real world, so she stormed through the wall into the stairwell to sulk.

Briar liked Gretchen. Though testy, she helped him with potions and teased him affectionately, too.

She also chafed in a way he found familiar.

Given it was Linden's grand opening and the night of the festival, partaking in the festivities and schmoozing seemed a better use of Briar's time, so he closed early. He wore Gretchen's curtain, as promised, but he'd turned the cape into a cravat. It was a struggle to open his shop door into the crowd, with people holding pints, cameras, and their phones blocking the way.

The air smelled of smoke and cider. A dais was erected in front of Linden's shop, swathed in silk bunting. The drunken revelers mixed uneasily with the professional photographers and journalists. A few witches hovered on brooms above the crowd to get a better view.

The clock struck six, and a plume of red smoke erupted on the dais. Linden emerged from it, Atticus draped around his shoulders. He looked splendid with his hair charmed to twinkle with stars. People with color-changing sparklers waved them vigorously, cheering. A red ribbon tied itself across Linden's door, ready for cutting.

"It's time," Linden said, "to announce my new work here in Coill Darragh! For much of my life, I devoted myself to creating clothes I hoped would bring harmony and happiness to the lives of everyone who wore them. I put love into every stitch. I'm blessed to say I have no regrets.

"However, the time has come to revisit a chapter from my youth. Many have asked whether I will return to the noble path set out by my family. For some time, I didn't know the answer. The loss of my gifts left me uncertain of my future in the art of healing."

Some murmurs of sympathy went through the crowd.

All were aware that Linden had big boots to fill, as his parents ran one of the most successful potion chains in the world. That Linden had departed from it was common knowledge, even controversial. He'd chosen something considered frivolous—fashion—over something noble and altruistic—healing. That he'd been prodigally talented in both only reinforced the public opinion that he was wasting his powers.

Those expectations must have weighed heavily on him. They were the same age, Briar reflected. Linden had only been a boy when he came into his fame.

Vatii, unaffected, said, "What tripe."

"Hush."

Linden's voice rose. "Well, I've thought long enough to give you my answer."

He directed everyone's attention to banners waving on the dais. The logo upon them changed, transforming into a caduceus staff. The head of the snake was still his customary cat's face with a witch's hat. Fireworks popped across the long banner until it dropped, revealing the freshly painted sign over his store.

Fairchild Enchanted Elixirs and Remedies

The crowd frothed with the flash of photography and the snappy dialogue of reporters conveying the news to their camera crew. Linden descended the dais, his hair and robes floating in defiance of gravity. He conjured a pair of scissors, then cut the ribbon. The door swept open on its own.

Standing in the aperture, light forming a halo around him, he told the waiting crowd, "Though inspired by the work of my family, this store is still my own. Many of the enchanted objects here incorporate magic from my family's potion recipes, or new ones I made myself. You might wonder why I've come to Coill Darragh, and you'll find your answer in the forest surrounding it. As it is one of the last sources of wild magic, I wish to study it and see if any secrets of healing can be found within. Beyond that, I wish to serve everyone here, whatever their needs may be. Any problems you have, bring them to me. I'd like everyone to feel comfortable within these walls."

With that, he declared Fairchild Enchanted Elixirs and Remedies open.

The crowd surged forward, Briar pulled toward the entrance with them. By some miracle or magic, an orderly queue formed, weaving down the street. The banners, which once obscured the window display, curled up like scrolls, revealing an exquisite array of items on velvet pillows and tiered platters: from tiny jewels to candles to statuettes of animals in delicate china. Handwritten cards next to each described the effects they'd have on a room or a wearer.

Briar had a goal to introduce himself to Linden, but the simplest excuse to speak would be to buy something. The question was whether he could afford anything; even the smallest trinkets in the window display were pricey.

They were only a taste of the flavors within. A display of clothing—winter robes in Linden's characteristically neutral palettes and block patterns—turned on a pedestal. Longing and disconcertion flooded Briar's heart. He would give anything to own a garment made by Linden's hand, but the competition would set him back in his own pursuits.

Knowing he wouldn't like what he found, he pressed between a few other customers to finger the tag hanging from the sleeve of a coat. It proclaimed to grant the wearer a year of luck in affairs of the heart. *If you are looking for your beloved, your soulmate, wear this, and the search will not last long.*

"Not like you need *that*," Vatii said. "Since you and Linden are *destined* to be."

Briar's insides twisted. It would cost him a year's supply of medicine for this coat alone.

Setting his sights on something smaller, he perused the shelves of trinkets. Enamel pins, hair ornaments, tea lights. Even these were expensive, but he could always use more candles. He selected two. One would grant him sweet dreams if burned an hour before sleep, the second banished fatigue if he needed to pull another late night.

He followed the gold arrows on the floor to queue.

"Are you nervous?" Vatii asked.

"Excited."

But the closer he got to the register, the less that was true. Linden manned it himself, his smile blinding. Briar's heart beat a staccato rhythm against his sternum. He had to say something to leave an impression, but nothing adequately expressed the depth of Linden's influence. *You made my life bearable when I lost everything.* He couldn't very well say that.

Then it was his turn.

Stepping through a portal and into Linden's presence had the same surreal effect of crossing through worlds. His aura didn't carry through the camera, and on the day of the Miracle Tour years ago, he'd been protected by wards blocking Briar's abilities. Usually, Briar noticed a person's aura before anything else. But instead of the wash of sensation he was so used to, Briar felt . . . nothing. Just a careful blankness. Like Linden's aura existed beyond tinted glass. He must have utilized some kind of charm still, to keep prying eyes away.

A mask.

Maybe he really is my destiny, Briar thought. He'd joked but never really believed.

"Find everything all right?" Linden said.

Briar came back to himself. "Yes! Actually, I wanted to introduce myself. I'm Briar Wyngrave. I'm the other Reded witch, your neighbor. Just next door."

He shook Linden's smooth hand. Touch didn't bring his aura into sharp relief either. On the counter, Atticus licked a paw. Vatii clattered over to introduce herself, chattering in the strange language of familiars. The cat turned its head, ignoring Vatii. She looked tempted to pull Atticus's tail but returned to Briar's shoulder with an insulted squawk.

"Lovely to make your acquaintance," Linden said. "That's twelve pounds, by the way."

Between them, charmed tissue paper wrapped Briar's tea lights. Briar counted out coins. "Perhaps we could meet for coffee sometime? There aren't many witches in town. We could get to know one another."

He was pushing the envelope—Linden's shop looked straight out of a magazine, and Briar's still looked like it was available for rent. They had disparate reputations, but fortune favored the bold, and Briar was brazen.

"Oh," Linden said. "Perhaps. I'm very sorry, it's just that there's a queue—"

"Of course. I won't hold you up any longer." Briar ignored the scornful look of the woman behind him with an armful of talismans. "Congratulations on your grand opening."

"Thank you."

Linden looked to the disgruntled woman. Briar's time was up. He took his bag and wandered outside, where the queue still snaked down the lane.

"What a stuck-up prick," Vatii exploded. "I hate cats. That man better *not* be your destiny."

"He is," Briar said. "I'm sure of it." He replayed the memory with a sense of both curiosity and wonder. "He's nothing like what I expected."

"And that makes you sure of it, why?"

"Niamh said the man who'd lead me to my destiny wore a mask to protect his heart, which made it stony. I think it's a veneer. Would you be any different if everyone knew your name and wanted something from you? Maybe once we get to know him, he'll warm up."

"So what's the plan now?" Vatii grumbled.

Briar grinned. "I think we deserve a drink."

* * *

The Swan and Cygnet overflowed with people clutching pitchers, light glinting off their wardstone bracelets. Briar waded toward the bar. Vatii perched on his head, annoyed at the other patrons for bumping into her long tail.

Maebh cleaned a glass and ignored the pointed looks of rowdy tourists. They were tended to, instead, by her frazzled barmaid. Seated on a stool in front of Maebh was Rowan, his hands dwarfing a pint of stout. The two of them spoke low, with heads bowed, Rowan's strong profile wearing a grim scowl. As usual, strangers avoided him, so it was easy for Briar to sit next to him, bumping shoulders.

"Fancy meeting you here."

"Briar." His name rolled over Rowan's tongue, the *r*'s gone both soft and solid, like melting butter.

"Nice to see you again, Maebh," Briar said politely. Vatii hopped onto the bar top, probably not helping him into Maebh's good graces as she pecked at biscuit crumbs.

"What can I get you?" Maebh asked.

Had he imagined that her tone was warmer? "Do you have another recommendation?" He nudged Rowan. "Something traditional for Saor ó—" Briar struggled with the pronunciation. His accent didn't wrap around the vowels the same way.

Rowan raised his pint. "Stout's traditional."

"I'll have that, then."

Maebh hit Rowan's arm with her dish towel. "Give him a try of yours first, like."

She was *definitely* warmer than Briar remembered. She also didn't shy away from Rowan like everyone else. Obliging, Rowan passed the pint, filled with liquid so inky dark it could have been bottomless. Briar took an experimental sip. Creamy froth left a moustache on his upper lip, which he licked off. It was a bitter and deep-flavored beer, more meal than drink.

"Like it?" said Maebh.

"It's—good!"

Maebh said, "What are you really after?"

"Mulled wine?"

"I'll tell Aisling. Can you get that, Aisling?"

From the other side of the bar, Aisling called back, "Now in a minute."

"Never mind, I'll get it myself."

"You missed some—" Rowan's big hand was suddenly in Briar's periphery. After startling a second, he froze, and Rowan wiped a bit of froth from his upper lip with the pad of a thumb.

It set Briar's heart skipping. The cacophony of the bar fell away for just a moment. Rowan's by-now-familiar aura rubbed against him like hands bracketing his waist.

Maebh returned just as Rowan's hand dropped back to his pint.

Briar chastised himself internally for leaning into the touch, for the thoughts that crooned in his mind about what those big hands would feel like cradling the back of his head or hitched up under clothes. Maebh was right there, giving Briar a look of calculated scrutiny.

It was difficult to tell if the gesture had been an idle, platonic thing.

It hadn't felt like it, though.

Maebh slid him the mulled wine. He reached for his coin purse, but she held up a hand. "Leave it. You helped my Sorcha. Seems you're friendly with my Rowan, too. So that drink's on the house."

Briar felt both grateful and stupid. Looking at Maebh closer, the resemblance should have been obvious. She was their mother.

"Is everyone here related?" he blurted.

Maebh's barking laughter eased his fear of causing further offense. "Ours is a large family, but you've met the best of them."

Rowan grunted. "Mam."

"Right, I'll leave you before Aisling has a canary, but you best enjoy yourselves this evening, all right?"

She ambled away. Briar took a sip of his mulled wine, the tart, fruity brew and warm spices bringing a flush to his cheeks. Rowan considered him, quiet as usual. It was difficult to pin him down. He wasn't quite brooding, just less warm, and a cord of discontent furrowed his brow.

"I thought you'd be enjoying the festivities," Briar said.

"Hmm." Rowan tilted his head from side to side.

"Sorry if I interrupted a serious conversation with your—mam?"

"No, nothing like that." At Briar's inquisitive look, he took an evasive sip of stout. "Have you been enjoying your night?"

Briar leaned in close. He could see the individual white hairs of Rowan's beard where his scar branched along his jaw, up his cheek. "I think I'd enjoy it more with a guide."

Rowan took that in, then raised his pint to tap against Briar's. "Best finish our drinks, then."

A voice rose above the crowd, a young man climbing atop the other end of the bar. He called for everyone's attention with a braying laugh, ignoring Maebh's venomous look for tramping his boots on her bar top. Briar recognized him. The harried man who'd bought the engagement ring a while back. Enough patrons noticed him to fall quiet. He announced he had something very important to tell everyone before they went back to their merriment, then turned to Aisling, the barmaid. He pulled a velvet box from his pocket, Briar's magical signature hovering around it.

The young man jumped off the bar and got down on one knee, presenting Aisling with the ring. She looked ecstatic, pink cheeks turning red. Tearfully, she accepted, and her new fiancé rose to place the ring on her finger.

A tickle of joy and heartache went through Briar. He'd sold those rings, played a part in this joining of hearts, and left a little mark on the community. But he also ached for the wedding he'd probably never have.

Briar took the last sip of his wine and nudged Rowan, who'd been watching him and not the engagement. "Ready to go?"

They emerged into the crisp autumn air, breath frosting in swirling clouds. Briar interlocked his arm in Rowan's. The alderman looked briefly shocked but accepted the contact.

Vatii clicked her beak in Briar's ear. "I thought Linden was your destiny, huh? What happened to that?"

He couldn't answer without Rowan overhearing, so he shrugged her off. Vatii, who'd prefer he take up nunnery, huffed crossly. He didn't know for certain who the prophecy referred to. No harm in a little flirting, either way.

In the streets, a group of friends all crowned each other with laurels of autumn leaves. A woman wove through the crowd with bundles of them over each arm. Rowan in tow, Briar asked her for two. She granted him one with leaves arranged in fiery colors and another in different shades of orange and brown oak. Briar took the former and held it aloft for Rowan.

"I think this one will suit you."

Rowan hesitated, then bent his head. Briar rose on tiptoes to place the laurel, an undisguised excuse to casually touch.

"What are they for?" Briar arranged his own on his head. "Seems everyone's wearing one."

"They're meant to grant protection from the woods."

Briar raised his eyebrows. "I guess my sorry arse needs that more than most. How do I look?"

Rowan haltingly straightened Briar's crown, then quickly withdrew his hand, chest inflating. "Good. You look good."

Briar linked arms with him again, and they wound through the crowd, chatting as they went. There was a market propped up along the high street, orange lanterns hanging from the beams to make each stall an amber-lit hideout.

"I never properly thanked you for saving me," Briar said. "In the woods."

"No need."

"What were you doing in there, anyway?"

"Ehm . . ." Rowan rubbed the back of his neck, casting Briar a sidelong look. "It's a long story."

"We have all night. We should get some food. You can educate me about other traditions. Or anything else that's common knowledge to locals but could actually kill me."

Rowan pointed to a stall from which the smell of fresh-baked bread floated toward them. "Berry buns are traditional on Saor ó Eagla."

The buns were round, fat rolls the size of Rowan's fist, powdered liberally with icing sugar and stuffed with different flavors of jam. Rowan ordered an apricot one. Briar doubted he could finish a whole bun himself, they were so large.

"It's traditional to share, too," Rowan said sheepishly. "If you'd like to—"

"Love to."

They walked to a tarped-over area with heat lamps and picnic benches. The furniture looked crafted for children with Rowan sitting in it. Briar sat next to him, shoulder to shoulder, hip to hip. Rowan tore the bun in half and gave Briar the piece with more jam.

The first bite was heaven, the buttery dough melting and soft, the jam sweet and tart.

"Everything here tastes so good," Briar groaned. The coffee chains of the big cities had nothing on Coill Darragh's mom-and-pop shops. At Rowan's smirk, he added, "Don't get smug. You didn't tell me how you happened to find me in the big magic, evil woods."

"You didn't tell me why you were there either."

"You first." He took a bite of his bun. Vatii fluttered onto the table, looming pointedly. Rowan, to her flapping surprise, tore off a chunk of his own for her, which she gobbled down. She took up an expectant pose in front of him.

Rowan said, "I don't really know the answer. I have blackouts. That day in the woods was one of them."

"What, you have no memory of it?"

Rowan's eyebrows drew together. "Woke up when I found you. Carried you out. I don't know how I got to you."

"Does that happen a lot?"

"Mm. More and more."

It sounded terrifying. Briar took another bite of his bun. "Rowan, why does everyone avoid the forest? Why are we wearing crowns to protect us from it? Seriously, it's starting to freak me out." His curse felt like a stake through his ribs. He didn't understand why the forest first cursed his mother, but he'd come to believe it had, and he wanted answers.

"We're a suspicious lot, Coill Darraghns. Plenty of stories about bad things befalling those who mess about with it. Most will say they don't believe it. Just tall tales. Still, won't catch any Coill Darraghn going in of their own accord."

"But you went in."

"Not of my own accord."

Briar shivered. Thinking he was cold, Rowan leaned closer. A subtle gesture, but one Briar basked in, sidling up to Rowan's ribs. Rowan was a small sun next to him, warmth seeping through Briar's hip and arm where they touched.

He considered telling Rowan about the tree. About the mark on his arm. About the curse cast by the forest they all feared. He didn't, though. He swallowed his last bite of apricot bun and the story with it. He felt stupid for ignoring Gretchen's warning, but he didn't know how else to get ingredients for spells. Besides, he was marked for death already.

"It's your turn to tell me why you went in," Rowan said.

"I needed some lichen for an elixir."

To Rowan's credit, he didn't ask why Briar hadn't just bought some. "Next time, come to me."

"You're the alderman, my fairy-tale rescuer saving me from murderous trees, and now you're a herbalist too?"

"No, but I have a garden."

Hope struck like flint in Briar's chest, but there was something dark and fearful with it. Rowan's idle generosity was one thing, but Briar couldn't allow himself to depend upon it. In the end, this was his quest, his fate to meet alone.

"You and Sorcha have already helped me."

Rowan shrugged. He finished his food, and with no napkins available, licked the jam from his fingers, behaving as though his kindness was the norm and naught else. Some of Briar's gratitude swelled and stuck in his throat. The words "thank you" seemed paltry.

Rowan gave him a quizzical look, and Briar realized he must be blushing. He was spared having to explain by a child's shriek and the sudden assault of tiny arms around his waist.

"Ciara, what have I told you about jumping on people—"

Ciara stepped back, holding up the ends of her cloak and twirling. Behind her stood a man who could only be her father. Ciara shared his red hair and freckled complexion.

"Didn't mean to interrupt. She saw you and just—"

"It's no trouble," Briar assured him and got up to introduce himself. "I'm Briar."

"Connor."

Ciara blew past the introductions. "Look, we match!" She spun again to demonstrate. She pulled up her star-speckled hood and grabbed Briar's hand. "Dance with me."

"Ciara, you can't interrupt their evening."

"I'd be happy to dance with you," Briar said. Quieter, he told Connor, "It's really no trouble. Rowan and I don't mind, right?"

Rowan shook his head. Vatii, jostled by the dancers, took up a perch on Rowan's shoulder. Rowan only looked a little surprised, but Briar was gobsmacked.

Vatii never liked touching anyone except Briar.

The jaunty music picked up. Ciara took Briar's hands and skipped around in a circle. She twirled and bossed him around, teaching him the "right way" to dance. In a game that made Ciara shriek with laughter, Briar would deliberately perform the steps wrong and ask her, "Like that?" It was an effective way to banish the cold, but it was not just the dancing that lit a fire in Briar's breast. Rowan watched them. Normally, his expression fell somewhere between solemn and contented. Now, a look of genuine affection crossed his face.

"Another!" Ciara cried as the fiddler struck up a new chord, but Connor intervened.

"It's nearly your bedtime. Leave go of Briar's cloak," Connor said while pulling her away.

"One more song?"

"Your mam will have my hide."

"Where is Sorcha, anyway?" Briar wondered aloud.

He immediately regretted the question. An unspoken conversation transpired in the shuttered look on Rowan's face and the one Connor cast his way. Ciara alone remained immune, jumping up and down to the new song.

"Sorcha's taking the night off," Connor said.

Briar knew a bruise when he saw one, particularly when he'd just prodded it. "Give her my love, then."

"I will. Come, say good night, Ciara."

She wrapped one of Briar's legs in a hug, then Rowan's. Connor whisked her away into the crowd, leaving Briar to wonder why a night of good food, music, and dancing was the cause for soreness. He didn't feel comfortable asking. Rowan had divulged enough about his blackouts; it seemed invasive to push for more, especially since it involved his family.

The dancers began a different dance, spreading out in a large circle. Rowan started to guide them away, but Briar caught his hand.

"It's your turn now."

Disconcerted, Rowan's gaze flicked to the people around them. "I'm not much of a dancer."

"Everyone but me seems to know all the steps. Teach me."

The dance involved everyone standing in a circle, counting steps into the center, then out again. Spinning. Breaking into pairs and turning, hand in hand. It was a fun, uncomplicated dance, mostly spent skipping and laughing as you bumped into people. Rowan looked uncomfortable when surrounded by others, not least of all because they were unnerved by his presence, shying away from him as much as the dance would allow.

Briar resented them for it, could see how the casual cruelty wounded Rowan. But then they were linked arm in arm, and the smile Rowan gave him made the anger melt away.

It was ridiculous that anyone should fear him.

The song ended. They left the dancers, though Briar didn't unlink their arms, huddling closer for warmth as they walked. The stares of the townsfolk followed. Barring his own family, nobody seemed to know how to interact with Rowan, and Briar's disregard for this particular tradition earned them a lot of attention.

They shared another drink. Briar wished he had opted for something hot instead of a cider, his fingers going numb around the cold cup. They walked the winding streets, making up the path as they went. Though he didn't want to bring up another potentially sore subject, his curiosity couldn't be dissuaded any longer.

"There's something I don't understand, Rowan. You're the alderman. You've been kind to me since I arrived. You and your family. Why does everyone here . . ." He didn't know how to phrase it without coming across as insulting.

"Avoid me?" Rowan supplied.

Briar let out a breath. "Yeah."

Rowan fell quiet. His brow scrunched. He took a drink from his cup in a measured sip. Briar felt a little guilty, but Rowan's reaction seemed muted. If the way people treated him hurt, it was a hurt he'd grown used to.

"I've no idea, only clues," said Rowan. "The more interesting question is: Why do they avoid me but you don't?"

Briar replied earnestly. "Because you're lovely."

Rowan ducked his head, looking away so Briar couldn't see his expression. Briar wished to turn him with a hand on his jaw, feel the prickle of beard against his fingertips. Had no one ever told him so? How long had Rowan spent isolated from the people of his home?

"You said you have clues?"

"Mm. It started after I got this." Rowan touched the scar on his cheek. Briar traced its path with his eyes. A branching thing, it traveled from his temple to his jaw, then disappeared into his cloak. Briar wondered how much farther it went.

"How did you get it?"

"A long story." He winced. "Another time, maybe."

Briar finished his drink and tossed the plastic cup into a bin they passed. Rubbing his hands together did little to bring feeling back to his numbing fingers.

Gruffly, Rowan said, "C'mere to me." He stopped them at the darkened window of a store and set his drink on the sill. Cupping Briar's hands between his, he raised them to his lips and breathed warm air over them. A different sort of shiver raised the hair on Briar's arms and set his blood to boiling. Rowan rubbed feeling back into his fingers. He avoided eye contact, keeping his gaze low. Briar had only two drinks down and knew the fuzzy feeling steeping in him had less to do with alcohol than the way Rowan's aura wound around him. Like the sensuous curve of a body warm against his back, it made his toes curl in his boots.

This close, though, an undercurrent of something else polluted his aura. Just a creeping sense of unease and a smell like wilted plants. It got stronger when Briar leaned closer to Rowan's left side. It gave him an idea.

"I can read auras, you know."

Rowan's hands stilled but didn't drop Briar's.

"It's not a common skill, but I've had it as long as I can remember. It's the first thing I notice when I meet someone. If someone has an aura that tastes or feels bad, it's hard to be around them." As Briar spoke, Rowan's thumbs rubbed warm lines into his palms. "I've met people whose auras taste and feel like I just bit my tongue. Someone whose aura smelled like a field of wildflowers. It's hard not to make an immediate judgment. Yours . . ."

Rowan waited. Briar didn't know how to say it. Briar, who could scream all the pet names Celyn used to call him in a crowd of their peers, who was usually immune to embarrassment, felt shy to describe this part of himself. It wasn't something he often shared.

"Mine?" Rowan asked.

"Yours is warm. The first sensation I got was the taste of hot stew on a cold, rainy day. It's . . ." He was toeing a line. Vatii's reproach echoed in his mind. *I thought Linden was your destiny.* This seemed misleadingly romantic. Too intimate for the idle flirting Briar had intended this night to be. "It's wonderful. But you have more than one aura. There's your aura. And there's your scar. It's different. Most people don't get a sense for auras the way I do, but everyone has some intuition when it comes to magic. Especially when it comes to something dangerous. And I think . . . I don't know, but maybe the energy of your scar makes them uneasy."

Rowan absorbed that, his thumbs still tracing lazy patterns in Briar's hands. Much as Briar enjoyed the touch, he pulled his hands free. He'd never talked about his abilities to anyone in this depth, and now that he had, he felt vulnerable.

"It makes sense," Briar finished. "Since you said they only reacted like that after you got it."

Rowan retrieved his drink from the windowsill and finished it. "Could be. Thank you, Briar."

"For what?"

"For telling me." He searched Briar's face. He opened his mouth as if to say something else, then shut it again.

Whatever it was, he instead opted to walk Briar home. Though he offered Briar his arm, he was even quieter than usual. So much so that

Briar wondered if he'd made a mistake in telling him. By the time they reached his doorstep, Briar's stomach had tied itself in knots.

He'd spent a good portion of the evening in Rowan's company. Admiring the strong planes of his face, his dark eyes. The way his bicep felt as they strolled arm in arm. How his rich baritone filled Briar's chest. He'd thought idly about how the night would end, and in his imaginings, it had always ended one way. He'd skirted over the thought, never looking at it directly.

Now they stood under his eave, he confronted the fact that he hoped Rowan would kiss him goodnight.

It was a treacherous thought. Perhaps Vatii was right. He shouldn't risk even a casual affair with destiny on his doorstep. Rowan stood close enough that Briar could smell bonfire and ash on his clothes. Close enough to hear the slight shiver in his breath. It would take only a half step, tilting his head, Rowan leaning down—

Rowan took a small step toward him. Briar swayed on the balls of his feet, looking up and into Rowan's face. The breath that had warmed Briar's hands became shallow, puffing in clouds on the cold air between them. Rowan's hand rose, knuckles just brushing Briar's chin, a tremor in that barest touch. The way Rowan looked at him, dark-eyed and wanting, made Briar's heart beat mightily, made him rise on tiptoe.

But Rowan didn't lean in the rest of the way. His voice tripped over his words as he said too quickly, "Have a good night, Briar."

He left.

CHAPTER 9

Briar opened the shop the next morning in a dreadful mood, convinced he'd offended Rowan with his aura babble and deprived himself of a kiss goodnight in the process.

It should not have been his focus. He needed a strategy to better acquaint himself with Linden, but from their interaction yesterday, he didn't know how. Linden was an enigma. Fame elevated him. Without good reason to strike up a conversation, Briar's attempts could look sycophantic at best and self-serving at worst. Grasping for a piece of his power, a touch of his fame. Briar couldn't very well say *Hi, a seer told me we're destined to be together, so how about a kiss?* either. The tithe of silence forbade it. Plus, he'd sound like a numpty.

The stiff competition left Briar hurting for work. He spent a good deal of time hunched over a sewing machine. He'd scraped the bottom of his ingredient stores for enchantments and started resorting to flesh tithes. It was exhausting, so Briar interspersed his work with something he found easier: moping.

Gretchen appeared at fifteen minutes to noon looking uncharacteristically cheerful. At the sight of him, she blanched. "What's wrong with you?"

"Nothing. I'm just an unkissable failure who couldn't sell a carrot to a hare, and my entire future hinges upon my relationship to a man who doesn't know I exist. No big deal."

"Yeesh."

Vatii yawned. She'd been kept up late by his whining.

Gretchen said, "Well, I'm feeling great, thank you for asking."

"How was your roam around town while I was at the festival?"

"Wonderful. I searched the town for clues on how I died. Do you know what I learned?"

"I thought you didn't care about that?" Though he had wondered.

"I don't. I mean—just listen! I found out I can—"

The bell tolled to announce a customer. Briar looked up from his work just as Gretchen blinked out of existence. Rude of her to leave him guessing, but she did have antisocial tendencies when it came to customers.

Linden Fairchild stood in the door. He wore pinstripe pants and a waistcoat with an emerald cravat. A traditional witch's hat, dripping a single string of crystals from the brim, tilted smartly on his head.

He looked too elegant in Briar's humble store. With a cursory scan of the room, he spotted Briar and smiled. "Ah, hello. I believe we met briefly yesterday. Briar?"

Briar suppressed a scream. *He remembered my name.* "That's me."

"I was wondering, I've just filmed a little tour of my shop for Alakagram, and I wanted to introduce my followers to the other places in town. Do you mind if I stream a tour in here?"

"Of course, make yourself at home." Briar glanced at Vatii to confirm she was hearing all this. She rolled her eyes at his exuberance.

Linden's grin broadened. He tapped open the app on his phone, held the camera aloft, and spoke to his followers with casual familiarity, showing them around the shop, saying, "This winsome place belongs to Briar Wyngrave, another Reded witch next door to me. Looks like we have ourselves an enchanted clothes shop. Man after my own heart."

Vatii muttered, "Kill me."

Linden joined Briar behind the counter, a sweet fragrance like lilacs perfuming him as he sidled close, holding his camera up in selfie mode. A number on the screen showed half a million viewers were already watching. Their commentary scrolled past, along with a spray of stars whenever they tapped the magic wand icon. Briar spotted a few complimentary messages. One person wrote, *Is it just me, or is he kind of cute?* Another replied. *It's not just you.*

A few disagreeable watchers said, *I don't see it,* but Briar paid them no mind. Despite very little sleep, he *did* look good.

Linden beamed. "This is Briar, owner of—"

"Briar's Bewitching Boutique," he answered, creating the name off the cuff. "That's a working title. I could give you the tour?"

Linden glanced into the camera as if sharing a secret with his fans. "Isn't he charming?" Then, to Briar, "Lead the way."

Briar tried to appear calm, but internally he vibrated with enthusiasm. "I'm only getting started, but here's what I'm working on for my winter line." He led Linden to the window display, gesturing to the garments with a flick of his wrist. He reeled Linden closer to show him the embroidered detail, or to run the fabric between his fingers and comment on its quality. He dropped Sorcha's name, insisting Linden check out her textiles. He spoke quickly and energetically, doing his best to keep the tenuous attention spans of Linden and his fanbase. Lastly, he pulled up the cloak he'd been working on.

"Not to be cheeky, but you inspired this one." Briar took a step back and whirled the cloak around his shoulders. It still needed hemming, but he was quite proud of it. The emerald green was a trademark of Linden's, and the high collar gave it an interesting silhouette. "I'll be adding embellishments to the hem with a charm to repel rain."

Linden touched the front of it, his long-fingered hand playing along the buckle. Briar hoped he couldn't feel his heart thumping. He'd jumped to showmanship, and the pause awaiting judgment felt infinite. So many eyes on him through the lens of that camera. This could highlight his work or condemn it, depending largely on Linden's opinion. In a private meeting, Briar might have been brave enough to turn up the charm, to lean in, to enjoy his proximity to a star upon which he'd made wishes from the time he was a boy.

Linden's eyes met Briar's. "I can see you're incredibly talented." On his phone, stars exploded, and a number of people gushed, *That would look soooo fab on Linden.* "You know, I've been looking for something fresh. What do you think about making something for me?"

Briar matched the sly smile with one of his own. "You'll have to give me your measurements."

Someone in Linden's chat typed, *DID HE JUST?* Someone else said, *Oh my God, are they flirting???* Another person just put loads of crying emojis.

A shocked laugh bubbled from Linden. "Oh, I like you. As bold as your taste in clothes."

Briar held his breath while watching Linden jot down his measurements.

Finished, Linden held the paper out to him. "I look forward to wearing it." Briar ensured his hand brushed the tops of Linden's fingers, long enough to be deliberate, brief enough to feel casual. Linden said quietly, "I'll see you again later, then."

He returned to filming, giving his fans one last look at the shop. Briar waved to them with a theatrical curtsy.

The doorbell echoed after Linden's departure, leaving Briar with the sense that he'd just cheated on a very complicated exam and gotten away with it. His short-circuited mind refired with a single thought. "Did that just happen?" he asked the empty shop.

Vatii said, "He's better without the cat. But still a ponce."

"Did that just happen, though? I have a job."

"Is he even going to pay you for it?"

"A job from *Linden*," Briar continued. "Half a million people just got a good look at my designs." The significance hadn't sunk in. He deflated into his chair, still holding the cloak that had won him Linden's business.

This could change everything.

For the rest of the day, Briar cut patterns to the sound of rain pattering against the windows.

At closing time, the hazy sun tucked itself behind the rooftops. Gretchen poked her head through the stairwell wall. "So, do you want to see what I learned yesterday or not?"

Briar thought he should spend the evening making clothes, but he'd felt bad his conversation with Linden had seemed to scare her off. And he wanted to see what had Gretchen so excited.

He locked up and put a sign on the door, tying the curtain-cravat around his neck on his way. They walked out to the failing light and bone-cold drizzle. The street was a sea of umbrellas. The weather in Coill Darragh had taken a cold turn, wind and the nip of winter on the air. It blustered through his clothes, making him wrap his cloak tighter. A few residents cleared up litter and decorations from the festivities the night before.

In the town square, the statue wore a pile of leaf crowns. The statues of Briar's hometown got a similar treatment with traffic cones, but the wreaths looked more dignified. Tokens of respect.

Gretchen floated over to the wall of the church. A chunk gouged from the stone pulsed with a magical scar, exuding an aura of pins and needles.

"Watch this," she said, and touched the scar.

The question of how Gretchen could see the scars died on Briar's tongue.

The town square transformed. A hazy vision superimposed over it, a memory made manifest. It looked so vivid, Briar stumbled into the wall to make way for the witches stampeding through. There were three, hands raised to enchant deflective shields. The wail of something high and horrifying droned in the air. Terror rendered the apparitions hollow-faced, the whites of their eyes shining wide around their irises. These visions collided with the real residents of Coill Darragh, only revealing their phantasmal natures as they phased through the living, who didn't respond with more than a slight shiver.

With a whining, reverberant song, a wave of magic reared after the fleeing witches. It ripped through the square, stripping paint from doors and shutters, chipping the walls. Briar cringed as a fist-sized chunk of stone tore off the spot Gretchen touched and collided with the shoulder of a witch. She hit the ground on hands and knees, scrabbling away, but a glut of magic climbed over her like the vines had done to Briar in the woods. Drowning, smothering.

She evaporated like smoke. Briar knew he'd just watched her die.

The vision ended. Gretchen retracted her hand, looking gleeful despite the horror they'd witnessed. "Isn't that cool?"

Briar felt queasy. "Gretchen, that was awful." Clutching his chest, he looked away from the spot where the witch had collapsed. Vatii ruffled her feathers. "Did we just watch a woman die?"

"Oh, that." Gretchen crossed her arms. "I forgot how squinchy you lot get about dying. Once you've done it, it's no big deal. Besides, the dying lady wasn't the point. The point is, I can access the history of Coill Darragh this way! We could find out more about what happened, what's going on now with the woods, maybe even learn how I died."

Briar touched the stone, the rough edges of the divot worn semismooth with rain. The magic there turned his veins icy. "I didn't know you could see the auras of these scars too," he said.

"See? No, I don't *see* anything, I just kind of . . . felt like this spot was weird? I don't know, I touched it, and this happened. You can see something here?"

Briar nodded. He could see the scars' auras. Perhaps Gretchen felt them because the magic tethering her was somehow linked to what had happened. Much as she insisted death hardly mattered, the hazy details around her own seemed like a thorn that needed excising.

"You said things are going on here *now*?" Briar said. "What do you mean?"

"Do you think roots destroying bits of fabric and eating hares is normal?"

He didn't. Vatii looked uncomfortable but didn't comment. Though he didn't understand much from that glimpse, Briar felt the draw of it, too. Something stirred in Coill Darragh that went deeper than a few strange phenomena. They had to investigate, even if the notion made him long to curl up at home with a cup of tea instead. It could lead him to answers about why the forest had cursed him. He could help Gretchen.

"There's another scar here," he said.

Between the gaps in the cobbles, a slash of magic fizzled, fainter than on the church. He pointed to it, and Gretchen hovered near. She asked if he was ready before kneeling to touch the violet aurora.

The vision didn't last long. In Gretchen's place, a witch took to his broom. A siren scream of magic roared through the square, and the same pulse that had taken the first victim snatched this one from the air, dashing him apart like dandelion seeds.

The vision left him clammy and corpse-cold. It seemed to drain Gretchen too, her apparition flickering. This vision was no less unnerving than the last, for all its brevity, but it offered nothing new, except—

"His shoes," Briar said. "The witch had beetle-wing embellishments on his shoes. Those were in fashion ten years ago, before people boycotted them because the beetles were endangered. It gives us a time frame."

"Of course the thing you notice is his *shoes*," Gretchen said. "We should try another location."

They traveled through town and paused at intervals to survey scars marking a street sign and a garden wall. Both played out the same. Witches running. A wave of malignant magic. A death, and the vision ended.

There was one anomaly—a vision wherein a civilian's arm erupted with roots—but Briar couldn't tell whether this was a misfired spell or a result of the magic wave.

One thing became clear. The wave discriminated in who it killed. Some perished in its grasp, others remained unscathed.

Beyond this, they learned little. The noise of the cataclysm set Briar's teeth on edge. He despaired at the devastation. With no sign of its cause or new information, he wondered if they'd wasted their evening. And he was keenly aware he had less time to waste than most.

On a stone footbridge, leading over a brook and out of town, there was a smear of magical scarring along the left parapet. It looked no different from the others. When Gretchen touched it, though, the ringing noise Briar expected didn't come. Instead, footsteps of an encroaching figure pounded closer. A witch blocked the bridge, casting a web of magic that walled off passage, spreading over into the brook, stretching several meters in either direction. Her fingers flexed as if drawing upon a well of magic from deep within, except that couldn't be possible. To create such a barrier, she would require a tithe of enormous power, yet her arms were unmarked, her hands empty.

Beyond the barrier, a running figure got close enough to see. A man with a jutting chin, his hair flying away from its leather twine, and his eyes alight with desperate rage.

He was unmistakably the man in whose likeness the statue in the square had been built.

Gretchen said, "Éibhear."

Briar didn't have the breath to ask how she knew him. All the air was stolen from his lungs as he watched the two witches on their collision course. If Éibhear ran into that barrier, it would eviscerate him, much like the wards should have done to Briar when the woods broke his bracelet.

Éibhear did not slow. He drew one arm back like a lance. As he did, thorny vines rose from the bedrock of the brook. They reared back and punched through the other witch's ribs like a serpent's strike.

Her barrier dissolved. She hit the parapet. The vision ended.

They'd just seen Éibhear, the man commemorated with a statue, murder another witch.

Hot bile rose in Briar's throat. He didn't know how the vision was significant, only that it made his skin crawl to see two witches wield magic like that.

Vatii whispered, "I don't like any of this."

"Me neither," Briar agreed. "How did they do all that without a tithe?"

"I don't know." Gretchen's hands clenched in fists. "I don't know how, but I don't know *why* either. I *remember* Éibhear." Her voice came out gritty and frustrated. "Or at least, I think I do. He was my mentor. He could be a strict teacher, but he was kind to me."

Briar struggled to reconcile that description with what they'd just witnessed. "What else do you remember about this battle? That magic wave thing?"

Gretchen scowled, clenching her jaw. "I . . ." She hesitated, squinting into the middle distance, a look of growing consternation in her dark eyes. "I don't know. It's like the memories are all locked up. I remember something Éibhear told me about the forest? He said it was special, that there were other ancient sources of wild magic a long time ago, but ravaged for tithes, those places weakened in power. But here, in Coill Darragh, it's different. Protected and protector." She squinted, searching for the memories, the details. "I . . . That's all I've got."

She sounded scared, and that scared Briar too. Not even death frightened her, but *this* did.

He searched the fields beyond the bridge, the woods within sight. The vines that killed the hare and destroyed the curtain scrap looked ominously like the vines Éibhear used to murder his foe. This forest claimed it had cursed Briar's mother. Now they'd discovered some terrible event had transpired ten years prior, around the time his mother was cursed.

Briar wanted to help Gretchen, but deep down, he understood this involved him, too. He feared the woods and what secrets they contained, but curiosity pulled him toward those woods anyway.

They crossed the bridge and followed the dirt lanes into the fields, following the direction Éibhear had run from in the vision, misty rain pestering their progress. The path split left and right ahead. Beyond that, grassy knolls bowed before the towering trees of Coill Darragh. At the edge of the wood, a line glowed in the reeds. The closer they got, the greater a sense of malaise settled over Briar. The scar blazed a swath in front of the woods, six meters across, grass growing over the crater.

Briar paused, the forest's voice echoing in his ear. *You, soon. Your mother.*

He bristled. He didn't want to get any closer, so he skirted around it, but Gretchen had to touch it to weave her strange brand of magic. With hand extended, she hesitated. Though blood no longer pumped through her veins, and no pulse could make her hand quiver, it shook visibly. She steeled her resolve, clenched her fist, and plunged it into the grass.

Éibhear appeared. Unlike the other vision, he stood alone. His shoulders rose and fell with harsh breaths, gaze cast up into the looming canopy. A moment of paralyzing indecision wrote itself in the sweat of his brow. After a beat, he shucked his cloak into the grass. Then his shirt.

Briar gasped. Even Vatii ruffled in surprise.

Across Éibhear's arms were rune tithes.

Countless, more than triple the number Briar had accumulated. They coiled up both arms, several more along his lower torso. Briar jolted with a nauseating thrill. He wanted no comparison to this man who killed witches with impunity, couldn't ever imagine using his magic the way Éibhear had.

Yet a powerful and celebrated man bore the same sordid tithes Briar did.

Éibhear took something out of his robes. Charcoal. With it, he drew upon his chest. He had no mirror, so the marks sometimes went awry. He smeared these away by licking his fingers and rubbing. It took some time. A sigil over his chest, runes around its circumference, circles interwoven at its center, more lines and symbols arrayed down his stomach, over his ribs.

Finished, he dropped the charcoal and stared into the trees. He tilted his head back and closed his eyes, lips parted. Stood frozen like that.

Nothing happened. Nothing that they could *see*, but *something* transpired. A silent communion of man and nature. The forest's heartbeat throbbed underfoot.

Then Éibhear bent backward, chest surging toward the sky as if drawn there by a needle and thread. He floated upward. The new runes on his skin glowed, and the agony of so many rent a bloodcurdling scream from him. Gooseflesh broke out over Briar's arms. The earth below Éibhear moved, bubbled, lumps of earth roiling. Roots burst forth in a shower of soil. They spiraled and coiled around Éibhear, thorns biting into skin, his blood hissing where it streamed into the open earth. The roots and vines enveloped him until only his face was visible. For a moment, he was more a tree than a man.

Then the roots pulled Éibhear under. Like a meteor hitting, he and the vines plunged beneath the loam. Dirt sprayed. The earth rumbled like a hungry stomach.

It went quiet. So quiet. Briar clenched his throat to keep from being sick.

Gretchen's voice quivered. "It's not over."

From the tree line, a sound rose. For all its familiarity, it still made Briar shudder. A high whine, like ringing in his ears. Then a rumble. The two frequencies wove together in a sickening, undulating tune that got louder and vibrated in Briar's core.

The trees bled. Not red, but a thick, semitransparent ooze that spread into a viscous pool. The dark purple of a bruise, it turned up bits of dead leaf and detritus from the forest floor, moved like a living deep-sea thing. Slow but picking up speed, it advanced toward the town.

The magic cataclysm swept past. Briar closed his eyes. He could feel it coursing over him, even if it was only an echo. He could envision it hemorrhaging through the town like poison through an anthill, killing with its peculiar discrimination. The purple ectoplasm covered everything as far as the eye could see and reached upward. Briar turned in a circle to behold it. A wall rose, stretching like fingers into the sky, until the wards of Coill Darragh painted the entire horizon in an amaranthine sunrise.

When the vision ended, it left them standing in the cold and the dark and the rain—in a funereal miasma. Briar clutched Vatii to his chest, where she was tucked into his robes, though they were soaking cold. He unstuck his tongue from where it was glued to the roof of his mouth.

"Gretchen, what was that?"

Her specter shivered like she felt the rain too. "We just saw the creation of the wards."

"It killed people," Briar said, and she nodded. "Why?"

She rubbed her eyes beneath her glasses. "I don't remember *any* of this, I can't—but I know who you can ask."

"Who?"

Gretchen gave him a queer look. "Rowan."

It made sense. He'd lived through it. He even had a scar reminiscent of the ones left by the wards. But something in the tone of Gretchen's voice made Briar think that wasn't all.

So he asked, "Why Rowan?"

"You really don't know, do you?"

"Know what?"

"Éibhear," she said. "He was Rowan's father."

CHAPTER 10

Soaked to the bone and head stuffed with grim images, Briar returned to his creaky flat. He hung all his sodden clothes next to the wood stove and got a fire going to chase out the chill. He made himself chamomile tea to warm his frozen fingers and bundled up in pajamas.

Normally, Vatii would opt to dry herself by the fire. Instead, she stayed close, slick feathers pressed against Briar's neck while he steeped his tea. Mug in hand, he dragged a chair to the stove and sat there until sensation burned back into his numb fingers. Gretchen had vanished to replenish her energy and give him space, but his thoughts blurred together. With an idle hand, he rubbed at the swirl on his wrist left by the tree, its image shivering in the flickering light of the fire.

He couldn't comprehend the conflict which had precipitated the creation of the wards, nor the strange collusion of man and forest that had been its architects.

"What have we stepped in, Vatii?" he asked.

She didn't answer. One evening, when he was twelve, she'd appeared at his window, pecking until he let her in. Familiars were a strange part of being a witch. His magic called her into being, and she'd been harassing him ever since.

But she was quiet now.

Saor ó Eagla commemorated Éibhear and the creation of the wards. It seemed sadistic in hindsight. Why would anyone celebrate that grisly event? Was the celebration a mix of fear and respect, like the town's feelings about the woods? Or maybe, Briar thought with rueful sarcasm, he'd fallen in with a cult.

Harder still to absorb was Rowan's relation to Éibhear. Generous, soft-hearted Rowan—he was nothing like the ruthless man in those visions. Yet the whole town feared him. Perhaps that wasn't a tragic side effect of his scar, but of his father's deeds.

Perhaps Briar should fear him, too.

There was one thing Briar needn't wonder about any longer: Rowan and Sorcha's solemnity on the night of the festival. It had been the anniversary of their father's death.

He took a sip of tea, its heat a soothing thaw.

He had to speak to Rowan, and for the first time, that notion unnerved him.

In the morning, a small group had gathered outside his shop and was waiting as Briar woke up. Composed mostly of teens wearing wardstone bracelets, they peered in the window and stared into the void of their phones.

"You're Briar," one girl said as he opened the shop. "From Linden's Alakagram?"

Still in shock from the visions he had seen with Gretchen yesterday, Briar nodded. The girl bounced, looking between her friends. "We were wondering if we could have a look through your store."

He recovered his senses. "Of course!"

In minutes, they cleared out the majority of his stock. On top of the cost of the garments themselves, most agreed to pay extra for fittings, thrilled that Briar accommodated for their different shapes. One girl liked a design in Briar's sketchbook so much, she asked to commission it for an upcoming Christmas party.

They left, chatting animatedly about their purchases. Briar felt a swell of pride. He'd just made more money in a day than he'd ever made in all his years at Wishbrooke covering shifts.

For the rest of the morning, Briar tried to push aside all thoughts of Éibhear and the wards to focus on work, but the memory prickled like a sliver he couldn't tweeze out from under his skin. He scribbled designs, but nothing felt worthy of Linden. Accomplishing so little left him agitated by day's end.

As he dumped his dishes in the sudsy sink to wash, Gretchen materialized in the kitchenette, her head bowed, chewing her lip in contemplation.

"There you are," Briar said. "You know, you could have warned me you were taking me on the serial killer tour of town. I can't clear my head of it. I keep seeing those horrible visions, and I know you think death is no big deal, but I'm sensitive! I have work to do! I can't be distracted, and I haven't gotten a single good sketch out."

Gretchen barely looked up. "Oh. Sorry."

That gave him pause. He'd expected her to retaliate or banter along with him. "You all right?"

She folded her arms across her stomach. "I've been thinking. What if the wards—what if they killed me, too?"

Briar hadn't considered that. For all her protests that death meant little when you'd already died, her face told another story. "What makes you think that?" he asked.

"I'm not Coill Darraghn. Seemed like the wards killed anyone who wasn't. I don't have any memory of it, but this is where I would have been when it happened."

Briar didn't know what he could possibly say. He understood how discomfiting the visions were. History hoarding the locked parts of her past, the mysteries surrounding her death. His curse could be linked, too.

He couldn't hug or comfort her. She looked more transparent now than she had last night.

"I'm sorry."

"What? Why?"

"For what I said earlier. And, I don't know, you seem down about it."

"I'm not—I mean, I am, but it isn't your fault, and anyway, I'm just—" She scrambled for the words. "Pissed off! I remember things in bits and pieces, and I *knew* Éibhear. He mentored me. He saw how good I was with potions and encouraged me to make my own. It doesn't make sense, what he did. Because if it's all what we think, that means he murdered *me*. And countless other people besides."

"And the whole town celebrates him for it," Briar added.

"Right? If I could just remember what the conflict was about, where I was during the ward spell . . ."

Briar, unthinking, put a hand on her shoulder to quell her. His fingers passed through her, and a shot of embarrassment went through him in turn. She didn't shy away, so he kept his hand there, even as her chilly influence numbed his fingers.

"We'll figure it out. I'll ask Rowan. Okay?"

She sagged with relief. "Thanks."

Gretchen lingered while he finished washing dishes. He couldn't tell if his chills came from her or the notion of speaking to Rowan about what they'd seen. Rowan had never mentioned the dark history behind the wards' creation, nor anything about his father. His father, who tithed himself to the same forest that cursed Briar's mother.

He needed to know more. Flipping open his phone, he tapped out a quick message to Rowan, asking if he could come by. It didn't take long to hear back, his phone trilling like a wind chime.

>>*You're welcome anytime. I'm up Old Mill Road. Mine's the cottage with the chickens.*

Briar looked at his vision board, the colorful swatches like mermaid scales in the dark, and his focus zeroed in on his most pressing list of objectives. Some he'd accomplished already, but the fifth—making a gift for Rowan to thank him for his help—had not been. Perhaps that would help to smooth his jagged feelings around their upcoming interaction.

Or at least bribe his way into Rowan's good graces in the event he was secretly a maniac.

A few more messages to arrange a time, and it was settled. He'd visit Rowan tomorrow, on Saturday.

So, up in the wee hours of the morning, Briar knitted a scarf. There was something meditative about the process. The gift needed to express Briar's appreciation for Rowan's help, and looping every individual stitch by hand felt appropriate.

"You know about the sweater curse?" Vatii said as he counted stitches.

"I don't want to talk about curses, Vatii." His hands had started shaking chronically of late, and he didn't know if it was from overworking himself or Bowen's Wane.

"It's said that if you gift a hand-knit sweater to a lover, the lover will end the relationship. Or end it before the sweater is complete."

He rolled his eyes. "Tragically, Rowan and I aren't in a relationship."

"Yet."

"And this isn't a sweater! Besides . . . I don't know how I should feel about him now. Not after—all that business with Éibhear is really ruining my beauty rest, let's just put it that way."

"Well, good. Fancying him was a recipe for disaster, if Linden is your prophetic lover."

In the morning, after very little sleep, Briar set out with directions to

Rowan's house. Winter's chill invaded autumn, some of the bright fire in Coill Darragh's canopy had gone a sullen brown.

How to broach the topic of Éibhear? *Hi, Rowan. Lovely place you've got. Thanks so much for feeding me, rescuing me, just generally being a stellar human being. By the way, did you know your dad died in a horrific magical bargain with a forest to create the wards, which protect the town but also murdered every foreigner within its borders? The hell was that about? My poltergeist roommate is figuratively dying to know.*

Bringing it up at all seemed about as tactful as a claw hammer to the face, but he needed to find out. For Gretchen's sake and his own.

The directions led him up country lanes, fields of sheep watching his passage with baleful *baaaah*s. He knew Rowan's house when it came into view. In the shade of a poplar tree stood a thatched cottage with its door and shutters painted blue. A few chickens clucked around the dirt path. One such chicken, butterscotch colored and alarmingly large, took one look at Briar and decided it didn't like him. It charged. Briar had only a few seconds to backstep before the chicken was upon him. It leapt and flapped its wings in such a furor it rose to eye level.

Vatii, the coward, took flight. "Watch out! I think it's hungry."

Briar did what any sensible man would and screamed. He tried to run but tripped on his fashionable-but-not-functional boot laces. He landed in the dirt. When he raised his arms to defend himself, the chicken seized its opportunity and landed on his elbow, clucking furiously.

Rowan emerged from the cottage, drawn by the noise, to find Briar curled up in the fetal position, his poultry nemesis stalking around him in furtive circles.

To Briar's shame, Rowan laughed. "Ah, Maude won't hurt you."

He picked her up and tucked her under his arm. She regarded Briar in a manner he deemed unfriendly. Rowan helped him up with one hand, the other keeping Maude at bay.

"You all right there?" Rowan asked.

"Great! Fabulous. Just a little grimy. And wondering why nature has it out for me."

"Maude'll only cluck round you like that if she likes you." Rowan gave her a pat, set her down, and gently shooed her away nonetheless.

Briar's nerves returned. To dispel them, he held his gift bag out at arm's length. "I made you something. As a thank-you for all the help."

Rowan's face was inscrutable as he opened the bag and unfurled the scarf within. It was cable-knit and burnt orange, like the autumn leaves, and long enough it could wrap twice around Rowan's broad shoulders.

He looked at a loss for words.

"If it's not your thing, I won't be offended."

"No, it's—thank you."

Rowan looped the scarf around his neck, the ends trailing to his knees. Briar's breath caught as he stepped in to help. He arranged the scarf snugly so the ends didn't hang too long. He had to stand on tiptoes to do it. It brought them very close, and despite all Briar's fears, he didn't want to step away. Something about Rowan drew him in. A fire to warm his hands by. Or to burn him.

Rowan raised a hand. Visions reared in Briar's head too: Éibhear raising his hand just like that to strike a witch through the heart. Éibhear's arms dangling limp as the forest claimed him. Briar startled back like a spooked horse.

"S-sorry." Rowan's hand fell back to his side. A look of muddled hurt and confusion crossed his features. He cleared his throat. "I mean, thank you."

"No worries. No problem. Just wanted to return the kindness."

An awkward silence fell. An internal war of rebuke waged in Briar's head. Logically, he understood Rowan was not Éibhear, but the images that had played out in the shadow of the woods hadn't been hauntings; they'd been real.

Rowan broke the silence first. "The gardens. I'll show you round?"

The cottage backed onto acres of farmland, with a paddock for two horses, a greenhouse, and neat rows of outdoor crops. Rowan took him through the gate behind his cottage and into an altogether different variety of garden.

Densely packed flower beds sprouted all manner of rare potion ingredients. From sea holly—whose growing conditions were better suited to tropical climates—to a variety of belladonna Briar had only seen in textbooks. A plant he didn't recognize sprouted in a firework from an old cracked pot. A wisteria-covered trellis shaded half the garden. Without the summer blooms, its vines were reminiscent of the ones that devoured Éibhear. More reminiscent still was the purple aura hanging over it, uncomfortable as socked feet soaked in a puddle.

"Rowan, how are you even growing some of these things?"

"Ehm, I haven't. Was my da's. Still grew after he died."

Before he could suppress it, Briar shuddered. He hoped Rowan wouldn't notice, but of course he did. "If it isn't what you need, we can check the greenhouse—"

"No, honestly, it's perfect, Rowan. Do you know how rare some of these plants are?"

Rowan offered a shrug, which hid many unsaid things. "I've no idea what to do with 'em. Fill your boots."

He handed over some pruning shears. The garden had an unsettling effect on Briar as he knelt and snipped a few spiny leaves into a pouch. Part of him felt like he was reaching for a branch of lichen again, wondering what it would cost. He plucked a few flowers from the winter honeysuckle next. Despite the prickling aura of the garden, it gave him the perfect opportunity to broach the topic he'd feared touching.

"Your dad grew all this?"

"Mm. Cottage was his workshop. I converted it into a home after he passed."

Passed. As if in a hospital, not the grips of a sentient wood. Briar's head pounded. He didn't know how to push for more or if Rowan deliberately withheld the rest. Briar stood to pick leaves from a fern. The plants' combined perfume smelled thick and soupy, turning his thoughts in circles.

Vatii, perched on the retaining wall, pecked at his fingertips to snap him out of it. "You look peaky, maybe we should—"

Before she finished, Briar swayed on his feet. His head boiled like one of his potions. In his murky periphery, he registered movement.

Rowan caught him, but the garden's aura, combined with a chaotic stew of memories, triggered the same instinct that had made Briar shy away from Rowan before. He recoiled, tripping, landing in the grass, backpedaling into a garden wall. Rowan, usually so stoic, looked down at Briar and then at his own hands with undiluted pain and bewilderment.

Too late, Briar realized the cruelty of his reaction. How many others shied away from Rowan at the slightest glance, the barest brush in a crowd? A haunted look crossed Rowan's face, and Briar was immediately sorry he'd been the one to put it there.

"Sorry, I'm just . . . I think the garden's had a weird effect on me."

Vatii said worriedly, "It could be the curse, not the garden."

He flinched. He'd just lost too much sleep, or the memories from the town's scars were affecting him oddly.

"You don't look well," Rowan murmured. "Can I get you anything? Tea?"

At Vatii's urging, Briar agreed. Rowan ushered him through the back door into a kitchen. It was both tidy and cluttered, a pastiche of country crockery. A painted rooster decorated the bread box, and all the chairs were mismatching shades of weathered pastel.

Briar sat at the breakfast bar. "It's nothing. Just my fainting-damsel routine. No need to—"

"It's not a bother. Sit."

Rowan didn't ask how he liked his tea, just put the kettle on and fetched mugs. "Does that happen often?"

"What?"

"Fainting spells."

Briar traced the wood-grain whorls on the breakfast bar. Vatii nudged his elbow. She'd always advised him to be forthright about his condition, but he found it easier to keep it secret. If he was honest with himself, he hoped Rowan looked at him and saw a sparkling future of possibilities. Difficult to do that when his future was terminal.

"Just lost one too many hours of sleep. Used to pull all-nighters during my apprenticeship no problem. Now I lose my senses if I don't get eight hours and three square meals."

The kettle boiled. They shared an awkward silence. Every encounter before this had felt like a rhythmic stitch drawing them closer together. Now, Briar had come looking for answers and was finding that all the questions created buckles and snags in the growing intimacy of their relationship.

Rowan frowned down at his hands, laced before him. "Ehm . . . Briar, I—" The words caught on the way out, his voice rougher than usual. "Have I done something wrong?"

Guilt clawed its way up Briar's throat. "No, nothing."

"Is it my scar? You said the aura—is it affecting you too, now?"

"It's your dad," Briar blurted. The rest tumbled out in a rush. "I see more than people's auras, I see auras all around town. They show me memories of the past, and I saw your dad killing witches. Then he made a pact with the awful, freaky forest that tried to kill me, and the wards slaughtered people, and you didn't tell me, and I didn't know if you were involved or how to ask, but now I feel stupid for ever doubting you because you've been stupidly kind this entire time, so I don't know what to do!" He took a heaving breath. "What *happened*? Here? Why has he got a statue? I don't understand."

Rowan stared, shocked, and Briar thought, *Tactful as a claw hammer to the face.* He expected to be kicked out, told to go spin on it after dredging up a painful memory and unfairly conflating Rowan with the actions of his father.

The kettle whined. Rowan startled, glancing toward it. He ran a hand over his face and sighed. "Tea first."

Instead of handing it to him, Rowan set the mug on the breakfast bar. Possibly because Briar kept leaping away like his proximity caused electric shock. Heat wafted off the drink, carrying an herbal smell—some combination of peppermint, chamomile, lemon, and ginger. It seemed less a tea than a potion.

"Should help your dizziness," Rowan said.

It was too hot to drink yet. Briar waited, watching Rowan gather himself to speak.

"All of what happened, I was told about it after. Still don't understand the whole of it, but if you've questions, I'll try and answer."

Briar took a deep breath. "Why'd he do it?"

"Keep in mind, most of what I know's secondhand. Seer Niamh told us about it. At the time? I hadn't the faintest idea."

Briar wasn't a bit surprised to hear Niamh's name come up. Of course the meddling biddy was involved.

Rowan continued, "My da wasn't just the alderman—he was the forest's Keeper. Charged with protecting Coill Darragh—the wood and its people. As I understand it, witches came looking to take the wild magic for themselves."

"How do you just take wild magic?"

Rowan shook his head. "Don't know. Only know that we Coill Darraghns are connected to it somehow. So when the invaders took it, the forest sickened, and so did we. To sustain itself, the forest started taking things from us." A frown darkened his features. "Limbs, mostly."

Briar shuddered. He remembered seeing a woman in one of the visions, her arm entombed in vines. It painted Éibhear in a slightly more flattering light, although Briar couldn't be sure the extent to which he'd gone was a measured response.

"Who were they? The invaders."

"We don't know. The wards left no bodies behind. Strange, because no one came looking."

That was horrifying, as if the wards had erased those witches from existence. Something else about the story crept under Briar's skin. Gretchen claimed the things happening in Coill Darragh—like the thorns ensnaring the hare—were not normal. As if the forest was lashing out again.

"He was meant to teach me all this." Rowan pointed at the door into the garden, holding aloft his mug of tea-potion. "Sorcha's the eldest. She didn't want to be Keeper, so it fell to me, but he never taught me the ways."

"Did *you* want the position?"

Very quietly, Rowan said, "I think I only wanted my da to pay me mind."

Whatever clemency Briar might have granted Éibhear before, he couldn't now. From Gretchen's telling, the alderman had been an attentive, encouraging mentor. To his own children, however . . .

The judgment must have been plain on Briar's face. Rowan shrugged. "Sorcha and I weren't witches."

"That's no reason. Now it's your responsibility to protect Coill Darragh, but he never taught you how?"

Rowan's forehead creased. Briar was no empath, but even he could see that a dam held back a well of pain in him. "Sometimes," Rowan said slowly, "I don't think I needed teaching. If the time comes when I'm needed, the woods'll take me."

The pain in Briar's head hit a peak. The way Rowan said it, it sounded like Éibhear had passed a curse down to his son, just as Briar had inherited his from his mother. His mind called up images. The unnatural bend of Éibhear's body. His blood watering the earth. Was Rowan implying the same fate awaited him? Briar drank deeply of his tea. It lessened the ache in his temples, but didn't erase those images.

"Can I ask you something, Rowan?"

"Mm?"

"Your dad had an apprentice. Did you know her?"

"Not well. Kept to herself, like. Hardly left the house except to go on trips to the forest with my da. Why do you ask?"

Briar saw no reason to hide it. "She's sort of haunting my flat, so I'm trying to find out why she's trapped there. Her memory's a bit spotty."

Rowan's bewildered expression revealed plainly that he hadn't known. "She's not dangerous, is she?"

"No. Well, she threw some knives, but we get on now. Do you know what happened to her?"

"I've no idea. The wards could have . . ." He trailed off. "Though I can't imagine Da wouldn't have warned her. He took a shine to her."

To her, but not Rowan. The wound that had left was all over his normally impassive features. Briar could imagine him, at nineteen, just having lost his father, scarred and avoided by everyone. It broke his heart. He found he couldn't blame that version of Rowan for being too confused and overwhelmed to wonder about the girl who went missing amongst the chaos. Briar took his last sip of tea, the throb of his head waning.

"Is It helping?" Rowan asked.

"Yeah." Briar smiled to himself. "My mum used to always say that the best potion is tea."

"Used to?"

Briar didn't talk about her with anyone but Vatii. Yet Rowan had shared so much about his father, so . . .

"She died of a curse two years ago." He could say that much. Curses didn't always pass through generations.

"Ah, Briar. I'm sorry." He looked it. A soft bowing of his brow. "What sort of curse?"

"The unfair, totally random, inexplicable kind." Briar bit his lip. "Actually, Coill Darragh—the forest—it kind of . . . spoke to me? And said, or heavily implied, that it cast the curse on my mum. It said she belonged to it."

Out loud, it sounded ridiculous. But Rowan had grown up in the shadow of that wood, and he took it seriously. "So it took your mum and my da."

Briar breathed a mirthless laugh. "Aren't we a tragic pair?" He had no concrete answers after this conversation, but at least he had more information.

Rowan sat next to him at the breakfast bar. "What was she like? Your mum."

A wistful smile crossed Briar's face. "Brilliant. She was an empath, so she kind of knew my feelings before I did."

"She sounds like quite the woman."

"She was."

"You miss her?"

Briar did. Now they'd made the topic comfortable, he found himself telling Rowan stories about her. The elaborate scavenger hunts for birthdays to compensate for having so little money for gifts. How she taught him to walk in heels. How she'd given a homophobic priest what-for when he'd alienated Briar from the church.

Though he didn't say these out loud, he found himself drifting into memories about her last moments, too. Wasting away in a hospice bed and telling him she had no regrets because, even if her life was short, it was good because of him. Briar hadn't been a believer—not since the homophobic priest—but in that moment, he clung to faith because his mother spoke about graduations, weddings, the joy in his future that she was sorry she'd miss. He'd needed to believe in an afterlife from which she could watch. If there were ghosts, why not this small mercy?

They hadn't known the curse would pass on to him. That part he didn't speak of.

Rowan listened, and Briar found that the weight of loss lifted a little when shared between them. With the backs of his knuckles, Rowan reached to touch Briar's cheek, then hesitated. Twice today, Briar had shrunk away as if Rowan might hit him. He'd harbored unkind thoughts for the townsfolk who'd left Rowan estranged, and now he contributed to that alienation. Unfairly. Rowan was nothing like his father.

Briar leaned into Rowan's touch, and it still felt dangerous, but not for the same reasons. If Niamh was to be believed, the tender feeling unfurling in his chest was destined for another man. He shouldn't entertain his fluttering heart.

But at the blooming relief on Rowan's face, he couldn't bring himself to regret it.

Rowan's hand opened, tentatively cupping Briar's cheek in his palm. It sent a lance of heat through Briar's chest. Not just the touch—gentle in spite of Rowan's size—but the way Rowan looked at him. Like Briar could tell him every dark secret he possessed, and Rowan would carry on looking at him just like that.

"You'd be welcome at our church. If you wanted to come."

"I . . ." The prophecy loomed over him. This had not been part of it. Rowan was not a cold-hearted masked man. Attending church with him toed a line Briar was afraid to cross. "I'll think about it."

Rowan dropped his hand. "Of course."

Briar finished his tea. He should get going, but the longer he stayed, the less he wanted to leave. "Thank you for letting me at your garden. If you want, I could pay for—"

"Go 'way, you're grand."

Something tightened in Briar's chest. There was a lot more he wished he could give Rowan. "I don't know how to thank you."

Rowan touched the scarf around his neck. "You already have."

"You know that's not worth half as much."

Rowan considered. Reaching up, he flicked Briar's hair. "You can teach me how to plait. Ciara wants one like yours."

Briar's heart trilled. He knew this, too, toed a line, but he couldn't bring himself to deny Rowan this small thing. He hoisted himself onto the breakfast bar and shuffled closer. He ran a finger through the longer hair along Rowan's parting, white at the temple where his scar touched. Rowan froze.

"I can start with yours."

"It's a bit short"

"It's long enough for a small one."

The height of the bar allowed Briar to comb his fingers through Rowan's hair without reaching or standing on tiptoe. At first, Rowan sat stiffly. Back straight, shoulders set. Briar separated out three sections at his hairline. A barely perceptible lean backward, and Rowan brushed Briar's knees. He tipped his head. His chest slowly deflated as if after a long-held breath.

Briar took his time, plaiting from temple to crown. This wasn't teaching; Rowan couldn't see what he was doing, much less replicate it. Briar's fingers tingled where they touched the scar. For over a decade, for most of Rowan's adult life, he'd borne that mark. Aside from his family, no one went near him. He barely moved, made hardly a sound, but he seemed to Briar like a flower turning toward the sun one tiny, trivial measure at a time. Starved for contact and unable to fully disguise it.

Long after he'd finished the plait, Briar let his hands linger. When he could delay no longer, he touched Rowan's shoulder and said, "Done."

Rowan turned on the stool, looking up at Briar. It was a change from their usual height disparity. "Does it look all right?"

"Very dashing." Briar tucked in a bit of hair that stuck up out of it. As he did, he trailed his fingers behind the shell of Rowan's ear, watching his skin break out in goose bumps. The coffee brown of Rowan's eyes darkened. His pulse fluttered in his throat, visible and touchable under Briar's palm as he did what he'd told himself he wouldn't. He pulled Rowan closer, bent down like he was irresistibly falling, and touched their lips together.

Rowan stayed statuesque and shocked. Then he came alive. He tilted his head to kiss harder, his beard pleasantly tickling Briar's chin, his lips a soft contrast. Blood sang in Briar's ears. His skin tingled. Rowan paused to breathe, a silent question in the press of his forehead against Briar's. *Is this still allowed?*

And Briar couldn't deny him. Didn't want to.

Big hands wrapped around Briar's calves and slid up to the hinge of his knee, tugging him until he sat on the very edge of the breakfast bar. Then the rest of the way off it. Briar let himself fall, weight sinking into Rowan's lap. He glimpsed ruddy cheeks and the huffed breath of impatient yearning before Rowan kissed him again. Tongue parting Briar's lips to taste him. Shyness seeping away to leave room for bold hands grasping Briar's hips. Rowan only stopped kissing him for the brief seconds it took to drag in a lungful of air. Breathless, starving, hot-blooded.

And that did things to Briar. Turned his limbs soft and his cock hard at once. Not just the kiss, but the way Rowan held him like he and all his baggage weighed nothing. His thoughts spiraled, but he latched on to one.

"We shouldn't." The words broke the kiss, spoken into Rowan's lips.

Rowan's eyelashes fluttered. "Shouldn't?"

His thumbs, hiked under the hem of Briar's shirt, stamped two burning marks into Briar's hips. Quotation marks bracketing the scream of his growing arousal. With the pulse of those thumbs pounding through Briar's skin, it was difficult to say what he had to.

"No." Awkwardly, he slid out of Rowan's lap. It was only a kiss, but at the same time . . .

No kiss was like that one.

Rowan looked just as flustered, blinking to catch up with Briar. "Did I—?"

"No, that was—good. Great. I just can't because—" Magic bound his tongue. It choked him, robbed his voice of words. It had all happened so quickly. Vatii had said nothing, but she now fixed him with a chastising look. How was he meant to explain? The prophecy couldn't be spoken out loud.

"I'm only here for a year," Briar settled on. "Then I'm going to Pentawynn. To be a fashion designer. It's been my dream since I was little, and my mum wanted it for me, and I don't want to string you along or—"

"It's all right, Briar." Rowan's tongue traced his lower lip. "I understand."

And it sounded like he did.

But he also sounded stung.

CHAPTER 11

Vatii launched her interrogation the moment they got through his flat's front door.

"What was that?"

"Are you trying to sabotage your future?"

"Do you *ever* use the *other* head when you make decisions?"

On and on.

Briar collapsed face down into his bed and moaned. Vatii landed on his head. He had no defense. She was right. But Rowan . . . there was something about him Briar struggled to resist. For the brief duration of that kiss, he'd felt cozy, supported—safe?

Somehow, he wanted that and feared it in equal measure.

Vatii hopped across the duvet, regarding him with less scorn. "You like him."

"Of course I like him, Vatii. Look at him. He's dreamy."

"Have you considered that perhaps the prophecy is about him and not Linden?"

Briar sat up, his hair a fluffy mess from where he'd been tugging on it. "I'd considered it."

"And?"

"And it seems like wishful thinking. 'Known by all but known to none.' The town avoids Rowan even though he's their alderman, Linden's a celebrity, but no one really knows him beyond his public face. Could be either of them. But Rowan isn't masked or stone-hearted at all, and how is a relationship with him meant to make me famous? I'm not having a dig, he's bloody—"

Vatii gave him an arch look.

"He's a bloody good kisser," Briar finished. "But Linden's the fashion designer, the one whose aura I can't even read. Don't you think it fits him better?"

Vatii sighed. "What does your intuition tell you?"

"I don't have a single, solitary intuition, Vatii. Just a raging hard-on for probably the wrong man." He paused. "But . . . I don't know, it sounds like Linden to me. And that's a good thing, really. He's attractive, he's been kind to me, we've got things in common. I could learn so much from him."

"Then maybe," she said, "you should spend more time with him."

A half dozen sketches were spread out on the desk in front of Briar. Smears of pencil and charcoal expressed his vision in sweeping lines. He'd spent the week on them, and finally he was satisfied.

Following his trip to Rowan's farm, inspiration flowed more easily. Or perhaps he was only trying to distract himself from the ghost of Rowan's kiss, which lingered on his lips every time he closed his eyes to sleep.

He shuffled the sketches together and left to go next door.

Linden's emporium buzzed with activity. The interior's color palette had swapped to blue and silver for winter, an enchantment of songbirds trilling overhead. Briar's pulse ratcheted. Everything here filled him with whimsical longing and anxiety both. He'd never lacked confidence, stead-fast in his pursuit of dreams so many people had disparaged him for. He summoned his courage, but he wore it like an ill-fitting suit when surrounded by such powerful magic.

A clerk manned the counter. He was familiar—the same man who'd bought an engagement ring from Briar and proposed to Aisling on Saor ó Eagla. He looked tired, but he recognized Briar and smiled.

"Congrats on your engagement," Briar said.

"Oh, thanks, mate! She loves the ring."

"I'm Briar, by the way."

"Kenneth."

They shook hands, and Briar noticed something odd. Kenneth's wrist was bare, the wardstone bracelet gone.

Kenneth followed his stare. "Perks of true love and marriage round here," he explained. "It makes you one of the locals. Who's the lucky lad, lady, or gentlethem for you, then?" He pointed at Briar's equally bare wrist.

"I've had some wild nights, but last I checked I wasn't married."

"Ha, all right, keeping it out of the rumor mill. Fine, fine. What can I help you with?"

Briar's nervousness returned in full. "Just wondering, is Linden in?"

Kenneth looked dubious. "You, uh, got an appointment, mate?"

Briar offered his drawings as explanation, and Kenneth disappeared upstairs to check. He returned with an apologetic expression. "Sorry about that, mate. Just have to hold the line against fans, know what I mean?"

Given permission, Briar went upstairs, emerging in a flat so unlike his own he felt transported to another dimension.

An expansion charm made the low beams of the ceiling rise in a tall vault, spelled to look like a snow-flecked sky. Glittering trinkets suspended in the air cast prismatic lights in fractals over the walls. Every surface was draped in gauzy fabrics or home to curios that whirred and trilled soft notes. In the kitchen, a kettle billowed steam and whistled. It was dazzling yet overwhelming. Not a single place for Briar's attention to rest.

Linden sat behind a grand desk. "Ah, Briar. You're just in time." He snapped his fingers, and the dried petals in a jar beside him moved as though a few had vanished. The kettle rose to pour tea for them. "Would you like a cup?"

Most witches had to touch the tithe in order to use it. Linden's ability to use something without physical contact was extraordinary.

Briar tried not to appear too dazzled. "Yes, please."

While the kitchen contents floated and made them tea, Linden shuffled aside his notes and spun in his chair to face Briar. "Come! Sit."

Briar sat on the wing-backed sofa nearest, spreading his designs over his knees and smoothing the pages. He caught sight of the sheaves Linden had shoved aside on his desk. Many bore long alchemical formulas and scribbled-out potion recipes. Vatii hopped onto the coffee table, pecking at the swirling contents of a vase.

"Vatii, stop that! Come here."

Linden waved a hand. "She's all right."

"How are you enjoying Coill Darragh?" Briar tried not to feel self-conscious of his rollicking accent next to Linden's smooth, clipped one, or of Vatii, who'd begun bobbing for the berries floating in the vase. He would kill her later.

"It's lovely," said Linden. "A bit of an adjustment. I've never been away from Pentawynn so long. It's all very new."

"I've always wanted to go to Pentawynn," Briar said. At the mention of his home, Linden perked up. "I was dead set on it for my placement, actually. I thought my life was over when I got Coill Darragh, but . . ." He paused, wondering if his flirtatious nature would get him in trouble for overfamiliarity, but Briar struggled to be anyone other than himself. "The company's not so bad."

It was the right thing to say. Linden looked as smug as Atticus lounging over the back of his chair.

Vatii said, "Oh boy . . ."

"Yes, that is a surprise benefit. But please, you didn't come here just to stroke my ego."

Briar failed to hold his tongue. "I might have come to stroke *something*."

Linden's expression slackened with surprise. Vatii shot Briar a look of withering disappointment. Briar visibly cringed with self-reproof.

Then Linden burst out laughing. Not the prim, demure noise of before, but a true laugh. Briar eased. "You're even bolder than I first thought," Linden said. He held out a hand for Briar's drawings. "I'm more intrigued than ever to see what you've come up with."

Briar handed the pages over, and Linden spread them on his desk, a thoughtful finger tapping his lip.

"Just some ideas." Briar watched Linden closely. His blue eyes sparkled just as they did in pictures. His sleek black hair, tied in an elegant knot with wisps escaping, looked soft to the touch. Yet, his aura remained untouchable. It was frustrating. The Linden presented to Alakagram and the whole world felt more real than the private man sitting in front of him.

At last, Linden's lips bent in a smile. "I love them. Though, I have an idea. May I?" He hovered a quill over the page.

Briar nodded. Linden began scratching over the drawing of the waistcoat and pants set. As he leaned forward, something shiny slipped out of his shirt collar. A necklace. On the end of it dangled a talisman engraved with countless runes.

Briar's breath caught. He'd heard of such talismans. Famous witches often employed them as protection from unwanted photography, scrying spells, or—worst of all—curses from overzealous fans. They helped maintain some semblance of privacy.

Such a talisman could also block Briar's aura-reading abilities.

Linden hadn't noticed his attention. "I love the high collar on the other design, so I thought, perhaps . . . Yes! This would be perfect, don't you think?"

He turned the page to show Briar. He'd transformed the waistcoat into a vest with a collar reminiscent of the jacket. It would require stiffer fabric and gave the ensemble a different persona—hard-edged and tall.

"Very sharp. Powerful," Briar said, though part of him felt a sting of loss that the character of his design hadn't survived this edit.

"Oh, and what do you think of lacing in the back, like this."

Encouraged, Linden spent the next hour sketching as they discussed what details could be added to make the ensemble pop. With the grommets, lacing, and piping additions, Briar's heart rate soared along with the rising cost of materials, but he managed his blood pressure with a reminder: this would draw millions of eyes to his work. Linden had made no offer of compensation so far, and Briar understood that meant the exposure was the compensation. To Linden's credit, his attention had resulted in many of Briar's sales thus far. Hopefully those scales would tip in his favor. He'd just have to scrape together the upfront cost.

Once finished, Briar's lunch hour was through, and he'd only had the cup of tea, but he also had a pile of drawings in Linden's elegant lines. He stood to bid him farewell. To Briar's surprise, Linden clasped Briar's fingers in his own to say, "Thank you, Briar. I daresay, this is the most fun I've had since arriving in Coill Darragh."

If not for Vatii's claws on his arm, Briar might have needed pinching.

When Briar turned at the door to say goodbye, he saw Linden's expression shutter as he turned back to his formulas. Linden seemed every bit a showman. Polite, a little coy, but Briar couldn't help but wonder who the real Linden was.

For the rest of the day, it poured rain, so the shop was quiet, leaving Briar time to work on Linden's garment. He called Sorcha to get a quote for the additional materials and nearly choked. It would, he hoped, be worth it, but the fabric alone was costly. He would have to work hard to free up money for these extras.

A woman came in, shaking off an umbrella, to commission knitted scarves for her family—seven matching ones to be Christmas gifts. She'd seen Rowan wearing his and asked Maebh where he'd gotten it.

It made Briar's insides glow like embers.

No one else braved the rain. Sitting on the floor with paper to draw patterns on, he found himself looking at the spools of yarn stuffed in the cubbies behind the counter. The woman had given him creative freedom. "I trust your judgment," she'd said.

While he worked, Gretchen materialized to prod him about what he'd uncovered at Rowan's. Briar summarized, telling her about the mysterious invaders and Rowan's assertion that Éibhear wouldn't have cast the wards without warning her. The news failed to reassure her, as she scowled and picked at the holes in her tights.

The hope it would all jog her memory was for naught.

That left them with two options. Briar could speak to Maebh and Sorcha, but it was unlikely they knew more than Rowan. Alternatively, he could try to contact Seer Niamh.

This presented its own problem—Niamh didn't use a phone. The only way to contact her was by SoothSight or in person. A trip back to Wishbrooke would take an entire day by broom; with winter settling in, he'd be lucky not to freeze halfway there. That left SoothSight or a ferry ticket. Neither came cheap, but SoothSight had the benefit of time-efficiency. Briar wouldn't have to abandon his work for an impromptu trip.

He could see the sense in it, but he didn't have the means. SoothSight required a tithe of ghost orchid pollen, which was rare and expensive. He could make Linden's garment to his exact specifications or he could contact Niamh.

He couldn't afford both.

"Sod Linden," said Gretchen. "He's not even paying you! I help with your potions, and did you know? I managed to wash a mug for you. Once."

Briar rubbed his temples. Looking at his bank balance always triggered headaches. Years ago, whenever he'd been strapped for cash, his mother had helped scrounge something together. She'd usually include a bar of chocolate too, something to cheer him up. He'd been on his own for years now, with no one to ask for such help. The very notion turned his insides acidic. He never again wanted to find himself in the position he'd been in when his mother first passed, taking out loans for her funeral, selling off family valuables while mourning the person who'd given them to him in the first place. Tracking down and writing to a father he didn't know. Never hearing back. It was safer to depend upon himself alone, no one else.

"You're right. It's just, this project for Linden will probably bring in a lot of money—"

"Probably."

"—in the long term. And Christmas is coming. If I time it right, the promo from Linden will boost holiday sales too."

Puffing up, Gretchen said, "Fine! Postpone talking to Niamh. Not like I'm going anywhere. Because I *can't!*"

She stormed off through the wall into the stairwell.

CHAPTER 12

The last week of November, Briar did little more than work.

Many of the additions to Linden's project were things he'd never done before. He practiced applying piping with fabric scraps and tried not to blow a blood vessel when it came to doing the garment itself. By virtue of online tutorials and prayers, he managed. He'd never been able to afford formal classes, so he subsisted on self-teaching for every new technique.

It needed taking in, which meant Linden had to try it on.

Briar went next door, but Linden wasn't in, so he left a note and returned to fuss over the outfit. Though not a stray thread needed trimming, though he'd hemmed it perfectly, nervousness overtook him. He'd sunk all his time and resources into this in the hope it promised the best return, but if Linden disapproved . . .

He had no other way to make money. He'd go bankrupt. He wouldn't be able to create anything new, his business would fold, and in the end, he would die having accomplished nothing.

After downing a supper he barely tasted, he decided the best thing would be a distraction and a pint. Plus, he still needed to ask Maebh about the invaders. He donned his cloak and headed out the door, nearly colliding with Linden standing just outside it.

"Briar! I hoped I hadn't missed you. I received your message." Linden held a broomstick of white poplar and looked resplendent in a stormy gray traveling cloak. Atticus wasn't with him.

"I was on my way to the pub, but if you wanted to come in?"

"That would be lovely."

Briar stepped aside. Delight at seeing Linden gave way to indecision. It would only be polite to offer tea, and his flat was a state. Moreover, he worried the dinginess of his home might have a sobering effect on the clothes. His designs seemed far more likely to succeed in the splendor of Linden's enchanted rooms.

"I finished our project. I could make us some tea while you try it on, or—?"

"I'm very excited to see it. Lead the way."

No luck that he would offer to host. So Briar took him up the wobbly staircase and into the kitchen, kept serviceably tidy. The rest looked as though a fabric bomb had exploded. Colorful off-cuts lay shredded around the feet of the table. Half-constructed garments hung over the backs of chairs. Briar hastily cleared a space on one for Linden, piling it all on his unmade bed. As he turned, he caught the unsettled look Linden cast around the room before smothering it with a placid smile.

"I'm sorry it's such a mess. I've been so busy—"

"It's not a problem, I assure you. I called on you unexpectedly."

Briar felt out of his depth, wading chest deep into a world of etiquette to which he'd never been privy. He made tea, hoping his mother's methods weren't gauche in Linden's land of crystal decanters and bone china.

Linden didn't sit. Instead, he strode to the mirror, where the outfit hung.

Briar steeled himself. "Do you like it?"

"It's stunning. May I try it on?"

Briar thought about the mushrooms growing in his bathroom. He hadn't found an effective way to combat the damp, and they made good tithes, so he'd sort of . . . let them propagate. "I'll leave to let you dress. Just let me know when you're done."

While the kettle boiled, Briar closed himself in the stairwell. Vatii waited with him.

"Well. This is less than ideal," she grumbled.

"He said it was stunning. That's encouraging."

Another thought occurred to him. Linden might remove the talisman to change. Would he put it back on, or would Briar finally see a hint of the man behind it?

Linden summoned him back. He looked in the mirror, smoothing his hands over the fabric of the vest, fingers tracing the filigree, the gold embroidery of the collar. Briar held his breath. Linden looked beautiful, his dark hair in a knot at his nape, loose strands framing his face. Even without taking in, the garments fit him well, the billowing white sleeves a stark contrast to the crisp lines of the vest. But as Briar got closer, no whiff of an aura greeted him. Beneath the vest, he could just make out the lump of the talisman.

Trying not to let his disappointment show, Briar said, "Hopefully this doesn't come across as sucking my own dick, but you look incredible."

Linden coughed a laugh. "Quite a colorful way to put it. Thank you, though. I must say, you have a unique talent for this."

"I had a good teacher," Briar said. At Linden's quirked brow, he elaborated. "My mum taught me the basics. I picked up the rest from your tutorial videos. If you trust me with pins, I'd like to take the vest in a bit?"

Linden put it on inside out while Briar pinned the waist. This close, he should have drowned in Linden's aura. Instead, he only felt the tickle of the enchantment he'd imbued the clothes with. A simple fragrance to enhance Linden's charisma. Briar undid the zip, and the vest cracked apart like beetle wings, the thinner fabric of the white shirt beneath sheer enough to see the talisman. It should have felt intimate, but his lack of aura unsettled Briar.

He left again so Linden could change. Upon his return, Linden had crossed the room to the window and stood with a finger along the branch of Briar's broom. It still sat in its pot, though the elixir had long since gone stale, magic drained. Linden held his own broom in hand, its bark a pearly white.

"I didn't know you flew."

Briar couldn't blame him for the tone of surprise. The broom was the most valuable thing he owned. "It's been in the family a long time."

Linden's delicate brow arched. "What do you say to a flight around Coill Darragh with me?"

Briar's head ached after the enchantments used on Linden's clothes, but the offer gave him a jolt of energy. "Yes!"

He fastened his cloak and locked up the shop, fingers shaking a little from excitement. Vatii stayed in to nap. In the street, Linden swept a leg over his broom and floated a foot above the ground. A few people stopped to stare, one girl raising her phone to take a photo. She frowned at her screen.

So the talisman did affect recordings of Linden. Though, evidently not when he recorded himself.

"Ready?" Linden said.

Briar prayed his broom behaved. He got on, and the magic in the branch wove through him in a warm, airy current. Lifting their feet, they took off. The night sky bowed to meet them, a sea of stars and twilight. Linden flew with weightless grace, as if buoyed through the air not by his broom but by magic all his own.

"I will have to think of an appropriate event to wear your piece. It will no doubt attract attention," he said.

Briar's heart soared with them. Linden Fairchild, wearing something of his to a public event where cameras and other celebrities would ask, *Who are you wearing?*

"I'm glad you like it," Briar said. "Is work going well with your new business?"

"It is . . . challenging," Linden responded delicately.

"Oh." Briar had a litany of questions he didn't feel familiar enough with Linden to ask. Why he'd chosen to return to magical remedies, or if his healing abilities had made any reappearance. Selfishly, part of Briar wondered about the latter because his aching head reminded him that, short of a miracle, his time was running out.

At a loss, he asked, "Is there any way I can help?"

"Kind of you to offer, but this is a challenge I must undertake on my own."

Briar understood that at least. He'd felt the same in coming to Coill Darragh with nothing. "Can I ask, why did you return to medicine?"

Linden shot him a cool, assessing look. "I . . . I'll not find anything we speak of in a gossip column?"

"Is that why you're always wearing that talisman? To keep paparazzi at bay?"

"It protects against more than unwanted photography, but yes."

"More?"

"Curses," Linden said. His eyes scanned the forest, its magic slithering in the air like a heat mirage. Though their flight path remained over fields and rooftops, Briar's broom lilted toward the wood, as though yearning to return to its brethren.

Linden said, "You feel it too, don't you? It's only a forest, yet it hates us. I can't comprehend that people spend their lifetime living in its shadow. Few witches, though. I think it would curse us all if it could."

Did Linden know about Briar's curse, or had the conversation turned by coincidence? "Why did you come here, then?"

"Ah, several reasons," Linden said. "Something about the wood compels me. Wild magic is rare these days. Most natural places have been polluted by mankind, stripped for tithes by witches. Coill Darragh's is one of the last remaining. Possibly the oldest. So much of its power remains mysterious. It's why I've come—to study it. To see if, perhaps, there are healing secrets yet to be learned from the sources of magic themselves."

Briar considered telling Linden that the forest had cursed him. Perhaps he would know more. Perhaps he could find a way to heal *that*. The possibilities spun in Briar's head in dizzying circles.

"You know so much about these things. You must really love it."

"I admit, I do it mostly to fulfill my parents' wishes for me." A wave of disappointment came over Briar that he barely disguised. Linden's expression pinched. "I hope you won't judge me too harshly. I admire the art of medicine. I always hoped I would develop a passion for it, but since my talents fled me, I . . ." Slender, long-fingered hands tightened around the handle of his broom. "Never mind."

"Do you think you'll go back to fashion after?"

"I don't know. I believe my course was set long ago. My best hope is that I succeed at it and can perhaps pursue what I love as leisure instead."

It didn't sound so bad to Briar, whose leisure so far had involved a hike into woods that nearly killed him, and even that had been for work purposes. Aside from Saor ó Eagla, he'd had little time for himself. Linden looked serene, but beneath that, a little sad.

Briar tried to lighten the mood. "Well, I'm not going to complain. Let's be honest, I'd probably have sunk if I'd been in direct competition with you."

That sparked a genuine smile. "I do appreciate your candor with me. Most people only speak to me because they want something. It isn't often I can speak freely. You're quite . . . disarming."

Briar's feelings clashed. A flutter of flattery mixed with a sinking guilt. Had he done that? Approached Linden solely to establish his own success? He hadn't meant to. He'd looked up to Linden for so long and appreciated his talent. Linden inspired him. He'd wanted to be his peer, his friend. Maybe more.

Had he only wanted that for personal gain? He didn't think so, but Linden's words worried him. "I'm sorry. That must be lonely."

Linden waved it off. "The truth is, I often fly because I like being alone. Curiously, your company seems to be an exception."

That sounded flirtatious, and yet Briar couldn't find the words to flirt back. Perhaps because Linden still felt distant and untouchable. Because he was rich and Briar was poor. Because, if this was "speaking freely," he wondered what Linden was like completely closed off. And mostly because his lack of aura made Briar edgy. Like he'd never truly know the man.

"I try my best to be exceptional."

Linden said, "By any measure, I'd say you are that and more, Briar Wyngrave."

The Swan and Cygnet smelled of cider and mince pies. After his evening with Linden, Briar had decided there was still time to talk to Maebh.

A number of people crowded around tables, but few lingered at the bar, where Aisling washed an already-clean glass, moving in a perfunctory trance. From her puffy red eyes and despondent expression, she appeared to have been crying.

Maebh caught Briar's eye and came to greet him. "Briar, aren't you a sight for sore eyes? How're you getting on?" Powdered sugar dusted her fingers and mince smeared her apron. The first occasion they'd met, she'd been cross with him. The second, far warmer. On this third, it was as if he were an old family member.

"Good, good. And you?"

"Ah sure, I can't complain. Can I get you a mince pie?"

"If there's one going."

She disappeared and reappeared with a tray and jug. Briar was used to shoveling cold mince pies into his cheeks like a squirrel without bothering to warm them. Maebh presented him with a plate of fresh pies and a dollop of custard. The last time Briar enjoyed them like this, it had been with his mother at Christmas dinner. The recollection felt a touch bittersweet.

Maebh asked after his shop and how it was doing. Even mentioned she'd been meaning to ask for a scarf like Rowan's, now it had gotten colder. The fresh mince pies tasted so good, he burned his tongue in his eagerness to eat them.

He asked what had Aisling so down. Maebh cast a furtive glance toward her barmaid and sighed. "Her man Kenneth's done a runner, hasn't he? Got cold feet, I imagine. Bless her. I told her to take time off, but she insisted on the distraction."

Shocked, Briar looked over Maebh's shoulder at Aisling. Upon closer inspection, she no longer wore the engagement ring. With a pang of sympathy, he made a mental note to prepare a heartbreak tonic for her.

It seemed a shame to bring down the mood with his prying questions, but he couldn't put it off longer.

"Maebh, I have a question for you. It's about a witch who lived in my flat."

He explained about Gretchen. Maebh took the news that he lived with a ghost in stride. That it was the ghost of her late husband's apprentice didn't faze her either.

"She disappeared, didn't she?" Maebh said. "I remember her. Dark hair, glasses. Didn't leave the house much. I contacted her relatives back then, to see if she'd gone home. Terrible thing. Seemed she was quite estranged from most. Very work focused."

Briar didn't want to accuse her late husband of murder, but he had to point it out. "You don't think she might have died when the wards went up?"

Maebh raised her eyebrows. "I see you've been learning our local history. No, Éibhear could be an eejit. God knows I had words with him countless times about how he treated our own. Rowan in particular. But he'd never let that girl come to harm. Matter of fact, I remember him making her a wardstone bracelet like the ones Niamh makes for tourist folk. Made it the day before he died, after effing and blinding that he'd misplaced his journal and accusing me of rearranging his office, as if I'd touch it!"

Briar grasped at the threads of information. "Do you remember anything else? Who were the invaders?"

Maebh frowned. Usually unflappable, she looked quite flapped. "Never found out, did we? Died when the wards went up, thanks be to God. Nothing left of them after."

"Nothing? No idea even where they came from?"

"I'm sorry, Briar. The woods, the wards, and my husband all took those secrets and buried 'em." Seeing his disappointment, she said, "I'll get you another mince pie."

"Let me at least pay for this one."

"You're grand." She fixed him with a serious look. "I owe you the kindness, anyhow."

He snorted. "How do you figure?"

"My Rowan," she said. "He hides it well, sure, but what my fool husband did to him . . . left him scarred more ways than one, it did. A good husband, Éibhear was, but a dreadful father. So obsessed with work and magic. Not a word I said mattered. I says to him, I says, it's not that you love that girl, Gretchen, but that you show no love to your own children."

A hollow spot in Briar's heart hurt. Her words mirrored a grief he knew well, though it took a different form. His mother's passing had left a void in his life, but for Rowan that void had simply sat empty. Waiting. Even when his father was alive.

"I don't regret marrying him, you understand," Maebh said. "Wouldn't have my Sorcha and Rowan otherwise. But I regret that I left it so long thinking he'd turn a new leaf, only for what happened to happen and, well . . ." She glanced up at the potion bottles behind the bar, a terrible, weighty melancholy in the taut pull of her mouth.

When she turned back to Briar, her eyes shone with something like relief.

"You see the heart of him, and I'm grateful he has a friend in you. That's all."

CHAPTER 13

Briar left the Swan and Cygnet with a belly full of warm pies and a heart sick with the things Maebh had told him.

He didn't know what to make of the story about invaders, wards, and emotionally unavailable fathers. Instead, he fixated on her last words. *I'm glad he has a friend in you.* That word *friend* struck him through with guilt and longing for something different as he steeped in the memory of Rowan's lips on his.

Then, as he passed a gap in the houses looking out toward the woods, he saw something strange, and all those thoughts perished.

Coill Darragh's trees waved in the night, blacker than the sky above. Briar could see the bridge where Éibhear had cut down that witch. Farther still, the purple hue of the scar left by his sacrifice glowed like a ghastly sunset.

A shadow in the shape of a man bisected the glow.

From size and shape, even at this distance, he knew it was Rowan. He walked in a slow, stumbling trance, and he was heading toward the forest.

Heart in his throat, Briar ran. Down the street, over the bridge, up the hillock smothered in cold fog. Getting closer, he could see Rowan walked at a slow pace. One step at a time, and something moved by his feet. Briar's vision adjusted to the dark, and the shapes resolved—they were vines. Twisting tree roots grew up from the ground and curved around Rowan's boots and calves. When he took a step, they wilted and shrank back, shooting up wherever he placed his foot next.

He was only a few paces from the tree line. Briar put on a burst of speed, nearly tripping on the lumpy grass.

He stopped in front of Rowan, hands on his chest. The aura of Rowan's scar flared and fizzled like television static, so strong it nearly drowned out his true aura. The roots were cobras swaying around their legs. One hissed against Briar's ankle.

His breath was ragged as he said, "Rowan?"

Rowan stopped. His dark eyes had a milky film over them. He looked, unseeing. Briar clapped a hand to his chest.

"Rowan, wake up!"

Rowan blinked, and when he opened his eyes, the film was gone. The roots dissolved into ash at their feet. Whatever trance had come over him lifted.

"Briar?" His chest rose sharply as he sucked in a panicked breath. A grunt of pain, and one hand rose to clutch his heart, only to encounter Briar's hand. He held it there. "Was I—"

"You were sleepwalking. I think."

Rowan looked past him at the forest. Briar felt it like a cold breath on the back of his neck.

Ours.

"Every time, I wake up closer," Rowan said.

There was such a vulnerability in his voice, the likes of which Briar hadn't heard before. Rowan still wore the knitted scarf. To give his hands something to do, Briar tied it tighter to ward away the chill.

"Have you ever woken up in there?"

"Only the once. When I found you."

Briar swallowed. He didn't like this. Some of the trees looked . . . wrong. Wavering. Throbbing like they had sickened lungs.

He linked his arm through Rowan's. "I'll walk you home?"

It sounded ridiculous. He wasn't near as big or intimidating. Rowan accepted gracefully, though, walking alongside him through the grassy knoll, away from the glowing scar and the hungry wood.

"Have you ever tried to stop them?" Briar asked. "Your blackouts, I mean."

Rowan looked sheepish. "I, ehm, tied my ankles to the bedposts once. Woke up in the fields and got home to the ropes in pieces. Think the forest did it to prove a point."

"And Niamh didn't know of anything? A spell?"

He shook his head.

"Well, I've got an idea. We'll put a bell on you."

He snorted. "Like a cow bell?"

"No, a cute one. Like on cat collars, or those gold Christmas ones, you know? Then anyone will hear when you're off wandering at night."

They breathed easier the farther they got from the forest. Dew clung to their legs instead of vines. Moonlight filtered through the overcast sky, enough to illuminate the foggy patchwork of farmer's fields and paddocks. Rowan's scar stopped crackling, replaced by the mellowing effect his aura always had.

Briar said, "What were you doing out here anyway?"

"I wasn't *here* here. I was checking on the chickens."

"In the dark?"

"Some foxes were unsettling them."

Briar smiled, heart lighter already. The image of Rowan bent over a hen house, cooing to Maude and her brethren, tickled him.

"You been getting on all right at the shop?"

"Yeah, good! And you? Tourists still eating up your time?"

"Less since the weather's been pure shite."

Briar started to laugh, but as if the weather had heard and taken offense, a drop of rain hit his nose. Another on the back of his neck. An ominous pitter-patter followed. They looked to one another for a bewildered moment before they started to run.

Rowan's cottage was only a couple fields away, but they didn't make it. The heavens opened. Rain lashed down in a frigid deluge, soaking them through in minutes. Laughing helplessly, they ran for the closest shelter available: a crooked lean-to for horses, currently unoccupied. Rowan reached it first, turning to pull Briar in with him. Boots slipping on the grass, Briar couldn't slow. They collided, spinning with the momentum. Rowan's arms wound snugly around Briar, pressing them chest to chest. Briar could feel Rowan's racing heart through their soaked clothes, and as he came awake to the sensation, the quality of his own racing heart changed. Their laughter trailed off.

Words and warnings echoed in the recesses of Briar's mind. Vatii telling him, *Maybe you should keep your distance from Rowan.* Maebh saying, *I'm glad he has a friend in you.* Even his own words, *We shouldn't.* His prophetic future—cast in shadow by his curse—was a dreaded, distant mirage, while Rowan was firm and real and close and *holding him up.*

It seemed an age that Briar was only aware of the way Rowan's chest rose and fell against his own while rain played percussion on the roof. He looked into Rowan's eyes. Dark, they reflected a yearning Briar felt deep in his bones. A yearning he'd done a poor job of resisting. Rowan's next breath shivered. His scarf had come undone, so it was easy to grab the ends and pull.

Rowan leaned in by a tentative fraction, and Briar surged up to meet him the rest of the way. With the heady crush of lips, the cold became a distant thing. Briar pulled him closer, cursing every mote of space between them. He wanted to soak in the scorching bath of Rowan's aura. Rowan, who was breathless and beautiful, eyes half lidded in the slants of moonlight. Briar kissed him again, tasting rain.

The deep baritone of Rowan's voice rumbled with relief and longing all tangled together. As if Briar enchanted him more than the woods, he took a powerless, uneven step forward. Briar stumbled on tiptoes and instinctively wrapped both arms around his broad shoulders to stop from falling into the wall. Only Rowan was crowding him back against it anyway. Cold wood at his shoulder blades and Rowan pressed hot between his legs. Kissing him still but less guarded, and with his tongue, too.

Tangled in one another, they kissed until the rain hammering the lean-to quieted to a patter. By that time, what little resistance remained in Briar melted. He needed Rowan's hands on him without the barrier of clothes.

"Let's go."

Rowan, the consummate gentleman, said, "Ah—are you sure?"

Briar, not a gentleman at all, guided Rowan's hand between his legs to feel his certainty. "Do I seem unsure? If it hadn't rained, I'd tell you to just lay me down in the heather."

Rowan choked on whatever response he'd mustered. Taking Briar's hand, he led them across the fields to his cottage. They paused only at the fences, where Briar, in the process of crossing, instead sat and pulled Rowan in for more of what they'd had in the lean-to.

There was just enough time in between for Briar to think that this might be ill advised, and if Vatii had been there, she'd have laid into him for his indiscretion. There hadn't been anything about kissing mask-less aldermans in his prophecy. But Vatii was *not* there, and there hadn't been enough time spent *not* kissing Rowan for the blaze in Briar's heart to dwindle. Just once, he told himself, couldn't hurt. Just one moment to give in to whatever it was that burned between them.

Inside, the cottage was quiet except for the rain tapping the windows and dripping from their clothes. Rowan pulled his shirt off, letting it slap to the floor in a sodden puddle. It stopped Briar in his tracks. For two reasons.

The first was that Rowan, only half undressed and in the dark, made Briar's breath stop. He didn't have the wood-cut physique and washboard abs of Alakagram models—he was densely muscled under a layer of padding. The impressive breadth of his shoulders tapered to his waist, and a pattern of dark hair did the same from his chest down past his jeans. His belly hung a little over his belt, a sight Briar couldn't help but devour.

The other reason was that Rowan had never seen the tithes decorating Briar's arm.

Instead of undressing, Briar stepped in close, stroking his fingers through the hair of Rowan's chest. He rose on his toes to kiss him, slower. Rowan leaned in to his touch, shivered with an eagerness that turned Briar molten. To test a theory, he ran his hands down lower, stopping below Rowan's navel. The response was definitive. Rowan stifled a moan in Briar's mouth.

It had been a long time since anyone had touched Rowan like this. That scar had left him starved.

"Should I slow down?" Briar asked.

A strangled growl. *"No."*

So Briar helped him remove his pants, then let his hands roam where they couldn't reach before. Rowan's expressions captivated him. Caught between eyes fluttering shut at the overwhelming pleasure of being touched and opening to drink Briar in. Briar thought, *I want to give you everything you've missed since that scar made you lonely.*

The cold caught up with him, though, and he shivered, still in his wet clothes.

Rowan said, "You'll catch your death."

Briar bit his lip. Rowan misinterpreted his hesitation.

"If you've changed your mind—"

"I haven't," Briar said.

He just hadn't considered what Rowan might think of the tithes. Part of him knew Rowan wouldn't mind. Not because his father used the same magic, but because this was Rowan. The latter part unnerved him. When had he come to feel like he knew the man so well that this, one of his best-kept secrets, did not feel like something he'd ever been hiding anyway?

He peeled his shirt off. It splashed to the floor. Rowan beheld him with mouth slightly open, gaze sliding down. He took Briar by the wrist—the one with the tithes—and drew him close, turning his arm over to see the rest. Sigils and bands of runes covered his skin in a sleeve of inky symbols that started just below his wrist and ended below the shoulder. There were more now than there'd been when he first arrived, and Rowan slid his hand over all of them, then the naked skin of Briar's shoulder. His fingers traveled until they landed at Briar's hip.

"You're gorgeous."

Briar leapt into his arms and kissed him again, not chastely. Rowan walked him back through the hall. They lost the rest of their clothes as they went, stepping out of boots and wet jeans until they were in the living room where a ladder led up into a loft. Briar detached himself long enough to climb.

In the loft above, a blue swath of moonlight streamed in from the window, falling over the quilted bed. It smelled of campfires. A gas lantern hung from the ceiling beams. On the rough-hewn wooden bedframe, a tartan blanket was folded over the foot in case the quilt was not warm enough.

Before Rowan made it all the way up, Briar sprawled on the bed in what he hoped was a seductive lounge. It worked. When Rowan made it to the top, his eyes went dark looking at him stretched out on his back. He crossed the small space quickly, knocking Briar's knees apart to lie between them, and the soft crush of his body was enough to make Briar see stars behind closed lids as they picked up where they left off. Only now with no clothes, which made a great deal of difference. Briar could hardly grow a beard, so he reveled in the sensation of soft hair tickling his skin, the rasp of stubble against his throat when Rowan kissed him there. It set off flares of heat in him that steadily built.

Worse was the way Rowan's belly trapped Briar's arousal and rubbed against it without properly addressing how hard he'd become.

Patience lost, Briar pushed against his shoulders until Rowan rolled. Briar went with him, sitting atop his hips. An attractive flush had crept all the way from Rowan's neck to his cheeks. The barrel of his chest heaved unevenly.

Briar said silent thanks to the magic gods that water was the only tithe necessary to cast a spell leaving him squeaky clean. "Please tell me you have lube."

Rowan nodded. "Bedside cabinet."

Briar had to lean over him to root around in the drawer at the bedside. He felt the tickle of beard, then the suck of a mouth around his nipple, and quite nearly forgot what he was looking for. He found it, though, and retracted it before Rowan could distract him further.

Briar uncapped the bottle and held it high. Lubricant streamed down in a gleaming string that, when it connected, made Rowan's cock twitch. At the touch of Briar's hand, he came apart. His head tipped back. His Adam's apple bobbed around a halting groan. The noise reverberated, then shivered and shattered with each stroke. Briar's hands were delicate, but they looked even more so wrapped around the girth of Rowan. He was every bit in proportion, and for the first time, Briar considered that he might have overestimated his ability.

He knew what he wanted, though. He prepared himself next, impatient and perfunctory. When it was done, he leaned forward to brace both hands against Rowan's rising chest and looked him in the eyes. The scar, branching over his cheek and through his brow, held barely a trace of its usual aura. Rowan's own overwhelmed it, cloaking Briar in a warmth like a swallow of whiskey. His honey-brown eyes fluttered closed as Briar lowered himself.

The sting was familiar, but the sharpness of it less so. Briar gritted his teeth. He wasn't about to quit, but as he tried to let gravity help, a lance of pain went through him that had him clenching tighter. He'd clamped his eyes shut in the process. He only opened them when a hand touched his cheek.

Rowan's expression had transformed. Instead of aroused, he looked concerned.

"Is that hurting?"

"Well, you are huge."

Rowan started to sit up, and Briar rushed to stop him.

"I can manage!"

"I'm not interested in hurting you," Rowan huffed.

"I'm sure I'm just out of practice."

Rowan pulled him down by the wrists, kissing him to halt his babbling. His big hands, rough with calluses, slid down the line of Briar's spine and over the curves found lower. The kneading massage loosened some of his tension, stretching out his muscles like taffy. Then one hand snuck lower, the other spreading him, and—

Briar melted, cheek pillowed against Rowan's shoulder, muffling a moan there.

Rowan's breath brushed the shell of his ear. "How do you like it normally?"

Briar struggled for coherence with Rowan's index finger giving him a different sort of massage. "S-sex?"

A chuckle. "What else?"

Briar wet his lips, unsure what he meant by the question. "In—the—butt?"

Rowan's laugh was a pleasant peal of distant thunder under Briar's cheek. "Can you be more specific?"

"I don't know?"

"You don't?"

A note of exasperation, because Rowan was testing the pressure of a second finger. "Well, no one's ever asked!"

Rowan sat up at that, dumping Briar onto the mattress. Before Briar could protest the loss of what had been a very pleasurable fingering, he found himself flat on his back with a pillow pushed under his hips. Rowan handled him with a firm, indomitable gentleness. Despite what Briar could only assume was a very long dry spell, Rowan seemed unfairly competent. It made Briar's cheeks heat. And other places.

Rowan braced over him, one arm between them so his hand could resume what it had been doing before, only this time with Rowan's mouth teasing Briar's lips open the same way his fingers were. He worked out every knot of tension with methodical, almost ruthless, teasing. He tried different motions until he found the right ones, the ones that made Briar's back arch. His hands weren't small either, and it was a stretch, but the pleasurable kind.

Briar's toes curled in anticipation. "Come on."

Rowan drew back and gave Briar's hip a pat. Obliging, Briar turned over, the pillow still canting his hips at an angle for best advantage. The mattress sank on either side of Briar's shoulders where Rowan's arms supported him. Briar spread his thighs and waited.

A kiss dropped to the crook of his neck. At the same time, he felt the intrusion. Just a light, nudging pressure at first that bloomed into something harder. It still hurt, but not the same as before, not at all. Now it was the languid stretch after too long spent motionless. Now, there was pleasure, too. A long, tightly wound, keening thing that slowly, slowly gave way. It wasn't everything all at once. It was slow. A push and then a pause in which Rowan's mouth left pink marks on his neck and drew gasps from him. And then waiting until Briar pushed back against him. Trapped against the pillow, there was not enough stimulation to come, but Briar felt that the barest touch might set him off. He bit his lip and tried not to.

Rowan finally slotted all the way into him. His breath whuffed against Briar's nape in a long, shuddering exhale. His belly felt heavy against Briar's arched back. His mouth traced the shell of an ear, and his teeth grazed Briar's shoulder while Rowan gave his hips an experimental roll. It sent sparks shooting through Briar from the hot place Rowan was buried in him to the tips of all his fingers and toes. Rowan did it again, and again.

Outside the bedroom, Briar hardly ever shut up. Inside it, he didn't often voice his wants, but this pressed him to it. "Harder."

Rowan rose to that encouragement. His next thrust rang out in the quiet bedroom with the slap of his hips against Briar's arse. He didn't draw back immediately. He sidled his hips from side to side, let Briar feel him deeply before he withdrew and pounded in again. Again.

Lights winked in Briar's vision. Even as the pace became relentless, it was unlike any of the clumsy fumbles of Briar's years in college. Rowan's demeanor was considerate. Intent. Rowan took the time to figure him out and coax pleasure from him with an almost tender aggression. Only then did Briar realize, it wasn't competence, but a keener sort of communication than he was used to. Rowan touched and listened for the sorts of responses that meant Briar liked it, and he seemed to revel in each clue, each new discovery.

Moaning, Briar told him what he wanted. And Rowan gave it. Until finally Briar caved and pleaded for release, which Rowan gave also. He snuck a hand under him, and it was the softest touch before Briar was coming into his fist. Bright bursts of pleasure set his limbs trembling. He smothered sounds he'd never made before in the quilt. Rowan hooked his chin over Briar's shoulder, moving still, drawing out the rush of climax until he could no longer hold back his own. He made a sound like the ghost of him was being drawn out through his mouth, the breath of his groan hot on Briar's neck. A few more shuddering thrusts, and he was spent.

He rolled to the side and crashed into the covers, panting. Briar languished in the feeling of tingling skin and his pulse returning to normal. It took a long time. Long enough for him to wonder if that was that, and he should prepare to steal away into the night. It would be difficult. He doubted his legs would carry him, and he dreaded the notion of putting his drenched clothes back on.

But these things did not comprise the whole reason.

He turned his head to watch Rowan, whose chest still heaved. He'd closed his eyes, lips parted with each ragged breath, a sheen of sweat all over him. Briar wanted to lean in and nip the sharp edge of his jaw where beard softened it.

Rowan turned half-lidded eyes on him. A smile quirked the corner of his mouth. "What?"

Briar said, "You are egregiously sexy."

A gust of laughter. He covered his eyes with an arm. *"Egregiously."*

"Too much? I've been told I can be a bit much." Now could be his cue to leave.

Rowan lifted an arm to usher Briar over. "Not too much. C'mere to me."

Briar went gratefully, curling against Rowan's ribs with a hand against his rising diaphragm. He soaked in the comfort of Rowan's aura. Sleep crept in.

With his heart still racing more than it should, Briar thought he might have made a mistake.

He woke to a bright morning and a divot in the bed that once held Rowan.

He'd slept well. Better than he had in ages. He wanted to luxuriate in that feeling a little longer, but with consciousness came thoughts, many of them unwelcome. He'd missed a dose of his elixir while gallivanting last night. His hands trembled fiercely as a result. Vatii would have his hide.

Walking home in last night's clothes was not his favorite part of one-night stands either.

His clothes were downstairs, probably soaking still. He could hear clattering from the kitchen, so Rowan wasn't out, which meant skulking around nude or in something borrowed.

The floorboards were freezing underfoot, and it took a moment to practice walking normally. He tottered like a foal over to a discarded throw blanket. Picking it up, he found it was actually a check shirt in red, which fit him with all the grace of a rain mac. The neck was so large it slipped off one shoulder, the hem reaching near his knees. It smelled faintly of Rowan. It would do.

Descending the ladder, the first thing Briar spotted sent a shot of gratitude through him: his clothes, hung on the radiator. He touched them to find them slightly damp.

Footsteps behind him, then, "I made eggs."

Briar turned. Rowan stood in the door to the kitchen holding a fry pan. Briar said, "Eggs?"

Rowan said, "Scrambled, but I could—" He stopped. "Is that my shirt?"

"Sorry, I was cold. I'll change now."

"No! You can keep it. On, that is." Rowan suddenly had to clear something very stubborn from his throat.

Briar dropped the hem. He looked at Rowan's flushed cheeks and the amount of eggs in the pan. "You made enough for two?"

Rowan inclined his head toward the kitchen and led the way there.

A sense of confusion and mild panic took root in Briar then. This—a cooked breakfast, wearing one another's clothes—this felt . . . domestic. All Briar's past relationships had been the casual variety. They involved sneaking in and out of places, making sure he no longer smelled like someone else's cologne, and stolidly avoiding the topic of relationships when it used to come up with his mother. In witch's circles, relationships were either for mutual stress relief or they were for more. Marriage more. It wasn't even about keeping magic within families or any of that tosh. It had to do with the relative smallness of the witch community and the drama that would arise from having serious relationships with so-and-so's brother, so-and-so's ex.

When you were gay, that became doubly true, with the dating pool shrunk by an even greater proportion.

Not that witches didn't also date non-magical people, or that these measures didn't still result in drama. But the tradition of keeping it casual unless there was serious commitment in the cards held true.

Briar hopped up on the breakfast bar, accepting the plate Rowan handed him. Eggs, sliced cherry tomatoes, and a few rashers of bacon. He took a bite and forgot his worries. These were the best damn eggs he'd ever tasted. They'd probably been freshly laid and plucked out of the coop that morning.

Rowan had abandoned his own plate. He was still giving Briar a look over, brow furrowed in consternation. His eyes stuck on Briar's bare thighs, revealed from the shirt hiking up when he sat down. "How'd you sleep?"

Briar set his plate down. Against all his better judgment, he shifted so his legs splayed a little farther apart. "Good. And you?" *What am I doing?*

"Good. Yeah, ehm—"

"Last night was?" Briar said cheekily.

Rowan locked eyes with him. Whatever lust they'd slaked the night before, it simmered between them still. "Very good."

The heat in the kitchen seemed to rise by a degree. Briar leaned back on the breakfast bar, so that what was rising under his shirt could be more clearly viewed. He said what he wanted to, even though he was tempting danger. "Do you want to make it a more regular thing?"

Rowan opened his mouth, a breath that never quite became a word whistling between his teeth. After a beat, he moved. He sat in the chair between Briar's knees and dragged him closer by the hips. The shirt hiked all the way up, and the movement left Briar with nowhere to put his legs except to hook them over Rowan's shoulders. He did. Rowan's hot breath turned his thoughts in a spiral, but he managed the other important detail before they derailed completely.

"Just a casual thing, yeah?"

A brushed kiss and Rowan's beard tickling his thighs. "Yeah."

"We don't tell anyone? Just friends—hngh—friends having a little fun, y-yeah?"

Rowan paused, mouth inches from its destination, the next words breathed where Briar could acutely feel them. "Sure thing."

After that, Briar's legs fell open, and he could only clutch Rowan's hair.

CHAPTER 14

B riar didn't tell Vatii or Gretchen about where he'd spent the night. When asked, he sidestepped these questions with a prim "none of your business." He didn't want to put up with even more scolding from Vatii, and Gretchen would be tetchy he'd made so little progress about her tether while distracted.

They found out soon enough. The next day, Rowan appeared with homemade sandwiches for Briar's lunch break. It wasn't the only reason he'd come, as his wandering hands and mouth soon made clear. Gretchen vanished in a blushing kerfuffle, and Vatii screeched so loudly in surprise that it stopped Rowan in his tracks.

Briar shooed her with an "I'll explain later," determined to enjoy their quickie now that this was something he could indulge.

Vatii laid into him viciously once Rowan left.

"Irresponsible! You will invite destruction on us both, behaving like this!"

"Good grief, it's only sex, Vatii."

"Is it?" she hissed. "What about the prophecy? What about Linden?"

"You don't even like Linden!"

"I don't. He's a smug arse, and I wouldn't mind if his cat went and played in traffic. I don't like most people, though. And these two are meant to help you. I care more about your future than my fickle taste in the men you fancy! What if this thing with Rowan ruins that future with Linden? It isn't like we have an abundance of time!"

She had a point. It complicated things to involve himself with Rowan.

"Linden hasn't opened up much. I still don't know if . . ." *I feel that way about him.* Had he really been about to say that? Linden was beautiful, talented—the talisman was the problem. If only Briar could get a read on him, perhaps his foretold feelings would follow suit.

"Rowan and I talked. We established it's only casual. No strings attached."

"Hm," grouched Vatii. "Why doesn't that comfort me?"

Whether it comforted her or not was of no consequence to Briar, who found his increasingly regular contact with Rowan very comforting. It became a ritual to share lunch hours. After a week, Rowan invited him for dinner, and that became a ritual, too. To the extent that Briar spent many evenings eating dinner with Rowan, kissing Rowan, sleeping with Rowan, and then having breakfast with Rowan before going to work.

Vatii worried, but she worried less when Rowan started making her a small plate of food, too. Some of her caution was even disproven. Well fed and sleeping better, Briar's headaches afflicted him less. He only got the shakes on days he worked late.

Gretchen became scarcer, popping in to occasionally ask how his investigations were going. Vatii maintained that Briar and Rowan's fraternizing traumatized her.

It was only a matter of time before Vatii's warnings caught up to him.

One day during his lunch, when Briar and Rowan were busily testing how robust his kitchen table was, a knock came at the shop door. Half-dressed and pink-cheeked, they scrambled to pull pants on and arrange their hair so it didn't look quite so . . . pulled. Neither had caught their breath by the time Briar opened the door to find Linden there.

"Briar. It's been some time. I thought I'd pop in, if you don't mind?"

Vatii, who'd been watching the shop while he "fraternized" upstairs, bored holes into Briar with her gaze. Rowan pretended to peruse the rack of clothes.

"Ah, you have a customer," said Linden. "I can return later."

"It's no bother, I was just on my way," Rowan said quickly. He inclined his head to Briar. "Be seeing you."

Linden watched him go with a peculiar, pinched expression. "Are you two familiar?"

Briar tried not to let *how* familiar show on his face. "Yeah, we're friends."

"Ah. I don't know if you've noticed, but he has a strange way about him, the alderman."

"O-oh?"

"You haven't noticed, then? Ah, it doesn't matter. Please, tell me how you've been."

"Great! I finished taking in your clothes. Let me run and grab them."

"Shall I come up?"

"No! No, the flat's a mess." Really, Briar didn't want Linden sitting at the table he had just been bent over.

He came down moments later with the garments folded over one arm. He'd ironed the trousers into a neat pleat and ensured no loose threads hung on. The clothes gave off an airy, esoteric scent as Briar held them out.

"They're very fine," Linden said. "I can't thank you enough for putting your time into this. You've a rare talent."

Briar preened under the compliment. "You think so?"

"Yes. Perhaps it's superstitious of me, but it seems fortuitous that we should meet like this." Linden's keen, crystalline stare pinned Briar to the spot. He reached out and touched the back of Briar's hand with feather-light fingers. "I wondered if you'd join me for a drink tonight? To celebrate the completion of this project."

Briar's throat went dry. "I'd love that."

Beside them, Vatii shuffled back and forth on the countertop. He understood her disconcertion. If this was a date, it would be best to clear that up right away.

Linden took the hangers of clothes, folding them over his arm. "I still haven't thought of an event to wear this to, but I will. See you tonight?"

"Tonight," Briar confirmed dizzily.

"I look forward to it."

Linden turned to go. Before he reached the door, Briar summoned his courage to ask the question he didn't really want to know the answer to. "So, is this a date?"

Linden turned by a degree, looking over one shoulder. "Let's call it a precursor."

After the door shut behind him, Vatii broke her edgy silence. "What the bloody hell does that mean?!"

Briar didn't know. He'd never been on a "precursor" date, whatever that was, and it did not clear up the difficulty this presented. If Linden was courting him seriously, then Briar had every obligation to break things off with Rowan. If Linden only wanted a casual affair, that was another thing altogether and would require a different conversation about exclusivity or lack thereof. What the hell could he infer from a "precursor," though?

It was frustrating. Not least of all because the longer he thought about it, and the more Vatii badgered him, the stronger the realization was: he didn't want to be courted. At least, not right now. Not yet.

He and Rowan were having fun, and with work stealing so much of his energy, he'd come to prize their time together. Time was something he had little in reserve, but still . . .

He didn't want it to end so quickly.

Gretchen popped her head through the wall then, glaring after Linden's retreating back. She said, "Is all this boy drama going to interfere with getting me out of ghost prison?"

Briar could feel a headache coming on. Whether because of stress or his curse, he couldn't tell. "Please, Gretchen, not now."

She stormed out again in a huff.

That evening, tourists stood outside the Swan and Cygnet, steaming drinks in hand, their chatter and merriment oddly conspiratorial in nature. Upon entering, Briar saw why. A corner of the pub was cordoned off with velvet curtains—not a usual part of the decor. They'd been conjured there. Aisling confirmed Briar's suspicions: Linden had paid to reserve a private space for drinks and conversation.

"Bit excessive, don't you think?" Vatii said.

It *was* a lot of effort for a drink and a chat.

Before seeing Linden, Briar pulled from his pocket a small potion bottle, a thimbleful of milky liquid swirling inside with ribbons of red. It hadn't been easy to brew, requiring three days of steeping in cranberries and cinnamon sticks to ensure its potency. Heartbreak tonics were time consuming and expensive to buy, but he felt responsible for worsening Aisling's grief. The ring he'd sold her ex-fiancé had been enchanted to heighten emotions post engagement.

He handed her the bottle. She recognized its distinctive color immediately.

"A heartbreak tonic? For me?"

It might have been presumptuous of him—they didn't know each other well. "If you want it. Maebh told me about Kenneth, so I thought . . ."

She rolled the bottle in her palm. "I don't have enough money."

"It's a gift."

"Briar." She closed her fist around it, and after a contemplative moment, tucked it into her apron, her eyes glazed. "I don't know what to say. Thank you."

He couldn't delay any longer. Aisling led him through the kitchens, where a conjured portal hovered between the refrigerator and the oven. It seemed a lot of effort to make his entrance discreet, but he went through. On the other side, noise from the pub patrons muffled to a distant hum. The curtains concealed the corner from view, but it seemed an anti-eavesdropping charm had been added, too.

Linden sat in a booth with his back to Briar, phone to his ear. In a tense voice, he said, "I'm telling you, the formula is impossible."

Briar froze. He could guess this wasn't a conversation he was meant to overhear. He thought about going back through the portal, but then Linden snapped.

"The main ingredient is nowhere to be found. Do you doubt my credibility? Perhaps you'd like to come and confirm it for yourselves."

A buzz of noise from the phone implied the response wasn't favorable. Linden spoke over it, voice lowered to an exasperated hiss. "The risk that my research will result in nothing is mine to bear. I'd appreciate it if you ceased stooping to criticize whatever leisure I find or who with. It does not affect you."

Briar stiffened. Did Linden mean him? Linden claimed he didn't share his company often, so who else?

Linden finished the conversation with a curt, "That's enough. I have an engagement now. We'll speak more later. Goodbye."

Briar hadn't meant to eavesdrop, but the ferocity in Linden's voice pinned him to the spot. Though he'd come on invitation, it felt like a terrible time. He waited a few breaths. Linden gripped his hair, staring at his phone on the table.

Briar cleared his throat. "Are you all right?"

Linden shot up. "Briar. Ah, how much did you hear?"

"Only the end."

Linden's normally calm veneer wavered. "It's my potion work. Apparently, my progress is insufficient." He rolled his eyes. "My parents, they expect no less than miracles."

Briar took a seat across the table. "I remember you performing miracles once upon a time." At Linden's curious expression, he continued. "I witnessed one of them a long time ago. Your miracle tour."

His eyes widened. "Which city?"

"A little town called Port Haven. I grew up there." He didn't mention that he'd brought his mother for curing, only to find she wasn't yet ill. It was a dark topic Briar would rather avoid.

"Lovely place," Linden said. "It had a wonderful seafood restaurant, if I recall. Yes, that would have been one of the last times I could—" He cut himself short. "Well. It doesn't do to dwell on what we've lost."

"You've never felt any sign of your healing gifts coming back to you?"

"No. I exhausted everything on that tour. My parents, well, I wanted to make them proud."

Vatii rolled her eyes. "Boo-hoo."

Briar had more sympathy. He didn't understand how Linden's parents could be anything less than ecstatic to have a son capable of healing. They'd pushed him to such lengths he'd lost those abilities altogether. He recalled his own mother, dying and devastated she wouldn't get to see him grow up, saying she was so proud of him. And he'd done little back then.

"I'm sorry," Briar said. "That's not fair."

Linden said, "Ah, but I didn't ask you here to burden you with my family's squabbles. We're here to celebrate the success of this first project, aren't we? And to get to know one another better."

Briar allowed Linden to sidestep the topic, which clearly discomfited him. The sentiment didn't quite leave him, though. *I'd appreciate it if you ceased stooping to criticize whatever leisure I find or who with.* Linden's parents clearly didn't welcome Briar's involvement.

Linden ordered a bottle of champagne for them. As he poured, he asked Briar questions. Where he went to college, what type of magic he excelled at beyond fashion and enchantments. He asked all with an increasingly languid smile while twirling his champagne flute. For a moment, the bubbles and the private atmosphere warmed Briar enough to forget his confusion over the "precursor."

"What are you trying to create, if you don't mind my asking?"

"I wouldn't burden you with it. It's all very dull," said Linden.

"I can be the judge of that. Maybe I can help?"

Linden rolled his last gulp of champagne around in his mouth. "Perhaps. But we'll need more alcohol."

This was Briar's cue to get the next round. "What would you like?"

Linden said a nice Riesling wouldn't go amiss. Briar went to speak to Aisling and nearly fainted at the price of the bottle. It was well outside his budget, but the idea of telling Linden so was humiliating. The cost would set him back—he wouldn't be able to afford the ghost orchid pollen until after Christmas, weeks away. The only reason he could buy the pollen over food was because Rowan frequently fed him. He consoled himself with distant hopes. Maybe, if the night went well, Linden would offer him another job. A paid one. If Linden's promotion attracted enough attention, he might never have to feel sick at a three-digit price tag again.

Briar took it to the table and poured them both a glass, managing not to spill despite the slight shake in his hands. If Linden noticed, he politely pretended not to. He took his glass and sniffed, swirling the pale liquid before bringing it to his lips.

With an air of revisiting the grave of a relative with whom he shared a troubled history, he said, "My parents have demanded that I create a . . . panacea of sorts. A curse cure."

Briar's alcoholic haze sharpened into something bladed and acute. "A curse cure?"

"It's quite the conundrum, yes? Apart from killing the caster—a most sordid solution we needn't investigate—a curse can only be lifted by the person who cast it, so how to bottle that kind of individual intent and make it universal? So that anyone could drink the elixir and be relieved of their affliction."

"That is a challenge," Briar said faintly.

"It's impossible. Near as I can tell, all tales of a successful cure are in the same league as Pandora's box and the Holy Grail. Utterly fabricated. And yet . . ." He raised his brows, taking another swig of wine. "I've heard stories of a genuine version created in Coill Darragh. So here I am." The wine mellowed Linden's nature. His words blended instead of ending in clipped consonants. "Complete bollocks, if you'll excuse my language. I've searched and found no evidence whatsoever. Folktales for children, I suspect."

The proclamation sank in one sick degree at a time. The wine, the private atmosphere, and the hooded look from Linden nearly compelled Briar to speak of his own curse, yet he held back. He knew well the look of pity that people wore when he told them, and he did not want his relationship with Linden to be based on charity, or the idea that Briar needed saving. Intent on earning his own station, he grasped the confession tightly behind clenched teeth.

Privately, he also thought that it felt a bit like fate. Another confirmation Linden was the man from his prophecy. A cursed man's life entwined with the one who sought a cure.

"Why would your parents give you an impossible goal?"

Linden snorted. "They presented the hypothesis of my inferiority long ago. They would rather be correct in their assumption than admit they were wrong."

Briar couldn't help it. "That's horrible."

Linden's fuzzy expression resolved into something curious. Intense. "Pardon?"

"I said, that's horrible. They're horrible."

Linden's smile felt like a long-held breath, finally released. "Ah, there's that candor I admire so much in you. No one else would dare speak ill of my perfect, powerful parents."

"Well, I don't know them," Briar said. "But I'm getting to know you. I think you can do it, by the way. Find the cure."

Linden's smile wavered. He leaned across the table and laid his hand over Briar's. His cool fingers warmed against Briar's skin, a spark of something hopeful in his eyes. Then his expression turned troubled, and he withdrew. "Your certainty is misplaced, but it means quite a lot to hear. From you. Ah! But it's getting late, and I haven't even asked you the very thing I invited you here for."

"Oh?"

"This project of ours. You've created something better than I imagined. Not to say that I ever doubted your talents, but you've outdone yourself. So what would you say to a collaborative business partnership? Perhaps on a summer line to test the waters?"

Briar's heart fluttered in his throat. "An entire line."

"Yes. If it fits into your schedule—"

"Of course! I would love t— I'm honored. Of course, of course I will."

Linden beamed. "Wonderful! Then all that's left is the contract."

He rolled out a sheaf of parchment from within his robes and set it down on the table. Rising, he produced a pen and told Briar to take his time reading it while he fetched another drink for a toast. While he was gone, Briar scanned the pages. It detailed a partnership in which they would create a summer collection of twelve garments, to be promoted and taken to runways both national and international. They would collaborate on design. Linden would provide materials while Briar provided the labor. That seemed fair enough, but under Section C, it dictated Linden would receive ninety percent of the net profits. Briar supposed the basis for this discrepancy was that runways were expensive to put on, and Linden would be providing the capital for their collection. Aside from that, Linden's name had the clout Briar's lacked.

Still. It seemed skewed.

At his elbow, Vatii clucked and tutted. "That's ridiculous."

The alcohol left Briar fuzzy headed, and he didn't have the experience necessary to estimate what their profits could be. The amount listed as Linden's investment capital was significant, so presumably he expected a return on it. Briar put his head in his hands, the persistent ache returning. Pushing for a greater percentage of the spoils felt greedy, but of the two of them, Briar had the most to lose if this venture failed.

Linden appeared with two wineglasses in hand; Briar accepted his with a smile he hoped masked his nerves. Linden offered a sympathetic nod. "Paperwork is hardly my favorite part either. Is everything in order?"

"It looks great, I was just wondering . . ." Briar wrestled for the right words. "The profit split seems a bit . . . skewed."

Linden's smile didn't budge. "How much more would you like?"

Put on the spot, Briar wished he'd had longer to contemplate a figure.

Vatii croaked, "Remember what your mum told you about haggling."

Figure out what you want, then ask for more, and always know when to walk away. He'd watched his mum stare down a car salesman after listing a litany of reasons his car wasn't worth the asking price. He tried to be as much her son now as ever.

"I want more. Thirty-five percent."

Linden's expression didn't change. "You've seen how much I'm investing."

"Which means you're pretty confident in our success."

"Hm, a third is steep," said Linden. "Twenty percent."

"Thirty-three," said Briar.

"Twenty-five."

Briar didn't respond. He thought his heart might cave a hole in his ribs, but he waited in the awkward silence.

Linden unfolded his hands. "I do admire your boldness. Thirty, then."

A wave of relief and triumph both. "Done!"

Linden snapped his fingers, and the line about profits was erased. It never ceased to boggle Briar's mind that Linden didn't have to touch the tithes at his belt to use them. With a pen, he wrote the amended figure and turned the parchment for Briar to sign.

Contract complete, Linden lifted his glass to toast their partnership. They finished their wine, discussing ideas for the collection, but it had gotten quite late.

Linden slid toward the end of the booth. "I've had such a good evening, but I'm afraid it's time I turned in." With one hand, he reached out and covered Briar's on the table. "However, I must tell you how pleased I am we get to work together again."

His hand lingered a moment longer. Long enough for Briar to recall through the slosh of alcohol what Linden had called this night.

"So . . . the precursor? How'd I do?"

Linden's radiant smile snuffed out. "Briar . . ."

"Sorry. Too bold?"

"No, not at all, I'm flattered." He took a step closer, the proximity bringing with it the scent of sandalwood and cauldron fire. The blue of his eyes looked darker, more contemplative, as his hand touched Briar's cheek. A flutter of cold went through him. Not butterflies, but a nervy fear. Fear of breaking away and of leaning closer, because the name *Rowan* tangled his heart in complicated knots. So he remained still. His breath fell against Linden's bare wrist. He saw Linden's slight shiver, barely disguised, and then his flash of self-reproach as he broke away.

"I'm sorry, Briar. My parents . . ." He looked askance at their empty glasses. *They wouldn't approve.* It went unsaid. "Perhaps, for the sake of professionalism, it's best we remain friends."

A queer combination of relief and uncertainty overcame Briar. That Linden's parents wouldn't approve failed to surprise him, but it seemed strange that Linden caved to their pressure. He didn't strike Briar as obsequious in nature. Beyond that, he'd thought for certain Linden was the man from Niamh's vision. He matched the description exactly: cool, enigmatic, difficult to know. His cure, if he ever found it, could save Briar's life.

Yet, Briar was relieved. "Of course," he heard himself say.

"Thank you for understanding."

Linden fastened his cape and took a pinch of gray dust—powder ground from bat bones—from a pouch at his belt. He tossed this in the air to open a second portal, the icy decor of his flat sparkling beyond. He stepped through and, on the other side, turned.

"Ah, before I go, be sure to leave through the kitchen, won't you? Best not give the press anything to gossip about."

At Briar's mute nod, the portal shut, and he was left alone.

He went through the remaining portal into the kitchen, and it dispelled behind him. As he made to leave, Aisling mimed a zip over her lips. Something about the way she averted her gaze . . . Briar knew Linden had already insisted upon her discretion.

It stung like a papercut, forgotten about until you squeezed a lemon.

Linden's preoccupation with privacy reminded him of Celyn's reluctance to be associated with him. It wasn't the same; Linden's celebrity status attracted cruel rumors, and this had nothing to do with Briar and everything to do with the disapproval of Linden's parents. Otherwise, Linden wouldn't have entered a business partnership with him.

Despite his hurt, Briar had to admit the dominant emotion he felt was relief.

"I can keep seeing Rowan," he said to Vatii as they left the Swan and Cygnet.

"I thought you'd be more excited that you have an ongoing collaboration with your childhood idol," Vatii said.

"Well . . . that too." But that required a lot of work, and Briar already had so much to do.

These thoughts fled his mind at the sound of a scream splitting the night.

It silenced the pubgoers who'd spilled into the street. More screams followed. A center of pandemonium separated the crowd, people backing away from a crooked figure on the ground.

The power of the forest pulsed in the air, in the burn of the mark on Briar's arm. Dread curled in his heart.

Maebh appeared, pushing through the crowd. She crouched next to the figure, who shook fiercely while holding her arm. Briar's stomach turned.

The arm was desiccated, ending in a nearly mummified and unmoving hand. And through it, sunk beneath flesh, twisting up over her limb, was a dark, thorny vine.

CHAPTER 15

Maebh looked up and spotted Briar. "Get Rowan," she said.

Briar, glad to look away from the horror of the woman's arm, ran into the night.

The high street through the center of town was the fastest route to Rowan's cottage, but Briar didn't have to go that far to find him.

He stood speaking to Sorcha outside her shop with a paper bag in his hand. Sorcha saw Briar first, waving to him. Rowan turned and started to smile, but he must have seen the fear in Briar's face because the smile extinguished.

"What happened?"

"The forest. I think it attacked someone."

Back at the Swan and Cygnet, the patrons had dispersed. Linden's conjured curtains had vanished, leaving the pub cavernous and empty except for Maebh and the other woman, seated together. The woman had her arm across the table, the vine still carving its way through the gray limb, more alive than the flesh from which it had sprung. Rowan beheld it and went pale.

Maebh pushed a glass of brandy into the woman's uninjured hand. "All right, Orla. Help is here."

Sorcha said, "I'll call Connor. He's still at the clinic."

"This will need a different sort of care."

Briar thought she meant magic, but Maebh's eyes flicked, not to Briar as the only witch in the room, but to Rowan. Worry shone in her stern gaze. Rowan's answering stare might have appeared cold to the casual observer, but Briar could see the ashen fear plainly.

Comprehension dawned. *To sustain itself, the forest started taking things from us. Limbs, mostly.*

Whatever had afflicted the people of Coill Darragh ten years ago, it had returned.

Only now, Éibhear was dead, his responsibilities passed down to Rowan. This attack was within his domain to fix. Rowan took a step toward Orla, but she shied away from him. Maebh's expression hardened.

"Don't be a tit, Orla. Let him see it."

Maebh ushered Rowan closer. Shivers walked up Briar's spine as Rowan set a hand gingerly upon the thorny branch, another upon the desiccated arm. The wild magic of the wood reared up at his touch, making the air in the pub smell like ozone.

To Orla, Maebh said, "Have another sip of brandy." To Rowan, she said, "You saw what your da did when this happened last. You'll have to do the same to break the forest's hold."

Orla gulped the brandy. "Do it."

Rowan snapped the branch.

It didn't splinter like wood, it snapped like bone. Orla let out an ear-splitting howl. Something dark that could have been blood or sap spurted from the branch's broken end. Briar's stomach twisted, everything he'd drunk threatening to reappear. With the branch broken, the remains of it crumbled, sloughing apart like dead skin.

Rowan murmured "I'm sorry," but the screams drowned it out.

Though the threat of being sick persisted, Briar stepped forward. "I can cast something to ease the pain."

He hadn't brought his pouches or tithe belt, but Rowan knew what he meant and inclined his head. "If you're sure."

Everyone under this roof would have known Éibhear, who used flesh tithes liberally. Briar felt less wary pulling charcoal out to draw arrowheads on his outstretched arm. Orla whimpered, bowed over by waves of agony. She shuddered at the touch of Briar's fingers, but slowly the tension loosened in her bunched shoulders as the magic seeped through him into her. It took its time, slow to answer his call, dredged up from the bottom of his waning well. His pounding head reached a splitting ache, but he imagined it did not compare with what Orla had just endured.

While they waited for Connor to arrive, Maebh pulled Rowan aside to speak. Sorcha took one look at Briar and told him to get some air. Gratefully, he went, and as he left, Orla called out a thank-you.

The cold air helped relieve Briar's nausea, but he could still hear an echo of the branch breaking. It rang out in his head, along with Orla's awful scream. He didn't have long to contemplate it. Sorcha stepped out to join him, crossing her arms against the December night.

"Feeling better?"

He sidestepped the question. "What was that?"

Like her family, Sorcha had something of the forest in her manner. Strong and unwavering, but at this question she looked weary. "Someone took something from the forest. So it took something back."

Briar remembered the sickened tree extending an olive branch, only it was a branch of lichen polyps. He had given something back, hadn't he? It had been months ago. If he'd taken more than his due, the forest would have lashed out then, not now. Still, the fear that he shared the blame stuck. "Who took something? What did they take?"

"It will fall to Rowan to find out, and he isn't prepared. Our father—" Sorcha bit down hard on her lip. Her chin dimpled like she barely held grief at bay.

"I'm sorry," Briar said. "You must miss him."

"No. It's been a long time. It's my brother I'm afraid for. If the forest is taking bits of us, piece by piece, like it did before . . . He's marked by it, Rowan. If things get worse, it will call on him like it did Da, I know it. And it's my fault, 'cause I wanted no part in it. Refused to take up Da's mantle, so it fell to Rowan instead."

Briar's jaw ground so tightly he couldn't open it to speak. The image of Éibhear engulfed in tree roots played out in his mind with one nightmarish change: instead of Éibhear, it was Rowan the forest devoured. The very thought made a muscle in his shoulder seize, and he twitched with it, Vatii hopping and hovering in the air as the movement startled her. She settled back down with a look of concern.

"I won't let that happen," Briar said.

With a watery smile, Sorcha elbowed him. "I'm glad he has you looking out for him."

Briar wished he felt worthy of her words. Truthfully, he feared he'd played a part in all this. His evening with Linden had cost him savings he could have used to call on Niamh and ask for guidance. But he hadn't known. At the time, he'd wanted to speak to her about events of the past, not present ones threatening Rowan's life.

Rowan finally emerged, face wan and shaky. Briar volunteered to walk them both home. They stopped at Sorcha's house first, where she gave her brother a hug and made him promise to call her tomorrow.

They walked in silence after. Some color returned to Rowan's face, but his hands still shook. It was dark and the streets were deserted. Briar snuck his hand into Rowan's and held it all the way to the cottage.

At the door, Rowan turned with a look of awkward trepidation on his face. "You can come in. Don't know if I'll be good company, but—"

Briar understood. "We're friends first. I could make you a cup of tea."

In the kitchen, he turned on the gas lantern and gathered mugs, putting two bags of chamomile in each. Though the kitchen wasn't his, the motions felt as habitual and automated as they did at home.

Rowan hovered next to him, accepted his mug, and led them back to the living room, where he sank into the sofa. Briar curled up beside him, their knees just barely touching. Rowan's hands dwarfed his mug, and Briar thought about the gentleness he knew the man for, how profane it seemed to ask those hands to do what they'd done tonight, even if it had been to help someone. Wordlessly, Rowan dropped one hand to his knee, palm up in invitation. It was a relief to be asked for comfort instead of guessing at what kind was welcome. Briar set his tea on the coffee table, shuffled closer, and twined his hand through Rowan's. He dropped his head against Rowan's shoulder.

"Are you okay?"

Rowan said, "I am now, yeah."

"I have to tell you something." Through his guilt, Briar recounted the events that had led him into the forest and the bargain he'd made with the tree. He showed Rowan the mark on his arm and asked the question that plagued him. "Do you think all this could be my fault?"

"No, Briar." Rowan's tone was resolute. Fond. "You've nothing to do with it. Though it wasn't your brightest idea, making bargains with trees, you'd have to take more than a branch to anger the wood like that."

Briar wasn't so sure. If his presence by Rowan's side subverted a preordained destiny, could that throw off the balance of magic in Coill Darragh? Though he couldn't know for certain, something about the possibility niggled at his instincts. It felt true.

He needed to ask Niamh. He considered asking Rowan or his family for help with the cost of the orchid pollen, but it would be graceless to ask for money after everything they'd already done for him. No. He'd take on extra Christmas commissions to cover the cost. Besides, he'd promised Gretchen he'd look into this. He didn't want to let her down.

"Should we go investigate it, then? See what's hurting it?" he asked.

Rowan looked uneasy. He touched the spot on his chest where his scar started. "I'd prefer to leave that as a last resort, if you take my meaning."

"You think it would hurt us?"

"If it had to."

Briar looked up into Rowan's worried eyes. "How do you know?"

Rowan's gaze turned inward. "Just instinct, I suppose."

Briar supposed he understood. A similar intuition was coalescing inside him, too. Telling him he really ought not be here.

Rowan yawned, tipping his head to lean against Briar's.

Briar said, "I can stay the night or head home after—"

"Stay."

So Briar, ignoring his instincts, stayed.

In the week that followed, Rowan got pulled into town meetings to discuss what could be done about the attack on Orla. These, he lamented, went nowhere, because it was a forest and could not be reasoned with. This much he conveyed when he could see Briar for lunch, which was less often than they liked. Briar pulled all-nighters, rushing through commissions and working on designs for Linden.

The first proper evening he had to relax was a Saturday. He went to Rowan's cottage, intent on being wined, dined, and rolled into bed. Instead, it pissed rain on his walk so that he arrived half-drowned and shivering like a small dog.

At the sight of him, Rowan couldn't contain his laughter. "C'mere to me and we'll dry you off." Rowan, in his pajama bottoms and oversized— even for him—jumper, could not have looked cozier.

So Briar stripped out of his clothes and exacted vengeance. Without warning, he crawled under Rowan's jumper to leech his body heat. Vatii flicked off her wings, showering him in rainwater for good measure. Rowan didn't so much as shudder at the touch of Briar's cold hands, just gathered him up and went to the sofa, unzipping the hood of his jumper enough so that Briar could poke his head through.

"How's your ghost been?" Rowan asked.

Briar hadn't seen Gretchen very much, and she was often irritated with him when she did appear. But a fire in the hearth crackled and spat over a new log, giving off radiant heat, and Rowan himself was a campfire. It was difficult to worry about Gretchen. Briar's shivers abated, but he didn't extract himself from Rowan's jumper. He couldn't help but steep in it. The hearth's smoky smell mixed with the shepherd's pie baking in the oven, all warm, earthy herbs and braised meat. Rowan's rich voice in his ear as they murmured in conversation about their days, their jobs. The silky comfort of Rowan's hands wrapped around his lower back.

He'd never had anything like this. He warred with himself over how badly it scared him, and how much he didn't want to let it go. Nothing so solid or comfortable had ever lasted in Briar's life, and this was no different. Destiny called. A city across the channel sea awaited him. And his time kept slipping through his fingers, like the magic he struggled to call upon with every spell and enchantment cast.

"I'm going to make tea. Want any?"

Rowan smirked. "Shall I get you some clothes?"

"Please."

In the kitchen, Briar put the kettle on. Vatii perched on the bread box, assessing his actions with beady scrutiny.

"This is all very domestic," she said.

"I know."

"You said it was just sex."

Briar sighed. "I know." He couldn't carry on like this. Waiting for the kettle to boil, he held up his hand and found it trembling.

A whiskery kiss tickled the nape of his neck, and Rowan's hand twined with his shaking one. "Still cold? I brought you a jumper. Won't fit, but—"

Briar turned in the circle of Rowan's arms. "I've got another idea to warm me up."

Rowan blushed and looked askance at the magpie on his bread box. "Oh. Ehm, excuse us a minute, Vatii."

The tea and the jumper they abandoned in the kitchen, but they didn't make it to the bedroom, instead stretching out on the fur throw in front of the fireplace. Briar went from soaked in rain to soaked in sweat. To his horror, a beep went off from the kitchen, and Rowan—quite close to bringing Briar satisfaction so deep he got the bends—rudely stopped all activity to get up and take the pie out of the oven. Briar whined the whole time about the injustice of it all, sprawled on the fur rug, legs and arms akimbo. Evidently, this was a sight and sound so funny it had Rowan doubled over laughing upon his return. Then he doubled over Briar's body, picking up exactly where they left off.

They showered together, ate dinner together, then fell soundly asleep together—though slumber didn't last long.

Briar startled awake at an aborted shout from Rowan. Even in the dark, he could see Rowan's eyes were closed, violent shivers wracking his body, his scar's aura bleeding wild magic. Briar shook him by the shoulder and found his skin damp with cold sweat. Panic crept in when he didn't wake. It took several tries, and when Rowan's eyes did fly open, a milky cataract covered them. It faded as he beheld Briar.

"I think you were having a nightmare," Briar said. He tried laying a placating hand on his shoulder, but Rowan recoiled and grabbed his chest where the scar started, a flinch of pain twisting his features. "Sorry, did that hurt?"

"It's fine." But he said it through clenched teeth.

Briar leaned over the edge of the bed to root through his discarded clothes. He fished charcoal from the pockets and started drawing. He'd run out of room on his right arm. The runes covered his shoulder too. He drew one on his collarbone, craning his neck to see.

Rowan said something. It might have been "You don't have to."

"Shh."

Briar completed the line of arrowheads and placed his hand over Rowan's scar. Just as he had with Orla, he drew upon the tithe, letting the healing magic flow through them. Only "flow" was no longer the right word. It dripped and dredged as though sucked through a straw when there was little at the bottom to drink. He felt cold and hot at once. One day, he would reach into his magic well and find it empty, but it should not be so soon. He could think of a few reasons it might be exacerbated. His proximity to the wood, or his proximity to Rowan, who seemed less and less like the man from his prophecy by the day.

The spell worked its magic, Rowan relaxing a degree at a time. His breathing evened. Tithe spent, Briar felt woozy himself. He reclined next to Rowan, propped up on an elbow. This time, when he laid a hand over the scar, Rowan didn't flinch. The deep furrow in his brow smoothed, and he gazed back at Briar.

"You do me a lot of good."

There was such a deep affection in his eyes that Briar almost looked away. If he'd been present enough, he'd have known that moment for what it was. There was nothing casual about the way they looked at one another.

"Can I do anything to help?" Briar said.

Rowan squeezed his hand. "You already are."

"Not enough. Not to be overdramatic, but I'd rather the forest didn't eat you." Briar leaned closer. Though dark, he could still make out the fine tracery of Rowan's scar, like fronds of frost curling up one side of his face, thin and fractal. "Your dad didn't warn you about this?" He traced the lace over Rowan's cheek.

"No. Nothing." He winced. "I tried to make magic. Spells. Tea was the best potion I could manage."

"You make good tea."

Rowan's expression was pained. "Not to Da. *It's not enough.* That's what he'd say."

Briar's heart broke. He turned Rowan to face him, hands on his cheeks. "You, Rowan, are so much more than *enough.*"

Rowan's eyes went bright in the dark before he closed them and leaned in to kiss Briar. Soft and grateful, opening his mouth to drink Briar in. Briar gave in to it, pressing close, crushed in the warm fold of Rowan's arms. And he wished it didn't scare him so much, how their kisses filled the empty places inside him. Knowing it couldn't last.

Nothing like this ever did.

When they pulled apart, he traced the path of the scar where it turned Rowan's chest hair white. "I wish your dad had given you anything else to go on. Or just been kinder. Did he even say goodbye?"

"In a way. Only, I didn't know it was goodbye at the time." While Rowan's other scars seemed worn smooth with time, this one had jagged edges, roughening his tone. "He told me, 'I'm sorry, but you won't always be alone. Have courage.' That's all."

Rowan looked raw, crushed, and Briar thought he knew why. *You won't always be alone.* But for ten years, aside from his family, no one had worked past the barrier that scar left. It sounded like Éibhear had known what would become of Rowan after his sacrifice, and he'd gone through with it anyway.

When Briar had been young and learning the ways of men, suppressing feelings and squashing them all into angry shapes, his mother had noticed. It had been his twelfth birthday, and he'd opened a card from his father. Only, it wasn't actually from his father. He'd seen this card already in the grocery shopping, where his mum had forgotten she'd hidden it. He realized then she'd forged them all. Likely in the hope that if his father ever decided he wanted a part in Briar's life, they would have some small connection to start.

Briar had tried to hide how angry he was, but she knew. She'd wrung the feelings from him like soiled water from a sponge. She hadn't tried to tell him that, as his mother, she knew best; she admitted it was a mistake and held him through the wash of emotion he failed to tamp down.

Briar did the same with Rowan now, drawing him close. Rowan rolled willingly into the embrace, snuggled under Briar's chin, their disparate sizes made inconsequential when lying down. Briar kissed his temple. He wanted to say, *You'll never be alone again.* But like his mother's ill-advised cards, it wasn't something he could promise. His future, even foretold by a Seer, felt too cloudy.

Words whispered against his neck. "I've been meaning to ask you something."

"What's that?"

"You don't have to accept."

A snort. "You haven't told me what it is yet."

"Ehm. Christmas. Have you got plans?"

Briar thought about his mother saving up for a turkey and how, for two years, he had missed those turkeys. And her. "Not unless you count sewing and cold sandwiches with my dead flatmate."

"Then you're invited to dinner with me and mine."

Briar said, "I wouldn't want to impose—"

"Could feed the town with what we cook. It's no imposition."

"It wouldn't be weird?"

Taking his meaning, Rowan said, "I'd tell them we're only friends." He tucked a strand of hair behind Briar's ear. "I'd love for you to come."

It felt dangerously intimate, sharing a holiday meal with Rowan's entire family. Especially with the way Briar's heart fluttered. Especially with the way Rowan looked at him now. He could see the courage it had taken to ask wrought in the deep quotation mark between Rowan's brows. The hope, too. Open longing thrummed like a thread of tangible magic between them, and Briar knew it was tempting fate to give in to it.

He said, "Yes."

Ill-advised decisions aside, it gave Briar something to look forward to while the holiday season left him inundated with orders. He scraped hours out of mealtimes and sleep with the most ancient of enchanted potions: coffee. He used up his charmed candles for enhancing mental acuity and began using flesh tithes when desperate, but he oftentimes wondered if this only exchanged one type of exhaustion for another.

Rowan's visits were his only respite. He came, sometimes only for five minutes, but always bearing food. On one such afternoon, Briar had been working behind the counter on a gift for Rowan and, in a fatigued melt-down, told him he was spoiling Christmas.

"You're knackered," Rowan said. "I don't want you to make me anything."

"Too late," said Briar. "You've ruined the surprise."

"I didn't see a thing." A lie.

"You'd better act surprised."

A few days before Christmas Eve, Briar hadn't slept in two days aside from an hour-long nap when a tremor started in his left hand. He stopped sewing and flexed his fingers. He told himself the trembling was from the coffee, but as he began pushing linen through the machine, his arm gave a sudden jerk. Pencils and a case of beads spilled off the edge of the desk. The motion tugged the fabric askew, the stitch bunching into a messy clog in the machine.

Vatii squawked, "Are you all right?"

"I'm—"

He gagged on the words. His shoulder jerked. Electric white light crowded his vision and blotted out the world one shock at a time, and then he fell from his chair. He felt the impact of his head on wood, the ringing afterward like a television set to a vacant channel. He was vaguely aware of Vatii flapping above him, begging him to come around.

He lost consciousness to her shrieks of alarm.

When he came to, the acrid taste of milk thistle elixir soured his tongue. Vatii perched on his chest, chattering low in her throat. Looking to his left, he nearly jumped. Huge blue moons peered down at him. Atticus, his white fur aglow in the lamplight, got up and bounded off the bed, giving Briar full view of his room. The floor was a chaotic sprawl of things Briar had torn down with him when he fell. Beads glittered like tiny jewels, trapped in the cracks of the floorboards, winking from under the dresser.

In the desk chair, hands steepled before him, face a wan mask, was Linden. His expression held a confusing glut of emotion. Troubled, disturbed, guilty, concerned. On the desk beside him, a vial of Briar's regular potions sat empty except for a few drops at the bottom.

Vatii said, "I screamed until Atticus heard me. They were the closest ones who could help. Gretchen tried, but she couldn't pick anything up."

Briar had the most ungrateful thought. He wished it had been Rowan he'd awoken to.

"You never told me you've been cursed," Linden said.

Briar tried for levity. "Don't take it personally. I don't tell anyone."

"I told you I was working on a curse cure, and you didn't think to mention your own? Did you know about my work prior to our meeting?"

Even foggy as he was, Briar recognized the barbed accusation. "You think I've been spying on you."

"Are you insinuating it's only a coincidence? My work was prompted by the emergence of Bowen's Wane specifically, and you so happen to have it."

Briar swallowed, head still reeling. "I didn't know. Linden, I promise you, I had no idea."

Linden stood up. He paced, heedless of the beads sent skittering away. With a hand, he rubbed at his temples. Briar had never seen him so agitated. After a moment, he stopped and said, "Yes, of course. You must forgive me for finding it all suspect. It's just that my life has often been dogged by—it doesn't matter. Perhaps I'm paranoid, flinging such a baseless accusation. What matters most is your health. Are you all right? How far along is it?"

Briar winced. The last time he'd had a blood test, the results came back fine. Less than ideal, but not bad. Yet, what he'd just experienced—a fit, loss of consciousness, violent muscle spasms. These were symptoms his mother had in her last year alive. The thought winched around his throat like a wire. On his chest, Vatii blanketed him with her wings for comfort.

"Not far? I inherited it recently."

"Inherited."

A deep breath. "My mother."

Linden's face fell further, distraught. Briar might have felt touched if he didn't feel so sick.

"She died two years ago."

"And how long have you been performing flesh tithes?"

With a spasm of horror, Briar looked down at himself. In his dazed state, he hadn't noticed. His shirt, its ties undone, had slipped over one shoulder to reveal the scrawl of tithes creeping across his skin. He startled Vatii off him in his haste to cover it, though it was too late. He held his shirt collar together like a maid protecting her virtue.

Linden huffed and sat on the edge of the bed. He brushed Briar's hand aside and swept his shirt down enough to expose the marks. If Briar had been smart, he might have started using his legs. Easier to cover those. His sleeve of them, like a tattoo, and a band around his thigh, meant never wearing T-shirts or going to the beach. But he lived in a cold, rainy country with two weeks of decent weather. He'd deemed it a reasonable exchange. Most witch's clothes involved long sleeves anyway.

He prepared himself for judgment, but Linden's gaze softened. With a thumb, he touched the arrowheads on Briar's collar. The ones he'd used to soothe Rowan's pain.

"You wound me by presuming my question comes from a place of judgment. I ask out of concern for your health. These tithes could be exacerbating the curse."

To Briar's embarrassment, tears pricked at his eyes. His doctor had said there was no evidence flesh tithes had negative effects, but then, so little was known about his condition. Linden's family likely knew all sorts of things he didn't, with their knowledge of magical medicine. He should never have tithed so much in the past week to keep working. "I didn't know."

Linden moved his hand to Briar's forehead, smoothing back his hair. "How do you feel now?"

"I feel like an idiot."

Linden gave a surprised laugh. "You are very strange."

"You aren't the first to say so."

"If you're well enough to joke, then that's a relief." Linden stood, straightening his clothes. "I'm going to mix you some more milk thistle elixir. The ones you've got aren't potent enough."

"You don't have t—"

"You should also see your doctor."

Alarm shot through him. "I have too much work. And I have a blood test after Christmas anyway."

Linden looked at the state of the flat, and Briar's cheeks heated. After a beat, Linden dispensed a handful of berries from a pouch at his belt. He closed his fist around them, and a flare of magic lit the room. Beads rolled and floated back into their trays. Fabric scraps put themselves in the bin. Dirty mugs flew to the sink, which filled with water and soap. Even the skewed fabric unstitched and righted itself in the machine. As all this happened, Linden went around the room and folded a few half-finished garments over an arm.

An objection rose on Briar's tongue. Every muscle in his chest clenched, rebelled against the charity. He wanted to prove he deserved a place at Linden's side as his equal, but looking at all the other half-finished projects, now neatly arranged on the table, he had to admit he couldn't do it. Not all of it. Ridiculously, he thought of Celyn strutting into his flat to boast about his placement in Pentawynn. Briar had said he would succeed without help. On his own.

Watching Linden gather his work up felt like leaning upon a crutch too tenuous to hold him.

Vatii said, "You need the rest. Let him help."

Briar knew she was right and hated it. He couldn't place where this ingrained sense of independence had come from, why it felt so dangerous to need someone else, but it all bruised worse than the phantom pains of his fall.

Linden sat on the edge of the bed again, his blue eyes downcast. Haltingly meeting Briar's gaze, Linden took his hand and squeezed. "I told you it was a miracle, what my parents asked of me. That it was impossible. I want you to know that I've changed my mind."

Briar couldn't be sure whether it was the silky touch or the crushed velvet of Linden's voice, or simply what he was saying, but he froze.

"I promise you," Linden said, "I will find the formula that rids you of this curse."

CHAPTER 16

On Christmas Eve, it snowed.

Briar woke to a text from Rowan.

>>*Happy Christmas. Be by around 4PM to pick you up? xxx*

He held the phone inches from his face and couldn't contain a smile.

Since his episode, he'd completed all his custom orders and finally made enough money to buy ghost orchid pollen. He hadn't told Gretchen yet, waiting to surprise her. Vatii fussed over him and promised not to chide him too often, since it was Christmas. He felt brighter.

The sky was navy by four. Rowan arrived early with a bag of gifts in one hand and snow in his hair. He set the bag down in the doorway and drew Briar out into the cool blue air just to cup his cheeks and kiss him.

It should have set off alarm bells. People could see. They were in the street, only a few steps out the door, aglow in yellow lantern light and—

And Briar didn't care.

They drew apart. Rowan said, "Happy Christmas."

Briar rose on tiptoes to kiss him again.

Maebh lived in the flat above her pub. It was a riot of smells and commotion, a roaring fire chasing out any trace of cold. Christmas carols played on an old radio from the kitchen, where everyone gathered to prepare food, except Ciara, who prodded presents under the tree.

"Ey, no spoaching," Rowan told her as he placed his own gifts there.

Briar brought presents too, wrapped fastidiously like showroom props. Ciara saw these and yelled, "Pretty! Which is for me?"

After letting her shake her gift and chase Vatii around the living room, Rowan led them into the kitchen. Maebh smothered Briar in a hug and a kiss on the cheek. She poured him mulled wine from a pot on the stove, brewed with caramelized oranges. Rowan started preparing dessert—rhubarb pie and custard.

Briar insisted on helping somehow. As he peeled potatoes over a newspaper and the convivial atmosphere seeped into him, Ciara came to sit next to him, a pink diary in hand with a cartoonishly enormous lock on it. She leveled Briar with a serious stare.

"Briar?" she said.

"Yes?"

"When you and Rowan get married, I'm going to be your flower girl. Okay?"

Across the kitchen, Rowan choked audibly on his mulled wine. A bubble of hysterical laughter rose in Briar's throat. Given how Ciara looked at him, it sounded like a threat.

"I'll let you make my dress for me," she added benevolently.

He pointed to her diary. "Are you planning weddings in there?"

She gave a theatrical, long-suffering sigh. "I can't."

"Why not?"

Sorcha said, "She hid the key and can't remember where she put it, didn't she?"

"I put it somewhere safe!"

"I know a bit of magic that could unlock it," Briar said.

Ciara's eyes grew wide, and she picked up the diary to slam it in front of him. "Show me, show me!"

"Say please, Ciara, how many times have I told you?" Sorcha said.

"Please!"

Rowan came over to watch as Briar lowered his voice to a conspiratorial whisper. "It's an old type of magic. It needs a different kind of tithe. You've got to tell a secret, something you've never told anyone." Though a rare spell, certain words, or their meanings, held power. The confession of a deeply held secret unlocked the truth, and thus could free something sealed away.

A deep frown of concentration came over Ciara as she searched for a secret to tell. At a loss, she cast about the room, eyes falling on the turkey. She said, "I don't like cranberry sauce on my turkey."

The lock did not open. Sorcha burst out laughing. "Ciara, you've been giving out to me about the cranberry sauce *all day*."

"I never told Briar!"

"It's got to be something you've told no one else," Sorcha said. "Not something you've told half of Coill Darragh."

"I've a secret for you," Rowan said with a sly smile.

"Tell me!"

"You've got to promise not to tell, or it won't work."

He mimed a zipper over his lips. Ciara did the same. After a moment, Rowan, Ciara, and Briar all put their hands on the diary. Rowan leaned down to whisper in Ciara's ear. As a conduit for the magic, Briar felt it surge through him into the diary, but as it did, something else leaked through. It tickled his senses like fall leaves scuttling along a windy street. A magic signature, but not his own.

The lock on the diary popped open with a click. Shrieking triumphantly, Ciara pounced on it and ran from the room saying, "Don't look, it's private!" Unaware of the irony that if she had any secrets therein, she wouldn't have needed Rowan's to open it.

Briar watched her go. "I think your niece might be a witch, you know."

"Wouldn't surprise us. She's a right spitfire," Rowan said.

Briar had wondered why Ciara never showed the same unease around Rowan as others. Perhaps she had an ability, like Briar's aura reading, that helped her see through it.

"So." Briar smirked up at Rowan. "What's the secret you told her?"

Rowan made a production of shrugging and returned to stir the pie filling without answering.

The kitchen became a thoroughfare for every O'Shea in Coill Darragh while the cooking continued. Cousins, aunts, and uncles poured in with bottles of wine or a "How ya doing, hey?" They all introduced themselves to Briar and asked in a roundabout, friendly way how he found himself in Maebh's kitchen, and had he tried her gravy yet? When he said he was a friend of Rowan's, none concealed their shock. They seemed genuinely glad, if surprised, that Rowan had a friend. One of them put it like so: "He's a face for scaring children, but he wouldn't hurt a fly."

They greeted Rowan, warm but with an underlying discomfort. Briar could see them reaching across the void of that scar's influence, and he could see Rowan on the other side of it, resigned to the distance the chasm created. They were all family. They'd known him before. But none seemed to understand what had become of him.

Some of the hubbub moved into the living room, a distant hum of activity. As Briar set the pots of veg in the kitchen, he felt a warm hand at the small of his back.

Rowan said, "When I invited you, I didn't mean to put you to work."

"I'm happy to help."

"Well, you've worked enough. C'mere to me." Rowan reeled him in close and wiped the corner of Briar's mouth with his thumb. "Gravy," he said, by way of explanation.

"Your mam seems famous for it."

"Ah, sure." He looked askance at the potatoes, a furrow in his brow. "Look, I asked Mam about Da's work. She says she's kept his office right like the day he left it. If you wanted to have a look and see what we can find about . . ." He gestured to his scar. "All this."

"Of course. If you're okay with me seeing it."

"It's fine for me. Just don't want you working on your holiday."

"Rowan." Briar nudged him. "Let's go look."

They went upstairs through a door at the end of the hall. Inside, something half office, half bomb site awaited. Sandwiched between towers of books and papers was a desk. A curious number of instruments, both for potion making and aesthetics, decorated it. Some moved, whirring and spinning in an eternal loop, powered by invisible magic that had endured since the caster's death. Framed botany samples and scientific illustrations covered the walls, and the dust of a decade coated everything in gray film.

Some of the clutter looked less natural. A couple desk drawers had been removed and upended.

"It looks like someone ransacked it," Briar said.

"Could easily have been Da who did that. Mam mentioned he'd given out to her about his missing journal the day he disappeared. He was always misplacing things."

"Any chance the journal wasn't lost, but stolen?"

Rowan frowned. "Could be. I don't know where to start."

"I'll start with the desk. That stack of books over there looks . . . well used? Maybe there's useful information there."

They sorted through the contents of the office, though with little idea of what to look for and so much to sort through, it made for a frustrating task. Vatii perused the spines of books stacked against walls and overflowing from shelves. Briar sifted through desk papers—spare parchment and Post-its with only a few scrawled reminders or phone numbers on them. The one drawer not strewn across the floor was locked. Briar asked about a key, and Rowan said he'd have to ask his mam when she wasn't preparing to carve a turkey, as she was liable to carve him up instead.

Rowan leafed through ledgers and history books with one hand, the other fidgeting in his pocket. A small frown tugged at the corners of his lips.

"Anything interesting?" Briar asked.

"Hm?"

"In the history book. Anything about the invasion?"

"Oh, ehm, no. Doesn't cover anything so recent," Rowan said distractedly.

Briar turned back to the desk. There had to be some clue here, yet the only thing Briar gleaned was an interest Éibhear had with a particular plant called the red carnella. A handwritten treatise of Coill Darraghn flora had been consulted so many times that the spine fell open to a specific, tea-stained page. On it was an illustration of a red flower shaped like a string of hanging bells. The same flower was painted and framed on the wall, along-side scientific lino prints. In the margins of notes, Briar found doodles of the plant. It seemed like an obsession. The botanical book claimed it was rare and endemic to Coill Darragh—something about the soil being the exact acidity necessary. Briar had never seen one before.

He sighed and closed the book. Nothing else jumped out. Nothing about the invasion, or Gretchen, or the responsibilities Rowan would inherit. Nothing that might have precipitated the loss (or theft) of the journal, nothing to indicate why it might be worth taking.

He looked at Rowan, profile aglow with the lamplight behind him. He seemed far away, still holding the same book, open to the same place. Briar admired the fall of dark lashes over warm brown eyes, the slope of his nose, the pursed shape of his lips.

Rowan still fidgeted with something in his pocket. On closer inspection, he looked agitated.

"Find anything?" Briar asked.

Rowan sat up straighter. He blinked, looking down at the book in his lap. "Ehm, nothing." Sheepishly.

"Are you all right?"

"Yeah! Yeah, fine."

Briar looked around the office—a museum to Éibhear's history. He stood and reached for Rowan, who got up and stopped fidgeting to put his hand in Briar's. It was shaking. Even towering over Briar as he did, the hunch of his shoulders made him seem small.

"Is it hard having so much of him around?" Briar asked. "We don't have to keep looking now."

"It's not—" Rowan broke off. He looked incredibly lost.

Unsure what else to do, Briar reached on tiptoes to embrace him, and Rowan gratefully stepped into it. He dropped his head into the crook of Briar's shoulder, and a shaky exhale shivered against Briar's neck.

"Rowan, you're shaking."

"Just a bit cold." It was sweltering in the house.

"Are you sure you're okay?"

From downstairs, Maebh's voice shouted, "Boys! Supper's about ready!"

With dry humor, Rowan said, "We'll get it in the neck if we let the food go cold."

Briar debated pushing the subject. Something ate at Rowan, though he couldn't seem to articulate what, and Briar didn't want to dredge it up right before dinner. He would ask later.

Downstairs, the dining table had expanded, place settings arranged with gold crackers at each. There was even one for Vatii. Briar sat squashed between Rowan and Ciara, a vast spread of food before them. Succulent turkey, roasted potatoes crisped at the edges, thick gravy you could stand a spoon in. Honey-roasted ham pricked with oranges and cloves. The smell of turkey stirred a cauldron of nostalgia in Briar's heart. No matter how skint they were, his mother always made a turkey for them Christmas Day.

This feast was bigger. This family was, too. They filled Briar's heart in places his mother had left empty.

He helped himself to only a little of everything, which still resulted in a tower of food he struggled to finish. Luckily, Rowan's size reflected his appetite, and he finished what Briar couldn't.

Rowan's family gossiped about the disaster of cutting a Christmas tree down so it fit in the living room. It barely squeezed through the door, shedding needles everywhere. For dessert, they enjoyed Rowan's rhubarb pie and custard, the perfect mix of tart and sweet, served with vanilla ice cream.

Briar, stuffed to the gills, insisted on helping clean up. As he did, Maebh came in with a drying cloth. Briar said, "You cooked. Shouldn't you be resting on your laurels now?"

"Oh go 'way. I've ulterior motives anyways."

Briar's heart thunked, though he couldn't be sure that wasn't impending cardiac arrest from all the carbs. "Oh?"

"It does this mammy's heart good to see her shy boy find a friend in you, is all," she said. "My Rowan's a good man, but not many see it."

"I noticed. I think it's the scar."

"Aw sure look it is." She put a stack of dried plates in the cupboard. Briar thought she wouldn't say anything else about it, but as he scrubbed the bottom of a wineglass, she added, "What I'm saying is, thank you. For making him happy."

It struck Briar like a lightning bolt, shocking and heating him through. From where he stood, he could look into the living room and see Rowan sitting on the sofa. Ciara bounced on the back of it, putting bows in Rowan's hair. Rowan glanced Briar's way and met his eyes for just a second, and his smile grew.

He makes me happy too, Briar thought, petrified, like he'd stepped atop a very tall place and looked over the edge at something beautiful and perilous, then lurched with the desire to step off.

Pain lanced through his wrist, and his hand spasmed, dropping the glass he'd been holding into the water.

"You all right there?" Maebh asked.

"Yeah. Yeah, just clumsy."

Everyone gathered around the tree, wine in hand, to exchange gifts. Rowan's family got Briar decorations for his flat. Buttercup curtains. A houseplant with leaves shaped like coins. A fur throw for the end of the bed or to soften the wood floor. Briar had knitted them all scarves and enchanted them to feel perpetually dryer-warmed. Ciara buried her face in hers.

While the others were distracted by the giant, hideous portrait Sorcha had painted of Connor as a joke, Rowan tipped a gift into Briar's hands. A small box that fit in his palm, with a silky blue bow that glided as he pulled it free. Inside, an earring sat on a bed of tissue paper. A silver antler with teardrop jewels dangling from it.

Briar thought it was very unfair he couldn't kiss Rowan right then.

Rowan shifted nervously. "If it's not to your liking, I can—"

"Put it on me."

Briar held his hair away, and Rowan gently attached it to the cuff of his ear with fingers that fluttered like bird's wings. When he finished, Briar turned his head this way and that, making the jewels swing and glitter in the lights from the Christmas tree. Vatii, always keen on sparkly things, nipped at it.

"What do you think?" Briar asked.

Rowan didn't say anything, but his expression said plenty. Briar went to grab the gift he'd made from under the tree, wrapped like origami with mistletoe tucked in the folds. "Remember, you have to pretend to be surprised."

"I told you, I didn't see anything."

He unwrapped it one corner at a time, lifted the lid. Inside lay a necklace of leather twine. At the end, one of Vatii's feathers was tied with a gold Christmas bell that didn't ring when Rowan picked it up.

"It's charmed," Briar said. "I've enchanted it so if you ever find yourself wandering into the forest again, the bell will ring, and it will alert me that something's happened to you. See?" He pulled on the neck of his jumper. A rune in the shape of a diamond with a dot in the center sat in the middle of his chest.

Rowan didn't respond for long enough that Briar wondered if he'd miscalculated, if this gift served only to remind Rowan of something terrible rather than expressing how badly Briar wanted to protect him.

Then Rowan put the necklace over his head and whispered, "Thank you." He made the two words sound grand.

They spent the rest of the evening playing board games until Ciara had to go to bed. Basking in good food, drink, and company, Briar caught himself reminiscing over nights spent like this with his mother before she'd gotten ill. Watching old black-and-white films. Making elaborate cheese boards. Sharing a box of chocolates, his mother always leaving his favorite caramels. He hadn't felt like that in a long time. The only thing tarnishing his good mood was the flicker of a muscle in his hand.

Rowan made motions to depart, and it was another fifteen minutes of saying goodbyes and thank-yous, then lapsing into conversation, then goodbyes again. They finally made it out the door and into the chill night. Snow fluttered down in big fluffy flakes.

"I have something to show you," Rowan said.

He led Briar into the alley behind Maebh's pub. There, under a blanket of snow, was a long wooden sledge. Rowan picked up the rope tied to its front.

"Asked Sorcha if we could borrow it. Have you ever been?"

Briar grinned. He hadn't.

They traipsed through town, snow crunching underfoot, the sledge dragging behind them. Rowan took him to the fields where they'd had their second kiss. At the top of a steep hill, he set the sledge facing the incline and instructed Briar to hop on. It had been made for more than one, but Rowan stood behind it and shoved.

Briar let out a yell. The nose of the sledge angled downward, and he got a good look at how steep the ground went and how far down the bottom was as gravity took hold. Cold stung his cheeks, a laugh stolen by the wind. He hit a bump that sent him swerving, but he managed to swing his body sideways as counterbalance. He wobbled and slid the rest of the way, coming to a sudden stop in a drift at the bottom. Vatii winged after him, cawing joyously.

He turned around to see Rowan, a faraway waving shape on the hilltop.

Euphoric and dizzy, Briar grabbed the sledge rope and started up the hill again. Rowan came to meet him halfway.

Briar insisted they both go. Rowan didn't think they'd both fit, but Briar was determined. He sat in the front, Rowan wedged behind him with both legs stuck out to either side.

"It's going to crash," he said in Briar's ear.

They did crash.

As they sped down the slope, Rowan's weight dragged the sledge leeway. They tipped out, rolled and skidded down the hill, snow rucking up under their clothes. They came to a stop with Rowan half atop him, breath frosting the air in silver puffs. Briar shuddered, laughing, teeth chattering. Rowan had snow in his hair and all over his face. With mittened hands, Briar wiped it away.

Cheeks glowing red, Briar moved to kiss him at the same time Rowan did. They knocked foreheads, burst out laughing and groaning. Rowan kissed the throbbing spot where Briar would have a goose egg later, and then kissed his mouth. Briar's entire body felt heavy, drunk on the desire tasted between them. Rowan pulled off his mittens to put hands as hot as irons under Briar's clothes, making him gasp. He broke away to apologize, only for Briar to chase his mouth and drag him into the snowbank.

It was the sort of joyous moment Briar thought only happened to people with richer, luckier lives than his.

Rowan's heart was a hearth, the circle of his arms a home, and Briar felt sick with the longing to stay there forever.

He realized, with a drop in his stomach, that he was falling in love.

This wasn't casual.

He wasn't sure it ever had been.

Rowan drew away, panting. His nervousness from earlier returned. With one hand, he reached for his pocket. At the same time, splintering white light formed a halo in Briar's vision.

Rowan said, "Briar, I— Briar?"

Briar tried to answer but choked. The lights in his vision spidered and spread. His body jerked. For the second time that week, the curse took him.

CHAPTER 17

White light clouded his vision when he lost consciousness, and white light greeted him when he came to.

Briar squinted at the fluorescent strips overhead, reacquiring his senses one at a time. Starchy, stiff sheets. The soft hum of machines and the clip of distant footsteps. An acrid taste in his cotton-dry mouth, and the unmistakable, sterile smell of antiseptic.

He was in a clinic.

Vatii roused next to him, a low chirrup of greeting in his ear.

He didn't have long to recall how he'd blacked out before the door opened and Sorcha's husband appeared. It was surreal to see Connor changed out of the ugly Christmas jumper into blue scrubs. All Briar's illusions about keeping his curse a secret dissolved. Connor would have seen it in his medical files.

"Ah, Briar. Sure good to see you're awake." But something in his voice said otherwise. "Not your favorite place to be on Christmas Day, I imagine. How are you feeling?"

"Exhausted. Where's Rowan?" He knew what Rowan would have seen. Part of him was embarrassed. He'd seen his mother have these seizures. They were terrifying.

"He's in the waiting room. He'll give out to me in a minute for not letting him know right away that you're up, but we have to talk. Doctor-patient confidentiality comes first 'n all that."

Connor pulled up a chair, metal legs squealing, and sat next to the hospital bed. He folded his hands in front of him. The pose told Briar he wouldn't like what he was about to hear. No good news could come from such a posture.

"How long have you been afflicted with Bowen's Wane?"

"Two years. And a bit."

"That's all?"

Defensively. "Yeah."

Connor looked at a loss for words, like he didn't often have to deal with delivering terrible news, not in this small town, not to someone he'd just shared Christmas dinner with.

"Just tell me."

Connor met his eyes. Steeled himself. Possibly, he dug into the persona he would present to any patient. "It's as if you've had this curse for a long time, Briar. Your health has degenerated so badly, I don't know what to make of it. It's as if you've had it ten years, not two."

"Ten," Briar heard himself say as if from underwater. He expected to follow a list of things he would need to do to rectify his devolving health. A new dosage for his potion. Something.

Instead, Connor said quietly, "I'm trying to contact your specialist, but it being the holidays . . . I managed to speak to someone in Pentawynn, and they said some things can accelerate the curse's symptoms. Unrelated illness. Too little sleep. Stress." He didn't mention the tithes, though he must have seen them while treating Briar.

"How long do I have?" Briar repeated it before the panic took his voice. "How long?"

Connor's eyes crinkled at the corners. A kind, pained sympathy. "Months. Six, at most."

In a wash of dread, Briar unstuck his jaw enough to move it, but words failed him. That couldn't be right. That just could not be right. He had to look away, up at the lights, but their brightness made his eyes sting harder. He choked on a well of things rising in his chest. A roiling bile of emotion that burned and scraped like a flood full of debris was trapped in the shivering prison of his ribs.

He remembered holding his mother's hand while she lay dying, how he'd been speaking to Vatii, because it took a long time to die. And they'd had no idea when it would happen. And he remembered thinking, *It's been a long time since Mum breathed.* Those breaths had been loud in the quiet hospice room, each one a rasping struggle. He'd waited, and the room was silent.

The feeling that had come over him then, and the one that came over him now, were not dissimilar.

Connor started to stand. "If you need a moment—"

Impulsively, Briar grabbed his sleeve to stop him. "Don't tell Rowan." It just came out.

"Why don't you want him to know?"

Because he had a plan to fix it. Because he didn't want the fondness with which Rowan looked at him to change into pity. Because he had a destiny that didn't involve dying, and maybe this—his growing affection for Rowan—had derailed that destiny. Not stress or sleeplessness or flesh tithes but an unbidden love affair, accelerating the rotting curse in his brain.

Because all of these things, and because he didn't know how to tell Rowan.

Connor deflated. "I won't tell him. Patient-doctor confidentiality 'n all that. But he'll want to know. He'll ask. And he'll want to see you soon, like."

"I know. I will talk to him. Just give me five minutes? To think."

Connor nodded and left. Briar sat up, his head swimming. With the heels of his hands, he pressed at his eyes to stymie the threat of tears. Vatii hopped into his lap, and he gathered her up in his arms. Her little body weighed next to nothing, her heart fluttering fast in her chest. This prognosis was as much hers as his. If he died, she'd go with him.

She nibbled at the ends of his hair.

He had months to live. Anything could have affected the curse. Stress. Insomnia. Briar had them in great supply, but he had something else looming over him too, and now he couldn't avoid it any longer.

He was never meant to fall for Rowan. Linden was the man with the mask, the man with a heart of stone that would turn golden, the man with all the connections to Pentawynn, fashion, and the success Briar longed for. The man searching for a *cure*. He'd deviated from that path.

Something else burned deeper beneath all those things: he'd come to rely too heavily on Rowan. Rowan, who fed him and kept him warm and supported him through the burnt-out wreck of his weeks leading up to Christmas. He'd come to count on it, and that dependence terrified him more than the curse. What became of you when you built the brick and mortar of your life on the support of a single person? Briar knew. He'd sat in the rubble left to him after that support strut cracked once before. Briar couldn't let Rowan be that strut, but moreover, he didn't want to be that strut for Rowan either. Only to die six months later.

Rowan was waiting to see him. He'd want to know what had happened, and Briar couldn't very well hide it. But there was something *else* he would have to tell Rowan, and thinking back to their kiss in the snow, this alone made his chest burn.

He took a stabilizing breath. He set Vatii down in his lap and stroked her feathers. She understood without speaking what he was preparing for.

A soft rap at the door. Connor poked his head in. "Are you ready to see anyone, or do you need more time?"

"No, it's fine. I'm fine."

Connor nodded and shut the door. Moments later, it burst open. The room filled with the breadth of Rowan and his calming aura, though he himself was not calm. He moved swiftly to the chair Connor had vacated. Worry furrowed his brow and drove his hands to flutter aimlessly. He looked to the shut door and back, then put one hand to Briar's cheek.

All the grief Briar had stuffed down threatened to spill out. He wanted to hold Rowan's hand. He wanted whatever last scraps of comfort could be had, but knowing what was to come, couldn't take them. It wasn't fair.

"Are you all right?" Rowan asked.

"I'm fine." His lack of dramatics proved it a lie.

"Briar."

He raised his eyes to meet Rowan's. How could he say it? He didn't want to believe it. The words tasted like copper and iron as he summoned them and held them behind clenched teeth, as if chewing on them might soften the blow. When he did say it, he saw the words sink in one at a time in the splintered look on Rowan's face, and that feeling was mirrored in his own heart.

"I'm dying."

Like his lungs had collapsed, the air punched from them, Rowan doubled back against the chair. He took a moment to absorb it.

Briar couldn't bear the silence. "Remember how I said my mother died?"

Rowan nodded.

"It was the kind of curse that gets passed on. I have it." The rest of the words he squeezed out from the narrowing passage of his throat. "I don't have a lot of time left."

"How much time?"

"Months."

Rowan slouched forward, elbows on his knees, and he wiped at his face like he could smother all the feelings worn on it. Even in his most open moments, Briar couldn't be sure he'd ever seen Rowan look so untethered. He took Briar's hand in both of his.

"Why didn't you tell me?"

"I didn't want it to change anything."

He expected Rowan to push for more of an answer, but he didn't. Perhaps it was that he, too, lived with some dark, unnamed magic that made him understand. This sort of magic meant people kept their distance. Only Rowan wore it like armor he couldn't shed.

"What can I do?" Rowan said.

"Do?"

"To help. To stop it."

Briar felt hollow telling him the answer. "Nothing."

"There's got to be something. Magic?"

"Curses like this either have to be lifted by the one who cast it, or they run their course. My mum had no idea who cursed her, but the forest here claimed it was behind it. And I don't think it has any intention of letting me go."

"Potions, medicine—"

"People are searching for a cure. Nobody's found one. I take a potion to slow it down, but—"

"I will find something," Rowan said. His surety startled Briar more than anything else.

"Rowan . . ."

"No." His tone hardened. "We will find something. You've been helping me with my problem, now I'll help you with yours. It can't be coincidence we're both connected to the woods." He lifted Briar's hand and pressed a kiss into the palm, then over the pulse of his wrist.

Vatii's feather and the bell dangled against his chest, a reminder of everything Briar had done wrong to land himself here.

He'd been so incredibly stupid. So reckless. Casual fun, he'd told himself. Just something simple and uncomplicated that he could enjoy before destiny whisked him away. But there was nothing simple or uncomplicated in Rowan's unbroken gaze. Nor in the tangle of real emotion threatening to ensnare him.

He should have ended it long ago. He should never have let it start.

Now he had to pay for his reckless stupidity.

He took his hand away. He folded it in his lap. "I think we need to stop this."

Rowan froze. "This?"

It was cowardly, but he couldn't look at Rowan when he said it. "Our relationship. It's—I think it's better—simpler—if we didn't."

Comprehension dawned. "Oh."

"I'm sorry."

"No, no."

"Just, there's stuff I'm supposed to do, and I'm dragging you into my mess."

"I understand."

Briar looked at him finally. Rowan's expression was unreadable. He looked at the floor as if it was very far away. If it tore at him as much as it did Briar, it didn't show, and for a moment, Briar felt even more stupid. Perhaps the delicate feeling that had bloomed when Rowan kissed him in the snow had been one-sided. That, if anything, should make it easier.

Briar said hopefully, "We can still be friends, though, right?"

Still very far away, Rowan answered, "O' course. O' course."

CHAPTER 18

With nothing more the hospital could do, Briar was discharged and sent home.

He climbed the stairs of his flat as if going to the gallows and only got halfway before he had to sit and rest, head between his knees, a bag of potion bottles set at his feet.

His new prescription came with further bad news. It cost more than five months' worth of his previous supply. Connor kindly informed him the hospital in Coill Darragh had a loaning policy that would cover him. He hadn't extrapolated on how Briar would go about repaying that loan, but it seemed clear he didn't expect Briar would survive long enough to do so.

This debt, added to the loans he'd taken out for his mother's funeral, was another stressor. He could hope Linden would brew him the new dosage, or continue digging himself a financial grave. All this, and he'd been told to relax. *Don't work so hard, it will worsen your symptoms.* How could he afford to survive if he didn't work?

And Rowan . . .

Briar squeezed his eyes shut. Rowan had stayed with him. He'd more or less carried Briar home. At the door, Briar insisted he would be fine the rest of the way. Rowan reluctantly left, though he clearly didn't want to leave Briar alone on Christmas. He hadn't spoken much the whole way, and Briar felt like he'd ruined something precious.

His legs trembled too much to hold him, so he crawled the rest of the way up the stairs and across the floor of his flat. Vatii hopped along beside him. At the edge of his bed, he tried to pull himself up but found himself too weak. The seizure had taken everything out of him. He managed to sit up and lean against the bed.

Only then did he notice Gretchen. She sat cross-legged in the center of his kitchen table, arms folded. Her sour expression spoke volumes.

"Good night?"

He snorted. It was almost funny. She thought he was hungover. "I wish."

"I'm fine, thanks for asking," Gretchen said. "No, actually, I'm not. Know why? I'm still *stuck* here."

Briar closed his eyes. He hadn't forgotten. Things had just piled up. "I've been a bit busy."

"Yeah. I noticed. Busy sucking Rowan's beard off. How very nice for you! Do you know what I've been doing?"

The mention of Rowan made him flinch. "I—"

"Nothing! Surprise, I've been doing nothing, because the only person who can let me out of ghost prison is too busy flirting his way up the class ladder."

Briar felt sorry, but the longer she railed, the more his sympathy curdled. He'd gotten the ghost orchid pollen, finally. He'd planned to tell her, well . . . today. Christmas Day. "I'm trying."

"You haven't tried anything new! You've used all your money on fancy things for Linden's project instead of calling Niamh. And then there's all those potions you're taking, and that seizure you had—"

Briar stiffened. He hadn't realized Gretchen saw that.

"It's as if I don't even exist! You didn't even tell me you had a bloody curse."

The guilt in Briar went flinty and sharp. He kept thinking, *I'm dying, I'm dying, I don't have time.* "I'm sorry."

"Are you?" Gretchen's specter crackled like the sparks of a roaring bonfire when the kindling finally broke apart in blazing heat. "You don't sound very sorry, but you don't sound like anything much anymore because you *never* talk to me!"

"I am sorry!" The volume of his shout surprised her into silence. "I'm sorry I haven't figured out what's tethered you here, and I'm sorry I haven't had time to look, but I've had my hands fairly full with—"

"With Rowan's dick?!"

"With staying alive!"

She gave him an incredulous look.

"I'm dying." He said it as much to her as to stop the cycle of it repeating in his head. "The curse is killing me fast, and there's little I can do to stop it, but I'm going to do what I can, and I'm sorry if that means your imprisonment is lower priority, but I can't—" He didn't finish the sentence. He didn't know how.

For a moment, he thought it had gotten through to her. She sat stock still, mouth half-open.

Then she said, "I keep telling you, death is no big deal. Figure out how to get me out of here, and we can just be dead together."

Briar stared in mute disbelief. The news of his impending doom was a grievous wound. Splitting up with Rowan had left it open and raw. Now Gretchen was throwing salt on it, sounding delighted that his life would end soon.

It took all his energy, but he stood. His legs wobbled, so he used the furniture to support himself.

"Where are you going?" Gretchen demanded.

He made his painstaking way to the kitchen and grabbed the salt shaker.

"Wait, what are you doing?"

He unscrewed the cap and started distributing salt. On the floor, on the counters. It scattered in a hissing stream.

Gretchen's image flickered worse than when she'd been angry. "What— Briar? You can't be serious!"

Exhausted as he was, fury made for potent fuel. He poured salt into his open palm and threw it over the kitchen table where Gretchen stood. It dissolved her apparition like an acidic rain, passing through her in tiny holes that grew and stretched. Her betrayed expression and garbled shout of alarm were the last he saw or heard of her before she vanished altogether.

The flat went silent. Briar held himself up on the wall. After a moment, he dropped the saltshaker to the ground. It clattered and rolled away. With the last dregs of energy available to him, he shuffled to the bed and collapsed into it.

Vatii fluttered across the room to settle on the pillow beside his head and nuzzle his cheek. She'd been uncharacteristically silent in the hospital and the whole way home. Now she finally spoke.

"It'll be okay. There's hope. Linden's looking for something."

Briar clenched his eyes shut. It was somehow worse that she sought to comfort him when, under normal circumstances, he'd be bracing for her reproach. For banishing Gretchen. For his foolish behavior with Rowan. For all his terrible choices.

Instead, she preened his hair.

He stayed in bed for hours. Connor had recommended rest, and Briar couldn't move if he wanted to. At some point, there was a knock at the door, but he couldn't muster the energy to go downstairs. He stayed in bed and drank his potion at the times instructed. He dragged himself out of bed on two occasions to make toast. The potion tasted even worse at this potency, but he couldn't stand long enough to cook something without collapsing.

Christmas Day passed this way. By morning, he felt cold to his bones and wanted to soak in a bath, but his tiny flat had no such luxury, so a shower would have to do.

He managed the trip to his bathroom and turned on the showerhead. He removed his clothes and sat on the toilet while waiting for the water to heat. It took only two minutes of standing under the spray for his legs to shiver so precariously he had to sit. The water was hot, though, and it helped to ease the aches spreading through his limbs.

How had it gotten so bad so quickly?

He tipped his head back and waited for the heat to soak into his bones, but it didn't quite penetrate, and as time wore on, the water cooled. When it reached lukewarm temperature, he tried to stand. The slippery bottom of the shower and his tottering lamb legs prevented it. He tried grabbing hold of the faucet handle, but his arms couldn't lift his weight. Concluding that he would have to crawl out and partially flood his bathroom, he pulled on the sliding door, only to find it had come off its tread. He tried to force it open, but after all his attempts to stand, his arms were too weak for this as well.

A steadily rising hysteria threatened. He had been eating and laughing and sledging and kissing only a day ago. How had one episode left him so incapacitated?

After a few more pathetic attempts, he curled up against the shower wall, as far out of the cooling spray as he could get, and let out a mournful wail. It was very theatrical and on brand for him.

Vatii came to perch on the edge of the shower door. "Do you want me to get someone?"

"No!" Briar howled. He was committed to having a well-deserved meltdown.

Fate, twisted in its machinations, had other ideas, because there came another knock at the door. Briar whipped his head up and regretted it. His vision swam.

Vatii flapped away. Briar heard her winging down the stairs, then the manic scrabbling of talons against a window. She couldn't open the door, but she could alarm someone enough they might break in to see what was wrong. Humiliated as he felt, trapped naked in a cold shower, he hoped it was Rowan.

It was not Rowan. Moments after he heard the door open—not with a crash, but a click and jingle—Linden appeared on the other side of the shower glass.

He whipped around at the sight of Briar naked, sputtering. "Oh, pardon me, I'm sorry! Vatii seemed distressed, and I thought you might have been ill again."

"I am," Briar said. "The door's stuck. Don't look at the mushrooms!" The bathroom still had a fungus problem.

Briar appreciated the irony that, a year ago, if someone had told him Linden Fairchild would burst into his bathroom to rescue him dripping naked from a locked shower, he would have tithed the skin off his left leg to fast-forward in time and arrive at that exact moment.

Now, he lived in a mirror world where everything he'd seen as decadent and delicious had spoiled. He couldn't even think of a teasing repartee to deflect from his embarrassment as Linden picked the door up out of the tread to wiggle it aside. He looked stricken at the sight of Briar. Without hesitation, he leaned through the spray and pulled Briar to his feet. Drops of water speckled his glasses, and a sheen of water soaked through his hair and clothes. He lowered Briar onto the toilet seat and wrapped a towel around his shoulders, then turned off the shower, something he should have done first.

They looked at one another, neither sure what to do.

Briar broke the silence. "This is not as sexy as I hoped it would be."

And Linden responded with a gust of indignant laughter.

Briar almost laughed too. "No, seriously, please wipe our memories of this moment. This isn't how I imagined you seeing me naked."

"Nor I, but I'm afraid memory spells are quite outside my ability."

"Shame," said Briar. "I'll have to use the traditional method." He leaned over the counter and knocked his head against it. Gently.

"I'd appreciate it if you didn't. Come, let's get you dried and dressed."

Linden found and brought him clothes. He allowed Briar to lean on him as they hobbled back into his flat. A plastic bag sat on the salt-covered kitchen table, which hadn't been there before.

"Someone left it at your door," Linden explained.

Briar detached from him and put a stabilizing hand on the table. With the other, he peeled open the plastic bag. Inside were several clear containers filled with leftover Christmas dinner. His stomach growled looking at it, even though it was cold.

A note stuck to the top read: *I'll be by with more later —Rowan*

"The alderman?" said Linden, looking over his shoulder. "Are you two close?"

"I don't know anymore," Briar answered with honest melancholy.

Linden raised an immaculate eyebrow but made no further comment. He took one of the containers, snapped his fingers, and opened the lid to a puff of steam. The smell made Briar's mouth water. He sat at the table and hardly waited for Linden to fetch a fork before eating.

Linden watched in contemplative silence. Under other circumstances, Briar would be mortified by anyone seeing him like this, let alone Linden, but the past twenty-four hours had left him devoid of superficial worries like how grotty he looked.

"What's happened, Briar? You've been taking my potions, haven't you?"

It took less effort to summon an explanation this time. He'd already told Rowan and Gretchen. Between bites of food, Briar summarized his episode and the trip to the clinic. Linden listened, tight-lipped, his features pinched. When Briar told him the prognosis, he rose from his chair and began to pace. The salt crunched under his shoes. By now, Briar understood Linden paced when thinking. The leftovers restored some of his vigor, but looking at the various projects strewn around, he didn't know how he'd get back to work.

"I might be a little late with our collaboration."

Linden stopped pacing. "Pardon?"

"Our project. I'll get to it as soon as I can, but—"

"Absolutely not. You're not to strain yourself, do you understand? This is very serious, what you've told me. It's abnormal how quickly this has progressed, and if you continue to overextend yourself, it will only worsen. I want you to rest."

He said all of this very fast, in his usual clipped annunciation, but the note of panic was new. Briar might have been touched, but he felt like a fried circuit board, all emotions numbed from a power surge.

Linden looked around the flat. He'd tidied it magically a week prior, but it was back to a state best described as an invitation for rats. "Did you have an accident with the salt?"

"I had a fight with my roommate." When Linden continued to look confused, Briar added, "She's a ghost."

Linden's eyes narrowed. "I see. I've trained in performing exorcisms, if you wanted a more permanent solution."

"No! No, we just had a falling out. We'll sort it eventually. I just needed space."

Linden still looked dubious. It was unusual, entertaining the presence of a restless spirit, but Briar was adamant. Angry as he was with Gretchen, he still hoped to salvage their friendship. She'd kept him company when he first arrived, a stranger in this town, and besides . . . it felt important, given the proximity of his own death, to help her find closure in hers.

Maybe. When he was feeling less bruised.

"Very well," Linden said. "I have an enchantment that will work in place of salt. I will return shortly. Do you need anything at present?"

Briar said he didn't. To his surprise, Linden came forward and cupped the back of his head before pressing a kiss to the top of his hair. It happened so quickly Briar thought he'd dizzily imagined it.

"What is happening in here on this day?" he said to the room after Linden left.

Vatii replied, "Your destiny is being put to rights?"

Briar didn't know how to feel about that.

Linden came back soon after. He used magic to tidy up again. In place of salt to keep Gretchen at bay, he tied a charmed ribbon to a desk lamp, ward runes shining along its length. Incredibly, he transfigured Briar's old, single bed into a double, piled with fluffy pillows and comforters, a feat of magic that required tithes aplenty, the pouches at his belt shrinking with the expenditure. It made Briar ache for the time when his own magic had risen to his call with spirit.

In minutes, Linden transformed the flat into a comfortable oasis, easier to navigate for someone in Briar's state.

Linden vanished into the bathroom. Light glowed from within, and several sounds like fireworks went off. Briar waited, bewildered. Linden emerged and helped him over to see his work. The bathroom, magically expanded, now contained a bathtub with a seat and detachable showerhead, along with several fluffy white towels, plush mats, and renovated fixtures that shone brand new. No more mold or mushrooms.

Briar wished he felt gratitude. Instead, he felt sick. This was precisely what he'd feared—becoming a charity case incapable of making his own success, dependent on someone else's. Plus, he'd needed those mushrooms. They made good tithes.

"You didn't have to do all this."

"If there's anything else that could make you more comfortable, you have only to ask."

"More comfortable." The phrasing bothered Briar. It sounded too much like it could end with *before your time comes.*

"No, not like that," Linden said.

Briar leaned on his shoulder for support, so their faces were very close. He could make out every crystalline eddy of Linden's blue eyes, every fine, flyaway hair from his plait.

"I told you before. I will find you that cure."

CHAPTER 19

B riar woke to a missed call and text message from Rowan.
>>*Just checking in. How are you feeling?*

His heart tripped and sank. Rowan used to sign his texts with three
kisses.

He almost flopped back into bed to weep, but he needed to eat so he
could take his potion. Vatii, perched on the headboard, took her head
out from under her wing and followed him into the kitchen. He heated
another container of Christmas dinner. While the microwave hummed,
he looked at the enchanted ribbon from Linden on his desk lamp; it
still shone with the runes keeping Gretchen at bay. Briar wasn't ready
to reconcile with her, but calling Niamh couldn't wait any longer. He
needed to know what was going on in Coill Darragh in regard to his
curse, Gretchen's death, the forest's involvement, and Rowan's peculiar
connection to it.

There was something else he wanted to ask Niamh, too.

The microwave dinged. He retrieved his leftovers and tucked in. Even
reheated, the smell pulled him through a tide of memory. Jostled between
Rowan and little Ciara at a table sagging under the weight of its feast.
Looks exchanged across the room like love notes passed in secret. Little
more than a day since then, but it felt like an age. The moment in the
hospital had carved a gulf between then and now.

He texted Rowan back a quick, >>*Feeling better today. Thank you for the
food, it's helped like magic.*

Sending it without the *xxx* on the end felt like a lie of omission.

Pushing aside his empty container, he filled a bowl with water and took it to the kitchen table. Then he fetched the packet he'd stowed in his tithe belt, the pollen inside like fine grains of sand.

This tiny portion cost him everything he'd earned knitting custom mittens for an entire family.

The ghost orchid pollen caused hardly a ripple as he poured it in. As before, the water turned metallic blue, and he hovered over it, picturing Niamh. Her dark clothes and graying hair. The sharp scrape of a knife sharpened on a whetstone and potpourri smell of her aura.

The water rippled, Niamh's face resolving within, wavering so badly that her features warped.

"Is—Briar I see?"

"Niamh! I have to ask you something—"

Her response came through garbled. Anxiously, Briar wondered if the apothecary had underestimated the amount of pollen needed for the spell. He called Niamh's name while the bowl vibrated on the table, then it stopped, the surface turning placid as a lake. Niamh's hand retracted as the grains of pollen tumbled from her fingers into the scrying bowl on her side. Briar's vision narrowed. The chair he sat in seemed to tip forward and dump him into the bowl, his flat falling away, replaced instead by the rough-hewn furniture and esoteric incense of Niamh's shop in Wishbrooke. Her familiar—a leathery black bat—hung from the curtain rail and twitched its ears. Briar couldn't be there physically, but the more powerful tithe had strengthened the connection to such effect that he might as well have been.

"That's better," Niamh said. She shuffled a pack of weathered tarot cards with split corners. "Had a feeling I'd be hearing from you. You showed up in my dream, bawling about only having a few months to live."

Briar said, "It's true."

"You were also a lizard in the dream."

"Well, not that part," Briar said, annoyed.

Rearranging her skirts, Niamh sat across from him. "Let's do a reading for you. That should sort it out. It will cost your silence again, but that's old hat by now."

"I don't have time for—I need to ask you about what happened in Coill Darragh ten years ago. With Éibhear, and Gretchen, and the invaders, whoever they were, and—"

"Ah sure, nasty business. But you already know as much as I do about it, I can tell you that."

Briar's hopes floundered. "You must know more. What the invaders came for, what happened to Gretchen."

"All that's for you to find out. Shuffle the cards."

"But you're a seer!" His skull felt like it could crack. "You're meant to see things, know things. You told me I'd find success here, and now I've got a few months to live."

"I see you're still sharp as a tack with some things and thick as a plank with others. The Sight doesn't make me omniscient. It doesn't work like that. Now, shuffle."

"But—"

"Shuffle!"

She pushed the deck toward him. Frustration caught in Briar's throat like a snared thread. He'd been so certain Niamh would know more than he'd managed to ascertain so far. All that effort to contact her, and all she'd give him was a tarot reading and some flaky nonsense about how The Sight Doesn't Work Like That.

He took the deck and found he could feel the cards' worn backs. He shuffled, uncertain if the act was a figment of his imagination or magic, but he could feel the toll of silence wending around his throat. Niamh took the deck from him, licked a finger to peel the first from the top, and laid it out, then another. She assembled a spread, two cards atop each other, and two columns of three beneath.

She flipped the first, bowing its surface so it snapped flat.

The Ten of Swords. It depicted a man lying prone with ten swords stuck through his back like the world's saddest pin cushion.

"That's you," said Niamh.

"Great."

"Things appear bleak. You're pinned under the weight of your ambitions and the relentless passage of time. There's also a sense of betrayal."

Briar folded his arms across his chest. Yes. He felt betrayed. He was meant to have *years*.

"Knowledge and truth are the only means by which you might free yourself from despair," Niamh said.

"Which is why I'm *here*—"

She hushed him and flipped the next card. The Lovers. Briar cringed.

"You've come to a crossroads," Niamh said. "A choice is before you. It comes down to more than love, but life, too. Of embarking on a journey or remaining home. Who you choose to take with you will shape your fate."

She turned over the two cards below. On the left, the Six of Pentacles depicted a man distributing coins to people on bended knee. On the right, the Knight of Cups serenely offered a bountiful, golden chalice.

"Hm," said Niamh. "The Six of Pentacles tells us an influential figure with wealth and power will present you with extravagant gifts, while the Knight of Cups offers humbler comforts and emotional fulfillment."

Briar thought those sounded a bit on the nose.

"The cards beneath will reveal what each can give you, and what it will cost."

She flipped the two cards beneath the Six of Pentacles first, revealing Temperance and the Three of Swords. On the first, an angel stood with one foot in a stream, balancing water between two cups. On the second, a heart was stabbed through with three blades.

Niamh scowled, eyebrow raised. "In undertaking a journey with this influential figure, you'll find balance and healing. Great wrongs will be brought to rights, harmony restored to you and those close to you. A river of health and fortitude will flow through you, reinvigorating you after this painful journey. However . . . it will cost you in love. It will break your heart."

Briar nearly screamed. "So I'll have harmony and health, but I'll be heartbroken about it?"

"No need to take that tone. The other cards might be more illuminating." She flipped the last two underneath the Knight of Cups. Briar's heart leapt into his throat. The first was the Two of Cups, the second was—

"Death," said Niamh.

"But that just means change, doesn't it?" He'd paid *some* attention to Niamh's teachings.

"No," she murmured. "In this case, I believe it means what it says on the tin."

The weight of Briar's curse felt leaden and physical. "And not in the 'we all die eventually,' long-term, tricky word-play sense?"

"No . . . I'm afraid it will come much sooner than that."

"Don't sugarcoat it or anything."

"You came for answers. Here they are." She tapped the Two of Cups. "With your humble man, you will find a heart that can hold yours. A soul divinely paired to your own. True—"

"Don't say it."

"True love."

Briar's gaze stuck to the card beneath, where a skeletal rider on a pale horse grinned back at him. "But I'll die."

Niamh spread her hands above the cards, the many faces of which stared dispassionately at Briar. "Yes," she said. "You'll die."

It hurt. It confirmed every instinct that had told Briar to keep away from Rowan, but still it hurt. He bit back the vinegary sting, the lump of things he couldn't say lodged in his throat. "So I can choose to live or love. Not both."

Niamh considered Briar across the table. She'd never been the nurturing sort. Cudgel blunt and sensitive as an iron maiden. He didn't expect to see the sympathy brimming in her eyes. "I'd say it's a sight more complicated, but yes. These are your choices."

Her face began to blur. Mortified, Briar swiped at his eyes, thinking he'd let himself cry. He hadn't, though. The SoothSight spell wore thin.

"It's time you went and met that destiny of yours, Briar," Niamh said, her voice distant yet sonorous. "I'm sure as anything I'll be seeing you soon."

Then the real world grabbed Briar by the scruff and pulled. Niamh's desk melted away. He heard the caw of birds as he slammed back in his chair. It rocked hard enough he nearly tipped over. Vatii, the source of all the screeching, regarded him with beady concern.

"You started shaking something awful," she said.

He felt awful. While scrying, his symptoms had been distant. Now they swarmed in. Holding his head, he went to the kitchen and opened the cupboard reserved for all his potions, unstopping one and draining it. Connor had said to take them whenever his symptoms worsened, but the current dosage should have been enough. He'd taken one that morning—

He looked out the window, the sun blearily high in the sky.

"You were gone a long time," Vatii said. "I was afraid to call you back. It must have been important. What did Niamh tell you?"

The impotence of his answer drained him. "Nothing good."

Vatii commiserated over the cryptic content of Niamh's reading. It hadn't illuminated anything about the mysteries of Coill Darragh, but at least it put one theory to bed. The man from her initial vision had to be Linden. Rowan, according to Niamh, would only bring a swift death.

Briar didn't want to think too long or hard about his love life, so he returned to the trusted method he'd always employed when he didn't know what to do with himself: his vision board.

Reviewing the goals he'd listed upon arriving in Coill Darragh had a sobering effect. He'd accomplished most. He'd brewed Diarmuid his potion, made amends with Maebh, knitted a scarf for Rowan. He'd created a number of garments and sold them. Even, he liked to think, made many clients happy. He recalled the woman he'd knitted mittens for holding the small ones for her children. "The kids'll outgrow them in no time, but maybe they can give them to their kids." It touched him to think he could make something that became a family heirloom.

Now, as he pulled out a purple card to write his goals on, the first thing that came to mind was, *Don't die.*

Composing himself, he came up with something to redirect his focus.

1. *Create a collection that leaves my mark on the world.*
2. *Uncover the secrets in Coill Darragh.*
3. *Free Gretchen.*
4. *Find a cure for my curse and free Rowan from his.*

He pinned it between sketches of tailored jackets and trailing gowns, teacup dresses and pantsuits. Ideas Linden had overhauled, but Briar liked his own versions enough to keep them. For later, he told himself.

There might not be *a later.*

A knock interrupted his brooding. Vatii, who'd been helpfully picking up Linden's sketches from the desk and chucking them on the floor, flew to the window.

"It's Rowan," she said.

A blend of relief and trepidation came over him. Rowan, dressed in a winter coat and—still, even after everything—the scarf Briar made him, smiled with equal relief when Briar opened the door. Since the trip to hospital, they hadn't seen one another. Briar wondered if he'd wrecked everything they had, if the leftover food had been a bit of charity due to his worsening health.

"Briar. I came to check in, see if you're all right." He looked nervous. "How are you?"

"Bit better. Thank you for the leftovers. They really helped."

Rowan held up another plastic bag. "I brought more. Well, not Christmas dinner."

In the wash of winter air coming in, Briar shivered. Rowan kicked snow off his boots and shuffled inside. He set the bag on the counter next to the till.

"Thank you," Briar said again. "I haven't been able to cook. You don't have to do this, though. Especially not after I, well—"

"Ah, Briar." Rowan held up a hand to hush him. "We're still friends, aren't we?"

The hook in Briar's heart twisted. "Yeah. Of course."

"Good. You look good. I mean—I'm glad you're feeling better."

"I am."

"Good. And taking it easy, like?"

"Yep. Getting loads of beauty rest."

"Good." He'd said "good" a lot and seemed to know it. He frowned. The anxious fidgeting that had marked his discomfort in Éibhear's office returned. "I've something to show you." From his pocket, he pulled something spherical, along with something smaller that glinted gold. Perhaps a coin, as he quickly put it back in his pocket. He held the first item in his open palm. It looked like a soap bubble made of semitransparent obsidian. Inside, violet-and-ruby smoke undulated in a storm. Briar took an involuntary step back from it. It had an insidious aura—polluted like rusty water from a groaning tap. He hadn't noticed at first because Rowan's aura dominated.

"What is it?" Rowan asked.

"I don't know, but it's disgusting. Where did you get it?"

"Mam had a key for the drawer in Da's office. This was inside. Drawer was marked with runes. Look."

He showed Briar a photo on his phone of the inside of the drawer. A chain of black runes bisected the bottom and sides—rune wards. Not as powerful as the wards protecting Coill Darragh, but they would protect the thing in the drawer. Or contain it.

Briar said, "Not to put too fine a point on it, but I think that thing is evil, and we shouldn't be touching it."

Rowan's brows rose. He looked at the sphere in his open palm like it might sting. "What should we do with it?"

Suppressing a gag, Briar took a fabric scrap from the counter to wrap it in. "Let's set up the same containment in one of my drawers. I want to know what it is, and why your dad had it."

Briar led the way upstairs. He'd forgotten, until seeing his larger bed and Rowan's ever-rising eyebrows, that the flat looked much different from before. He set the cloth-bound sphere on the desk and emptied a drawer of its contents.

"Linden's been helping me while I've been ill," he said by way of explanation about the bed.

"I see," said Rowan.

"You sound surprised. You don't like him?"

"He's very . . . posh," Rowan said neutrally.

Briar studied him. He wasn't sure what he'd expected. A selfish part of him hoped for jealousy to mark that his feelings were reciprocated even if circumstances prevented him from acting upon them. Instead, Rowan looked conflicted and confused. He shoved his hands in his pockets and resumed fidgeting.

Vatii flapped over to greet Rowan, walking along his shoulder to sidle up to his beard, the traitor.

Briar set to work replicating the runes from Éibhear's drawer. He worked by lamplight, with Rowan's phone on the desk showing the photo for reference. The silence was filled only with the scratch of charcoal on wood.

Rowan's phone buzzed. A quick notification slid a text from Sorcha across the screen.

>>*Have you told him yet???*

Briar's heart knocked hard against his sternum. He returned to the drawer and pretended he hadn't seen it, but the words stuck in his head. Did she mean the magic sphere? It wasn't the first idea that sprang to mind. The first idea made him heavy with hope and hurt both. He wished he could lock up his feelings with the same ease he would this magic bauble.

"Finished."

He put the sphere in the drawer and touched the pads of his fingers to the rune chain. Unthinking, he cast the spell, taking tithes from the natural wood of the drawer. He had not considered that, in his state, it would drain him too much. A wave of dizziness turned the room to runny watercolors, and he swayed.

Rowan caught him. He'd moved quickly, Vatii exploding off his shoulder, and Briar found himself cradled in strong arms that carried him to the bed.

"I'm fine."

"Briar."

"It's nothing, really! I just forgot, spells can be tiring."

Brow creased, Rowan looked over at the drawer. "Then you should rest."

Briar didn't argue. He lay down and watched Rowan close the drawer with the sphere inside, then put the food he'd brought in the fridge. He paused, hovering halfway between Briar and the door, uncertain how best to say goodbye. It occurred to Briar that Rowan struggled to express himself with words. Where before he could kiss Briar, now he didn't know what to do.

Briar tried to help, his bed already making his eyelids leaden. "Will you come by again tomorrow?"

Rowan's shoulders sagged. "I will, yeah."

CHAPTER 20

After a nap, Briar cracked a few books to search for information on the strange enchanted sphere, but discovered nothing.

Vatii suggested, gently, that he ask Gretchen. Though a good idea, Briar's pride still stung. The news of his impending death had made him emotionally volatile and thin skinned. Perhaps his reaction had been overblown—Gretchen had spent most of her death trapped in spectral limbo, unable to manifest through the layers of salt keeping her at bay, and he'd thrown those fears in her face quite literally.

Still, he wasn't ready to reconcile.

He called Linden.

Minutes later, the shop door clicked open. Linden unlocked it with magic so Briar wouldn't have to limp downstairs. He appeared on the landing, Atticus weaving between his feet.

"What's the matter?" he said.

"Do you know what this is?" Briar opened the drawer.

In the pause before Linden moved, Briar wondered what he thought he'd been called for. Another emergency, perhaps. He seemed harried. Nevertheless, he straightened the linen of his shirt and came to look in the drawer. Seeing what was there, he stepped back.

"Briar, where did you get that?"

"Rowan found it."

"Rowan."

"The alderman. We were wondering what it is."

Linden's eyes narrowed. "How did he come by it? And why did he give it to you?"

"It's a long story involving curses and wards and the town's history of death and destruction. Are you sure you want to hear it?"

Linden's blue stare was indecipherable. He looked back at the sphere. "It's a siphon."

Briar had never heard of such a thing. "I wish I'd been more diligent in my apprenticeship, because you're going to have to explain that one to me."

Linden chuckled. "You seem more yourself today. Well, you needn't worry. They'd never teach you about magic like this. It's dangerous and taboo." His eyes flicked to Briar's arm. "So I suppose I shouldn't be surprised to find you in possession of it."

"Why is it taboo? What does it do?"

"A siphon hoards tithes from a hotbed of wild magic and contains them, to be used at the witch's whim for powerful spells. It drains these tithes from any natural source of relative purity. A river, a forest, the sea—wherever tithes can be harvested en masse. They're notoriously difficult to create and volatile to control when used. Highly dangerous magic." He hovered a hand over the rune chain containing it. "Though you seem to understand that."

"Where did it come from?"

"It appears," Linden said, using the drawer to tilt the sphere just slightly, "that someone wanted to know the same thing. That's a tracing rune on it."

Briar's eyes widened. It was difficult to see, but Linden was correct. A tracing rune had been drawn on the siphon to discover its creator. Had Éibhear discovered who made this and for what purpose? Had it led him to the battle, to his death?

Noticing his discontent, Linden shut the drawer. "You've done an excellent job containing it. I wonder, what do you plan to do with it?"

"Leave it there," Briar said. Or use the same tracing spell to see if he could discover its owner, but he wasn't sure he was ready for that.

"It bothers you. Why?"

"It feels off."

Linden tilted his head. He wore a smile so slight Briar almost missed it. "You're quite sensitive, aren't you?"

Briar puffed up. "I'd take offense, but yes, I am."

Linden straightened to meet Briar's eye. In the flicker of the candle-light, his expression softened like melted snow. "I meant no offense by it," he said.

Briar only had a moment to register the look Linden gave him for what it was. Then Linden leaned in and kissed him.

It was not quite passionate and not quite chaste. It was just as Linden was—poised and lingering. It lasted long enough for Briar to feel chastened that he hadn't closed his eyes or reacted at all.

Linden Fairchild was kissing him. Why wasn't he kissing back?

When Linden broke away, his brow folded in confusion. Alarm bells went off in Briar's head. This was the destiny laid out for him. He'd left Rowan to follow it, and he was about to spoil it.

"I'm sorry," Linden said. "I thought you—"

Briar broke from his trance and lunged. He kissed back, eyes clamped shut. With determination, he stuffed away the thoughts and feelings that made him hesitate and guided Linden's arms around him. He heard the pat of paws and flutter of wings as Vatii and Atticus left to give them privacy.

It was not difficult. These were motions with which he was well acquainted, and the past few days had left him harrowed, lonely, craving comfort. So it was not difficult to let Linden's cool, slender hands circle his waist. It was not difficult to reach and pull him closer. It was not difficult . . .

And it was the most difficult thing he'd ever done.

Something sharp dug into his breastbone when Linden pressed tightly against him. Briar cried out. They drew apart, and the talisman fell free of Linden's shirt, which trailed laces, undone far enough that Briar could see the arch of ribs expanding to draw in a sharp breath.

"Ah, stupid thing," Linden said.

He stripped, amulet and shirt both gone at once. It should have been a moment for admiring his lean frame or the flawless skin, unmarked by tithes. Instead, Linden's aura smothered Briar in an uninvited hug.

He'd thought it would taste like a jolt of coffee in the morning, feel like cashmere on bare skin, smell like sunscreen.

Linden was nothing like that. He was fog on the moors at dawn. The *snick-snick* of scissors cutting silk. He was the first breath of winter air you took after stepping outside in January, or the peculiar loneliness of feeling invisible in the middle of a crowd.

Briar couldn't determine if it was pleasant or unpleasant, only that it shocked him. Linden stepped in again, lips cool against Briar's throat, where his pulse scraped like fingernails underneath his skin. All the feelings he tried to suppress bubbled up, panic leading the charge. When Linden's hands shifted under Briar's clothes, he had to battle the instinct to recoil. He stilled Linden's hands with his own.

A look of confusion surfaced over the lustful bat of Linden's eyelashes. Briar had to explain. Wanting this should have come easy, so why was it so *hard?*

He knew the answer and didn't want to admit it.

"Can we take it slow?" It sounded uncharacteristically prudish. He'd never shied away from the bedroom before.

Linden looked chagrined. "Ah, I'm sorry. I didn't mean to—"

"I'm not feeling well, and I don't want to ruin it."

"No, of course! Your health is paramount." As if approaching a spooked horse, Linden pressed a hand to Briar's forehead. "You are a bit chilly. You should rest."

Remembering the cards and Death's grinning skull watching him, Briar added quickly, "We could . . . cuddle?"

Linden smiled softly and helped Briar to bed. Sat up against the headboard, Briar let himself sink against Linden's shoulder. Though he was the perfect height for it, though his touch was both gentle and firm, Briar found himself shivering. He tried to relax. Tried to imagine a world in which his feelings weren't so polluted by prophecies and lovely bearded men who cooed at chickens and baked shepherd's pies.

"You know," Linden said, his fingertips tracing lazy patterns against Briar's shoulder, "yesterday, I intended to ask if you'd let me court you properly."

This should have surprised Briar but didn't. Perhaps because a certain prophecy had ruined the surprise. "You did?"

"Shall I take this as a yes?"

"Yes." He wanted that still. Didn't he? "I thought you said we should stay friends."

"Ah. My parents' influence." He leaned his cheek against Briar's hair. "I'm afraid they did not approve."

"What made them change their mind?"

"They didn't. I'm here against their wishes."

Briar tilted his head to look up at him. Linden seemed completely at ease for the first time Briar could recall. It set off a chain reaction of pleasure and guilt. Pleasure that Briar had been the cause, guilt that his heart didn't quite reciprocate those feelings in spite of Linden's charms.

It wasn't fair to him, and Briar knew as much. To make this work, he had to forget Rowan.

So when Linden leaned in to kiss him again, Briar let him. He let Linden's fingers card through his hair. He closed his eyes, tried to close his heart, too. But kissing Linden felt a little too much like the few times Briar had kissed girls. The knowing how he ought to feel, yet didn't, was awful.

When Linden pulled away some time later, he said with mild self-reproof, "I should really get back to mine."

He shifted, climbing over Briar and out of bed, looking around for his discarded shirt.

"You could stay."

"Regrettably, I have much work to do, but . . . thank you. I could return later, if it would not disturb you."

Before Briar could answer, a knock came at the door. His brow scrunched. It was too late to be a prospective customer wondering over the state of their commission.

Linden said, "Do you get many night callers?"

"No."

"Shall I get it, then?"

"No, stay here."

The wood under Briar's bare feet was frigid, the squeaky stair creaking more quietly than usual. Outside, the wind whistled with streams of snow, and in the crescent moon window of his door, he could see a familiar shape.

Briar opened the door. Rowan stood there, as he had on so many days and nights past, but he looked very different. His face was open and scared. Wind and snow mussed his hair, and he breathed as though he'd run there. He had his hands in his pockets and pulled one out in a fist.

"Briar," he said. "I've come to tell you something. And it might not come out right or make sense, but I have to tell you. If you'll listen."

Briar heard himself say "of course," as if from far away. Internally, denial wrestled with intuition. There were few things he could think Rowan would come to tell him breathlessly in the dead of night. Either the forest had attacked someone again or this had to do with . . . them. Their relationship.

Rowan steeled himself. For a moment, instead of speaking, he looked like he'd be sick.

"I'm—" he said, but no more, because in the short intervening time, there came footsteps on the stairs.

Briar saw the moment Linden came into view. Rowan's head snapped up, his gaze following Linden's movement, until a long, cool arm draped across Briar's shoulders. Linden wore the amulet but not his shirt.

"Ah, the alderman," he said. "What seems to be the matter? It's quite late."

Rowan took in Linden's state of dress, their tussled hair, the arm around Briar's shoulders, and his harried breathing stopped. Briar would tithe anything of his to never again see Rowan look the way he did now. He thought about Rowan's hands on his cheeks as they shared a kiss in the snow. His laugh. The lit fire between them.

He wanted to say, *No, no, it's not what it looks like.*

It was.

I'm falling for you.

It didn't matter.

He couldn't even say *I'm sorry.* Not with Linden standing right there.

Rowan's normally stoic countenance wore a gutted expression for a beat too long to hide. Then he seemed to shore up the walls that had once contained and protected him before, the ones he'd let down for this moment, and he summoned a smile. Briar remembered learning in astronomy that a dead star's light still reached Earth years and years later, so distant that it took all that time to go out. The light of a dead star and the brittle brightness of Rowan's smile were the same.

"Never mind," he said, so quietly Briar almost didn't hear. "It doesn't matter. I'm sorry to have disturbed you."

He was already moving away, turning and hurrying down the street into the snow.

Briar watched him go with the sense that he'd just lost something perfect he didn't know had been his to claim.

CHAPTER 21

After Linden tucked Briar into bed, smoothing his hair away from his forehead and reminding him to take another potion if he felt unwell, he promised to return in a few hours.

But Briar wished to be alone. He couldn't sleep, Rowan's miserable expression painted onto the backs of his eyelids. He might as well have slapped him. On death's doorstep, breaking up with him, then a few days later hopping into a relationship with some savant celebrity like their time together hadn't mattered.

He took a whole roll of toilet paper into bed with him and spent hours weeping and moping. Vatii huddled close, but he could hardly abide even her company.

"You should be telling me off. This is my fault."

"I can't be hard on you when you're already so hard on yourself." At Briar's wretched sob in answer, she added, "Linden has been doting on you more and more. Was it not nice to get to know him better?"

He didn't know how to express how unhelpful that question was. Linden was the most buttoned-up person he had ever kissed. Kissing Rowan was bonfire warmth, and kissing Linden was cupping a candle in a blizzard. They hardly compared. He couldn't say it out loud through the guilt, though.

He might have wallowed for the entire week, but a confluence of previous engagements and poor fortune prevented it. He had to pick up an order of textiles from Sorcha.

She was sitting behind her till darning a pair of dungarees when he arrived. At the sound of his entry, she hardly looked up. On the counter lay the folded yards of fabric he'd ordered, but seeing them, he realized they would be too heavy to carry in his current state. His throat went dry.

"There you are," Sorcha said, pointing with her chin.

Caught between the carving knife of her mood and the immovable weight of the fabric, he went to try. He knew the second he'd wedged his arms under the pile it would be impossible.

"I . . . don't think I can lift it," he said.

Sorcha put down her darning. "I suppose you'll want me to fetch him?"

He winced. "How is he?"

"I'm not to speak of it. He isn't here, so I'll let him know to deliver it, shall I?"

"No, I'll just take it in trips—"

"Don't trouble yourself. You're touched by God he's better tempered than I am. Just go."

He took the bolt from the top of the pile and left.

Though the fabric was chiffon and light, it increased in weight with each step. Briar reached his shop with numb arms and a pounding head. It was less than he deserved.

Vatii, unusually merciful, did not agree. She thought Sorcha's behavior was unfair, and proclaimed this loudly all the way home, where Briar fell into an unintentional nap.

After waking, he unraveled the new fabric and cut the pattern for the bodice of a dress. He got out his embroidery hoop and stitched yellow flowers into the creamy blue chiffon. It would be a summery dress at odds with the snow pillowing outside, but with so little time left to him, all work seemed strange anyway.

He appraised the ribbon wrapped around his lamp. He could distract himself with projects as much as he liked, but he would have to face Gretchen eventually. Getting up, he went to unlace the ribbon. It fell away, and the glowing runes vanished, dispelled.

"Gretchen?"

Silence answered. He waited. She did not appear.

He would sulk too in her position. With naught else to do, he returned to embroidery. Not an hour into it, he'd made good progress, even felt a thrill at his own accomplishment. His phone buzzed a couple times while he tied off the threads of a flower stem.

Then it buzzed again. Again. Over and over, buzzing as if primed to detonate.

He leaned to pick it up and nearly dropped it at the sight of his Alaka-gram notifications. He'd received no less than two thousand in the span of a few minutes. Flicking open his phone, he checked what had prompted the sudden influx.

Linden had tagged him in a post. It was the first on Briar's feed—a photo Linden must have taken while they'd been cuddling and Briar fell asleep. His hair shone bright in the television's blue light, however his eyes bore dark circles from his days spent bedridden from the curse. And he was wearing his fairy pajamas, so faded after ten years of washing that the pat-tern was barely distinguishable. Linden smiled into the camera, eyes half lidded, as though he'd fallen asleep too and only awoken to take the photo on impulse. The caption read:

He looked too cute not to. Can you guess our secret announcement??

A wave of flattery and indignant fury came over Briar. What secret announcement? Why hadn't Linden asked before posting that? They were courting, yes, but they'd never discussed going public. The comments were a wash of congratulations and engagement ring emojis. Also, a few less-generous remarks about Briar. He did look haggard, but he was ill.

He tapped out a message to Linden, then erased it and typed out another, then erased that, too. He gave up and called but hit voicemail.

A rattling anxiety vibrated in his chest. He should be rejoicing, but instead he felt as though strangers had set up camp in his private bed of mourning and blown party horns in his ears. As he snapped his phone shut, it continued buzzing until he disabled Alakagram's notifications. He grabbed his coat.

Linden's shop assistant turned the color of a tomato at the sight of him. She'd clearly seen the post and recognized him. She didn't ask if he had an appointment, just let him bluster through.

Briar paused abruptly at the sound of Linden's voice, pitched loud enough to hear on the sixth stair.

"I don't see that it's any concern of yours who I court—yes, court! 'Fuck,' you say. You chastise me for 'fucking peasants,' but you have a peas-ant's tongue."

He spat each word. Briar's rocketing nerves spiked. Linden's parents would have seen the Alakagram post as well. Linden didn't bother correct-ing them on the current state of their physical relationship, either.

"If it is our family's reputation that concerns you, perhaps you should look to yourself for the sort of example you set! Regardless, it's done now.

It can't be taken back, not unless you can call upon a miracle to wipe ten million memories, which you obviously cannot. Now, I'm busy working *actual* miracles so, with no respect, as you aren't due any, *goodbye.*"

A brittle silence followed. Briar's mind reeled. He hoped never to get on Linden's bad side but had come here spoiling for an argument. Only now he felt terrible. Linden's affection for him flew in the face of his parents' wishes, and he'd just finished defending the legitimacy of their relationship.

He knocked on the door. "Sorry to interrupt."

Linden jumped. He'd been standing in front of a crackling fire, a cauldron brewing over it. He paled. "You overheard again."

"Yeah. I get it. 'Peasant fucker' isn't likely to sweeten your resume."

"You must know I don't think of you that way!" he protested.

"No, of course not." Briar frowned. He'd come for a reason, but he was losing sight of it. In light of his parents' reactions, Linden's big announcement was probably intended to be romantic. Briar had been furious with Celyn for hiding their relationship out of shame, yet he was still angry with Linden for doing the opposite. The irony didn't evade him. Whatever Briar planned to say, he tempered it. "I saw Alakagram."

Linden beamed. "I hoped it might be a surprise, given you've had a difficult few days. And that business with the alderman."

Briar didn't want to talk about Rowan. "It was a surprise! A nice one, but, maybe next time, a little less surprise would be . . . good?"

His face fell. "Oh?"

"Not that I don't appreciate it! It's very sweet. It's just, I didn't know we were going public, and my phone blew up, and I wish I'd had something to cover the dark circles under my eyes in that photo because I look seriously rough—"

"Ah," Linden said. "Ah, I hadn't thought."

"I do really appreciate it!"

Linden took a seat on the lounge. "Yes, yes, of course. Forgive me, I should have warned you. I forget you aren't accustomed to this."

"This? Relationships?"

"Fame."

Briar wasn't sure it was the fame that bothered him. But he also wasn't sure anymore which part *had* bothered him, so he sat next to Linden and opened his phone to the Alakagram post again. Linden eyed him curiously.

"Thought I looked cute, huh?" Briar said.

"You did. Do."

"And what's this big announcement?"

"Our summer line, of course. I think we should hold a press release—a party of sorts. It would be a brilliant opportunity to promote our collaboration, not to mention wear the first garment you made for me. What do you think?"

Briar gaped. "When?"

"Soon, I thought. The beginning of February, to usher in spring."

It sounded wonderful, exciting. It also sounded like a lot of work. The familiar scent of the potion brewing in the cauldron reminded him that these events would affect him differently now. "I'll take any excuse to party," he said. "Provided I'm, uh, still standing."

Linden took his hand and squeezed. "Yes, your health is my priority above all else. That is why I'm applying all my focus to researching a cure, and I think I've made progress. You've inspired me to explore other avenues, and I may be onto something."

"I have? Maybe I can help."

"I appreciate the offer, but you're not well. Besides, I believe this is something I must do on my own. I promised I would find this for you. I intend to keep that promise. Beyond that . . ."

Briar thought he saw a crack in Linden's facade. His distant expression belied an unidentified yearning, some passion he normally protected.

"You can tell me," Briar said.

Linden's answering smile flickered. "The world views all my accomplishments through the lens of those previous. Nearly every week, some tabloid runs a story about my lost talents, and the frivolous waste of my mind on fashion."

"But you love designing."

"What I love—hell, *who* I love—has never felt like mine, though. I'm never allowed to . . ."

Briar's chest ached at that word *love*. A whole world of magic, yet nothing that could forge a new road that didn't end in death or heartbreak for *someone*.

"I'll show you." Linden pulled his phone out and tapped through the trending tags on Alakagram. One of the first was #pityprince. Scrolling, each post critiqued the nature of Linden and Briar's relationship, positing that it was a charity case—the prince and the pauper—a ruse to elevate Linden's image from frivolous to philanthropist. They referred to Briar as "some nobody." Among the comments, plenty of fans defended Linden, but these were answered with dismissive "bootlicker" accusations. Round and round it went. Briar could imagine what the gossip channels might say if they knew about his health, the curse, or Linden's research.

"These are tame compared to the more outlandish conspiracy theories. There's an entire website dedicated to the notion that my family are alien cannibals who devoured our relatives in order to sustain our power on Earth—because *that* is apparently more believable than losing everyone we loved to a terrible illness."

Linden had never spoken about his other family members and the plague that took them. From the pinched look on his face, it was a subject which grieved him still.

"It was short-sighted not to warn you what a courtship with me might entail. Truthfully, I've lived alone in it so long that I forgot not everyone's life is analyzed beneath a microscope. Or perhaps, selfishly, I was glad not to be alone in it any longer. I'm sorry to have exposed you—"

"Don't apologize," Briar said. "I've been called worse things than 'pity prince.' Who cares what they say? They don't know you."

Linden looked into his eyes. "But you do."

Did he? Briar still felt they had a lot to learn about one another, but this was a change. A peek behind the curtain into Linden's brilliant mind. Perhaps there was hope yet that Briar's feelings could change.

He bumped Linden's shoulder with his. With more confidence than he felt, he said, "We'll prove them wrong."

Despite his commitments, something else swiftly climbed to the top of Briar's priority list.

Rowan's visit, and Linden's untimely interruption, replayed in Briar's mind over and over, unhindered no matter how he distracted himself. Rowan hadn't answered his texts, and normally he'd take that as a painful indication Rowan wanted space. Yet, containers full of food appeared on Briar's doorstep, on top of the fabric shipment—neatly wrapped in cling-film—but Rowan was never there by the time Briar opened the door.

He had to apologize—not only because his mother would be rolling in her grave that he hadn't yet, but because he kept tripping into a sinkhole of grief over hurting Rowan. This, and he wished he could have heard what Rowan had been about to say that night. Even though he felt sure it would only hurt more to know for certain what he'd lost.

So he bundled up in every jumper and jacket he owned to visit Rowan's cottage.

It was too cold for the chickens to be out, but he heard aggressive clucking from the coop as he trudged up the snow-slippery path. Smoke curled from the chimney. At the door, he rehearsed what to say, bumping snow from his boots in a shivering tap dance. Finally, he knocked.

Thumping from inside, then the door opened.

And all Briar's prepared apologies died on his tongue.

Standing in a housecoat and slippers was Rowan, only a decade younger.

"Your beard," Briar said. "You shaved your beard?!"

Rowan reached to rub his disturbingly smooth jaw. "Ehm, yeah."

"Why?"

"Just . . ." Rowan shrugged. He looked rough and sleepless, but he also looked like a baby. "Just thought I could use a—Briar, what are you doing here?"

Briar hesitated. Normally, he'd ask to be let in to have this conversation in private. Now, he wasn't sure he could handle seeing the inside of Rowan's home with its stupid, cozy fireplace and stupid, cozy furniture carved by Rowan's stupid, lovely hands.

"I came to apologize."

"You don't have t—"

"No, I do. Rowan, I'm so sorry. I wanted to tell you that I was never with Linden when I was with you. Not ever. I promise, it only just started."

The calm in Rowan's eyes flickered. "I . . . That's good to know."

"And I'm sorry you found out like that, too. It was horrible, and I'm horrible, and I understand if you need space. You don't need to answer my texts or bring me food just because I'm ill and—"

"Briar . . . I'm your friend first. You were clear where we stood, and I—It doesn't matter."

"It *does* matter," Briar said desperately. "It did."

"You don't owe me anything."

Just like that. No jealous outburst, no demands to know more. Briar would never have been so gracious in Rowan's place. His breakup with Celyn came to mind. He wished Rowan would get angry, dare Briar to deny that whatever they'd shared could be so easily abandoned.

Rowan told him he should come in to warm up, but Briar insisted on heading home.

He trudged into his flat and went upstairs to continue embroidering with a healthy dose of sulking. When he reached the landing, he found his flat wasn't empty.

Gretchen sat just as she had before, cross-legged on the kitchen table. Her apparition wore the same clothes as the day she died, her hair still tangled in its messy bun. Even the streaks of dirt on her knees were the same. She couldn't wear the exhaustion of her time spent banished the way Briar wore the effects of his curse—in clothes hanging off his thin frame and dark circles under his eyes. Yet she looked . . . harrowed.

After lingering in the doorway, Briar pulled out a chair to sit facing the table. He was so tired. Slept-for-weeks-and-still-needed-more tired. Neither of them spoke. It was a question of who would be magnanimous enough to apologize first.

"You didn't have to throw salt at me," Gretchen said.

"You didn't have to wish me dead," Briar shot back.

The stalemate persisted.

Gretchen broke it. "It took me a long time to figure it out, you know. When I died. I didn't look down at my corpse like they do in dumb movies. I woke up in bed like I'd been sleeping and went straight back to working on a potion recipe. I could stir a cauldron, drop ingredients in. I went a long time without feeling hungry when I was alive, so it wasn't much different when I was dead. I only realized when people came and started taking away my things, and they couldn't hear me screaming at them to stop, but they sure felt it when I threw a ladle at their head. They ran away screaming, 'Ghost!' and that's when I knew."

Briar listened with a feeling like a clenched fist.

"Ever since, I've been trapped here. A new witch would move in, and every year they'd make sure I stayed trapped. No one bothered with the expense of an exorcism. Why bother, when salt's good enough, right?"

She looked around at the bed, at the various symbols of Linden's presence there. "It doesn't look like you'd struggle to afford an exorcism now."

"Linden offered," Briar said. "I'd never do that to you."

She looked sad, picking at a laddered tear in her leggings. "I'm not very good at admitting when I'm wrong. Wasn't when I was alive either." A shaky sigh. "I wasn't mad at you about the tether. I was mad because I thought we were friends, and you didn't even tell me you were cursed."

Briar said, "We are friends."

"Then why didn't you say anything?"

Because people looked at him differently when they knew, but that wasn't the whole truth. Where had he got this stubborn impulse to do everything by himself? At the heart of it, maybe he still felt he had something to prove. That wasn't the whole of it either, though.

He said, "Ever since my mum died, I've been on my own."

"Ever since I died, I've been on my own, too, until you showed up."

The last part she said with such dripping sarcasm that Briar chuckled. "Sorry?"

"Is that an apology?"

"I'm sorry for throwing salt at you."

"Well, I'm sorry for telling you to just die."

The pressure of the stalemate dissolved. Briar eased back in his chair. Spoken like this, the argument sounded ridiculous, for all it had wounded him deeply at the time.

Gretchen said, "I really am sorry. Are you . . . feeling better?"

It mattered most that she asked. "A bit."

Awkwardly, Gretchen said, "So, what have I missed? What year is it?"

They fell into companionable conversation, mostly about the bizarre occurrences lately, the increase in attacks from the forest, the acceleration of his curse. He skimmed over the events of his love life, though he doubted she'd ridicule him for it. He enjoyed the return of his friend so much, he almost forgot to tell her what he meant to.

"The siphon!"

He sprang up. Gretchen looked bewildered as he ran to the desk and reefed open the drawer. The siphon rolled around inside.

"Have you seen this thing before? Do you know who made it?" he asked.

Gretchen floated next to him, her head tilted to the side. She looked closely at the object, face scrunched in confused concentration. Then her jaw slackened, a strange mix of recognition and uncertainty coming over her.

"I used to go on the roof," she said. "I used to go on the roof to clear my head."

She glided toward the window. Briar had seen her move objects before, but it was something else to watch her curl her fingers in the handles and, in one hard pull, open the window. She leaned out but seemed to encounter glass and could go no farther.

"Do you still have that curtain?" she said.

Briar fetched the cravat and tied it around his neck. He put his cloak on, climbed across his bed to the window, and looked out at the sloping roof. It wasn't too steep, traversable, but the shingles were frosty with January cold. Briar held on to the frame and stepped out, making his cautious way up. The clay tiles would be easy to roll an ankle over, but he climbed on top of the dormer window, which was flat enough to sit on.

Gretchen waited there, knees tucked to her chin. "I used to come up here when I was stressed and too busy to take a walk, but I needed the air." She recalled it hazily, squinting into the night. Her memories seemed to return to her like drips from a leaky faucet.

Briar followed her gaze. Over the rooftops, the forest swayed, a dark inkblot seeping into star-dappled sky.

"I think it does bother me," she said. "Being dead."

"Why are you so determined not to care about that?"

"Come on. It's such a cliché."

Briar couldn't imagine not caring.

"I worked so hard, Briar. So damn hard, and for what? I thought I was doing good things, making healing potions. But I'd come up with one brilliant recipe, and it wasn't enough. I'd move straight on to the next thing. Never stopped."

The words felt sharp. They prodded Briar in places he didn't want to examine.

"I think the worst part about being trapped in this house," Gretchen said, "is that I hardly ever left it when I was alive anyway."

She hugged her knees. Briar understood the feeling—he'd come to Coill Darragh wanting to make something of himself. To do something that mattered. Now, with his breath coming short in his lungs, he sometimes found himself wanting something simpler. Happier.

"Did the siphon jog any other memories?"

She shut her eyes. "I saw it before, but not here. In Éibhear's office? Then he gave me something." Abruptly, she stood. "Something to hide."

She was moving again, gliding toward the chimney. It was an old thing of brick and chipping mortar. She stopped on the other side of it, staring. Briar made his way slowly, some of the roof tiles wobbling. When he'd crested the top, he saw what Gretchen was looking at.

There, shimmering on a corner of the flanching, was a purple scar.

They knew without speaking what they'd found. Gretchen moved to touch it, but Briar called for her to wait. "Are you sure you want to see?"

In answer, she slapped a hand to the scar. Briar sat back on the roof ridge, one leg to either side of it for balance, as movement reined their attention toward the dormer window.

Gretchen, the living Gretchen, emerged from it.

She wore everything her apparition did, but her cheeks burned red with exertion as she scrambled up the roof. She reached the spot where her ghost stood and, getting to her knees, started prying at the roof tiles until she found one wiggly enough to free. She pulled something out of the pocket of her jumper and, in the recess beneath the loosened tile, set a small wooden box. A rune glowed on its lid.

A noise from the street, and she whipped her head around, terror in her eyes. With harried movements, she covered the gap with the tile again. The noises sounded closer, beneath them, emanating from Briar's flat. Only it was her flat.

She said out loud, "Think, think, think!"

In a burst of inspiration, she tugged a few strands of hair from her own head, pulling her bun messy and looser. Her fingers trembled as she tied the hair into a knot. She pressed this to the tile, and the hair scorched and vanished, sealing the tile beneath.

Shaking, she made her way back toward the window, but someone else emerged from it, blocking her path. A tall figure, hooded and wearing a mask of ebony filigree, as if arriving from a party. A long tear in their cloak was soaked in blood from a cut to the shoulder. They stood on the eave. From the look on Gretchen's face, she was considering pushing this person, except there was a good chance they would pull her down with them. Behind her, the fall was treacherous.

Briar gripped the roof tiles beneath him. A charge ran through him that had nothing to do with magic or memory. He knew what he was about to see.

Gretchen's eyes flicked, searching for an escape route. The intruder lunged forward with something in their hand. Whatever it was imploded, their hand clenching around empty air. A shockwave of force hit Gretchen in the chest and sent her sprawling. Briar's teeth ground together seeing her head clip the chimney. She landed heavily on the roof tiles, then rolled, her limp body tumbling over the edge. In the seconds before she hit the concrete below, her murderer summoned a portal and stepped through it. Briar only got a glimpse of something glittering brightly on the other side before the portal vanished. The vision severed the second Gretchen hit the pavement.

The ghost of her still stood with her hand in the chimney. She withdrew it. A cold horror overcame her features.

"Gretchen, I'm—"

"Don't." She dropped to her knees at the exact spot where she'd hidden something under the roof. Her last act. She pried at the tile, fingers leaving trenches in the moss grown over it, but it didn't budge, sealed by her own magic.

"Help me!" she said shrilly.

Briar startled into action. He moved carefully, balancing next to her. Brushing away the moss, he found the faint scorch marks of the hair used as a tithe. "We need magic to open it."

"Then get something!"

"I don't have anything for unlocking something like this, and if I use a flesh tithe, I'll fall off this roof, too." He said it gently, which only made her angrier.

"There has to be something."

A stir of memory hit him. "A secret. Tell me a secret, and that'll undo it."

Gretchen started to say, "I have no secrets because I can't remember—" She stopped. She looked at the edge of the roof where she'd fallen. "I do remember."

Briar put his hand over the tile. He didn't speak, afraid to derail the threads of recollection she'd been gathering since laying eyes on the siphon.

"I remember," she said again, "going to the woods with Éibhear to harvest red carnellas. There was something special about them. This time was different, though. The forest felt . . . sick." Her eyes glazed, caught in memory. "We went to the place carnellas bloomed and found a crater. Everything—the carnellas, the trees, their roots, gone. Just scorched earth and that siphon *thing* at its center. Éibhear took the siphon to study and sent me to look for more carnellas."

"Why were the carnellas so important?"

"I . . . can't quite remember? They had special properties, but they were difficult to harness as tithes. We were studying them. Working on something with them? I looked for a long time and found only three, so I picked them." She folded into herself. "The forest reacted. It was all wrong. It lashed out at me, tried to *kill* me. I barely escaped. It had never done that, not in all the times we'd gone before."

Briar listened, his heart thudding like the unusual, rhythmic cadence of her speech.

"I found Éibhear in his study. It was in tatters. Everything trashed. God, everything was so wrong. Éibhear didn't have time to tell me what had happened." Her face was stricken with misery. "We heard noise on the stairs. No one else was supposed to be home. Éibhear told me to take the carnellas and hide them where only he would find them.

"Then I turned to go, and I saw *him*."

Briar shivered. Somehow, he knew it was her killer she spoke of.

"That mask. I had to run past him to get away, and he lashed out with a knife." She gripped her shoulder, where the fabric was torn, the cut underneath obscured. "I don't think I'd have made it if Éibhear hadn't struck him. He used some kind of magic I'd never seen before. Like he'd called the forest up to fight for him. I think that's when I knew how much danger I was in. That *mask*." She shuddered. "I ran. That's the last time I saw Éibhear."

The rest of the story they both knew. They'd just watched it play out.

Between them, the roof tile juddered as the secret, now told, worked its magic. Neither of them removed it to check what was beneath. Not yet. Gretchen sat frozen, racked by memories. Her murderer had chased her down. Not to take the carnellas—he'd left without them—but to get rid of her. Like she was a loose end that needed trimming, a stain to rub out of the carpet. Whatever she'd seen, she was never meant to.

Gretchen sniffed. "We should get that out." She pointed at the loose tile.

His fingers were going numb with cold, but Briar pried it up. There, just as she'd left it, was the box. It had cracked open, compelled by the powerful secrets in her story.

Inside, the carnellas, decades old, had wilted to papery shrapnel.

"We should keep them. They could still be useful," Gretchen said. Seeing him shivering, she added, "And you should get inside."

Briar made his way down, grip tight on the tiles, taking it slow. Images of Gretchen falling over the edge played in his mind in a nauseating loop. He climbed back inside, trekking dirt and moss onto his bed covers.

"Briar."

He turned around at the sound of Gretchen's voice. She floated there, just outside his window, when he and his cravat were inside.

He held the small box of carnellas tightly. Her tether, now unlocked. She was free of it.

CHAPTER 22

Linden said, "What's this?"

Briar showed him the dried carnellas the following morning, though not much of them remained to look at.

"Remember my ghosty flatmate situation? She hid this before she died. They're called red carnellas, and they were special somehow, but she can't remember everything, and now they're extinct. I wondered if you knew anything about them?"

Linden's eyebrows reached into his hairline. With reverence, he took the box from Briar's hands. "Where to begin? Did your, er, 'ghost roommate' remember anything about them at all?"

"Only that they had special properties that were difficult to harness."

"That's putting it mildly," Linden agreed.

"So you've heard of them?"

"I have. You recall I mentioned rumors of a panacea found in Coill Darragh? The red carnella was purported to be the primary ingredient."

Hope pulsed in Briar's heart.

"I know what you're thinking," Linden said quickly. "But I wouldn't put too much faith in this. Literature on red carnellas is spartan given their rarity, but from what I understand, the use of carnellas as tithes yielded nothing. They were fragile, temperamental. Whatever magic they contained was too easily broken down."

"Then how did anyone know a panacea was possible using them?"

"Ah, who's to say? Rumor, local legend. Perhaps someone, once, in a fluke bit of luck, managed something with them long ago, and no one's been able to recreate it since. I believe it's a myth, but—" He slid a finger over the lip of the box, a slight pinch between his eyebrows. "It's worth investigating further. Any hope of finding something that could help you, I'll take."

In the years since Bowen's Wane began devouring Briar's future, he'd avoided hope like it was a snare ready to choke his final days. It was easier to press himself to work hard and bury himself in distractions, all the while convinced he'd live what time he had to the fullest rather than pray for the impossible.

Now, hope was a feverish, desperate burn in his breast.

"May I borrow these for study?" Linden asked. "I promise to return them to you and your—friend?"

"Gretchen."

"Gretchen." He took Briar's hand, kissing the knuckles. "I'll return them to you both, whether I find anything or not. I . . . I very much hope I do."

The shy sincerity in his voice compelled Briar to grab Linden around the shoulders and squeeze. After a stunned moment, Linden hugged him back. His tactility still surprised Briar every time. Linden had made advances in the bedroom, but Briar shied away from anything more intimate than a kiss, using his health as an excuse. He felt guilty, and could see it wounded Linden, but he didn't know how else to handle his lingering flame for Rowan. But in moments like these, where the intimacy was spontaneous and emotional, Linden froze up.

When Briar drew away, Linden's eyelids fluttered. He looked as if he wanted more, even leaned forward to—Briar's instincts bucked, and he drew away. Seeing Linden's guarded persona snap back into place immediately, he said quickly, "I'm sorry. It's not—Can I tell you something?"

Cautiously. "Of course."

"I can read auras. Have since I was little, and it's always been comforting. It makes me feel closer to people. Like I can really see them. But with you—your amulet prevents it. I haven't felt your aura since that first night."

"Ah . . ." Linden looked even more uncertain. "I didn't know."

"I know why you need it. But I think it's why I sometimes feel like I barely know you."

Linden touched his shirt where it covered the talisman. "It's dangerous for me to go without it. There are plenty of witches happy to curse someone for the crime of being popular."

"I know. I'm sorry, I just thought I'd explain why I'm sometimes—"

Linden lay a hand on his shoulder. "No need to apologize, Briar. It's understandable, and it need not be forever. When you come with me to my estate in Pentawynn, I'll be protected there and can remove this blasted thing."

"Come with you? To Pentawynn?"

"Of course. I assumed you'd want—"

Briar flung his arms around Linden again. What he felt—for Linden, for Rowan—it was not a simple thing to untangle. But Pentawynn, that was a dream he'd had since he was a boy.

Linden cleared his throat. "Yes, well. Now that's settled, I best get back to work."

As he prepared to leave, someone knocked at the door. It was not the calm knock of a person just checking in. It hammered, sending tremors through the floorboards, startling Vatii off the headboard.

It was Rowan. He didn't even pause at the sight of Linden with Briar, just blurted, "It got Sorcha."

Briar paled.

"It?" Linden said.

"The forest. It attacked her. Taken part of her leg—she's barely walking. She told me not to go, but I'll not listen. It's my job to stop this, and I've put it off too long. I have to find what's wrong with the wood."

"You're not going in there," Briar said.

"I am. Came to tell you in case that spell goes off." He touched the magpie feather and bell hanging from his neck. Linden watched the motion with scrutiny. "Needed to warn you so you know it's not taken me and don't come looking."

"Bollocks to that, I'm going with you."

In unison, both Rowan and Linden said no, then looked at one another, annoyed.

"It's my job," Rowan said. "I won't risk it harming you."

"I agree. Don't be ridiculous," Linden said. "You're hardly in a fit state."

Briar stomped back into the house to grab his cloak, tithe belt, and several vials of milk thistle elixir. Vatii knew his moods and not to argue. "I'm not letting you go in alone," said Briar. "What if it attacks you, too?"

Rowan sputtered in protest.

"What if you need help? Or a spell, or just another pair of hands?"

Linden halted Briar's motions, holding his wrist. "And what if your curse worsens given proximity to the very thing that cursed you?"

Though Briar hadn't considered that possibility, Gretchen's words echoed in his mind. Her regrets. He pulled free and said to Rowan, "I'm not dead yet, but I won't be able to live with myself if I let you go alone and something happens to you."

They all stood quiet long enough that the wind wheezing through the eaves sounded over-loud. Linden's hard glare turned on Rowan. "You ought to have known he wouldn't simply sit by."

Rowan's returning glare weakened a little under the rebuke.

"The charm on his necklace would have let me know he'd gone into the woods anyway," said Briar. "I'd have gone in after him one way or another."

He wrapped his tithe belt around his waist and donned his cloak. Linden watched, stormy and lost. Briar grappled with the ties on his cloak. Somehow, this felt like choosing between them all over again. It wasn't the case—he didn't need tea leaves to know that if it was Linden in danger, he'd dive in after him, too. Still . . .

He didn't like to do it in front of Rowan, but he leaned in to kiss Linden's cheek. In his periphery, he saw Rowan turn away.

"I can't let him go alone," Briar said. "I'll be back soon."

The storm clouds in Linden's face broke. "You know me better than that. I understand you'd not leave a friend in peril, but I will not leave my lover to the wilds either. I'm coming."

Briar's instinct was to argue, but Linden was a powerful witch. They were more likely to succeed with his help. He relented. "All right."

They set out together, Linden expediting their journey with a portal to the edge of the forest. Stepping through it was like entering a rainforest pavilion at a zoo. The air hung heavy, thick and muddy, the forest's aura filling Briar's lungs with loam as though he was at a freshly dug grave mid-burial. On his first visit, the wood had been verdant with life. Now, winter had pruned its branches, leaving low shrubs and thick fog. Beyond that, it felt different, like cloud shapes that changed the longer he looked at them.

"Are you going to inform us what we should be searching for?" Linden asked.

"Anything out of the ordinary," Rowan answered.

"In a wood of wild magic, that hardly rules anything out."

"Anything that could harm the forest," Briar supplied. "Right?"

Rowan nodded.

They reached a fallen log blocking the path at hip height. Linden took Briar's hand to help him over it and didn't let go afterward. Rowan stared into the trees ahead while Briar's stomach churned—he was here to help, not remind Rowan of what they'd lost.

They continued searching for anything amiss. Besides the wind and their footsteps, the forest was eerily quiet. No birds sang, no small animals scuffled in the bushes, no insects hummed. Only the trees spoke.

Ours, they said.

The Keeper.

Briar longed to wrench Rowan away from this place.

They discovered why it was so quiet with a dry crunch underfoot. Not of twigs—the tiny skeleton of an animal, perhaps a squirrel. Not so strange a thing, until they found more. A tiny tibia, the scattered remains of rodents and birds. Some were shriveled, still wrapped in tight skin, fur or feathers, others nothing more than yellow bones. What killed them wasn't evident until they came across a mouse, freshly dead and caught in the ivy of a tree. The star-shaped leaves made a red halo around its body. Before their eyes, the mouse shriveled as the forest sucked the vitality from it.

So the wood not only attacked the people of Coill Darragh, but the animals, too. The remains, Briar sensed, were devoid of tithe magic, sapped dry.

"This place is cursed," said Linden. "I don't know why you don't just burn it to the ground."

"If you'd seen Sorcha today, you wouldn't ask," Rowan growled.

"Will she be all right?" Briar still couldn't speak to Sorcha—she was frosty with him, but he couldn't blame her for that.

"She will be, yeah. Scared Ciara something fierce, though."

That made Briar shiver. What if the forest came for Ciara?

"What's that?" Linden pointed ahead, where a mound of earth and twigs rose from the earth. It looked like a sleeping goliath, a bear, from afar. They picked their way toward it and found—

A hut.

It was stranger than the dead animals. A man-made construction in this forest defied logic; no one went into the woods, let alone lived here. Red ribbons hung like gore from the twigs, fluttering in the breeze, markings written along their length. Runes. The ribbons were wards like the one he and Linden used to banish Gretchen. Many no longer shone with the light of active magic, weathered and frayed. Others were naught more than scraps of fabric. The forest menaced the hut from all sides, shrubs and trees leaning in, reaching, held back from destroying the thing by the wards. But only just.

A ragged blanket hung in the doorway, obscuring the interior. Rowan's hands shook visibly as he pushed it aside. Briar wished he could reach out to steady Rowan, but Linden still held his hand tightly.

Inside, it was too dark to see until Linden tithed a strand of hair to cast a floating orb of light. The ceiling was low. Rowan couldn't stand straight, and things hung from the ceiling, tickling the back of Briar's neck. More ribbons. Countless. Baskets containing tithes littered the floor. The ground was uneven beneath Briar's foot. He scuffed dead leaves out of the way to find a sigil dug into the dirt. Wards and tithes for protection were every-where. Whoever had occupied the hut, they'd known the danger.

"Look at this," Rowan said.

On a table at the back were several leather tomes scrawled with runes, recipes, and treatises on old magic. Next to them, in a bowl of inky water, floated several spherical objects. Hesitantly, Rowan lifted one from the water. It was empty. No smoke swirled within, but it was clearly a siphon.

Linden said, "Use of those would be a swift way to invoke the forest's ire, I wager."

"You don't think—?" Briar asked.

"Yeah," Rowan said gruffly. "Whoever was behind it ten years ago, seems they've returned."

He dropped the empty siphon back in the brew. Briar hated to think what that water might contain to empower the glass spheres to capture swathes of life from the woods.

"This is only a hypothesis," Linden said, "but, if this exact thing hap-pened before, then perhaps the use of these siphons is what prompted the woods to curse your mother."

"But *why*? She'd never been here, far as I know," Briar said.

A thunderous rumble interrupted them. The forest moaned as if every tree was the mast of a great ship whose stays had snapped. Abruptly, all the silvery rune marks on the ribbons dissolved. The hut shook.

Linden said, "I think that's our cue to leave."

The trees said, *This way.*

"No!" Rowan swayed. For a frightening moment, Briar watched his eyes glaze over, the milky cataract covering them. Then he snapped from it and said, "There's something else."

He left the hut. Briar marched after him and was nearly yanked from his feet when Linden did not follow. At the same moment, the hut rent apart. The wards dispelled, their magic no longer powerful enough to contend with the forest, which took back its components greedily. Light spilled in through the cracks as vines crept in and tore apart the log supports. Wattle and daub fell in crumbling chunks. Linden didn't resist this time as Briar ran. Ahead, Rowan's back receded into the trees, following a call neither of them could hear.

Linden's face was wan. "Where is he off to?"

Briar didn't stop to speculate. Vatii flapped after him as he skipped over the heaving ground. Linden swore and stuck close. His amulet helped—the skittering movement of plants and wild magic shied away from him as they went.

Ahead, Rowan came to a halt in a clearing. It wasn't a normal glade—it was a crop circle of blackened ash, as though a fire had burned within the confines of a ring. Rowan stood before the only remaining tree in the glade, a crooked thing. He stared at something caught up in a cage of branches.

It was once a man.

Like the birds and animals, his skin had pruned, sucked tight over his bones. Bright teeth bared wide. The tattered remains of clothing draped in lank folds. Though it appeared old, there was something fresh about the corpse. It dripped.

Rowan stared down at its hand. It held something tight in a skeletal grasp, something with a glassy sheen. A siphon, only this one was full. It contained all the life, all the tithes of that barren circle, and it had cost the caster dearly.

"Who is it?" Briar asked.

Rowan shook his head. No distinguishing features remained.

Linden said, "Look." With thumb and forefinger, he picked up the arm of the corpse by its loose sleeve as if picking up a rat by its tail. The hand gripping the siphon fell open, the orb bouncing in clouds of ash. Something shiny fell from its finger. Linden bent to pick it up and dust it off. A ring. Custom made to match another one, which Aisling had happily worn on the night of Saor ó Eagla.

It was the ring Briar had sold to Kenneth.

It was difficult to extract the remains without breaking them, but Rowan managed to use his oversized jacket to bundle up the body.

Though Kenneth had been behind the chaos in Coill Darragh, it still seemed cruel to leave him there. They had to tell Aisling, but how to explain her lover had been tithing the forest, inciting its wrath against her fellows? She'd thought he'd gotten cold feet, skipped town to avoid breaking off their engagement.

At the news, she railed against her ex-fiancé as though he were alive to hear her. According to her, Kenneth's parents were dead. It not only explained why no one had come looking for him, but aligned with the events of ten years prior. If his parents started this war on the woods, they'd probably died when the wards went up.

Perhaps he'd believed Aisling's love would protect him from the forest. Perhaps he'd wanted vengeance for the deaths of his family. They'd never know. Nothing left in the disaster zone of his hut alluded to his motives.

It should have been a relief. The source of the forest's ire dealt with by the forest itself.

Instead, Briar returned to find his flat in havoc. A hurricane sent the contents of his desk and kitchen cabinets streaming across the flat, a dervish of fabric and sewing materials. He had to hold his cloak up to protect himself from flying utensils. A barely human howl screeched through it all.

"Is that Gretchen?" Vatii shrieked.

Sure enough, a spectral image of Gretchen flickered like television static near the high beams of the ceiling.

Horror gripped him. "Gretchen?"

"Briar?" Her voice sounded distant and too close at once, breaking up and distorted. Her image winked out and appeared closer, her face drawn in agony. "Briar, help, I think I'm—"

She couldn't get the rest out. Briar reached for her, grasped for her wrists and phased through them. The chill on his fingers was no longer like snow on skin; it was the sensation of coming into a warm house after you'd gone numb, the scalding pain of every nerve reawakening.

Vatii shied away, taking shelter under an upturned chair. "This isn't right, Briar. No poltergeist has this sort of energy."

Briar called out, "Gretchen, what's wrong? What's happening?"

"Feels like— Torn apart— I think someone's trying to—" Her voice sputtered in and out.

"Trying to what?!"

The tornado of furniture and objects in Briar's home halted, everything floating in suspended animation. Briar stood rooted to the spot. Gretchen's screech came through slowly, like metal rent apart. Just one word.

"Exorcism!"

Her cries died. Everything in the flat crashed to the ground in a cata-strophic rain. Briar dodged out of the doorway to avoid a bludgeoning. It took time for the debris to settle, the tinkle of sewing needles rolling away like delicate shrapnel.

"Gretchen?" The silence made him panic harder. *"Gretchen?"*

Vatii peeked out from under the chair. "Briar, I think she's—"

"No." Briar climbed over the wreckage of his flat, grabbing the candles he found and anything he could draw with. He cleared a space on the floor large enough for a person to stand and scrawled a circle on it in chalk.

"Briar . . ." Vatii said, her tone sad.

"Don't say it. We don't know for sure."

He finished the summoning circle. The same one he'd used to call Gretchen on that first day in Coill Darragh, only smaller and without iron. He lit the candles, pressed his hands together, and called to her. It was more of a prayer than a call. He felt the magic of the circle drawn through him, but it stoppered up. A blocked tap.

There were no spirits here to call.

He dropped his hands, released the magic. He felt faint and took one of the potions from his pocket to drink. Wiping his mouth, he looked at Vatii with shining eyes.

"She's gone."

CHAPTER 23

Linden came at Briar's call, blanching as he took in the rubble. He climbed over it to take Briar by the shoulders and demand to know what had happened, if he was all right. Briar held in his breakdown, explaining best he could, asking if Linden knew any means to call back an exorcised spirit.

He didn't.

Briar said, "Nobody else was here. She didn't want to go. Fuck." He didn't swear often, but the moment called for it. "If you only heard her."

Linden sat awkwardly next to Briar on the floor. "I'm sorry, Briar."

"I managed to break her tether to the house. Do you think it weakened her connection here? But she didn't *want* to go!"

Linden rubbed his shoulders. "The laws of magic don't always obey our wants. Perhaps it has to do with what we found in the woods today. If the forest helped to keep her here, perhaps it released her."

Though it sounded realistic, Briar was haunted by her final words, by all her regrets, which he felt he would share when his time came.

It was ridiculous to work after everything.

Gretchen's departure left Briar lonely as he hemmed skirts and cut patterns. Kenneth's death was not appeasement enough to release Briar from his curse, and Linden seemed no nearer an answer, but the press release party would be upon them soon, so Briar worked. It didn't occur to him what he would wear to the party until Linden asked. He'd been too busy trying to perfect each garment, but he saw an opportunity to design something flamboyantly his own.

The idea came together on an evening when the first green buds of March showed on the trees. Briar sketched and scribbled out countless ideas. In each, he encountered the same problem, one that made him want to scream. Then he remembered Rowan's hand trailing over his arm.

The idea felt transgressional, forbidden. It was anathema to the very problem he'd been attempting to solve with his previous designs. But once he set pencil to paper, the allure became impossible to deny.

Briar hid it whenever Linden came over to check on progress. He wanted it to be a surprise.

He finished with only a few days to spare before the press release. Standing in front of his mirror, turning this way and that to check for flaws, Briar had to admit he was proud. It was an expression of his time in Coill Darragh. A love letter to this strange place and the man he might have become if given more time.

The bell jingled downstairs to announce Linden. Briar turned to face the doorway, where Linden came to a stop, eyebrows raised, eyes skipping up and down Briar's frame.

"Briar, that's . . ."

It was a dress. A white train, dip-dyed in fading peridot, fell from his hips in an asymmetric line from a slit at mid-thigh. Flowers and sequins curled up around his hip and tapered off on their way up his waist. He wore the antler earring Rowan had given him for Christmas. White lace like frost fronds formed a sleeve down one arm and over his torso.

But his other, heavily tithed arm remained bare.

It was winter turned spring, it was entirely in defiance of fashion for men, and it was his.

And Linden said, "Is it finished?"

Briar might have felt less stung if he'd been slapped. "Yes?"

Linden strode forward. With one hand, he fiddled with the neckline, which scooped down one shoulder and under the opposite arm. He touched the first mark that started halfway across Briar's collarbone.

"There's magic that could heal these scars."

Suddenly self-conscious, Briar crossed his arms and rubbed a hand over the tithes. After hearing Linden speak out against his parents, he'd thought the rebellion of wearing proudly that which others found shameful would appeal to Linden.

"I don't want to get rid of them."

"Wh—Then perhaps a matching sleeve? It is a bit showy, with the slit leg as well."

Briar looked down at his clothes and felt naked. Perhaps it was the exhaustion or the mess of events that had led him here, or perhaps it was simply that his time was running out and these last moments of it were not the memories he wished to leave behind. A knot of shame that was wholly new tightened his throat.

Contrition replaced Linden's judgmental stare. "Oh, Briar, you must know I think it's beautiful on you. I hadn't meant to—Please, come sit."

Briar sat on the bed at Linden's urging, staring at his hands in his lap.

Linden took both in his. "Briar, look at me."

He did.

"I speak from a place of concern for your well-being. The press are jackals. The first whiff of controversy is a thing they'll feast upon for years. I only wish to protect you from that."

"I want to wear something that's *me*. The real me."

"That is precisely the vulnerability they hunger to exploit."

"Let them," Briar said heatedly. "What do I care? I'll be dead soon."

"That *isn't* true." Linden tilted his chin to look in his eyes. "Don't you believe me when I say I won't allow it?"

Briar wanted to believe it. By all rights, he should. Niamh's tarot reading left little ambiguity about his fate in Linden's capable hands. If she was correct, Linden would have a cure, and Briar would be healthy. Yet he still struggled with everyday tasks, with spells that used to snip as easily as new scissors through string, and frequently it was difficult to see a future through the fog of his own exhaustion. Through the ache of missing someone else's arms around him.

He still thought of Rowan far too often.

Briar swiped at the dampness in his eyes. "Then help me out of this. I need to rush if I'm going to alter it—"

"Briar." Linden cupped his cheek and said, "I only wished to warn you. Please, wear it. I can see how it matters so much to you."

But the knot of shame didn't go away.

Linden held nothing back in decorating Coill Darragh's central square for the press release. A temporary pavilion of bunting and silk banners fronted the fountain, blocking the view of Éibhear's statue. Throngs of people gathered, many wielding cameras.

Briar peeked through the tent flap at them.

The noise of the crowd muffled the moment the flap closed. Linden hadn't arrived yet, busy with preparations. Briar had hardly slept and risen early. He'd taken a larger dose of elixir to prevent any mishaps on this day, where he couldn't afford a mistake. Absently, he touched his arm. Though he'd never shied from the spotlight before, this was different. He couldn't help but think of Gretchen, whose complaints and company he missed. She would hate these crowds, if she'd been here.

The flutter of the tent flap and noise from outside drew his attention. He thought Linden said he'd arrive by portal to avoid being seen—

The outside din muted as the tent closed behind Rowan. He froze there, gazing at Briar, drinking in the sight of him with unguarded admiration. That look made something inside Briar twist. It was precisely the awestruck, reverent expression with which he'd hoped Linden might look at him.

After a stunned moment, Rowan cleared his throat, recovered himself, and took a few steps into the tent. "Thought I'd come wish you luck," he said.

Briar took a step toward him too. "Thanks, I'll need it."

"No, you'll be grand." The quiet of the tent got quieter. "There's a lot of people out there."

"Yeah. No pressure or anything. Just the whole world behind the cameras."

"They'll love you."

Briar's heart punched his chest. "I've never been this nervous. I've never shown so many people."

Without their noticing, the space between them vanished step by step. Rowan stood a breath away and raised a hand to hover awkwardly over Briar's bare shoulder. Briar tipped toward it, like a magnet subtly drawn to steel, but didn't make contact. Rowan's hand dropped.

He said of the dress, "You made it?"

"Yeah. I wanted something that was . . . me."

Rowan's eyes roved hotter than any touch. "I've always lo—admired that about you."

"You do?"

"Isn't anybody who tells you who you are. You just—are." His voice sounded hoarse as if from disuse. "Passionate, that is. Creative. That's what I admire, ehm . . ."

Briar couldn't speak. If he did, the words might not be the kind he should utter out loud.

"I should get back to work." Rowan didn't move.

"You should," Briar forced himself to say. "Linden will be here soon."

Rowan did take a step back then, frowning. He asked, "Is he good to you?"

"I think so."

A significant pause. Rowan brushed his hands on his legs as if they were dirty. "I really should get back, yeah. Good luck today." A hazy moment of hovering near the tent flap followed, then Rowan left.

Briar swore under his breath. "I thought this would get easier."

Vatii, perched on one of the tent poles above, watched with her head tilted. "You've never had an audience like this."

"I didn't mean the stage fright."

"I know. It would get easier if you didn't see him so often," she said gently.

That was no comfort at all. He wished the affection he felt was platonic and not this huge thing that took up too much space in his chest, bleeding out of him whenever Rowan was near.

A portal opened. Linden stepped through, and he was not alone. Behind him, two people, tall and elegant, came into the tent.

Linden wore the stark, iridescent clothes Briar had crafted for him. He'd made his own addition—a spray of white feathers, twinned to Briar's antler, crested over an ear. Atticus trotted in and immediately climbed a beam to sit a yard away from Vatii, who glared at Linden's feathered fashion like it had come into her house and murdered her family.

The man and woman with Linden were straight-backed and regal in robes of deep navy that faded to a nebulous storm of cloudy blues. They entered the tent as if it were a dodgy alley with campfires in bins and scurrying rats rather than opulent silk. They were clearly Linden's parents— they'd gifted their son with their delicate bone structure and exquisite bearing, although not with their smiles, which showed a lot of teeth and a decent portion of gum. A blankness in place of auras revealed they were wearing talismans. Their eyes stuck to Briar's tithed arm.

Linden hadn't warned him they were coming, but then, Linden looked annoyed that they were there at all, so he probably hadn't known either.

"Ah! You must be Mr. Wyngrave," Linden's mother said, extending a hand. "Adelaide Fairchild, and this is my husband, Gresham. So pleased to finally meet you."

Gresham shook Briar's hand, his grip like an alligator's jaw. A wardstone bracelet peeked out from under the cuff of one sleeve. "Yes, it's good to finally meet the man Linden speaks so fondly of. Apologies for not announcing ourselves, but an introduction seemed long overdue."

"We would have appreciated an invitation," Adelaide agreed.

Linden said, "I didn't want you to embarrass me."

"We'd never dream of it, darling!" said Adelaide.

"Well, it isn't the Whitestone Gala." Gresham eyed the tent. "But you've done well with what you have."

"Never mind the tent, Gresham. Briar, please tell us how you met. I've been dying to know, but our son is quite private, keeping you all to himself."

Linden rolled his eyes.

"We're neighbors," said Briar. "Linden came into my shop to look around and film, and then I made an outfit for him, and . . . I guess it all sort of started there?"

Linden put on his brightest smile and kissed Briar's hand. "Indeed."

"And this 'outfit' you made for him, was it enchanted at all?" Gresham asked.

"Yes," Briar started to say. "A basic charisma charm for—"

"Why don't you speak plainly about what you're insinuating," Linden interrupted.

Briar went cold with realization.

"You must understand our caution," Adelaide demurred. "No one has ever drawn so much of Linden's attention. You'll forgive us for wondering what it is about you that has our son so charmed." She said "charmed" with particular emphasis. Again, she looked at his tithes.

Briar tamped down on a tide of anger. He didn't know how to argue against the assumption, until Linden cut in. "I've worn this"—Linden pulled the talisman from inside his shirt—"for the duration of our courtship."

"The *entire* duration?" she pushed.

"I'm not bewitched by some fanciful love spell, much as you'd prefer it."

"We only worry because we care, darling."

Gresham strolled the tent, hands laced in front of him. "Well, there's no point arguing. We came to pose an invitation, didn't we?"

Adelaide said, "Yes. Mr. Wyngrave, we'd love to invite you to our manor for supper, so we can make better your acquaintance. I'm sure you'd never bewitch our son, but please understand that if you had, you wouldn't be the first to attempt it. I hope, once we're certain all's well, you can forgive us our accusations."

Linden scoffed. "You insult him, then demand he forgive you."

Briar put a hand on Linden's shoulder. He wanted to make a good impression—he had to. "No, I understand. Dinner would be lovely, Mr. and Mrs. Fairchild. I look forward to it."

If either were impressed, they only showed it with a faint raising of their brows. "Perfect!" Adelaide said. "We'll be on our way, but good luck with the press release, darling. We'll see you again shortly."

"Keep in touch," Gresham added.

They both left through the portal they'd come in by. The tent fell quiet. Linden said, "That could have gone worse."

"I didn't know they were coming. I would have—" Briar cut himself short. Would he have covered his arm?

"They came unannounced. It was deliberate, so you wouldn't have time to prepare." He sighed. "You did well."

"I barely said anything."

"With my parents, you'll find that's for the best." He turned to kiss Briar's forehead. "We shouldn't let it ruin this day."

Preparations flew by. Three models and a team of hair and makeup artists arrived to style the outfits. The tent became a flurry of movement and hairspray. Briar experienced it through a haze of unease, replaying the interaction with Linden's parents.

You'll forgive us for wondering what it is about you that has our son so charmed.

Briar didn't know the answer. He remembered Rowan wishing him luck, and a sore part of him appreciated Linden's parents' caution. He would be far from the first to try and wriggle into Linden's bed and, by extension, his family's wealth and good graces. And why was Briar there? For a cure, for a destiny that still made no sense to him.

He glanced across at Linden, who was reviewing makeup palettes. He gleamed, every inch a star, and yet the feelings Briar wanted so badly for him were not there. Something small and hopeful was, but it lacked the depth needed to prove Adelaide and Gresham wrong.

Briar fitted a dress with a pin to the waist of his model. She jumped a bit as he stuck another pin in. "Sorry! Did I catch you?" he asked.

"No, it's—your aura. It's a bit loud."

Briar's mouth fell open. He so rarely spoke of his own ability and had never met someone who shared it. "Loud?"

"And bright," she added. "Not in a bad way!"

"Loud how?" he pressed.

"It's hard to explain. Like a musical number when it hits a key change? That's not quite—"

"Yours is like peach fuzz. It's very summery," Briar told her. "I'm an aura reader, too."

She beamed. "Oh, I've only met two others! That's much better than what the last one said. She said I was like sunburn."

Her name was Abigail. She chatted animatedly about the other two aura readers she'd met, asking Briar about his experiences. What sensations seemed to come up most often? What were the worst auras he'd ever encountered? It took his mind off his apprehension.

Before long, the time had come. Linden appeared at Briar's shoulder, fussing over his hair and picking a stray thread off his dress.

"Are you ready?" he asked.

"I'm going to puke," Briar said.

"*Well*, I was going to ask for a good luck kiss, but now—"

Briar kissed him anyway. Partly for luck, partly to assuage his guilt.

The tent flap drew back by magic, and they strolled out hand in hand to raucous applause. Night had fallen, enchanted lanterns flitting through the air. Swaths of people thronged the stage and cameras flashed so bright that Briar had to concentrate hard on not blinking.

The noise and burst of applause faded, a hush of shock was followed by whispers as the crowd beheld Briar.

Not all the whispers and exchanged looks were kind, but Briar hadn't expected them to be. Something like exultant rebellion rose in him, and he lifted his chin.

They'd prepared the speech together, with Linden introducing Briar as a new partner in an exciting project. Briar told the crowd about himself. Where he'd grown up. The challenges of his apprenticeship in Wishbrooke. The beginnings of his placement in Coill Darragh, where his path crossed Linden's. The tithes were a mark of how far he'd come, how hard he'd worked. His humble origin story. The crowd listened, rapt and devouring.

Linden spoke of the inspiration for their line, then summoned the models.

Enchantments of spring flowers sprouted where the models walked, glowing sparklers unfurling in the air behind them as they swept out in trails of gauze. Briar's exultant feeling stymied just a little. The outfits were beautiful, but they weren't his. Crafted by his hands, maybe, but he was not their architect.

Still, it was a bright beginning to a career. He looked at the crowd and ached. His mother would have loved to be here.

When the show concluded, Linden linked arms with Briar, drawing him into the crowd to answer journalists' questions. They congregated at the foot of the stage, microphones in hand.

"How did this partnership between you evolve?"

"Would you say this line is an equal blend of your styles?"

Every question had hidden layers. It felt identical to speaking with Linden's parents, parsing the subtext and responding as positively as he could.

"Linden, you've never worked with a partner before. Why Mr. Wyngrave?"

Linden chuckled as if the journalist had made a joke. "You saw the show we put together. Just look at him. He's a vision."

Briar smiled, but a question followed like a knife point in the ribs.

"We can all agree that you look lovely, Mr. Wyngrave, but care to comment on your flesh tithes? That magic is taboo for a reason. Many consider it a dark sort. What are you trying to say by displaying them on the stage today?"

Briar spoke through the tension in his chest, as honest as he dared. "This magic is no different from tithing a blade of grass—"

"You value a blade of grass the same as your own skin?"

Bristling. "It's more powerful, but maybe the disdain for those who use flesh tithes has more to do with the divide between who can and cannot afford to buy tithes at a store."

A herald of murmurs. Linden squeezed his shoulder in reassurance—or warning.

"And would you say displaying them inspired your garment?"

Briar thought about his time in Coill Darragh, the bright moments and the darker ones. "It's inspired by my life. It's a reflection of who I am."

"And who is that?"

"See for yourself."

Linden smirked with pride.

Once the journalists dispersed, they were free to mingle. Briar stuck to Linden's elbow as he was introduced to one recognizable name after another. That they'd all come to Coill Darragh—a place not easily visited with its wards—was a testament to Linden's influence.

A designer who'd clothed half the actors Briar grew up idolizing told him, "I admire a man who dresses himself better than his models." The risk of wearing the dress felt utterly worth it for that comment alone.

While Linden asked how the designer's family was doing, Briar's gaze strayed through the crowd. He told himself he was not searching for Rowan, only Rowan was so large that he was difficult to miss.

He stood leaning against the wall of the church, and he was not alone. Speaking to him with exuberance was Abigail, her red hair pinned in tumbling curls down her nape. Like Briar, she was unafraid of him. Rowan looked like a deer in the headlights, nodding at whatever she said. Briar felt keenly aware that the neckline of her dress was very low, and she was very pretty.

Briar returned his attention to the conversation at hand. He told himself, forcefully, that he should be happy at Rowan finding someone who could truly see him, too. He instructed himself not to look over again. He smiled at a joke Linden told, nodding along as if he had a clue what they were talking about. As if his attention wasn't straining toward a point seven meters away.

His restraint broke. He looked over. Abigail tucked a strand of hair behind her ear and, with exquisite gentleness, laid a hand on Rowan's arm.

Jealousy burned like acid in Briar's throat.

Linden concluded schmoozing and pulled Briar away to ingratiate themselves to someone else. It was a blessing when they moved out of sight of Rowan, yet Briar's jealousy simmered still. He endured it. He had no right to these feelings, but he felt them anyway.

During a pause in the mingling, Linden pointed someone out to Briar. "See that woman with the coattails?"

Briar didn't recognize her. "Yes."

"Her name is Finola Cadwallader. She's director of the Pentawynn Witches Gala Runway. If we want our line to walk it, she's the person we need to speak to."

"Then let's go speak to her."

Linden caught him by the arm and said in a hushed voice, "Shortly. First, I should tell you, she went to university with my parents, and they've never been on the best of terms. I've done my best to get to know her beyond my association as a Fairchild. Alas, she's a bit prejudiced where I'm concerned."

Having just met the senior Fairchilds, Briar could understand, but it wasn't fair to tar Linden with the same brush.

"I think you will do a better job of it than I," Linden said.

"You want me to speak to her alone?"

"You just spoke to millions on camera. One woman should be no trouble."

Briar's nerves returned. "What do I even say?"

"Did you ask yourself the same when speaking with me?"

"Yes!" Briar exclaimed.

At the small of his back, Linden's hand guided him forward. "Be your charming self. It comes most naturally to you, and if she's not endeared, then she's got an iron heart. Go. I'll find you later."

Briar gathered his train. People had dispersed enough into the adjoining pubs to make navigating the crowd easier, but the few yards between he and Finola Cadwallader weren't enough for him to prepare.

At six foot, she was of a height with Briar. She cut a sharp profile, with a sloping nose and hair swept back in tight, even braids. She didn't wear a wardstone bracelet. Her dark eyes snagged on his approach and watched, almost wary. Within a meter, he got a sense of her aura—fresh tobacco and beach sand between bare toes. It relaxed him a little.

"Did you enjoy the show?" he asked, approaching.

"It was the usual for Mr. Fairchild."

That wasn't the answer he'd have liked, but he pressed on. "Nothing about this is 'usual' for me. I like your coattails. The pattern on the lining—who's the designer?"

She told him a name he didn't recognize. For a moment, he scrambled as if forgetting his research at an interview.

Finola said, "She's a student. You won't have heard of her yet, but you will."

"You commission work from students?"

"Yes. What they lack in experience, they make up for in fresh vision. Guts, you know?" At this, she cast a quick look over his dress. "Not that I need to tell you why guts matter."

Briar preened with the flattery. He still gripped his train in his hand and flung it out to spin with all the flair of an exuberant bird courting a mate. "I'm told I can be a bit much."

"There's no such thing," Finola said. "What do you drink?"

"Uhhh." Lately, potions by the pint. "Anything."

"But what do you prefer?"

"Honestly? Used to be sweet cocktails and ciders, but now they give me a rip-roaring hangover, so I'm looking for a new vice. What's *your* poison?"

She flashed a grin. "Whiskey. Come, I'm sure the pub will have something."

Finola walked into the Swan and Cygnet as if it were her home. As Briar found out over drinks, it sort of was. Her mother was Coill Darraghn, and her father had been born not far from Port Haven, where Briar grew up. From there, the conversation flowed with the same ease as the drinks, reminiscing over the pasty shop on the beach and bemoaning the seagulls stealing those pasties straight from your hands.

As they talked, Briar's phone buzzed. He'd turned off notifications for most things because his affiliation with Linden led to more attention than even he—a self-proclaimed attention whore—could deal with.

He glanced at the message in case it was important.

It was from Celyn.

>>*I see you're getting on great, even without Pentawynn. Congratulations on your fashion line. If you're ever in the city, let me know. We should grab coffee.*

"Hate mail from one of Linden's fans?" Finola guessed.

"A text from my ex." He twirled the phone on the table to show her. "Two years together, and he pretends we don't know each other because he didn't want my peasantry rubbing off. Now he's pretending we *still* know each other."

Vatii pecked the phone screen. "He was a rotting tip anyway."

Finola smiled wolfishly. "It's good that you're angry. Fame does strange things to relationships. Makes it harder to tell who's around for *you*, and who's gone green-eyed."

He took a sip of whiskey to hide the source of his frown and burn away the surge of guilt. Was Briar any better when it came to Linden?

"If it weren't for that weasel you're in partnership with," Finola said, "I'd invite you to my gala, you know."

"Linden isn't a weasel."

"Oh, he is. He's the head of his mummy and daddy. Just like them, but a lot better at pretending otherwise."

"He's been very generous," Briar said. "I couldn't have done this without him."

"That is the trouble, when no one can do anything without the help of someone more powerful. How much of the line is really yours?"

"It was a collaborative effort." Briar turned the conversation back on her. "What do you have against him?"

"I'll tell you, but only because I'm petty." She reclined so far back against the wall of the booth that she was nearly horizontal. "I went to Pentawynn University with his parents."

"He said you didn't get along."

She looked affronted. "No, we were the best of friends. Is *that* what he told you? Oh, that's rich."

"Then what happened?"

"Well, that's just it, isn't it? I don't know, but around the time of their Miracle Tour, his parents cut all contact. Refused to speak to me. This was before I had much to my name, you understand. Suddenly, they were too good to answer my calls. Over a decade we'd known each other. I kept their secrets. I changed Linden's nappies, a fact we're both keen to forget."

Briar said, "They dropped you because you weren't . . . famous enough?"

Finola ran her tongue along her teeth. Her iron gaze turned inward, contemplative. "I like you, Briar. Consider yourself invited to my gala, *but* on the condition that I see at least half the garments on that runway look as fresh as the thing you're wearing right now. Don't let the Fairchilds use you as their doormat."

Briar adopted her posture and, with a flourish, kicked up a heeled foot onto the table. It was his leg bared by the slit in his skirt so he had to be delicate about the arrangement of fabric, but it proved his point. "Do I look like a doormat?"

Finola laughed. She sucked back the last of her whiskey, slammed the glass down on the table like a judge's gavel, then rose, smoothing her hands down her coat. "That's what I like to hear."

Her headstrong posture reminded Briar fiercely of Gretchen, whose absence burned like an ember in his heart.

Finola left him sitting at the table with the last sip of whiskey in his glass and success fizzling dully in his veins. He'd done it. Reluctant as she'd been, he'd won her over. Linden's fears that Briar would blunder into a public controversy could be laid to rest.

He took the last sip of his whiskey. A spasm in his hand made him nearly drop the glass, but he caught it, setting it down with a heavy thunk. Like a thorn in his foot, his curse reminded him with every stabbing step of progress that he'd have to survive long enough to see Finola's gala.

Fatigue setting in, he slid out of the booth but found his way blocked by Rowan.

The alderman held two drinks. A stout and a cider, like they'd had on Saor ó Eagla.

"Room to celebrate with a friend?"

CHAPTER 24

riend. Briar kicked himself.

He shouldn't accept. Vatii's talons squeezed his shoulder. She sensed the tumultuous emotions Briar harbored and knew the danger in them. He was impulsive, driven by feeling. And Rowan made him feel *a lot.*

But Rowan looked so hopeful, and he'd already brought the drinks. Briar said, "Of course."

Rowan asked about Finola, and Briar explained the importance of her gala. When he shared the news that she'd invited him, Rowan beamed. There was a shard of glass in his smile. There always was, lately. That glass twisted in Briar, too. Pentawynn, a runway of models wearing his clothes, proving his teachers and peers wrong—he'd grabbed it all while wearing stilettos and taboo magic and a dress made from the twisted yarn of his life.

But then there was this. A pub full of people he knew by name. Aisling at the bar. Diarmuid teasing her. Orla, her arm still in a sling, playing a hand of cards at her corner table. He might have only had passing conversations with them, but it felt convivial in a way he'd never known.

And there was Rowan. Making him laugh. Celebrating, gamely, Briar's success, even if it could take him far away from here.

Abigail came into the pub, too—her ginger hair made her stand out in the crowd—and Briar noticed her making eyes across the room. But if Rowan saw, he had yet to return those looks. A more selfless friend would encourage Rowan to talk to her. Briar couldn't fault her interest. Rowan was a rarity, soft in all the places the world should have made him jagged, pillar-strong even after relentless isolation. That scar carved a moat around him, and instead of crumbling, he just kept building bridges in the hopes someone might cross.

Briar made himself say, "You know, Abigail's been batting her eyes at you this whole time."

"Mm." Rowan glanced aside.

"You should go talk to her. She seems kind."

Rowan said, "I know what you're trying to do, Briar, and I appreciate it. But we both know it wouldn't be fair to her."

And if that didn't turn Briar's insides to pudding . . .

"How are you?" Rowan asked.

"Good. Great. Busy," Briar answered.

"You know what I mean."

Briar scratched a fingernail down his glass. "I guzzle about two liters of revolting potion a day just to stay standing. Takes me ages just to get out of bed. Other than that, all right." Maybe it was the alcohol, or maybe the gentle look on Rowan's face, but the rest came out. "Actually, not really. I'm tired. Then I get angry that I'm tired and push myself to work, which only makes me more tired. Sometimes I think—"

He swallowed the rest. He couldn't tell Rowan how, sometimes, he thought about putting it all aside to live out what little time he had left here. In Coill Darragh. By Rowan's side. He sometimes questioned if his dreams had been the right ones, or if it was all a waste of precious time. Despite Niamh's prophecies, his faith that a cure could be found faltered daily.

That option felt a lot like surrender, though, and it would still hurt to die, even in the comfort of Rowan's arms. Gretchen had pretended her death didn't matter, but that night on the roof, he'd seen her grief, her regret.

He changed the subject. "What about you?"

"Surviving. Helping Sorcha best I can while she recovers. Sometimes still get . . ." He shook his head. "Ah, we'll be grand, won't we? No need to bring down your celebrations."

"You mean a countdown to calamity *isn't* lifting your spirits? Where's your medieval humor?"

Rowan snorted. "That would call for more drink or more games."

Inspired, Briar shoved his glass so that it slid to the other end of the table. He fished in the pocket of his skirt for a coin.

Rowan chuckled. "It has pockets?"

"Yes, I'm not an animal."

Briar put the coin in Rowan's hand. "For every one you get in the cup, you'll add a year to my life, and for every one you miss, you shave off a week—"

Rowan scowled playfully. "Games are meant to be fun."

"You wanted medieval games. I made one up. Give it a go, at least."

Rowan humored him and flicked the coin. It spun end over end, flashing. The sloppy clink of it hitting the dregs of Briar's cider announced his success. Briar cheered and pulled out another coin so he could try. He'd had more to drink and found it difficult to look away from Rowan smiling brightly at him. He tossed the coin.

In retrospect, Briar's first mistake had been accepting the drink. Drinking more after he'd already had whiskey was the second.

The third mistake was sitting in a semicircle booth. They sat, at first, a small distance apart, but Briar swayed against the curved back as he launched his coin. He lost balance and slid, coming to rest against Rowan's shoulder, whose aura swaddled Briar in a feeling whiskey could not match. His arm, once along the back of the booth, settled over Briar's shoulder instead. His hand dangled, loose and relaxed, but it tensed when Briar reached up to thread his fingers with Rowan's own.

The final mistake was to look up. Rowan's gaze was steady, curious, assessing. Possibly wondering if Briar had drunk too much. Fuzzy as he felt, Briar knew it was nothing to do with alcohol. He wanted this. He wanted it so badly he ached just looking at Rowan's soft eyes. Stubble grew on his jaw, but it was far from the magnificent scruff Briar had once loved running his fingers through while kissing.

He hadn't checked to see if his coin had made it.

"I miss your beard," Briar said. The ache worsened. "I miss you."

"I'm here," said Rowan.

Briar sucked his lips between his teeth. He was so caught in memory, he almost thought he could taste Rowan on them. The gesture affected Rowan. Briar could feel the corded tension in the muscles cushioning his head. If he didn't sit up now, he was going to reach up and drag Rowan by his unbearded face into a kiss and suffer all the guilt and regret that would cause.

Vatii flicked her tail and said, low in warning, "Briar . . ."

With arduous willpower, he sat forward. By some miracle, his coin was in the cup alongside Rowan's. "I'll get the next round," he said.

Rowan took a while to speak. "Ah, sure you shouldn't be heading home?"

"You bought the last. Just one. I'll be back." Really, he just needed space. He walked a remarkably straight line to the bar, proving to himself that his actions were his own stupidity and not a result of impairment.

Aisling smiled tightly, still not entirely herself after all the terrible news of Kenneth, though she put on a brave front. "Sure look who it is. What can I get you, Briar?"

"Stout and a cider?"

As she went to fetch glasses, Briar scanned the rows of drinks behind the bar, Éibhear's old potions still lining the topmost shelf. His eyes caught on the one he'd noticed when he first came to the Swan and Cygnet—a steely brew in a twisted bottle. Liquid courage. Only when he'd last seen it, it had been full.

He remembered Rowan, snow in his hair, standing on Briar's doorstep, breathlessly come to tell him something important.

He looked over to the booth. Rowan was already looking his way. When Briar met his gaze, a shy smile lit his features, a secret shared between them. Briar, helplessly, smiled back.

Two drinks slammed down next to him. He jolted, looking up to find not Aisling, but Maebh standing over him.

"Stop looking at him like that," she said.

"Like what?"

"Like you love the bones of him."

He couldn't answer her fury with anything honest. Vatii's discomfort manifested in a ruffle of feathers.

Maebh held the drinks still, so when he reached for them he had to wait for her to release the handles. She did and said, "He's told me to wind my neck in. God knows, I've tried. But you hear me right, I cannot watch you play him. He's not a ride you can hop on and off."

Briar said, "It's not—I'm not—" *Playing him.* He couldn't say that either.

She glanced toward the booth, where Rowan started to stand. "He'll give out to me for this. Just know, if you hurt him again, I'll have your head. And I don't mean that figuratively. I'll feed you to the feckin' woods."

Briar nodded and took the drinks back.

Rowan grumbled, "I told her not to give you a hard time."

"No. I deserved it."

They finished their drinks and headed out. Rowan helped Briar search for Linden, but the distinctive black and white of his ensemble was nowhere to be seen, so Rowan escorted him home. He made an admirable attempt to cheer Briar, but Maebh's words stuck like slivers under his skin. She was right. He had to do something to rectify the situation, and he knew—prophecies be damned—what the truest, most honest, *fairest* thing would be.

Tell Linden how he felt. Leave him. Live out the rest of his remaining time with Rowan and hope that, if Linden found a cure, he was benevolent enough to share it. Even with his earnings from the press release, Briar doubted he could afford it.

Or he could cut himself off from Rowan and devote himself wholly to Linden, but with the knowledge it wouldn't be fair to anyone involved. He'd be doing it for selfish reasons. He had a choice, Niamh had told him, but did he really when his life depended upon the right one?

Briar shivered. His jitters came on partly from his need for another draft of potion, and partly because the night had gotten colder, and he hadn't made a jacket to go with his dress. Rowan stopped to sweep his wool cloak off, wrapping it around Briar.

"You'll get cold too. We're almost home," Briar said, teeth chattering.

Rowan rubbed his hands up and down Briar's shoulders. It made all the thoughts Briar had been chewing on turn hooked and sharp, catching him up in memories of Rowan, cupping his hands and using his breath to warm them.

He forced himself to keep walking, but the sense of Rowan so near didn't abate. Slowly, slowly, his mind turned, arriving at its inevitable destination as they stopped at his front door.

He started to take the cloak off. Rowan lay a hand over his. "Keep it."

It didn't feel like he was talking about the cloak.

Under Rowan's hand, Briar's began to shake violently. It was a combination of things. His racing heart. The cold. The way Rowan looked at him.

Mostly, though, it was the curse.

Rowan caught him when his legs gave out. His arms wound around Briar's middle, stopping his fall backward, while Vatii startled off his shoulder and flapped up to the roof's eave. The world swam, and Briar groaned as he tried to stave off an incoming episode.

Rowan held him with one arm, the other finding his keys in the pocket of his dress among the coins and empty vials of potion. In a fumbling rush through the door, he got them up the stairs, setting Briar on the bed.

"In the right cabinet." Briar gripped the headboard, squeezing his eyes shut against the bright lights in his periphery. Rowan pressed an uncorked vial into his hand. He hardly tasted it going down. Gradually, the light speckling his vision faded. The splitting pain in his head didn't, like someone had put a wedge in the crack of his skull and taken a hammer to it.

Rowan hovered near him. "Tell me what to do."

"I don't know," Briar gasped. It took an effort to speak.

The bed sank next to him. "Please, Briar. Stay with me."

His broken voice cracked through everything. Briar couldn't do this. Much as he cared about Linden and didn't want to hurt him, that felt inevitable. His impending death felt inevitable. The only good in all of this sat next to him.

He had to tell Linden how he truly felt. End it.

Beyond this, he didn't really think. Just reached out and found Rowan's hand gripping his. Tethering him as the last of his jitters and aches faded in the wake of the potion.

"I should call Linden," he whispered. He only realized how that sounded when Rowan stiffened next to him.

"You should rest."

"Yes, but I should tell him about this." His declining health, and *this*.

"Can I get you anything?"

"No, no, I'll be fine."

"Briar." There was an edge to Rowan's smooth baritone. "I wish you'd let me care for you. Even if just as your friend."

Briar was no expert on withholding feelings, but he thought he'd done an admirable job of keeping it together. At the desperate concern in Rowan's voice, he broke.

"I'm twenty-five." He sucked in a breath that did nothing to calm him. "I'm twenty-five, and I'm dying. Rowan, I don't want to—I'm scared."

The dam shattered. Tears turned the world a blur, and each subsequent breath he tried to take failed to fill his lungs all the way. Without hesitation, Rowan dragged him into his arms, wrapping him up, holding him together while he fell apart. With anyone else, Briar might have been embarrassed. His words came through hyperventilating sobs.

"I—just—wanted—to—do something—important."

"You did."

"I'm—scared—I'm gonna—die and—nothing I've done have—mattered."

"It mattered. Trust me on that."

"I thought—if I can't live a long life, at least—at least, I wanted a memorable one."

"Oh, Briar." Rowan drew back enough to look at him. He must have been a snotty, blotchy mess. "Briar, you're mad if you think anyone could ever forget you."

Cradling Briar against him with one arm, he leaned to grab a box of tissues with the other. Briar accepted them and, once finished mopping his face, turned his forehead into Rowan's chest and wept. Vatii settled on Rowan's shoulder to nuzzle Briar's hair.

It took some time to compose himself. Rowan didn't rush him, but as the seconds ticked by, Briar had to return to reality.

"I should really get some sleep. My head is pounding."

"Can I get you anything?"

What Briar said next didn't sound even a little flirtatious, a testament to how tired he felt. "You could undo the back of my dress, or else I'll have to sleep in it."

Rowan helped him stand. The back of the dress had pearl drop buttons that hooked through eyes in a line down his spine. Briar gave instructions on how they worked. Rowan's fingers were gentle unlooping the first, his knuckles warm where they brushed bare skin.

He'd undone a third of the buttons when a portal opened by the door.

The sounds of merriment from the other side snuffed out as the portal shut, and Linden stood looking at them, an awful expression on his face. They all stood in silence, the situation too large for any singular exclamation to encapsulate it.

Linden broke the quiet first. "Of course. Shameless. In the bed that I made for you." His voice shook with betrayal, and Briar's guilt went sharp enough to cut.

"It isn't how it looks," Briar said. Only, it was, and it wasn't. His feelings existed, but he'd had no intent to act upon them now.

"Then tell me how it is."

Rowan spoke up this time. "Briar was ill. I was helping him so he could get some rest."

"I'm expected to believe that?" Linden said.

"It's the truth," Rowan said.

"Then, please, by all means. You say it isn't how it looks? Tell me." Linden pulled out his phone and flipped the screen to face them.

The photo on Linden's phone was a post on a gossip channel. Briar knew instantly where and when the picture had been taken. In it, he sat in a booth, leaning against Rowan's shoulder. He and Rowan gazed at each other like there was no one else in the room. The fall of Rowan's lashes, the brightness in Briar's eyes, they looked like a painting. It could have been a photo taken before a kiss or after. There'd been no kiss, but the look was intimate enough to be one.

Briar's heart clenched. "We were just having a drink—"

A blaze of hot pain sent him reeling.

The sound of Linden's backhand rang loud in the room. Briar caught himself against the sideboard, gripping it hard, more pain lancing up his elbow where it impacted. Blood speckled the wall. Distantly, he recalled that Linden wore a ring, and thought it might have cut him. Even more distantly, movement to his left.

Rowan grabbed Linden by the front of his shirt and slammed him against the door.

It didn't even shudder or reverberate on impact. Rowan was immovable, furious. Atticus sprang back and swatted at Rowan's ankles, hissing. Linden's eyes snapped open, wind forced from his lungs, his lips frozen on a rebuttal that wouldn't come. Genuine fear replaced the look of affront. Briar overcame his dizziness to move and put a placating hand against Rowan's ribs. Linden had magic. Linden could take vengeance. Combative magic was uncommon because most of it required *living* tithes, but that didn't mean the situation couldn't spiral.

The fact that Linden had struck him still hadn't sunk in.

Briar stood halfway between them. In that moment, he understood why the townsfolk were so afraid of Rowan. Under his hand, Rowan's huge chest swelled with each labored breath. It was grievously clear what a flimsy barrier Briar's arm made—if Rowan wanted to hurt Linden, there was no magic Briar knew that would be powerful enough to stop him.

And yet. Rowan's gaze did not falter from Linden's face. The rage written in every line of his brow did not unwinch. He lowered Linden until his feet touched the ground but didn't let go of his shirt.

"If you lay hands on him again," Rowan said.

He didn't finish the threat. Linden hardly reacted, but his returning glare was calculated. Rowan stepped back, yielding to Briar's hand like a draft horse bending its head to the yoke. For a brief second, the hand that had just pinned Linden to the door lifted to Briar's cheek but did not touch. Briar felt the tickle of blood there.

He pushed Rowan's hand away. "You should leave," he said.

Rowan wouldn't listen. "He hurt you."

Softly, Briar said, "I hurt him."

It was clear from the look on Rowan's face that he did not think the hurts equal.

"I need to speak to him alone," Briar said.

After a second that felt much longer, Rowan broke his gaze and turned to go. He paused in the doorway where Linden stood, disheveled and seething. Rowan's size forced Linden to press against the wall, and Rowan used that to his advantage, looking down with open menace. Then he descended the stairs. The shop bell jingled after his departure.

Linden unfroze. Briar fought to think what he should say. An apology seemed insignificant. At the same time, the weakness in his limbs returned, his head pounded, and he had to hold on to the sideboard to keep from crumpling.

"I think it's clear you should not see that brute any longer," Linden said.

Briar had expected an outburst of jealousy, of hurt, demands for an explanation. Linden's voice was cold.

His legs gave out. Ridiculously, he thought, *No, I need to stand, I can't make this about me.*

His body didn't care for the delicacies of his situation. His knees hit the floor.

Linden watched before grabbing him under the arms. He pulled him up. He took bone powder from his pocket and created a portal into his own bedroom. For some reason, this flagrant display of magic struck Briar harder than any other. A portal just to go next door.

Vatii swooped into the room, hovering nearby. Linden eased Briar onto a settee amongst the silken velvet and incense of his flat. He paced to a tower of shelves and pinched pink sand out of a jar. Sprinkling this along the front of his phone screen, the crack in it glowed and sealed. The phone must have gone flying, but Briar had been reeling too hard to notice.

Linden took a seat in an armchair, Atticus lying along the back of it, licking a paw and glowering. He set his phone on the coffee table between them, still on that photo from the pub.

"Are you even going to explain this humiliating indiscretion, or should I enumerate all the ways this has undermined our success tonight?"

"I'm sorry."

"Did you even speak to Finola Cadwallader, or did you head straight into his arms the moment I left?"

Briar couldn't defend himself or Rowan. "I spoke to Finola. She's invited us to the gala."

"Before or after you publicly sucked the alderman's face off?"

"I didn't kiss him."

Viciously, Linden said, "But you wanted to."

Briar couldn't deny it. "Linden, I'm so sorry. I didn't mean—Everything was meant to be casual with him, but I developed feelings, and I thought I cut things off early enough. We were just going to be friends, but these feelings won't *go*. And there's the pr—" Magic was a garrote around his throat, stopping the word "prophecy" before it got out. Impotent frustration boiled within him, but he pressed on. "I promise you, though, I didn't act on anything with Rowan. I didn't want to hurt you, but I think—" He held his face in his hands. The nearly dried blood on his cheek smeared on his palm. "I wish I'd figured it out sooner."

Linden leaned forward, wringing his hands. "Figured out what?"

"My feelings. None of this is fair to you. I think, maybe—maybe we shouldn't be together."

Linden recoiled. Poise abandoned, he slumped back in the lounge. "You wish to end things? With me?"

"I don't want to string you along. Or hurt you."

"And this is your idea of sparing my feelings? Did you ever feel anything for me, or was it merely the usual fascination with celebrity?"

"No!"

"Shall I become accustomed to this alienation, even from you?"

Briar closed his eyes. What could he say? He couldn't speak of the prophecy. He could walk Linden through every step of his thoughts and feelings, convoluted as they were, and it wouldn't make a difference. "I didn't mean for everything to be so messed up. It just spiraled and . . . I don't want to hurt you any more than I have. I understand if this means you're too—too upset with me. To find the cure."

"But Briar," Linden said, "I have already found the cure."

Briar thought he'd misheard. "What?"

"I found the cure."

White noise rang in Briar's ears. He thought this must be what people felt like when a bomb exploded near enough to knock out hearing but not consciousness. Vatii let out a warbling noise of uncertainty. Shock and an assault of questions battled to the surface.

"H-how?"

"I'm still awaiting resources I'll need." Linden stood, pacing a few steps toward the window, his silhouette touched silver by moonlight. With his back to Briar, he was stiff and unreadable. "I have the answer to the curse cure, I only need the tools to enact it. I hoped to make use of my family's facilities in Pentawynn to ensure its safety, but after that?" He swallowed audibly, choking down his emotions. "I intended to give you the cure as part of an engagement present."

"Engagement."

Voice quiet, Linden said, "Yes."

Briar could hardly believe his words. Their relationship felt stiff, distant. Or was that merely by comparison to the easy intimacy he had with Rowan? He and Linden had hardly done more than kiss.

Linden turned enough for Briar to see a sliver of profile. "Since my affections are not reciprocated, I suppose I will have to return the ring."

Briar felt wrung out and twisted. "It's not that I don't care about you, just . . ."

The weight of that sentence's conclusion hung in the air between them.

"Just not as you care for him," Linden finished tightly.

"I'm sorry."

"Do you love him?"

Briar didn't dare put that language to what he felt. "I don't know."

Linden walked back toward Briar, his expression rigid. Briar wished he would lash out again. It would be easier to deal with everything out in the open, not guarded within the fortress of Linden's mind. Linden sat on the settee, his knees straight and parallel, his hands laid upon them, sphinx-like. Only the bob of his Adam's apple betrayed how difficult it was for him to ask the next question.

"Do you believe you could ever love me?"

He didn't look at Briar as he said it. Briar struggled to read him. Now that he'd met Mr. and Mrs. Fairchild, he understood why their young prodigy might guard his feelings, why public mockery might trigger fight or flight. *A deified pillar of the people, stripped of humanity in the eyes of those who love him from afar.* Wasn't that how Niamh had described him? Briar wondered if Linden had ever known what it was to be loved up close. The curse of celebrity.

In all this mess, Briar found himself caught between two lonely men locked away from the world—by completely different circumstances, but the results were the same.

Linden's expression bowed under the weight of Briar's silence. In a crushed voice he said, "I see."

Remembering the prophecy, Briar said, "I could love you. I think I could. In time—I don't know. It's been hard to get to know you."

A brittle look. "I do not let anyone in with ease, it's true, but I have been incautious with you. Perhaps too incautious. I moved too quickly."

"I'm the one that screwed up."

"It hardly matters now. What will you choose to do?"

The words felt thick. "I can't string you along. I'd rather pay for the cure than use you for it. Whatever it costs."

Linden told him how much it would cost, in clearly enunciated digits, the syllables of which seemed to echo and carry on for a long time. It was far more than Briar had. Far more than he'd made from his work on the fashion line, far more than they'd make even if they scraped home every award at the gala, more than he could make in a lifetime.

"It will require an excruciating amount of power," Linden explained.

Something about the words prickled, but exhaustion both physical and emotional made it hard for Briar to parse. It was all too much to absorb. There was a cure. He couldn't afford it. He waited, knowing an olive branch was coming, and not understanding why he feared taking it.

Delicately, Linden picked Briar's hand up in his. "I would forgive you all of it," he said. "I can take you to Pentawynn, away from this ghastly place. Cure you of this affliction and spend the time we bought together where prying eyes can't meddle. Tell me, if it were a simple choice, would you give me your heart?"

Briar wanted to be true to his feelings. Now, it seemed selfish.

Beyond that, Linden had the cure.

He had the cure.

A chance at survival, and not just his own. A cure could free Rowan from the forest's hold, too. The effects of his scar nulled. Still, none of it felt right. If Fate held his hand and guided him down a path to prosperity and good fortune, why did he feel as though death awaited and sharpened its scythe?

Vatii nudged his arm. "If Rowan found the cure, he wouldn't hold your heart ransom for it."

And there it was. It had niggled, but he'd been too distraught to put a finger on it. Or perhaps too sick and ailing. Linden would charge him if he didn't agree to this elopement, and he knew Briar couldn't afford it. Echoes of the painful slap to his cheek throbbed in dim reminder.

The hairline fractures in Briar's esteem for Linden cracked. His hopes that their relationship might prosper foundered.

It was no choice at all. A heart with three swords stabbed through or a skeletal rider to take him beyond the veil. Heartbreak or death?

"Of course. Of course I'll come with you," he said.

Linden's smile was relieved.

And a tiny bit triumphant.

CHAPTER 25

Linden insisted they could discuss everything further in the morning after rest. He helped Briar back to his flat and undid the rest of the buttons on Briar's dress; Rowan's presence was a physical thing between them when Linden's fingers encountered the three pearls already loosed.

Then Linden pulled a shining slip of something from his pocket. A ferry ticket, its location stamped in gold-embossed lettering: Pentawynn.

"The city is quite spectacular to see from the water," he said.

Briar's throat constricted.

After Linden left, Briar collapsed into his own bed, Vatii crooning softly in his ear. He drifted into restless half-sleep, in and out of dreams. In them, he thought he heard a bell.

Pain like a brand snapped him awake. He sat up, clutching his chest, the tithe over his heart burning.

The tithe he'd used to charm Rowan's necklace.

But they'd found the culprit behind the forest's wounds—he was dead. There shouldn't be any more reason for the wood to call upon Rowan. Yet the tithe burned, calling Briar like a whisper from a dream.

He bolted out of bed and remembered too late how weak he was, stumbling, catching himself on the dresser. He needed help. If Gretchen had been there, she'd have a quippy remark or emergency potion recipe to help. But she was gone.

The forest has Rowan, the forest has Rowan.

First, get dressed. Find supplies.

He staggered his way to the dresser and changed. He fetched his tithe belt and stocked it with the most powerful ingredients he owned. Remembering the vines lashing him to the earth, he went to the kitchen and grabbed a knife, tucking it into his belt. He looted the cupboards next, drinking a vial of potion and stashing several more in a pouch. All this, yet he still felt underprepared. It would have to do.

Grateful Linden had given him a key, he let himself into the shop next door and hurried up the stairs, only to find an empty flat. Panic gripped him. Movement, and Atticus lifted his pale head off the comforter, staring bleary-eyed at the intruders. Vatii chattered at him, no doubt demanding where Linden was. Atticus gave his own chittering reply.

"He's gone to Pentawynn," Vatii said. "To prepare for your arrival. Atticus says he'll return by morning."

Morning would be too late.

Driven by impulse, Briar raided Linden's desk for bone powder. He measured out a portion for himself, saying to Atticus, "I'll replace it later, I promise." If he survived.

Then he was off into the night. A one-man rescue, and a severely hobbled one at that.

The mark on his chest tugged him in a specific direction, as the crow flew, but he had to navigate the twisting streets. Despite the cool air, his skin beaded with feverish sweat. He considered rousing Sorcha and Maebh, telling them Rowan was in danger, but their houses lay in the opposite direction from where the charm led, and he didn't know how much time he had. Regardless, neither Sorcha nor Maebh were witches.

He resisted the urge to run, instead walking at a steady clip. There would likely be a time he needed to run, and he had to save his energy. His health would not hold otherwise; it protested even this small abuse of walking quickly. The slow race to the woods was a torment, but he reserved his dwindling magic and the bone powder for when he'd most need it.

They went out into the fields, and as the forest drew closer, as they neared the edge of it, Vatii whispered in his ear.

"I feel like I should tell you not to go, but I know you won't listen, so I'll only say this . . . I'm quite proud to be the familiar of someone so willing to dive in to help those he loves."

"I've got to help him, Vatii. After all the ways he's helped me."

"You can admit you care for him."

He couldn't. He'd made a choice.

The forest loomed. Briar plunged in.

When he'd first entered, the forest had been intimidating and alive. The second time, eerily quiet, guiding them toward Kenneth's corpse with a trail of bones.

Now, the sway of the trees and the lurching of the mossy ground seemed more like the death throes of a limping animal than of something vivid and powerful. Tree bark sloughed like rotten skin. Rocks jutted up, white as broken bones. No vines lashed for his arms and legs, no whispers filtered through his mind. He passed like a ghost between the trees and wondered if they even knew he was there.

Vatii hunkered down on his shoulder, wings hitting him when she extended them for balance. The way was treacherous, the ground sinking and uneven, but he followed the pull of the mark on his chest like a compass.

His body twitched in warning. He drank a potion and kept going.

When he found the wound that had so injured the forest, it set his arms out in gooseflesh. The trees thinned, and he emerged into a blackened crater like the one that had contained Kenneth's body. Every inch of life was sucked from it. No trees or shrubs, just ashen earth and a halo of moonlight cascading through the hole in the canopy. Nothing lay at the center, no corpse and no siphon. Perhaps it was an old scar from Kenneth's earlier activities. But it didn't *feel* old.

It was not the only one. Briar picked up his pace and passed two more. The trees just on the fringes of each pocked scar bent backward, recoiling from the magic. Whoever had caused the destruction had already retrieved their prizes. None of the craters held a shining sphere.

The tithe on his chest burned more fiercely the closer he got to Rowan. He thought he knew where it was leading him. As if to confirm it, a reedy voice filtered through his mind.

You.

Angry, he spoke back. "Why are you doing this? I thought you already got rid of the problem."

More.

"More what? Why can't you just tell me what you need?"

Ours.

It was no use. The forest either couldn't communicate its needs, or it refused to.

Panting hard, three vials of potion depleted from his pack, Briar finally reached the tree.

It was the same, and yet nothing like how he'd left it. The stink of rot was an eye-watering punch. At first, Briar thought that the tree sang in a droning hum, but that was the flies. They hovered in clouds around its branches like buzzing foliage.

At its roots, Rowan lay. He stared, sightless, into the canopy with milky eyes. The forest crept over him in seeping mosses and curling vines, shredding his shirt apart, but the necklace remained miraculously intact. These were the least alarming things.

Briar crashed to his knees next to him. On Rowan's chest, a branch had sunk into the skin. Or sprouted from it—it was difficult to tell where it began and Rowan ended. It arced up, the other end buried in the loam a few feet away. Briar seized his shoulders.

"Rowan, wake up!"

Rowan did not wake, but his chest rose, even with the branch through it. The vines crept faster to thwart Briar's rescue. Panic set his hands shaking, or maybe that was the curse. Briar took another draft of potion—his last—and flung the empty bottle away. He scraped away the moss on Rowan's body with his fingers, shuddering at the squelching noise it made as it lifted. Underneath, it left angry, red wheals on Rowan's skin.

"Briar, hurry." Vatii darted around his knees, pecking at the moss attempting to creep over him too.

Stop.

Briar drew out the knife and started cutting the vines. They shrank from the slice of the blade. Not the large branch, not yet.

Stop. Ours.

"He's not yours," Briar said. He tried to wake Rowan again, to no avail. The knife trembled in his grasp, and he clenched it tighter. The big branch stuck through Rowan's chest was last, and he feared it the way he feared turning on a light when he'd heard a noise in the dark. He gritted his teeth, took the knife to it and sawed. It bit through the bark but sank no farther. He drew it back and, with all his limited strength, brought it down like an axe. A sickening burst of ichor seeped from the tiny wound, but the branch did not sever. Rowan twitched but didn't wake.

Panic grasped Briar. He sawed at the branch but couldn't get farther than a scant centimeter of bark, at which point it felt like trying to break through concrete. Vatii squawked in alarm as a vine tied her leg. Briar seized her, cutting the vine away, and she clawed his cloak to hang onto his back, away from the devouring forest floor.

"You have to wake him up," she said. "Remember Orla!"

Briar remembered. He'd just hoped this would be different. If this was like Orla, then only one person could break the forest's hold, and he was not responding no matter how hard Briar shook him. Briar could think of only one recourse. He had no tithe to bring someone back from the edge of consciousness or death, or whatever gripped Rowan now. The only thing he had on hand was his body. His weak, aching body.

He retrieved his charcoal and drew a rune on his bare wrist, cursing the shakes that made his lines wobble. He had to spit, wipe them clean and redraw them. Finally, he had a serviceable rune, and he reached into his magic well to the sense of his fingers trailing the sodden bottom. He pulled and pulled, dredged the scraps of a spell together. It drained his energy enough to make his vision spotty, but it worked.

Rowan's lashes fluttered. When he opened his eyes, they were brown, not white. Confusion took hold as he saw Briar swaying beside him.

"Briar?" The confusion quickly slid sideways into horror when he saw what protruded from his chest. Rowan didn't scream, but he tried to sit up, scramble away. He couldn't. The root had him pinned. With mounting panic, "Briar?"

"Rowan." Briar rushed to calm him, putting both hands on his cheeks and leaning in to block his view of the vine.

"It's okay, Rowan. It's going to be—you have to break that vine. We have to get out of here."

Rowan made a sound somewhere between a groan and a sob. It rent Briar's heart in two. He'd never seen Rowan look so afraid. He could do little to help, his reserves of magic so dwindled he doubted he could cast a pain relief spell without blacking out. He had enough to escape, nothing more.

"You can do this," he said. "I'll be right here to portal us home, you just have to break its hold."

Rowan looked into his eyes. He was ashen-faced, clammy, shivering as if submerged in ice, but he nodded. As Briar drew away, he wrapped both hands around the bend in the branch, where he'd have the most leverage to twist and snap. The muscles in his arms flexed, testing. He looked to Briar, perhaps for confirmation or encouragement, which Briar gave by squeezing Rowan's shoulder.

No! the forest shrieked.

The snap fractured through the air like a thunderclap. On the heels of it, Rowan's harrowing scream.

Liquid from the severed end striped hot as blood over Briar's arm. Black in the dark of the forest, but in flashes of dappled moonlight, it shone crimson. It *was* blood. The stump of the vine melted and congealed, molting away. Rowan's howl was ear-splitting. Briar did his best to hold him and draw him back to the present.

"It's okay, it's okay, you did good. We've got to go, Rowan. Can you stand?"

Rowan tried. He rose up on his elbows before vines lashed around his throat to snap him back. The forest, desperate, was not going to let them go easily. Briar reached for the knife and found it gone, swallowed by the earth.

Rowan didn't need it. In a burst of movement, he lunged forward and tore through the vines. He stood, lifting Briar, moss falling away from them. Vatii clung to the hood of Briar's cloak, flapping as he rushed to pull out a handful of stolen bone powder.

The forest said, *He's ours. Promised. We will have him. We need him.*

Briar had never made a portal before, but in the grips of fear and the drive to survive, he did not lack the intent needed to find his last drops of magic.

"Take me home," he shouted as he flung the powder.

The portal opened, and they fell through.

All the quiet noises of the forest had coalesced to deafening—the hiss of wind, the drone of flies, the rustle of foliage. The portal closed, and it was silent.

It took a moment for Briar to realize where they were. In the dark, he struggled to make out the hand-painted wooden furniture. Rowan's cottage.

They made their way to the sofa, no longer sure who held up who. Briar shrugged his shoulders until Rowan collapsed onto it, clutching his chest where the root had sprouted. It left no deep, gory wound, only a red mark on the spot where his scar began, but it pained him. His eyes closed, face drawn.

Though Briar badly wanted to collapse too, neither he nor Rowan had the energy to withstand another encounter like that one. He went through the back door into Éibhear's garden. Vatii helped him collect the plants he needed. He found clean cloths in the kitchen and wet them. He boiled water and made tea using some of the plants, adding cold water to the brew so they could drink it right away. When he brought these back, Rowan opened his eyes.

"C'mere and rest," he croaked.

"I will now in a minute," Briar said, not realizing until the flicker of a smile on Rowan's face what he had said. It was a phrase he'd picked up in Coill Darragh. He knelt on the floor and pressed one of the cool cloths to Rowan's forehead; the other he used to mop the wheals and specks of blood. In the back of his throat, Rowan made a tiny noise of relief.

Against his better judgment, Briar reached up and carded a hand through Rowan's sweaty hair, combing out dead leaves and twigs. Rowan leaned in to his touch and made that same, small noise again.

Briar said, "That was really close."

"Bit too close," Rowan said. "Thank you. For coming to my rescue."

"Didn't make this *just* to look pretty." He flicked the necklace.

"Hm. Rather not go through that again." He looked ashamed. "Was feckin' terrified."

"You were brave," Briar told him.

"You make me brave." He gazed at Briar steadily as he said it. Briar's heart could have burst. There was no mistaking the swell of affection burgeoning within him. In hindsight, the idea that leaving Coill Darragh would mean leaving these feelings behind seemed asinine. They felt as intrinsically a part of him as Vatii, or his tithes, or his own name.

He said, "Can you sit up?"

Wincing, Rowan managed to, accepting the mug of tea and taking a sip. Briar drank his too. It soaked into his bones, both vigorous and soothing. It would help them sleep and restore some of their drained energy, but it was no substitute for the milk thistle elixir. He'd have to pick some up from the apothecary, since Linden was away.

"Thought we found the reason the forest was acting the maggot," Rowan muttered. "And here we are again."

"There were more craters like the one Kenneth made," Briar said. "They didn't seem old."

Rowan rubbed his head. "So we're back to where we started."

Briar didn't think so. Something had shifted. They'd gone into the forest before, and it hadn't attacked them. He sighed. "I'm taking the ferry to Pentawynn tomorrow. When I'm back, we'll get to the bottom of this."

Rowan's face fell. "You're leaving?"

"Only for a little while, then—"

"He's going to ask you to marry him. Isn't he?"

Briar flinched. "Rowan . . ."

"Do you think he'll let you come back that easy, like?"

"Let me?"

"I don't trust him." Rowan tried to sit up, voice trembling with something long repressed. "He holds your hand like it's the end of a fecking leash."

"It's not like that. He's trying to help lift my curse, and he's been under a lot of stress because of me and his parents and—"

"He hit you!" The shout rang loud in the quiet of the cottage. Rowan held his chest like the pain of his injury worsened with his raised voice. "You were sick and hurting, and he hurt you *worse*, all because he was *jealous*. He's used your talents to make himself a fortune, wears you like a badge of honor. And now he's taking you off to Pentawynn, away from here."

"Away from *you*, you mean?"

"You know that's not how it is."

"It's not?" Briar's head pounded. The tangle of emotion rising in him was too convoluted to parse; he felt trapped and it was somehow worse hearing Rowan say it out loud. So he retaliated in kind. "Fine, you don't trust him, but what choice do I have? This is the only hope I've got. That *we've* got. Linden's got money and endless resources. And you'd have me pass up this chance because you don't like that it's Linden offering? So which of you is jealous and hurting me because of it?"

Rowan looked gutted by his words. "I won't pretend I'm not jealous. I'm trying, I am, but you—you made me feel—" He took a moment to collect himself. "It doesn't matter. Just hear me on this, because I'm no liar. If I believed for a moment that fecker would cure you, I'd see you off on the damn boat myself."

The words stung because they were true. Rowan's motives didn't require deeper interrogation. He'd see his own heart broken before he saw Briar's stop beating.

Briar could tell him Linden had the cure. He withheld it because saying so felt tantamount to admitting the cure was his only reason for pursuing a relationship with Linden in the first place. Once, Briar had believed loving Linden was inevitable, fate. Only now he realized the prophecy said nothing at all about him loving Linden back.

Weakly, Briar said, "We're exhausted. We should sleep."

Whatever energy Rowan had in reserve to argue fled him. Neither of them could even climb the ladder into the loft. Rowan tried to coax Briar into taking the sofa, but since he was much larger, it made no sense. Briar insisted he was comfortable in the armchair and curled up there. Rowan relented and started softly snoring moments later.

Briar couldn't sleep. He watched Rowan's back rise and fall, haunted by the idea that tonight he could have stopped breathing altogether.

Tomorrow morning, he would take the ferry to Pentawynn. Linden would cure him of his curse, and then he would set all of his ardor into convincing Linden to cure Rowan, too. He would give Linden whatever he wanted. As he contemplated that, he found he didn't really know what Linden wanted. He'd thought it had been all the same things Briar longed for. Love, success, recognition, a partner. Now, he wasn't sure.

It chilled him. It was the only plan he had.

He drifted off for a handful of hours. When he woke, Rowan still slept. Briar got up, joints stiff but serviceable. He knelt and put a hand on Rowan's chest to wake him, but he didn't stir. His lashes were dark fans against his cheeks, gilded gold in sunlight. For a moment, Briar allowed himself the fantasy of leaning over and kissing him awake. Like he'd done countless times in those bright few weeks mostly spent here at the cottage. He imagined Rowan coming slowly awake to the warmth of Briar's lips on his. He'd make that soft sound of relief again, cup the back of Briar's head.

Briar gently shook him. When Rowan saw who woke him, he smiled so sweetly—like their entire argument the night before was forgotten—Briar nearly kissed him anyway.

"I have to go into town and get more potion. I wanted to see if you needed anything first."

"I'll come with you." He started to get up but gasped at the pain of moving. Briar pushed to ease him down.

"You're staying here to recover. You should take pain killers or an elixir. Do you have any?"

"In my bedside cabinet."

Briar managed to climb the ladder. Rowan's bedroom looked untouched, the quilted bed still made. Rowan hadn't even slept in it before the forest's call took him.

Briar opened the bedside cabinet and found a brown paper bag that looked like it contained medicine. At first, he thought it was empty, but then he saw something glint, and his heart fell into his stomach.

Rings. Two of them. One, a gold plaited band with a crowned heart at its center.

The second was simple and delicate, a diamond set with four smaller blue stones at the corners like a star. It was beautiful, custom made to fit with the claddagh, and was unmistakably an engagement ring.

He cast for the most far-fetched conclusions in order to avoid what he already knew. Rowan had relationships from before his curse, maybe he'd bought this for a past lover and then, when they'd left him, kept it for whomever came along and stole his heart. But he knew it wasn't true.

A wave of emotion swept over him, so strong he felt sick.

He'd known in his heart the reason Rowan had come to speak to him that snowy night. But not the depth of feeling. Not the certainty.

Underneath the bag was a sachet of ibuprofen. He left the rings in the bedside cabinet. Pretended he hadn't seen them. He made his careful way down the ladder and repeated his plan to himself. Tomorrow, he'd leave on a ferry for Pentawynn. He'd see the city. Linden would give him the cure. He'd come back with it for Rowan. And after that . . . ?

Why did he get the sense Linden's engagement was not the sort he'd be able to call off?

He handed Rowan the ibuprofen, hoping nothing of the emotional war within showed on his face. He must have failed. Something dawned in the slackened expression on Rowan's face.

"Will you come see me off tomorrow?" Briar asked.

"Please don't ask that," Rowan said. "I can't say goodbye to you."

"It wouldn't be forever."

Rowan just gave him a heartsick look that said he knew different.

Deprived of its sacrifice, the forest lashed out at the people of Coill Darragh.

Briar saw it on his way home. People collapsed in the street, branches clawing up their bodies. Maebh appeared outside the Swan and Cygnet and herded people toward the church. It was safe there, she said. Just until they got everything sorted, she said.

Briar offered to help, but Maebh said not to bother. From people's faces, he could tell he looked like no help at all. When he got home, the mirror confirmed it. He'd always been vain about his appearance. He liked to dress nicely, to spend hours getting ready for a fancy party. Now, sallow-skinned and hollow-eyed, he looked near death. With leaden fear, he realized he was.

His ticket to Pentawynn lay in an envelope on the kitchen table. He sat and traced the edges with his fingertips. Vatii perched on his shoulder and nibbled his earlobe to console him. The anxiety between them was a pill swallowed with a parched throat and no water.

"You could leave Linden after," Vatii said.

Briar thought he'd misheard. "Pardon?"

"If Linden won't give you the cure out of the goodness of his heart, why give him *your* heart when someone else would treat it better? Why not take his cure and leave?"

Because it was cruel. Because it would make him the sort of person Linden had always feared. Because Briar could kiss his career prospects goodbye if the press sniffed out what he'd done. In his darker moments, he'd thought of it, and it disgusted him. Besides, he didn't need the cure for himself alone. He needed it for Rowan, too. Niamh's tarot reading had been unambiguous about what lay in wait for him if he pursued a relationship with Rowan.

Frustration boiled. "I don't understand. You've been pushing me to heed the prophecy this entire time. We might *die* if I don't."

"I push and question because whether I think your decision is the right or wrong one, I want you to be certain of it."

"Linden has the cure. I'd rather be worthy of him than a backstabbing—"

"But Rowan loves you."

"What does it matter?" Briar shouted. It burst out of him with such vehemence that Vatii danced away, talons clicking across the table. "If I stay here, we're as good as dead, and if I go and marry Linden, I break Rowan's heart. If I leave Linden after getting the cure, I'm a no-good user, just like he feared. I'd hate myself for it. You're my guide. You're the one who told me not to tempt fate with Rowan. You said all along it was a mistake. Well, you were right. Gloat if you like! You should! You were right." He put his head in his hands. "You were right."

Vatii hopped over to him and ducked under the cavern made by his bowed head and arms. She snuggled under his chin, her feathery head soft.

She said, "I wish I'd been wrong."

CHAPTER 26

The ferry docked at Bán Cuain, a fishing village neighboring Coill Darragh. Briar had seen it when he'd flown in. The houses were painted to brighten cold, gray winters. The air smelled of brine. Morning sun shone, but the brisk April wind stole its heat.

He stood with his back to the crowd, looking out to sea. The water lapped at the wood posts, where barnacles and algae clung. He wondered why this bay wasn't a hotbed for magic to siphon off, like Coill Darragh. Then he remembered the squadrons of fishing vessels on the opposite shore, waiting like an army, and figured that had something to do with it. The wards preserved Coill Darragh's purity against invaders.

Something was missing from it all. Briar thought of Gretchen rolling off the edge of a roof. He thought of Éibhear giving his life and cursing his son to stop an invasion of witches from destroying their home, his people. Kenneth, dead, but the effects of his actions echoing. All this set in motion ten years ago, and Briar found himself at the center with no clue how to stop it.

He breathed deep the sea air. On his shoulder, Vatii startled and looked behind them.

"It's a good day for sailing."

Briar whirled. Standing on the pier, the scarf Briar made for him wound several times around his broad shoulders, was Rowan, looking breathless and scared like he'd run there. He took a cautious step forward.

"I've never been sailing," Briar said. "Used to live in a town just like this, but we—well."

Rowan said, "I'd take you sometime."

Briar thought of his mother, and how she'd have liked that for him. "You came to say goodbye after all."

"No," Rowan answered. "I came to tell you something. Something I should have said ages back. And probably you know already. I've not hidden it well. But I've not said it out loud and it's been a weighty curse to keep it from you so . . ."

Briar couldn't bring himself to speak, throat stoppered. The yearning to hear what Rowan came to say warred with the need to set foot on a ferry bound for another shore, a different future. Rowan's jaw firmed. His Adam's apple bobbed. It looked like he might say nothing at all, like the words were lead, too heavy to summon.

When he did speak, it stole all the sound, all the air from the pier.

"It was never casual for me." The words knocked Briar in the chest, but Rowan continued. "I tried to pretend that it was, but it wasn't. I've feelings for you. I've had them a while, but been too afraid to tell you in case you didn't feel the same, or I scared you off, but I'm telling you now because if I don't, then I'll always wonder. And I know it's a terrible time. I'm feckin' terrified of what's happening to you. To us both. So if it's not the same for you, then I promise you I'll not ever mention it again. I'll go on being your friend and won't ever bring it up because I don't want you to feel this is all that matters to me, 'cause it's not. You've been a good friend to me, and I'd not ruin that for anything, but I had to tell you the whole of it. That I'm mad about you. You're bold and brave, and you've made me braver, too. Brave enough to say this. That I love you. I love you something fierce."

He opened his clenched fist. In his open palm sat not the claddagh, but the engagement ring. He'd held it so tightly that it left indents in his skin.

It was never casual for me.

Never, in all the time he'd known Rowan, had Briar ever heard the man speak so much at once. The monumental effort it had taken to summon the words weighed heavy as unbroken storm clouds between them. Despite the cool weather, sweat beaded on Rowan's brow, and he breathed hard, awaiting an answer.

Briar wet his lips and opened them, but no sound followed. Despair was a physical thing, and he choked on it. He couldn't say the one thing he'd longed to ever since that kiss in the snow.

What he said instead was, "He has the cure."

Rowan said, "Pardon?"

"Linden. He has the cure."

Slack-jawed relief bloomed on Rowan's face, followed slowly by confusion. "That's good news, isn't it? Wait, hasn't he given it to you?"

"He said he needs his resources in Pentawynn to prepare it." Briar swallowed the lump in his throat. "And that he wanted to give it to me as an engagement present."

"Engagement—"

"We have one show, and he'll propose and cure me. It'll be fine," Briar babbled, meaning none of it.

Rowan's tone grew suspicious, angry. "And if you didn't want to marry him? What then?"

Rowan's guesses cut too close to the quick. Regret that he'd let the truth out was a sour sting as Briar bit his tongue and tasted the ever-present, lingering fume of his potions. "It isn't—"

"How much would it cost?"

"Too much."

"We'll pool together, all of us. I'm sure the whole town would help, if we asked."

That struck a well-worn chord in Briar. He couldn't name the emotions bursting out of him, but the words that did were lies he'd told himself over and over. "I have to do this on my own."

"Why?" Rowan said. "Why's he charging you if he cares for you? Money or marriage, he won't just cure you because he loves you? If he's blackmailing you—I'll get a ticket myself and come with you, convince him to do right by you. You deserve that choice!"

If Rowan had hit the chord before, he'd jammed a nail through it then.

"Stop!" Briar shouted. "Just stop . . ."

Rowan's anger melted and came apart like a snowflake fallen on a bare palm. He spoke in broken syllables. "Do you love him?"

It was as much a question as a dare.

And what could Briar say in answer?

No, but I can't see a way to save us that doesn't involve tying myself to this man I thought I could love but who, now, in this moment, I loathe more than words can say.

No, I love you too, but there's no future for us that doesn't end in death.

The prophetic magic tied his tongue, but whatever he could say, the results would be the same. And perhaps the easiest thing, the kindest thing, would be to make Rowan hate him. So there was no room left to hope for the impossible. He blinked the sting from his eyes and summoned words he didn't mean. The only ones he thought would make Rowan relent.

"I'm sorry. I love Linden. It was never like that for us. This is what I want. It's . . ." He barely got the words out. "It's all I wanted from the start."

Grief cut across Rowan's face like a physical blow. His normally immutable features had worn a look of open entreaty all this time. Now, his brows pinched together, his jaw went slack, and his eyes flitted over Briar, over the ground, skipping across the waves and water, back to Briar. Searching. Probably for the future Briar had just cast away. Almost imperceptibly, Rowan shook his head in disbelief. A twitching, indecisive movement.

"You can't mean that."

"I do."

"Everything between us? It wasn't just . . ."

Briar's Adam's apple felt like an iron lump bobbing in his throat. He couldn't say that it was foretold. That Seer Niamh had said so. "This is how it's meant to be."

It was horrible to watch Rowan's conviction shatter. He believed it, and why shouldn't he? Briar had never lied to him before. Still, he could hardly hold steady at the stricken look Rowan fixed him with, at the way his aura went cold like tea left forgotten, like a long winter that stole too much time from spring.

Briar's eyes burned, and his throat constricted so hard he thought he'd come apart.

"Oh—" said Rowan. "Oh. I thought . . . I— Goodbye."

His voice cracked so the last word came out cloven in two. Already, he moved to pass, in such a rush to be away that his shoulder clipped Briar's. It was not this, but the pang in his chest that sent Briar reeling back a half step. Every bit of distance put between them tugged and tore him in that direction. He listened to Rowan's boots tramp up the dock. With one hand, he pressed at his sternum, as if he could reach inside and pinch closed the open seams of his broken heart. Smooth over the cracks like clay.

Rowan's footsteps faded. Briar stood, paralyzed.

Vatii nuzzled his cheek.

The horn of the ferry blew.

"Briar?" Vatii whispered. Her worry made the melancholy prick painfully behind his eyes.

He had to go.

Briar navigated up the ramp to the ferry, weaving through threads of tourists, avoiding eye contact for fear they'd see how distraught he was and ask the dreaded question, *Oh, are you all right?*

He didn't want anyone to ask because the answer was *no*. And, *I don't think I'll ever be.*

He found a vacant spot on the sunless side of the ferry, where the wind and the cool shade had everyone scattering for warmer views. Briar curled up on a bench, buried his face in his knees, and let the flood of tears overwhelm him where no one could see. Once the first sobs broke, it was impossible to stop them, sucked under, shoulders heaving. His vision darkened as Vatii extended a wing over his head to conceal him from anyone passing by.

He thought, *I'll be okay. I won't learn to love Linden, but I'll get to live in Pentawynn, show at the runways I've always dreamed of. Time heals all wounds, so maybe in a year or two, it won't hurt like this.*

But it hurt now.

Knees soaked in tears, he looked up when Vatii's wing retracted and she pecked at his hair.

"Briar, look."

Over the rail of the ferry, he could see the houses of Bán Cuain with their bright colors like a painter's palette smeared across the horizon. The docks were a dark strip stretching into the water. On them, at the end, was a figure too tall and broad to be anyone else.

Briar went to the rail. Wind whipped the tears off his cheeks to join the salt spray against the ferry's flanks. The figure on the docks didn't wave or move, or do much more than watch him go. It tugged at Briar so hard he thought he would pitch over if he didn't hold on to the rail.

Love was a burning brand in his chest.

He wanted to say it. No one could hear anyway. Not Rowan, not the people milling on the ferry, not even Vatii if he said it quietly. The roar of the wind, water, and the ferry's engine would steal the words if he voiced them.

But he didn't.

CHAPTER 27

The ferry sailed parallel to the shore, giving all aboard a long look at Pentawynn's glass spires winking in the sun. Briar had postcards of the skyline from every time of day—amber dawns and starlit nights. The crowning jewel was the Magician's Council Tower, a spiraling skyscraper like a unicorn's horn.

It was colloquially referred to as the Horn for that reason, which usually made Briar laugh.

He found it difficult to laugh now, but something exultant filtered through at the view before him. He'd dreamed of it for years, and now he was here.

Linden had arranged for a driver to pick Briar up at the pier. He'd expected a taxi. Instead, the driver took him to a horse-drawn carriage, splendid in white and gold and surrounded by paparazzi. They parted, flashes leaving Briar temporarily blind. Linden waited there, hand extended, dressed like a prince in a half cape, jodhpurs, and riding gloves, smart and sharp as the slap Briar's cheek still remembered. As Briar stepped up, Linden tilted his chin and kissed him chastely while the cameras flashed. Briar hoped they didn't capture his despondence.

Settling into the carriage, a tickle of magic passed over them. "There's a privacy spell to keep the press from eavesdropping, so we can speak freely here," said Linden.

"Thanks for coming to get me."

"Of course. I hope the ferry ride was to your liking."

Briar pushed out the memory of Rowan. "You were right. Pentawynn looks incredible from the water."

"Good, I'm pleased. There's much to discuss before your arrival at the manor."

The horse's hooves clopped against the pavement, and they pulled away into the streets. It felt like entering a jungle. Cars all around them, and buildings that increased in height the farther they went, until Briar had to crane his neck to see the sky. Bustling through the streets were countless witches, identifiable by their hats and skittering, flapping familiars.

Linden ran through a list of things he'd prepared for their showing at Finola's Gala Runway. He went into detail about the stories he'd fed the press regarding the photo snapped of Briar and Rowan. They were only good friends, the photo only gave the appearance of something more, Linden and Briar were deeply enamored with each other and this was another attempt by the press to defame him, etcetera.

Briar stroked a hand through Vatii's feathers, wistful for an alternate reality where he could fully enjoy this, where his eyes didn't feel papery from crying, where his body didn't ache like it was aflame.

The entrance to Linden's estate was accessible down a private road. As the carriage passed under an arched gate, a wave of wards like the ones guarding Coill Darragh prickled over Briar's skin. A thicket of trees obscured the grounds from public view. Through it was a long stretch of road framed by manicured topiary and symmetrical gardens. At the end, the manor strove tall and white toward the sky in pointed turrets and bas-relief colonnades. The carriage pulled up to the entrance, and the driver opened the doors.

Inside the main foyer, the grandeur of the manor sank in. Curving staircases framed a three-story atrium. A crystal chandelier suspended from the ceiling flung prismatic color against the walls, refracted from the sun coming through the skylights above. Everything was cut from the same cloth as the city itself. Glass, crystal, white walls, gold embellishments.

The grandeur and ostentation made him feel small. Such excess, while he'd pinched pennies for beans on toast.

Linden beheld Briar's awe with satisfaction. "I'll show you to my apartments. Well, *ours*."

They climbed the stairs to the third floor, flanked by a footman carrying Briar's luggage. A long hall from the atrium balcony led to a master bedroom. The doors off this hall were open to let in the sun, and through them were rooms for every occasion. A sitting room. A library. An alchemist's laboratory. A crafts room.

One door was closed. "My study," Linden said, and procured a key to open the door, revealing a tidy room of bookshelves and an oak desk with a stained-glass lamp. "It's nothing special, but there are legal and private documents, so I prefer the servants leave it." He locked it and returned the key to his pocket. Briar prickled at the mention of servants. Linden's home was so large it needed an HR department.

Linden's bedroom was enormous, with a four-poster bed so wide it was a ten-minute taxi ride from end to end. Enough room to spread out and not touch. Briar never slept in the same bed as Linden in Coill Darragh. Once cured, would expectations of a more physical relationship follow? Briar's stomach twisted at the notion, his meager breakfast threatening an encore.

Linden took off his jacket, a servant hurrying to take it from him. He pulled the talisman from around his neck and tossed it on the vanity amongst bottles of beauty potions. Briar noticed the talisman's surface was blackened and dented.

Following his line of sight, Linden tutted. "I'm afraid the effectiveness of my talisman is diminishing. It's a sign it's been under duress to protect me. I'll have to get another."

Atticus jumped up on the windowsill, eyes trained on a bird splashing in one of the shallow fountains behind the estate. Linden came to stand next to Briar. Freed of the talisman's influence, his aura swept through Briar like a cool wind sneaking through gaps in his clothes.

"My parents want you to join us for dinner. I've left clothes for you on the bed."

A waistcoat with a back panel of blue fabric speckled like the night sky lay on the coverlet. Trousers, a poet's shirt, and some jewelry came with it.

"How do I . . ." Briar didn't know how to phrase the question. "How do I make them like me?"

"It's not in their nature to be pleased by anything or anyone. It doesn't matter what they think. This is our destiny, not theirs."

A splitting ache in Briar's head made it impossible to contemplate things as large as destiny. "Linden, I don't mean to push, but the cure. Do you know when it will be ready?"

"Yes, I wanted to discuss that with you. I thought maybe after dinner, but—no. Sit, sit. I'll get your potion."

Briar abandoned his trunk, which he'd been struggling to open. He hoisted himself onto the bed. Linden returned with his elixir, which Briar drank.

"The cure is a complicated endeavor, I'm afraid. Not nearly so simple as drinking a potion."

"How much more complicated?" Briar said.

"Very. Before I explain, promise me you'll listen. When I first thought of it, I was convinced it would be impossible. Unreasonable. But I see no alternative."

Briar's heart kicked. "I'm listening."

"I researched the red carnellas. Seeing as you had a small sample, I thought perhaps something could come of them. However, my search bore nothing. What little I did find reported the same thing—the blooms are fragile. Whatever unique magic they possess, it breaks down easily.

"So I researched the wood they came from instead. Did you know? The red carnella's extinction occurred ten years ago—I thought that could not be a coincidence. Though I cannot prove my theory, I believe the erection of the wards destroyed the flower entirely. Made the land unsuitable to its growth. So—"

"You want to destroy the wards?"

"No," Linden said. "I want to destroy the forest itself."

Briar reeled. He harbored no love for the forest, but he'd seen what happened when people threatened it. At the revulsion on Briar's face, Linden took his hands.

"I understand your reaction. I felt the same, particularly after that business with that man—Kenneth, was it? But please consider, Briar, your time is short. We can waffle over theories and mythical panaceas, or we can cure you by the most sure-fire, expedient means, of which there are only two. The curse caster releases you, which it has refused to do, or the curse caster dies."

"But—" Briar sputtered. "H-how? How do you kill it without hurting, maybe even *killing*, all the people connected to it?"

"I had the same misgivings, but I discovered that, even all those years ago, and with the exception of Éibhear, the forest has never killed a Coill Darraghn. It has injured plenty, but I believe killing its people would be counterproductive. If it uses the energy of Coill Darraghns to heal its wounds or feed its power—like batteries, if you will—it can't lose them completely."

Briar absorbed that. "But how do you know it won't lash out at *you*. You're not Coill Darraghn."

"If you married me, I would be."

"I'm not Coill Darraghn either."

Linden pointed at his bare wrist. "The forest treats you otherwise."

Briar's brow scrunched. Many things crowded in his head, too many to voice all at once. He started with the most obvious. "It killed Kenneth, and he was technically Coill Darraghn after his engagement. He didn't wear his bracelet."

"I considered that. I believe Kenneth erred when he failed to nurture his relationship with Aisling. Spurned, she considered the engagement broken, or perhaps she stopped loving him, and his citizenship was revoked."

The theory picked at the scabs of Briar's wounds. If what Linden said was true, then Briar's own acceptance was conditional on Rowan's love for him. Given what happened on the pier, Rowan should hate him.

He didn't, though. He'd stood on that pier, watching Briar leave. His love held, dependable as the rising sun.

"Say we go through with this," Briar said. "How do you kill an entire forest? What spell could possibly be powerful enough?"

"A challenge, but mostly a question of resources. As we've already seen, siphons can damage it badly. It wasn't fully recovered from the wounds inflicted by Kenneth while we were there. I could create enough siphons to devour it like it's been devouring you—however, it recovers too quickly and harms Coill Darraghns in the process. I needed to discover its weakness. On this point, I was at a loss. I hate to admit it, but the alderman's predicament is what gave me the final piece to the puzzle."

Briar prickled with suspicion, but he asked, "Rowan's?"

"The forest calls upon him, doesn't it? In its time of need, it draws him in as a sacrifice to heal itself. Given what his father did, I thought it best to delve into the history of magical human sacrifices. A grisly topic, but I learned of an interesting principle. A sacrifice, willingly given, produces much more powerful spells than something stolen or traded. It explains why the energy the forest takes forcibly from Coill Darraghns fails to heal it satisfactorily, while Éibhear's singular sacrifice has powered the wards and the forest's magic for a decade.

"I believe Éibhear is the true source of the forest's power, and that his remains, wherever they are, continue to feed its growth. Destroying them would render the forest vulnerable, make it easy to clear with fire or siphons or any normal means."

"So you want to, what? Dig up Éibhear's body?" Briar couldn't disguise his disgust. "And do what? Burn it?"

Linden sounded frustrated. "I know it sounds crude, but think about what the forest has done to you. What it's currently doing to the alderman. I bear no love for that beastly man, as you *well* know, but the forest is a menace. It ought to be dealt with, and if it's the source of your curse, perhaps it cursed every person inflicted with Bowen's Wane. Had you considered that? Would burning one man's remains really be so criminal if it could free everyone ensnared by this malignant thing? We can grow more trees."

Vatii looked uneasy. "I don't like this."

Briar didn't either. When he'd gone into the forest last, it had been a shade of itself, ravaged by siphons. Had Linden planted them during his experiments, endangering Rowan's life? Even in pursuit of a cure, Briar recoiled at the thought of it. But their options were limited. If this could *free* Rowan . . .

"You're confident this will work?" Briar asked.

"More confident than I've ever been."

Briar hesitated before asking, but he had to know. "Would it hurt Rowan or free him?"

"It would likely unbind the sacrificial magic," Linden said with a hint of reproof. "He'd be safe."

Briar said, "Okay . . . In that case, yes. Let's do it."

Linden softened. "I knew you'd understand." He patted Briar's hand, and Briar wished that didn't make his skin crawl. Something still seemed wrong in all this. "We should get ready for dinner." He crossed the room. Atticus lingered, eyeing Briar, then followed.

Linden had a point—the forest was a terrible, malevolent force. It had killed Briar's mother. He should want vengeance, want it gone. It could save his life, Rowan's life, and countless others if what Linden said was true. But the plan rankled. Killing the forest outright? Was his hesitation borne of nothing more than spending so long in Coill Darragh that the tradition of respecting the forest as much as fearing it had sunk into him as well?

It wasn't this that irked him, though. Vatii put to words why he so distrusted this.

"He needs you to marry him for this plan to work, Briar."

Briar shuddered. Linden began courting him so suddenly, after he'd said he only wanted to be friends. So how long had he been planning this, really?

Briar called out, "Linden . . . are you only asking me to marry you so you'll be Coill Darraghn? So you can kill the forest?"

Linden turned. The softness in his voice had gone. "Are you here because you love me or because I have the cure?"

The ugliness of the question hit Briar in the sternum. Winded him.

"You should get ready for dinner," Linden murmured. "My parents won't like to be kept waiting."

A servant led Briar to the dining room, candlelit with a circular table and settings for four. A fireplace roared with cerulean flames. Suspended above the table in an enchanted glass sphere, an aquarium of tropical fish cast eerie, dancing lights over Linden and his parents.

"Ah, there you are," Linden said. "Thank you for joining us."

Both Gresham and Adelaide had removed their talismans; Adelaide's aura was a finger sinking through overripe fruit. Gresham's, the smell of a hospital.

A servant pulled out Briar's chair and tucked him in, unfolding the napkin shaped like a swan to lay on his lap. Servers glutted their glasses with wine in a synchronized dance. In the flickering blue light cast by the fire and the aquarium, Linden's parents frightened Briar, and he weighed the pros and cons of surviving the meal while plastered.

Linden led the conversation. First, to Briar's adept persuasion of Finola to invite them to her gala. Then, to Briar swaying the press to reconsider their views on taboo magic like flesh tithes.

"And that man? The alderman," said Gresham.

Linden let Briar answer. "A friend. The photo looked like more than it was."

There was a blessed quiet when the first course arrived—beluga caviar on blini with sour cream and chives. Briar would have watched to see how Linden ate it, but all eyes were on him, awaiting his verdict. Did he use utensils or just pop it in his mouth with his fingers? It was very small. Briar opted to use his hands. He hardly tasted the thing, too nervous to appreciate it. He said "Mmm!" and Linden's parents nodded, satisfied.

Briar drank more wine. He was glad for the aquarium, which gave him something tranquil to look at. Fish in rainbow colors danced through the water and corals. A particularly mesmerizing one had red fins like chiffon veils. More courses arrived, each with a list of ingredients Briar had never seen at the grocery store.

Adelaide addressed Briar, at first neutrally. "How do you like the food?"

"It's delicious."

"We hope you've made yourself comfortable. How do you find the estate?"

"It's beautiful. Like nothing I've ever seen."

"I don't think you told us where you're from?"

"I moved around a lot," he said. "But I grew up in Port Haven."

"Lovely place," said Adelaide. "Quaint, but friendly."

Summoning courage, Briar said, "You won't remember, but I saw you there, years ago."

Both Adelaide and Gresham stopped eating.

"During your Miracle Tour. I saw Linden cure people of so many fatal ailments, and I guess I was smitten from the start."

Linden smiled as he lifted a spoonful of bisque to his lips.

Gresham and Adelaide exchanged an indecipherable look. "You were there?"

"Yes. With my mother. It was—is—one of my fondest memories."

Gresham took a determined sip of his soup. Adelaide's mouth opened and closed. Briar couldn't determine if his praise had been well received. He didn't understand how it could be interpreted badly.

Gresham dabbed at his mouth with his napkin. "Son, I really think we should speak about this—"

"No," Linden said coldly.

"But darling, this engagement, this affair, it's all been so sudden," Adelaide said.

"No more abrupt than your own engagement," Linden returned. "How soon was I born? Six months after your wedding?"

Adelaide's attention shot to Briar, then back to Linden, a look of mortification melting into appeasement. "Maybe your father's correct. We should discuss this alone."

It had struck Briar as odd that they continued to bring this up in front of him. From the sounds of it, Linden had never given them the opportunity to speak privately, forcing them to engage him with an audience in the hopes they wouldn't raise the topic at all.

"I already told you there's nothing to debate," Linden said. "Briar and I are in love. We're a good match. That should be enough for you."

Gresham slammed a hand on the table so hard the bit of bisque left in his bowl splashed. "Dammit, Linden, we hardly know this man! We don't know how he might—"

Linden's hand clenched into a fist, and Gresham stopped abruptly. A horror-struck look crossed his face, which purpled with unuttered frustration. His moustache bristled.

Briar's insides froze despite the heat of the meal.

Adelaide looked between them, a hand to her breast.

"Oh, stop! I wish you wouldn't."

"You both," Linden growled, "are the ones who insist upon calling my judgment into question at *every* opportunity. My relationships, my choice in career, the way I conduct myself with the public—you've never approved, and I don't expect you to start. Your opinion of Briar is noted but irrelevant. You can either learn to like him or continue to air your misguided sentiments, but do so safe in the knowledge that mine won't change."

Adelaide gave a shaky nod. Gresham choked, hardly breathing, but finally nodded, too. He inhaled sharply, the room silent enough they could all hear it.

"Good." Linden's hand unclenched to pick up his spoon again. "Ah, it's gone cold."

It ended that conversation. Briar was almost sorry for Linden's parents.

When dinner was finally over, and they all got up to go, Briar noticed the red fish was missing from the aquarium.

There was a bathroom down the hall from Linden's master suite. It was Briar's now. Linden had an en suite to himself.

Briar's bathroom was palatial. He considered soaking in the tub, but he couldn't figure out what the different knobs did, and given his curse, he decided not to risk drowning. He showered and tied one of the fluffy towels around his waist. In the mirror, his reflection was a shadow of himself. His ribs showed. The inky tithes covered so much more of him than before.

He touched the one on his chest, the one linked to Rowan's charm. He'd come knowing that, if something happened, it would alert him that

Rowan was in danger. But what if the distance prevented it? Or the wards around Coill Darragh, around this estate, blocked it?

A new toothbrush had been provided for him. The toothpaste came from a crystal pump. He'd accidentally used the one that distributed soap first.

"It's going to take some getting used to," he told Vatii.

She shuffled along the marble rim of the sink. "I don't know if I want us to get used to it."

"You were the one always telling me not to mess around with Rowan. That I needed to embrace my destiny, all that. Now you don't want to get used to it?"

Vatii bowed her head, chagrined. "I know. I've tried to guide you down the right path, but the more time we spend with Linden, the more I wonder if I've done right by you, or if I've given you bad advice." She hopped across the counter and nudged his hand with her beak. "I'm so sorry, Briar. I've failed you."

Briar's anger subsided as quickly as it came. "It's not your fault, Vatii . . . I'm an adult. I'm past the point where I can blame my mentors and teachers or whoever else for my decisions."

She hopped onto his wrist and sidled up his arm to nuzzle his cheek. "I'm still sorry."

He sighed. "Me too."

Too tired to carry on, he combed out his plait, washed his face, and brushed his teeth. He almost didn't notice the figure behind him, but movement in the mirror made him jump.

Adelaide looked just as she had at dinner, except her hair was loosed from its knot. She took a step into the bathroom, blocking the door.

She spoke so low, Linden wouldn't hear. "I've come to ask you something. I want you to be truthful in your answer."

Briar spat a mouthful of toothpaste foam into the sink. "Okay."

"Do you love him? Truly?"

Briar felt like no response was the right one. "I'm not after his money."

"That's not an answer." Her voice was a hiss to keep from raising it. "Countless men and women have thrown themselves at him for years, and none got far. What do you have to offer? You've sullied yourself with tainted magic, you've already brought the vultures to our door, and they don't forgive mistakes. Not of people like us. So what is it about you that's worth the risk?"

Every mark on Briar's body felt hot as an iron in coals. She wasn't entirely wrong. It wasn't Linden's money Briar wanted, but the power to save his life. Was that, in the end, any different? Probably not to her.

"I'm cursed," he said. It seemed to echo off the bathroom tiles. "I'm dying, and he can save me. There. Is that the answer you wanted?"

Adelaide's face went white.

"I'd love to love him, and I'm trying," he went on, "but he isn't easy to get to know, and you haven't made it easier."

She didn't seem to be listening. "You'll be the ruin of us."

Briar's emotions flared and sank like a ship tossed in a violent storm. He couldn't settle on one. He'd never failed so badly to do the right thing, or to make a good impression, or to be liked. These were things that had once come easily. Chief amongst those feelings was a deep sense of unfairness. He'd worked so hard, tried with everything he had to do the right thing, follow a path to success that was hard won on his own. She made it sound as though none of it counted, and it had all been to Linden's credit.

Briar knew the irony in saying it, but he said it anyway. "Is it really so hard to believe I could make him happy?"

She grabbed Briar's tithed arm. He recoiled, but she held it hard enough that he couldn't pull free, and her nails dug crescents into the skin. Vatii let out a squawk of reproach.

Adelaide spoke every word like a string of curses. "You are not so charming that his affection could be genuine. If I find which of these you used to ensnare him, I'll burn it off."

Stricken, Briar couldn't reply. Her grip tightened enough to bruise.

"Mother!" Linden's voice was a whip crack.

Adelaide released Briar with a look like a chastised child. "Linden, please—"

"You will have your private conversation," he said, "but you will not like it. Get out."

Without question, she obeyed.

Briar couldn't put everything together just yet, but—the manor, the meal, the way the Fairchilds spoke to one another—all of it seemed off, an illustrious feast of rotten food glamoured to appear fresh. Briar's fear, once focused on Adelaide, pivoted to Linden.

"I'm sorry about my parents. They have no respect for boundaries."

"It's all right," Briar said. He suppressed a shudder as Linden came forward. He recalled the sharp sting of knuckles and a ring impacting his cheek. He recalled the vitriol with which Linden spoke to his parents. He recalled Gresham gasping for air, and a fish vanishing from the aquarium.

Linden tilted his chin up to look into his face. Briar held firm.

"I should lend you some of the skin elixirs I have. The curse is affecting you quite badly."

Briar said, "My vanity would appreciate it."

A soft chuckle. "Come to bed when you're ready."

Briar sat in Linden's monstrous bed with his knees tucked up, running his fingers over the fine cotton of the new bed shirt he'd been given, trying to calm his racing heart. The sound of running water issued from the en suite as Linden showered.

The bedroom doors were open, giving Briar a view of the atrium down the hall. Their floor was on a level with the chandelier, which glittered at the edge of Briar's vision like a shadow that vanished once investigated. The sense of déjà vu he got from it was potent and inexplicable.

His stomach churned. It was not only the meal, or the alienating luxury of the manor, or that altercation in the bathroom. It was the silk on his skin. The open door to the bathroom, where Linden showered. The condom on the bedside cabinet.

That he wanted no part of this was a crushing pressure cracking his ribs.

Linden emerged, mercifully dressed and drying his hair. "I suppose I'll have to go speak with my parents about privacy. I'll return shortly. Perhaps, then, we can finally spend time together properly." He pressed a kiss to Briar's forehead. By a strong resolve, Briar didn't shiver at the touch or the oppressive fog of his aura.

Linden shut the doors. His footsteps receded like the ticking of a clock.

Briar swept the covers back and got out of bed. He pulled his tithe belt from his luggage and withdrew a feather—one of Vatii's. Atticus was with Linden, and his hearing would be acute. So, with difficulty, Briar cast a spell that allowed him to pass without sound or trace, so long as he was careful and nobody saw him. He didn't have a tithe powerful enough for invisibility, and it drained him terribly just to use the silencing one anyway.

Vatii whispered with pride, "I'm coming with you."

The oiled hinges on the doors made no noise as he opened them. Vatii crouched on his shoulder. He hadn't used the silencing spell on a bird before, and didn't know if it would quiet her wings. Given his fragile state and the risk it could go wrong, they didn't chance it.

Finding Linden would be difficult. Three stories and two wings, the east and west, to cover. From the exterior alone, Briar could tell that each had hidden depths—guest apartments, additions to accommodate growing art collections.

Linden had said the art galleries were in the east wing, so Briar guessed the residences wouldn't share the same space and headed down the west hall.

No lights or open doors hinted where Linden had gone. Briar's steps, silent instead of echoing cavernously, were eerie. These rooms could have anti-eavesdropping charms, so he might not hear voices to follow. The doors he tried were all locked regardless.

At the end of the hall, stairs led down to the floor below. He tried to mark the place in his mind so he could find his way back.

At the bottom, Briar saw the first sign of life. A sliver of yellow light cut through the gap in a door at the end of the hall, and from it issued voices. He crept closer. Headless, winged statues thronged the hall, and he kept to these as cover in case anyone came out the door. He recognized Linden's voice first, loud enough to be heard several meters away.

"What have I said before? I do hate it when you undermine me."

His parents' side of the conversation was muffled, too difficult to hear. Briar gave Vatii a look. She was small and could fly closer, but it was unlikely she could do so without alerting Atticus. She shook her head.

Briar snuck closer, hiding behind the second-to-last statue. He could see, through the gap in the door, Linden standing with his back to them, Atticus seated at his heels. Both Adelaide and Gresham, still in their dinner clothes, looked fretful as their son laid into them. Briar thanked his luck that the hall was dark, but if Atticus turned, his lamp-like eyes would cut through it. Listening instead of looking was best. Briar pressed against the wall and held his breath.

"We only want what's best for you, darling," said Adelaide.

"And that stunt with Briar?"

"What your mother means is she fears the threat he poses. To you, to this family."

Briar scowled. What threat could he possibly pose?

"I had that under control. It is your interrogations that have made him suspicious, so to my mind, it is *you* who poses the greater threat right now."

"Linden, if you would only consider," said Gresham, "the risks if your plan fails could be—"

"Careful."

"—catastrophic. For us, but for you especially."

"You doubt me? And why should that ever be a surprise? You've never had any faith."

"We have had boundless faith in you!" Adelaide demurred. "We were happy to support you in every way we could throughout the duration of your Miracle Tour. We gave tithes of ourselves quite happily to make that all happen for you, don't you remember?"

Gresham said, "If it was any other cursed boy—"

Briar strained so hard to hear, held his breath so tightly that the world went still.

"It cannot be any other. He's the only Coill Darraghn."

Gresham's voice shook. "A Coill Darraghn with a close relationship to the alderman, who can read auras, and who lives in *that* house—"

"Silence!"

The bark of Linden's voice echoed down the hall, reverberating in the cage of Briar's straining lungs. What did Briar's flat or his relationship with Rowan have to do with it?

These questions were clogged gears screaming into motion. The ticking clock finally arrived on all the answers. Icy with dread, Briar's arms raised in gooseflesh.

He peeked out to see Linden taking a step backward. It was time to go.

Linden said, "You wanted this life for me, you wanted the fame and fortune. Well, this is the cost. We must take risks, we must protect what we have, and this is the best way, the only way. You've seen the papers. It isn't only idle gossip and conspiracy theories any longer—very reasonable people are calling into question what really happened to our family all those years ago, and it's only a matter of time before someone comes forward with proof. Unless we rectify the situation and cover our tracks, as I've proposed."

"But if he discovers that you were behind it all—"

"Our marriage contract will prevent him telling anyone, provided he agrees to marry me, which you've very much jeopardized with your rotten meddling. I won't hear any more of it. Next you raise your voice against me in front of Briar, you will find you don't have a voice at all. I'll tithe an entire sea of fish so that I never have to hear you again. Do you understand me?"

Linden and Atticus still had their backs to the door, but Briar could see Adelaide's and Gresham's faces. Wan, petrified, pleading. Adelaide said, "Of course, of course, whatever you like, my darling. We're sorry."

And Briar saw them as if for the first time. Not as the overbearing parents who'd burdened their son with the weight of impossible expectations, but who had spoiled him so thoroughly that he'd learned he was their master. Had they actually sent Linden to Coill Darragh, or was that just a story, a twisted perspective? Had all their disapproval actually been fear for his safety? He didn't know.

All Briar knew for certain was that they looked at their son and were afraid.

By now, Briar was sure of things that made his stomach churn like he'd eaten something spoiled. He needed proof, and he thought he knew where to find it.

First, he had to ensure he didn't get caught.

Clutching Vatii to his chest so she wouldn't flap, Briar ran back down the hall, casting a backward look as he reached the end of it. Just in time to see a hand push the door open, light spilling out.

He couldn't climb the stairs—Linden would no doubt see his feet disappearing up the top of them. He turned a sharp left and went as fast as his legs could carry him. This hall stretched all the way back to the atrium. Any second now, Linden would emerge behind him, and there were no more statues to hide behind.

Heart in his throat, Briar pressed himself into the shallow alcove of a doorway and prayed.

Linden's footsteps rang on the marble, louder as he reached the spot where, if he or Atticus turned, they might see the sliver of a shape sticking out from a doorway. Under Briar's hands, Vatii's little heartbeat fluttered. He watched as Linden passed without looking to his left, making his way up the stairs. Atticus trotted at his heels, sweeping up the stairs.

Briar waited a few seconds, let out his breath, then hurried the rest of the way down the hall.

He came to the atrium on the second floor. Heading for the stairs, he heard footsteps again and, looking up, saw Linden emerge from the hall above. Briar was in clear view. Still hugging Vatii, he whirled and pressed himself behind the thick column of the banister.

Linden hadn't noticed him. His footsteps receded down the hall, but now Briar had a different issue altogether.

Linden was about to return to an empty bedroom.

Climbing the stairs, Briar peeked down the hall to see Linden quietly open the door and push through.

Briar ran, wondering what to do, wondering what to say when Linden inevitably questioned him about where he'd gone. From the bedroom, Linden called his name.

In a fit of mad inspiration, Briar dove left into his own bathroom, not bothering to flick on the light. He managed to shut the door without making a sound and, hurriedly, yanked the pull chain to flush the toilet. The sound of the swirling water seemed deafening. He busily washed his hands, spitting to dispel the silencing charm. He dried off, trying to get his panic under control, trying to convince himself there was no need to fear Linden.

Linden wouldn't harm him, he thought, but then he remembered the slap and Rowan saying, *You were ill and hurting, and he hurt you worse all because he was jealous.*

He opened the door.

Linden waited on the other side of it. "Ah. There you are."

"Er, yes, had to use the toilet." Briar pointed to it.

"You could have used the en suite."

Puffing up and doing his best to sound funny instead of out of breath, Briar retorted, "But this toilet's *mine.*"

After a suspicious pause in which Linden seemed to doubt his sincerity, he finally laughed.

"Glad to see you're making yourself at home, then."

But he held Briar's hand back to the bedroom.

Inside, Linden closed the doors, offering Briar a last glimpse of the chandelier winking at the end of the dark hall.

The recognition hit Briar threefold.

The last time he'd seen that chandelier was in the window of a portal, through which Gretchen's murderer fled.

Linden turned back to him. The look he gave Briar then made him feel like a rabbit in a snare. Satisfaction and seductive intent coiled lazily together in the hooded flick of his gaze. He set a hand on Briar's neck and leaned in to kiss him. Revulsion hit Briar so strongly his memory blanked. Next thing he knew, Linden had pulled away, a smirk playing across the lips Briar couldn't believe he'd kissed.

"It's so good to finally be alone with you without the usual barriers. Amulets. The public," Linden said.

Briar squeezed his eyes shut when another kiss came. He silently screamed into it. This man was a murderer. He could summon sweet words, but Briar could no longer pretend they weren't sickle-sharp lies. He knew the truth, and it made touching Linden abhorrent, unforgivable. At the same time, it felt dangerous to deny him. Suspicion already clouded their every interaction.

He couldn't alert Linden to what he knew.

He couldn't let those hands touch him, either. He'd be sick.

But then, he was already sick.

He feigned a stumble, eyes fluttering, then hit the floor.

Now Linden's hands were on him, but at least not sneaking under clothes. "Briar?" he said. How had Briar ever thought that voice could sound *kind*?

"The curse," Briar said. "I'm—sorry. I don't think I can do this until I'm feeling better."

"No, of course, how insensitive of me. I apologize. Ardor overcame me. We will have you feeling better soon. For now, you should rest."

He helped Briar into bed and kissed him goodnight.

Briar held his breath and hoped it would be the last touch he ever endured from Linden Fairchild.

It took a while for Linden to fall asleep. Revelations spun in Briar's head, and the curse ailed him with dogged conviction. He lay on his side with his back to Linden, a gulf of mattress between them.

He'd formulated a plan, and now he waited for the moment to execute it.

The issue was Atticus. Sneaking out of bed without disturbing a person, that was a feat, but not impossible. Without alerting a cat? He had to await the perfect moment, when Atticus was too deeply asleep to notice anyone casting spells.

Mostly, he depended on Vatii for this. She settled on the mattress within reach of Atticus's pluming tail. Every once in a while, she'd give the hairs a gentle pluck. If Atticus twitched his tail or swiveled an ear, she pretended to sleep again.

Finally, she whispered, "It's now or never."

Briar took the feather she gave him and cast the same silencing spell. Vatii went to his belt of tithes and pulled out a small bottle of fine white sand. Normally, he used it to enchant pajamas to make the wearer feel cozy and sleepy. This time it would ensure that, when he moved, neither Linden nor Atticus would wake.

Every incantation now felt next to impossible—dredging moisture out of desert air—but adrenaline helped. The pinch of sand in his palm vanished. Nothing seemed to occur, except Linden took a long, deep breath. A sleepy sigh.

Briar rolled to his feet. If the spells didn't hold, and he was caught now . . . well, he had a few lies prepared, but he doubted they would hold water.

It took some searching to find Linden's keys. The trousers he'd been wearing when he tucked them in his pocket were gone, collected by a servant. Briar looked through the walk-in closet, searching cubbies and drawers. Eventually, Vatii swooped to his shoulder and nipped his ear.

"The bedside cabinet," she said.

Sure enough, the drawer was slightly ajar. Sleep charm or no, Briar held his breath as he pulled it open, watching Linden for signs of waking. The ring of keys lay amongst a few pouches of tithes. Linden color coded them, and the blue one contained bone powder.

If Briar got caught, that was his escape route. He took out the jar that had contained his sand and scooped a measure of bone dust into it. Before he shut the drawer, he noticed something else. A familiar bracelet, the stone shining in the low light. Linden might notice if he tampered with it, but Briar could not allow him to return to Coill Darragh. Making a snap decision, he took the knife from his tithe belt and sawed through the bracelet, severing it. Then he gently shut the drawer, leaving it slightly ajar like before.

Keys clutched in his fist so they wouldn't jingle, Briar crept out of the room and to the shut door amongst all the open ones in the hall. He slipped the key into the lock. The *plunk* of the heavy metal sliding open mimicked the heavy beat in his chest.

The inside of Linden's study, dimly lit by moonlight, was just as he'd left it. Mahogany bookcases housed heavy tomes. The tidy space left fewer places to explore than the ransacked contents of Éibhear's office, but Briar's time was limited. He started with the desk drawers. In the first he found nothing but pens, parchment. He opened the next, and his stomach lurched.

A dozen siphons rolled around inside. Similar runes to the ones Briar had drawn were scrawled in the drawer, disguising their foul auras. Briar shut it.

The big cabinet at the bottom housed books with cracked spines and weathered pages. The titles all related to curses and the wild magic of places like Coill Darragh.

None of it was the thing he searched for. The thing he was now certain Linden possessed.

He found other alarming things. Sheaves of paper, notes cataloguing the effects the forest had on his talisman, and on a "Subject K." Subject K appeared in many of the notes, sometimes carrying out instructions at Linden's behest, sometimes as a test subject, until a note dated in January which marked him as deceased.

Beneath that, in Linden's curling script, it read: *Engagement or marriage conveys safety, but disruption of relationship possibly responsible for forest's attack.*

Subject K. Kenneth. It had to be.

On the wall, a photo of Linden and his beaming parents caught Briar's eye. In it, Linden looked no older than sixteen. Shining banners above his head read *Fairchild Miracle Tour*—it could have been taken at Port Haven, for all that the image sparked Briar's memory.

And on Linden's shoulder, faint after spells and probably a good deal of makeup, was a ragged scar that looked like it could have been made by a thorny vine.

He bore it no longer, but it had been there.

"He killed Gretchen, Vatii." A lump rose in Briar's throat. "God, he killed her, and he was *fifteen.*"

Vatii's feathers shivered. She was likely thinking the same thing, following the dark line of dominos to its inevitable conclusion.

Shoving aside despair, Briar thumbed through book spines on shelf after shelf. Something cold stirred inside him, like the shade of an aura. Not powerful, more of an echo, but he followed it until his fingers stopped on beaten leather. Blood pounding in his ears, he pulled the book out.

Éibhear's journal cracked apart in his hands, the spine broken from being opened time and again to a single page.

Red Carnella Curse Cure, it read. Below that, a recipe.

His hands trembled. There was blood on the pages, Éibhear's untidy scrawl partially obscured, but the recipe was complete, with careful instructions that seemed impossibly simple.

"Why would Linden hide this?" Vatii asked. "Why wouldn't he just use it?"

In answer, Briar pointed to a single word in the ingredient list. He could have sobbed, but there was more he needed to do. He couldn't stay here, he couldn't marry Linden, but if he tried to leave now, he wouldn't get far. He needed a plan, or he would end up like Gretchen.

Gretchen . . .

Briar ran a finger over the bloodstains on the journal. They could belong to Linden, but the faint echoes of aura attached felt . . . different.

He dug charcoal from his tithe belt.

Vatii made a warbling noise. "Be careful."

Briar lifted a rug off the floor and drew. He could cover it after. He worked as quickly as he could until the summoning circle was complete. He set the journal in the center, its bloody pages open. Pressing his palms into the floor, he concentrated his magic into the circle, drawing on the spirit attached to that blood. He shut his eyes and pleaded in a desperate whisper that it was a tether strong enough to draw a ghost back, that a full exorcism had not been possible when so much evidence of her foul end remained.

Light flickered. Not from the lamps, but from the center of the circle. A lavender flick of smoke. A haze that condensed into the shape of a girl.

Gretchen's ghost opened her eyes.

CHAPTER 28

Backstage at the Pentawynn Gala Runway was a mill of models, makeup artists, choreographers, and designers. It reminded Briar of Gretchen's exorcism in his flat, a typhoon of frenetic movement and swirling fabric. He waited in the wings, wringing his hands.

Their line would walk the long, lit strip beyond, and it should have been a moment for celebration, but every inch of Briar trembled with sick nerves.

His plan had come together in the wan hours of dawn light while Linden slept.

Vatii's talons gave his shoulders a squeeze. "You can do this," she whispered.

Still, it wouldn't do to lose what little breakfast he'd eaten.

Briar prepped the model wearing his dress from the press release. It had to be adjusted to fit. He resented letting anyone else wear it, but it had been his greatest creation yet, and he'd be damned if he didn't make good on Finola's bargain that he bring something of his own to the runway.

Finola appeared, wearing her braids piled in a colorful scarf on her head, the long sleeves of her robes trailing like wings. She spoke, to his surprise, with Linden's parents. There were stilted laughs and polite, overly wide smiles. She caught Briar's eye, said her farewells, then whisked over to him.

"Nervous?" She gave his shoulder a pat. "You look a bit pale. Can I get you a glass of water?"

"No, no, I'll be fine. Is it strange to just want to get it over with?"

In a conspiratorial whisper, "You seemed to love the cameras before. What's so different now?"

"I've waited for this day my whole life." It was half the truth.

"And your nerves have nothing to do with Linden?"

She'd been so reticent to let the Fairchilds near her show. Briar said, "Are you on better terms now?"

"You know, at first, I thought it was rich. *Now* they want to talk to me. Now that I'm *somebody*. But after speaking to them today . . ." She tapped a finger against her elbow. "They said they'd missed me, and they sounded genuine. Makes a girl wonder, you know?"

Once, Briar might have considered the implication ridiculous. Linden was their son, their junior. How could he possibly have that kind of influence?

Now, he knew Linden better.

"Shit, speak of the devil," she said. "Oh well, it's time to start. Knock 'em dead, yeah?"

Finola left at Linden's approach. His garments were forest green with gold embellishments like scales. His hair had been drawn up into an elegant knot, a decorative pin dangling jeweled drops from it. He appraised the models, each wearing something Briar's fingers had bled to create. It raised all the hairs on the back of Briar's neck to feel him stand so near, their arms touching from shoulder to elbow.

"It is a fine thing we've created," he said.

"How much longer until it starts?"

"Ah, these things always run over. It feeds the anticipation of the crowd. You need not be nervous."

Briar held his arms tightly around himself and, with a hand, felt along the edge of the journal hidden within an interior pocket of his vest, magically masked from sight. Not that it needed much. The curse rendered him thin enough that it probably wouldn't show anyway.

"I have something that might take your mind from it," Linden said. "I thought to surprise you, but . . ."

Briar knew what he would pull from his pocket. It was a velvet box, which he flipped open to show the ring inside. An enormous, glittering thing, a band of tiny diamonds set with one huge gem and a waft of magic—the enchanted contract that would prevent Briar from ever speaking a word against Linden to anyone. It did nothing to stifle Briar's terror.

He pretended to be awestruck. Linden tucked it back into his jacket before anyone else could see. With a smug laugh, he said, "Our work will be the star of the show, but you will be the envy of everyone."

Outside, the crowd hushed, spotlights spun, and Finola's voice rang out, magically projected to the audience of fellow designers and celebrities. She introduced herself, the show, talked about how excited she was to present the stunning, innovative work of many new and untried designers.

Then she called their names.

Linden took Briar's hand, and they walked out together. Briar plastered on a smile, though his jaw felt like rusted iron. He squeezed Linden's hand hard. The lights shone so brightly that many faces were mere shadows, for which he was grateful. After the applause died down, Linden told the story of their meeting, their project, how their work together brought them closer.

Briar spoke his rehearsed lines verbatim. *So lucky to be here.* And the one line that mattered most to him, "This is for my mother, without whom I'd have never made it this far. I wish she was here."

It was the only moment where the painful, stilted speech made his voice bubble with real tears. He hoped she would be proud of what he was about to do. He hoped, if her spirit watched, that she did not feel responsible for what he'd landed himself in. If his resolve to do it alone, to prove himself, had been for her, he understood now that she would never have wanted that loneliness for him. She'd tell him it was okay to need people.

They retreated backstage, and the models strutted out in an even stream, garments billowing, springtime cherry blossom charms dancing around them. From backstage, Briar saw appreciative nods, some murmurs of approval, but he could also see Finola. She watched the outfits with a pursed mouth, recognizing Linden's trademark influence, which had consumed Briar's vision. Until the second-to-last garment.

Linden hadn't allowed Briar's to take the runway as the show-stopping finale. He'd insisted it be the penultimate. Still, Briar felt a small glow of pride as the model glided across the stage with a train of flowers sweeping behind him. The dress Briar had made and worn himself, not long past. Finola's stern expression melted into one of nodding approval, her eyes following the outfit to the runway's end and back again.

Briar saw the last two models return as if watching the blade of a guillotine slide toward him.

Linden took his hand again. They walked out to applause and the standing ovation of some. He and Linden bowed deeply, twice. Blood rushed to Briar's head, made his vision swim. To the tune of many hands clapping, Linden pulled the ring smoothly from his pocket and got down on one knee. The noise of the crowd was a crescendo of applause and cameras clicking. Briar ceased breathing, steeled himself. Vatii gave his cheek an encouraging touch of her cool beak.

Linden said, "Briar Wyngrave." A hush fell over the crowd. "You have fulfilled my life in ways I can never hope to articulate. These past months with you have been a dream, and I ask you now to ensure I never wake from it. Would you do me the honor of marrying me and being my husband?"

In the long hours of the night in which Briar had not slept, he had wrestled with two truths.

The first was that he could not fight Linden on his own. He knew what would become of him if he confronted Linden at the manor. He would disappear; nothing but a sad casualty of his curse. Linden would post mournful stories to Alakagram, beautifully shot photographs of funeral lilies. No one would know what had really become of Briar, and no one—save for a lonely, love-struck Coill Darraghn—would care.

The second truth was that he didn't have to do it all alone. Any of it. His job, his success, some things were more powerful when shared.

If he wanted to fight Linden, he had to do it with millions of eyes watching.

The gasps and clapping subsided the longer Briar stood unresponsive. Murmurs began to spread.

Briar looked down at Linden and the ring. He didn't melt into his arms or hold his hands to his face in blissful surprise. He waited until the crowd's enthusiasm for a live proposal went out like the tide before a big wave. Until it was quiet enough they could clearly hear him say,

"No."

Linden's blinding smile hardly changed. It froze there. "Excuse me?"

"I can't marry you."

"Briar, this is hardly the time for jokes."

"I'm not joking." Briar took a step back as Linden reached for his hand. "I cannot marry a man like you."

Linden's beatific features locked in a rigor of shock and, briefly, anger, but he smoothed this, turning to the audience, to the cameras. "I'm so sorry. He's confused. He's been ill."

"Yes. I've been ill with a curse. A curse you might as well have cast on me."

Linden said quickly, "That is preposterous. Briar, really. We both know the source of the curse is an accident of unpredictable, wild magic. I'm wounded that you could say such a thing."

Linden was turned toward the audience, speaking as much to them as to him. Briar did not waver from staring directly into Linden's face as he began to explain, as much for Linden's benefit as the people watching, just how well he understood.

"Ten years ago, an invasion of witches came to Coill Darragh to pilfer its woods of the powerful magic and rare tithes found there."

"Oh, you can't be serious."

"The forest retaliated. To survive, it took energy from the townsfolk. The alderman at the time sacrificed his life to build wards that would keep the invaders out. It killed the invaders. Most of them."

"You're sick, Briar. Delusional. We should get you to a hospital immediately."

Briar clenched his hands into fists and willed himself to go on. The audience of high society watched, riveted but skeptical.

"You escaped," Briar said. "You left the witches to die by the wards. Those witches were your own family. You claimed they died of a mysterious plague. Aunts and uncles. Cousins. The Fairchilds didn't die of an ailment, they were killed paying for your avarice. Avarice you paraded around proudly! You never had a talent for healing. You used the powerful siphons collected from Coill Darragh to go on a miracle tour, curing people of their sickness and earning yourself a tidy fame and fortune, while the siphons caused curses to strike anyone unlucky enough to witness your so-called miracles. My *mother* included."

Linden's face paled, but he maintained a smile. An ugly, bared-teeth smile that failed to convey any of his usual charms. "How could you say this of me? I cured the sick and the dying. I've been trying to do the same for you."

Briar said, "No, you've used me as a token example of your charity. A poor, dying nobody you lifted up. You want to marry me so that taking what's left of Coill Darragh will be no challenge to you, so you can cover up your misdeeds, so you can claim to cure the very people you cursed. You've been studying the forest, trying to harvest its power without incurring its wrath. You even hired a helper, a man called Kenneth, to carry out your research. I wonder what you promised him, but I know what he got.

He became a convenient scapegoat for all the terrible things that arose as a result of your research. All so you can harness more power and bury your past. And if your actions pass on more curses, what's that to you? On and on, in an endless cycle. And for what? Your reputation?"

Linden stood. He'd been kneeling the whole time, as if expecting Briar to name this all a joke. The expression of heartbroken misery he wore chilled Briar. "I can't believe that you, of all people, would believe me capable of all that."

"It's the truth."

"Where's the proof? When this took place, I would have been—what? Fifteen?"

This rippled through the audience in whispers of disbelief and dissent. Fifteen was young to tithe half a forest, to kill most of your family, to use dangerous magic in pursuit of fame. Who was Briar to level these accusations? He had no reputation or accolades to lend his word credit.

"I do have proof," Briar said.

He opened his vest and showed Linden the journal. Old, creased, and dappled with blood.

"This is the other reason you came to Coill Darragh. You heard about a panacea, something powerful enough to compete with your family's recipes. You stole the formula from the alderman, Éibhear O'Shea. There was a single witness. A girl named Gretchen, who you threw from a rooftop in order to cover your crime."

Linden scowled. "That is hardly proof."

"The journal isn't my proof."

From the journal, from the spots of blood, her apparition rose.

Violet and smoky, seeping from the pages with spectral drama, Gretchen materialized. Non-magical people might not see her, but they would feel the room go frigid, and there were enough witches to behold Gretchen's testimony.

"Linden Fairchild," she said. "You killed me."

Now, Linden truly looked ashen. He stepped back, a livid aura enveloping him. The crowds' noise changed in quality again. More raucous, outraged. Here stood a ghost, a girl who looked no older than Briar or Linden themselves, to confirm Briar's words.

"Linden killed me," Gretchen said, "and tried to exorcise me so I wouldn't tell anyone. I can attest that everything Briar told you is true. I lived with him in Coill Darragh for the better part of this year. I was not an easy companion, yet he befriended me and did his best to help me. He freed me from the prison of the house I haunted, helped me reclaim my lost memories, and now he's given me the opportunity to tell my murderer who I am. Who he killed."

She rounded on Linden. "I was twenty-five. I was young and idealistic. I wanted nothing more than to make potions and medicine and help people. I gave up every minute of my time in pursuit of that, and you ended my life and took everything Éibhear and I worked for! You robbed me of my future. You've robbed Briar of his mother, and now of his future, too. You robbed the planet of life-saving medicine and tithes. You're a liar, a thief, a murderer, and I hope you *rot* for what you've done."

Linden's eyes darted to the faces of their audience. Some wore frowns of disapproval, others slack-jawed shock. Briar knew, coming into this, that his chances were small, but he'd also known what Linden feared most. The ever-turning tide of public opinion. Humiliation.

And lucky for Briar, he himself was immune to embarrassment.

Linden, cornered like an animal and watching all that he'd fought for slipping away, turned to desperate action. Briar saw the motion too late. Linden reached into a pocket and pulled out something dark and shining.

A siphon.

Briar thought, *No.* Would Linden freeze this moment in time, reverse it, wipe the memories of the audience? Everything had been televised. Could he control Briar, force him to discount everything he'd said?

Linden clasped the siphon in his hand. At the same time, Gretchen launched herself at him. Never had she been capable of affecting another living being. Throwing knives had been an exhausting use of her energy. Yet her fist connected with his jaw and sent him sprawling. She landed on his chest, drawing back for a second attack.

She said to Briar, "Go! Get out of here!"

At the same time, the siphon in Linden's grasp shattered into dust. The malodorous aura contained within spread, the magic seeping through the air like a toxic cloud.

Briar grasped the tiny vial of bone powder pilfered from Linden's stores, uncapped it. In a second, he could be through the portal with the journal and drag Gretchen back home.

But the siphon acted faster. Gretchen had a second to realize what was happening as her apparition flickered. There came a noise like water sucked down a drain, only it was a roar.

She turned in time to look at Briar and smile. It looked as though she mouthed the words "thank you." Then her specter melted, ink diluted in rain, and she was gone.

The magic of the siphon, like a thick blanket over the entire room, receded back to the spot where Gretchen had been.

Linden wrestled to his feet. He moved like a bull, like he never had in public before.

The bone powder felt thin and measly between Briar's fingers as he flung it in the air and thought, *Take me home.*

CHAPTER 29

B riar knew something was wrong the moment he stepped through the portal.

He'd come believing the wards could protect him since he'd broken Linden's bracelet. Those wards should have also prevented him from portaling directly into Coill Darragh. He should have emerged on the border.

Instead, he stepped into Rowan's living room.

With creeping dread, Briar called out for Rowan, but no reply came. Slowly, the tithe on his chest began to burn.

"No, no, no."

His vision swam at the edges. Vatii, recognizing the signs, fluttered her wings to fan his face while he drank his potion. Standing up to Linden, escaping here, that was as far as his plan extended. He'd hoped to have a few hours to prepare for whatever counterattack Linden launched. He'd hoped Gretchen would be by his side, but she was gone.

He stumbled out of Rowan's house to a sky of crumbling wards, their light pocked through with giant holes, held together by gossamer threads. A collapsing web instead of a shell.

"How?" said Vatii. "Éibhear sacrificed his life for those wards."

"The forest. If the forest maintains the wards, and Linden's been destroying it . . . maybe the power of the sacrifice is running out."

Which meant it would need another.

The tithe on Briar's chest ached. He had to find Rowan.

He went down the garden path, pulled by the tithe. Ahead, he saw a figure close to the forest, too hunched and small to be Rowan.

Niamh ambled, hands behind her back, in no particular rush. The sight of her made Briar flush with anger. He had a bone to pick with her, but of course she would choose now to appear, when he didn't have the time to rail against her stupid, deceptive, confusing prophecies.

"You're just in time," she said, once they were within earshot.

He moved past her. "I don't have time, actually."

"Of that, we're both aware." She kept in step with him.

"Everything's a mess. And it's my fault. And a bit yours! Linden's a megalomaniac, *not* the man of my dreams like you said. He's probably on his way here to kill me. I'm dying anyway. Rowan's in danger *again*."

"I know. I sent him into the woods."

"You *what*?" Briar's anger stopped him dead. What was he going to do? Punch a ninety-year-old woman? He turned and kept marching. "You're—you unbelievable, selfish, miserable—Why would you do that? Are you trying to get us killed, or are you just senile? You sent him in there? *Deliberately*?"

"I sent him in with a message from his father. Which, I suspect, was a message from the forest. Or maybe they're the same thing. Anyway, I don't decide how Fate chooses to use me as its voice."

That made for a convenient excuse. "Great. Perfect. Any more confusing pearls of wisdom before I go in after him?"

"No, no wisdom."

"Then wha—Agh!" His ankle gave under him. He nearly rolled it, going down on his hands, grass stains on his knees. The curse sent spidering fingers of pain through his head like an oncoming migraine.

Niamh knelt in front of him with a humbling amount of grace for her age. She held a piece of charcoal.

"Fortitude," she said, and drew a symbol on her arm. She clasped Briar's hand, and the sharp pains turning his vision white shrank away. Strength returned to his aching limbs. It felt like drawing breath after months of drowning, like taking off heels after wearing them for a year. He'd been tired for so long.

He was still so angry with her, but as he rose to his feet without feeling it in every joint, he said, "Thanks."

She handed him the stub of her charcoal. The forest loomed, a different beast than before, mangey, rabid, and desperate. Briar feared it, but he feared losing Rowan more.

"Are you coming?" he said to Niamh.

"No. This is your fate."

"Fine." He marched toward it, Vatii swooping from his shoulder.

"I do have one piece of advice for you, if you'll have it of me," Niamh said to his back.

He looked over his shoulder. "Yeah, all right. What have I got to lose?"

"Everything," she said. "But Rowan, he thinks he's already lost it. He thinks he's alone. My advice is, don't let him believe it."

Briar didn't understand her. Not her motives, not her prophecies. If he survived this, he would ask her. This piece of advice, though, this he understood.

He dove in. Navigating the forest never felt the same. In its current state, desiccated trees crumbling like columns of ash, it didn't seem like a deep source of magical power. Farther in, he saw signs of desperate life. Foliage sprouted. Trees groaned as they grew. Brambles shot up under Briar's feet, making him skip away. Nothing was green, not even the fresh sprouts. Everything was gray and sickly.

Magic pushed and pulled, killing the wood and trying to save it, and Briar felt something new—sympathy. Kinship. The quiet indignity of justifying one's continued survival.

Linden's siphons had taken too much, pushing the forest to desperate action. It drew on the townsfolk, on the power of Éibhear's sacrifice, and now on Rowan.

The tithe drew him onward. He went as quickly as he dared but still had time to think. A dangerous thing. His thoughts felt a lot like the forest—wounded, tangled, grasping, lost. They circled back to that painful moment on the pier when Rowan bared his soul and Briar burned it to ash. Regret was a sour bile in his throat. He didn't know if Rowan could forgive him, but he wouldn't forgive himself if Rowan lost his life to this.

He pushed onward, forging a path through brambles.

He knew where the tithe would lead him. Deep in his bones, he felt the influence of the tree. It called through the gloom and the tithe on his arm. Something didn't feel right. Did it ever in this place? He started to run, panic rising.

He realized what was wrong. The bell. Its muffled jingle reached him as though he had gauze in his ears. Too quiet.

He burst into a clearing. Everything living had withered to ash, a crop circle of soot enclosing the tree. It stood alone, and at its roots, something gold and ringing caught the light.

Briar lurched toward it, feet kicking up dust as he crossed the infinite distance. He knew what it was, but his mind recoiled. Vatii got there first, landing next to the thing and nudging it free of blackened leaves and dirt. By no fault of the curse, Briar fell to his knees.

The bell and the iridescent magpie feather were tarnished with soot, the leather twine snapped in two, rent from Rowan's neck.

An ugly noise, trapped in Briar's throat, struggled free. He started to dig. His fingers made furrows through the ash until they reached soil, which squelched sickeningly in his palms. His hands came away streaked with muddy red. With another stifled sob, he stopped. Did the blood belong to the forest or Rowan?

"He can't be gone, Vatii." But saying it out loud made it feel real, and the tears came in earnest, watering the greedy forest that had stolen the brightest part of Briar's vanishingly short, sad future.

His sobs became a scream. A railing, throat-shredding keen.

Vatii flew to his knees, walking up his arm to push her head against his wet cheek.

He thought that the croaking croon in his ear was her consoling him. But it was too loud, too wooden. He looked up to see the tree moving. Not uprooted and falling, not swaying and creaking in the wind. Its bark peeled back, the long scar in its trunk opening like sutures ripped apart. Strings of its meaty interior, held together by threads, snapped. From within, something stirred. A creep of moss, the flash of bone.

It emerged in stages. A leg. A gnarled arm. Vatii shrieked, and Briar backpedaled away.

The thing rose near twenty feet tall, vaguely human in shape. A skull, suspended from a vine where a man's head would be, sprouted broad antlers thick with moss. Sticks and bark replaced eroded bone. Roots arced in a cage like ribs around the heart of the thing, which was a scrap of torso, covered in a sigil of tithes Briar recognized.

In a reedy voice like the high wind whistling through leaves and the low creak of wood, the thing said, "You. You weep for my son."

Briar swiped tears from his cheeks, leaving streaks of dirt. His own voice was raw yet vicious. "What have you done with Rowan?"

Éibhear, or what remained of him, took a long, hollow breath. As he did, some of the bone in one leg crumbled and reformed into wood.

"My influence wanes," he said. "You must come now, if you wish to save him."

A flicker of hope stymied all the hateful things Briar was about to say. "He's alive?"

Already, Éibhear moved. He took one long stride and passed Briar, heading for the trees. There wasn't time to consider whether this was a trick or a trap, and Briar would risk it regardless. He followed, hastily picking his way over tree roots back into the forest. The dryadic thing moved easily, the trees bending to permit him. Briar didn't see them move to make way, the path simply was.

Countless questions burned on his tongue. "Are you Éibhear?"

"*I* am. *We* are not."

"That makes no sense."

"Éibhear is one of us, but he is himself, too. A tree, but never wholly of the forest."

"Then why did you—he—ask Rowan to come here, knowing the forest would kill him?"

"*I* didn't. *We* did. I'll tell you the story. You'll need to know."

Leaves and dead things crunched underfoot. Briar had to jog to keep up. Short of breath, he pressed on. Niamh's tithe had helped, but fatigue bayed at his back like a pack of hounds.

The thing that was and was not Éibhear spoke. "In every leaf, in every twig, in every branch, in every tree, there is magic. But in the forest, there is power beyond your reckoning. Connected by root and vine, *we* existed long before there were witches and tithes.

"The first witches knew this. Feared and respected us. They took tithes, and when they died, conveyed their bodies unto the loam for us to feast. Now, you bury your dead in concrete and coffins, tombs and sarcophagi. Witches take their tithes and give nothing back. We grow hungry, but not in Coill Darragh, where our Keeper kept the old ways and the people have roots. Éibhear."

Upon uttering the name, a hiss of breath issued forth in a rattling sigh.

"I was to train my son in the old ways." The switch to a singular pronoun made Briar shudder. He'd spoken to ghosts before, but this was different. Not wholly the spirit of the man whose name it bore. "Witches came to tithe what didn't belong to them. We fought back, but they had protection and numbers, so I did the only thing I could to protect my people and the forest. I offered myself as a willing sacrifice and cursed my son to take my place if the wards were to fail and the forest was invaded again."

"It wasn't your life to give!" Briar's fury flared. Not for the forest, which seemed a mindless collective will of survival, but for Rowan's father. "He loved you, and you marked him for slaughter."

A twitch of wood and bone. "*You* exist in minutes, hours, years, and decades. We are centuries, millennia. We have learned what it is to survive that long."

"At the price of his life."

"One life for many. It is an acceptable exchange."

"And my mother? Me? Every person cursed by the siphons made from your magic?"

"Casualties of greed, from which we slowly sustained ourselves after the damage suffered in the siphons' making. Éibhear's sacrifice was enough to create the wards, but not to heal. That is what those witches failed to comprehend. They thought what they stole came free, but in the short term or the long, a price will be paid."

"It doesn't make sense. You've attacked countless people. Surely what they've given you is enough. How did Éibhear's sacrifice sustain the wards for a decade, but the rest isn't enough to heal?"

"Because," said the woods, "there is more power in a gift than something stolen. His sacrifice was worth more than any tithe, any exchange. It is more than the commerce you call magic."

"And now?" Briar gestured at the forest, which grew and withered. At the sky, where the wards were evanescent.

"Now, we are under attack again. We use what remains of Éibhear to sustain both ourself and the wards, but it is not enough. Another sacrifice must be made."

Briar's voice broke. "But he didn't agree to this! Rowan isn't like Éibhear, he isn't giving himself to you, not willingly. You said that's not as powerful."

"This is true, but he is a Keeper. There is magic in his blood, in the fulfillment of responsibility, in a promise kept, even if that promise was not made by him."

Upon saying this, it stopped and swept aside a bush, revealing a low hill on the other side, a tree atop it. Bound to the tree was Rowan.

Briar sprinted up the hill, relief chased away by worry. Rowan was unconscious, eyes closed, head drooping. Roots entombed his feet, and vines held his arms outspread so he hung like an insect caught in a web. Thorny branches had once again shredded his shirt, and upon his chest a snaking tendril of thorns cut into his skin, drawing the beginnings of a sigil. Briar seized it and tore it away, but more snaked up his calves and pulled his legs out from under him. He hit the ground, wind knocked from his lungs, and scrambled to pull the knife from his tithe belt before remembering he hadn't worn it. He'd taken only the bare minimum to the runway.

Desperate, he turned to Éibhear's construct. "Stop! Didn't you bring me here to rescue him?"

"*I* did. *We* didn't. My influence is limited."

Briar tore at a vine and kicked the remains from his ankles. He got to his feet and held Rowan by the face, begging him to wake. More vines seized him.

"You have to do *something*," he pleaded. "He's your son!"

"That's why I brought you."

Still fighting. "But I can't *do* this alone! Rowan can't either. He deserves to know you tried."

The construct shook. "I . . . I—"

"You cursed him with this fate! You can undo it. You're the only one who can."

Éibhear's grinning skull took in the spectacle of his son's prone body and the plaintive words of the dying witch, and it froze. It looked inanimate, a motionless tree like any other. Then the skull blackened and crumbled. It raised a hand of branch-like claws. It slashed.

Briar thought it would strike him down. But the air whistled at either side of his head, and the vines holding Rowan came apart, wind shrieking through the trees like a wail. The last scrap of Éibhear, the tithed skin by which Briar had identified him at all, burned up in the last efforts of his will. The rest, sticks and claws and bark, all crumbled like a skeleton no longer wired together.

The last twinkles of purple winked out of the sky, the wards gone with their maker.

On the wind, a voice said, "Tell Rowan I . . ." The rest faded.

The buzzing, malignant energy of Rowan's scar slowly, slowly dwindled. But did not vanish entirely.

The creeping ivy of the forest gave a sudden surge of motion. It wound up as far as Rowan's waist in defiance of Éibhear's last efforts. Briar yanked them away, but it was not like the time before. The forest, ferally desperate, wouldn't release him. Éibhear might have promised his son to them, but his withdrawal of that vow was not enough, for in the moments before death, he had been as much the forest as the forest was him. Both would have to surrender Rowan.

Briar despaired. He could use a flesh tithe to wake Rowan, but his arms and legs were both encased in vines. Rowan would only be able to struggle, and he would be conscious while the forest consumed him.

Briar thought about what Eibhear had told him, and wished the only option open to him wasn't so dire. But he had so little life left. What better way to use it?

With Niamh's charcoal in hand, he undid the buttons of his shirt to draw on himself.

"No, Briar!" Vatii cawed. She snapped at the charcoal in his fist.

"What good are we dead in a few months' time?"

She clawed the charcoal away before he finished the circle on his chest. He swore, leaning down to look for it in the grasping mulch. He couldn't find it, but the vines and thorns had cut him enough times. He used the blood in place of charcoal.

Ours . . . whispered the forest.

"I will be." He finished drawing and grasped the vines around Rowan. "Release him and take me instead."

The vines ceased to grow. The forest went still, considering his offer. The wind caressed his bare skin, a susurration through the leaves like a chorus of voices.

Without warning, several roots around Rowan drew back and lashed around Briar with flagellating speed. A howl of pain escaped him, cut short when he impacted against Rowan's chest. The limbs of the forest bound them together with crushing force. Briar struggled to draw a full breath.

No, he thought, pain stealing his voice. *This wasn't the deal.*

Too weak. No time left. Cursed. Ours anyway. An unfair trade. The forest's answer chilled him through. *We will have both.*

He struggled. Vatii flapped and clawed at the vines, to no effect. Choking and ensnared, the last guttering candle of hope in Briar's heart went dark. Rowan's forehead lolled against his shoulder, but he didn't wake no matter how many times Briar screamed his name. Locked in this last embrace, the unfairness of it all struck him.

Rowan had given Briar so many things. Simple gifts of fresh-baked pastry, help with tithes and spells. He'd invited Briar into his life, shared his family, his meals, his home. He'd opened his heart. If there was magic in gifts, as the forest claimed, then Rowan had been an incantation all his own. It seemed the most brutal of injustices that Briar couldn't give anything back. There wasn't a spell he knew to break the forest's curse, he couldn't even give his life—it was of that little value.

He hadn't even gotten the chance to tell Rowan . . .

"Vatii!"

"I'm trying, Briar, there's too many—"

"Never mind the vines. Come here. I need you to draw a rune on me. Use your beak. I can't use my hands."

"What? What rune?" She fluttered to his shoulder, dodging ivy. Briar described what he needed. "But what will waking Rowan do?" she protested.

"Trust me, please."

She had to smear her beak with his blood and avoid the grasping fingers of the forest, but she managed to draw a mark on his neck of a closed eye half opening. Briar let the magic flow through him. The energy Niamh had bestowed on him went out like the tide, stealing his vitality with it. If not for the vines, he couldn't have held himself upright. Rowan barely stirred, and for a moment Briar feared it hadn't been enough, or that Vatii's messy writing had skewed the spell. Then Rowan moved. Bound so tightly together, Briar felt Rowan's heartbeat speed. His eyelashes fluttered against Briar's shoulder.

Then he snapped awake, and a look of horrified betrayal overtook his face. "Briar?"

"I need you to listen to me."

Angry panic tinged Rowan's voice. "Briar, what are you *doing* here?"

"I came to tell you something."

Rowan began struggling, trying to rend free of the vines. He did a better job of it than Briar, loosening them enough that Briar could get his arms up and hold Rowan's face in his hands.

"Listen to me!"

Rowan ceased struggling.

"This is important. Remember what I said to you? On the pier?"

Rowan flinched, his eyes shutting. "Briar—"

"I lied!" With every ounce of suppressed feeling, he said, "It's you I love, Rowan. It always was."

Until he said it, Briar wasn't sure it would work. Was it really a secret at all? It felt so obvious.

But for Rowan, who was hearing it for the first time, and who up until then had believed the lie, it was the most powerful secret ever told.

The vines slackened and fell away in looping coils around their feet. The forest blurred and spun around them. It snarled, a wheezing cough of impotent rage. Briar felt a wave like dizzy vertigo as the wood that had sought to lock them away was prized open, and the magic of the spell spat them out.

No! screeched the forest. *Ours! Promised!*

Briar and Rowan were freed of its grasp, magic transporting them.

They landed in a heap on the grass just bordering the woods. Briar rose to his knees. The aches and pains Niamh had temporarily relieved returned, but he hardly cared because Rowan was alive, whole, and looking at him with barely restrained hope.

"I love you," Briar said again. "I'm so sorry for everything I said. I know I hurt you. I was trying to save us both, and I thought Linden had the cure, but he was a liar and a cheat just like you thought, a *murderer*. And he killed Gretchen and might as well have done in my mum and your da, and I don't know if you can ever forgive me, but I will do anything to make it right. If I have to spend every day I have left making it ri—"

By then Rowan had risen, crossed the space between them, drawn Briar into his arms, and kissed him into silence.

Shock froze Briar only temporarily. Then he was grasping Rowan's shoulders, climbing into his arms. And kissing back. Furiously, desperately kissing back. Relief washed over him. Rowan clutched him close, breathing raggedly between their parted lips. His aura was as soothing as stepping into a warm bath. Briar ached, his body barely held together by hope and dogged willpower, but he felt safe in Rowan's arms.

"Just like that?" There was barely any space between them for Briar to speak. "You can forgive me just like that? I thought you'd be angry."

"I'm feckin' fuming." One of Rowan's big hands carded through Briar's hair, and his brown eyes were anything but furious. "I'll give out to you something fierce later."

He tilted, fitting his mouth over Briar's, and nothing was perfectly fixed, there was still so much they had to do, but for a second Briar could let his muscles go lax and slump into arms that held him steadfast. Briar might have marveled at Rowan's willingness to forgive if there was anything surprising about it, but Rowan was not like the trees whose shadow he'd lived in. He was the sort you could sit under when you needed rest, the sort to shade you from the sun, to bear fruit when you were hungry.

Briar had rejected his help for fear of the day none was forthcoming. He thought he'd needed to achieve everything on his own to make his mother proud, but she'd never have wanted him to feel ashamed of asking for help when he needed it, like he was too burdensome.

She'd have wanted this: a man who saw his heavy heart, his scars, his dreams, his mistakes and could carry it all. Strong and brave enough to make all that baggage lighter.

Reluctantly, Rowan pulled back. A look of confusion crossed his features.

"What did you mean, Linden might as well have done in your mum and my da?"

A thunderous crack of splintering timber and the toppling of a tree sent them skipping back. The forest groaned in lament.

Briar took Rowan's hand. "I'll explain on the way."

CHAPTER 30

They walked, navigating cowpats, as Briar told Rowan what he'd learned in Pentawynn.

Rowan listened with a darkening scowl. If he had disliked Linden before, he loathed him now. When Briar finished, he remained silent, eyes stormy.

"You can say I told you so. You knew Linden was no good. I should have listened."

Rowan shook his head. "I thought he was a pompous toad, I thought he was taking advantage of you, but I never thought he'd done—all I'll say is he best not show his face here again."

Briar didn't think it was the last they'd seen of Linden, though.

It had only been twenty-four hours since Briar left Coill Darragh. Many of the townsfolk were still sheltered from the forest's wrath in the church. Rowan and Briar burst inside, interrupting the pastor mid-sermon. Rowan didn't need to raise his voice; his baritone carried to the high ceiling.

"I'm sorry, Father, but we've an emergency."

From the pews, Maebh and Sorcha stood. No doubt they'd come to pray for Rowan. There was one other who stood too, near the front.

Niamh regarded them overtop her spectacles. "The time has come, I take it."

Briar conveyed, quickly as he could, everything he'd just told Rowan.

"The forest is sick," he finished. "It will keep taking tithes from Coill Darraghns until it returns to its former strength."

"Unless Rowan sacrifices himself," Sorcha said. She shook with fury. "And Da did this? He knew?" At Rowan's affirming look, she let out a snarl of frustration. Briar remembered her, on a cold night, admitting that it would have been her, except that she'd given up her father's mantle. She'd chosen a family. She wanted nothing to do with the responsibilities that had torn her father from his. Now they tore her brother away, too.

"I'm not letting it have him." Briar had contemplated their problem on the way here. He had no perfect answer. If they didn't give the forest its sacrifice, then it would continue to savage the town. There were no wards to prevent Linden returning for vengeance.

Briar's whisper sounded loud in the quiet of the church. "I don't have long to live."

Rowan whipped around. *"No."*

"It can have me, but I won't be enough," Briar said. "Not to heal it and erect the wards."

"Briar, *no*." Rowan's voice shook. Softer this time, "No."

Briar met his eyes. Squeezed his hand. "I brought this down on us."

"It's this Linden's doing more than yours," Maebh interrupted. "Knew I didn't like the look of him, mind. I say we throw *him* to the woods."

She wasn't joking. Briar said, "It wouldn't be the same. It has to be a willing sacrifice. That's why the tithes it takes from people only help a little. The forest said there's more powerful magic in a gift than something stolen."

Everyone fell silent. Rowan hadn't looked away from him, his fierce eyes drinking Briar in. It felt sacrilegious in church, where you weren't meant to love anyone more than God.

"I won't let you," he whispered.

Briar said, "You can't stop me."

"No."

The conversation was quiet but impossible to keep private.

Maebh, dusting her hands on her skirt, said, "Well, that settles it. I'll be doing the sacrificing."

"Don't you start," Rowan said.

"You aren't the boss of me. I'm your mammy. Will be always. Hasn't changed now you're grown up."

"You've a lot of years left," said another voice. It was Diarmuid, wearing dusty dungarees just like the day Briar fixed his gate. "Briar's done us a few favors too many in this town, and I don't rightly blame him for this mess. We've not been doing right by our ancestors if the woods are this angry. I'm old. Let it have me."

"That's not—" Briar started to say.

Then another older woman said, "Or me. I'm ancient. Can't get out of bed without effin' and blindin' anyway. Might as well be me."

To Briar's surprise, Aisling spoke next. "I'm not old, but this is home to me. If my man Kenneth died 'cause of this Linden . . . And here I thought he'd left. I'd join him."

Before she could finish, another person stood in a pew and said they wanted to help. And another. Briar suspected they didn't understand it would mean the end of their life, a transformation into something other-worldly like Éibhear. He didn't know how to put voice to all this, but an idea had started to take root in his mind.

Every leaf, every twig, every branch, every tree has magic. But a forest has power beyond your reckoning.

He recalled giving a small flesh tithe and receiving an entire branch of rare lichen. He recalled standing in front of the cameras, knowing he could not face Linden alone, but with all those eyes on him . . .

He had no idea if it would work. He was no master; his apprenticeship hadn't prepared him for a spell of this magnitude. With his curse, he didn't know if he had the reserves of magic necessary.

But if it did work . . .

Everyone argued, everyone with a different take on who deserved more time. Niamh cut through it, her voice echoing off the high eaves.

"I think," she barked, "Briar has an idea."

Had she known? Or only suspected? Was this all part of her prophecies, in the end?

"Will it work?" Briar asked.

"You haven't told us the idea."

Briar released Rowan's hand and drew up the sleeves of his shirt, revealing the marks beneath. "If we all gave a tithe . . . If everyone in the town did willingly, would that be enough?"

Niamh smiled cannily. "One way to find out, boy."

Someone got Briar a piece of charcoal. It felt too light in his hand for what he was about to do. Rowan knelt in front of him first. He trusted Briar, even after everything. The whole town was willing to try. It moved something in Briar that had once felt unshakable. A sharp, painful support strut was now dislodged, but the people around him were enough to keep him standing.

"Should we put it somewhere less visible?" Briar said.

Rowan said, "I'd wear it proudly."

There was no symbol Briar knew for a spell like this, so he invented one. From the hollow of Rowan's clavicle to the bump of his Adam's apple, Briar drew a vertical line. Then two diagonal ones, so it looked like the letter Y. From this, he added branches, making it more treelike. It seemed right. The forest was nothing without its trees, and Coill Darragh was nothing without its people, who were not unlike trees themselves. Sturdy, long-lived, entwined together.

He finished drawing. Rowan stood, and Maebh took his place. Her stern expression softened a little as Briar began to draw.

"If he's forgiven you, then so have I," she said.

Briar blinked back a surge of feeling. "Don't speak or I'll mess it up."

Sorcha came next. Then Connor. Ciara was too young—despite her tantrum, everyone agreed only adults would give a tithe. Then came Diarmuid, Aisling, countless faces Briar recognized from his time in Coill Darragh. Some wore clothes he'd crafted himself, tinged with the familiar touch of his magic. With each tithe drawn, he felt a burgeoning need to tell them how much he'd come to love this place. He sensed they already knew.

Niamh was last. Briar hesitated. "You already tithed to help me."

"No need to twist my arm. I'll give another."

As he drew, many of Briar's burning questions rose to the surface. The wrinkles of her neck made it impossible to make the lines completely straight, though he did his best. "You were wrong," he said. He could at least talk to Niamh about the prophecy, if no one else. As he opened his mouth, he felt magic enfolding them, their words transmitted only to one another. "You told me Linden was the man who'd lead me to success."

"I said nothing of the like."

"You said a man with a mask and a stone heart."

"The prophecy refers to Rowan, not Linden."

Briar stopped drawing. "But he's not masked at *all*. Not even a *little*. He's been himself the whole time. He's not stone-hearted or difficult to read. And besides, your tarot reading said I'd die if I chose him." He paused. "Which, I suppose, I still will."

She waited as he finished a finicky line. "He is different with you than he is with me. Or anyone. So, I suppose, I spoke the prophecy using what I knew of him."

"Well, how's that helpful?" Briar muttered, finishing another stroke. "If I'm the one living the prophecy, shouldn't it account for *my* perspective?"

"Perhaps it did," she said. "It's funny, the way Fate works. I often wonder if it misleads us on purpose. What would have become of us if you hadn't gone to Pentawynn? If you hadn't discovered Linden's true nature? I believe, by the way, you already made the correct choice set out by the cards. You *did* go on a journey with Linden to Pentawynn, though it broke your heart to do it. There's hope yet for your health and prosperity to follow."

Briar could have screamed. He didn't know if he could hold out for that hope, not with his hand shaking so badly he struggled to draw. The pitfalls of her prophecies irked him. "You made it sound like I had to choose one of them as my soulmate. Forever!"

"You interpreted it that way. It's not what I said."

Briar scoffed. "You're saying I was destined to misinterpret it so I could fulfill everything properly. If it was all preordained, why give me a prophecy at all? Why not just let me walk the path set for me?"

"Who knows how much your path diverted as a result of hearing what I saw?"

Briar stopped. He only had one line left, but he was furious. "Niamh. I hate that!"

She laughed.

"It's not funny!" He waited for her to stop laughing. When she did, he decided to have the last word. "I'm not stupid just because I don't see things the same way. You shouldn't be telling your apprentices they're stupid."

She hummed. "You could be right about that."

The tithe was done. Everyone had one. It was time.

As they left the church and walked together through the streets, people who hadn't been at the church joined their throng. The charcoal was in pieces to share between them. People brought more from their homes. Some cast guilty looks at the pastor for missing Sunday Mass, and he said, "Oh, you're forgiven, just come along." They all helped draw the tithes.

By the time they reached the edge of town, their company numbered in the hundreds. It was most of Coill Darragh. Briar thought the air should have carried heavy solemnity or fear. The forest garnered respect, but also suspicion. Instead, everyone seemed electric, all of them filaments in something grand, and Briar was overwhelmed with gratitude to play a part in it.

They'd nearly reached the forest's edge. A portal opened, so close Briar nearly fell into it. He stumbled back, his way barred by Rowan's formidable arm, flung across his chest like armor.

Linden stepped out of the portal.

He looked as pristine as he had on the runway—nothing of the experience besmirched his silky clothes—but his blue eyes were wild, the pupils distant black holes. Atticus stepped out too, back arched, hackles raised along his spine. Before the portal closed, Briar glimpsed the Fairchild manor, the bedroom where he'd lain awake in fear. It was torn asunder, clothes and smashed perfume bottles strewn over the floor. Something he glimpsed lodged a stake in Briar's heart. It could have been a spilled potion, but it could have been blood.

The portal closed. With the wards down, Linden didn't need a bracelet or a marriage to ensure his safety while he pillaged Coill Darragh for all it was worth.

Somehow, the thing that Briar's mind caught on, of all the jagged glass in his relationship with Linden, was only this. "Your parents?"

"They could not bear to see what you'd done to me. They went willingly." From his belt, he pulled a dagger. In the other hand, he held his broomstick of white poplar.

Rowan started to put himself between Briar and Linden, despite Briar's resistance. He was large, had greater reach. Rowan could disarm him. Linden was also outnumbered. His sharp gaze ricocheted between Rowan's and Briar's throats, to the townsfolk, all bearing the same mark. Carefully, he sheathed the dagger in his tithe belt, but his hand lingered there.

"I'm going to finish what I started," he said.

"The hell you are—" Rowan began, but Briar cut him off.

"What for, Linden? It's over. The whole world knows what you did."

"I can fix it!" Linden's words came through bared teeth.

"You don't want to fix it, you want to cover it up and pretend it never happened."

Linden's shoulders rose, stiffening, holding himself back. "You don't understand, it was never meant to go so far. None of my research said anything about curses resulting from wild magic! I know it can be tamed. I have the power now, my parents died to—"

"You killed them! You killed them, and my mother, and Rowan's father, and who knows how many other people while you scrambled to fix it, but you only made it worse!" Briar's chest heaved. At his words, the people of Coill Darragh formed a wall of bodies at Briar's and Rowan's backs.

Linden snarled. "You think I don't understand that? I led my entire family to their deaths. I thought we would find a wealth of magic that could heal. I thought I would change the *world*, but this forest is malignant. It must be destroyed, and with it, all will be rectified, resurrected!"

Linden spoke with the conviction of a lie told so many times it had become ideology, a belief held to so firmly because to accept the reality would be to see himself for the first time, and to loathe what he saw. Briar could imagine a young, idealistic Linden finding rare texts about the power of wild magic. He could see the family, who'd funneled so much of their adulation and energy into this talented witch, rallying behind him in his quest to make their fortune. Charismatic, beautiful, a prodigy. He'd only been a boy, and Briar didn't know if he could blame that boy for his terrible mistakes over the adults who enabled him, but he absolutely faulted the man before him now.

"The forest can't be killed," he said, "not without more suffering, maybe lost lives. Just leave."

The mad look in Linden's eyes subsided. That was somehow worse. He straightened, fixing Briar with the imperious expression he so often wore. "I should have known you were just like the others. Fine. I'll prove it to you."

Before Briar could stop him, Linden took to his broom, Atticus leaping astride it. They sped into the skies above the forest.

Briar took Rowan's hand. "Make a line, everyone! If I can cast the spell all at once . . ."

People crowded nearer, everyone holding a hand or touching a shoulder, everyone connected. Briar looked to his left and right at the lines of people fanning out around him.

A crack of thunder erupted in the twilight. Briar jumped, his hand clenching around Rowan's. The noise had not been another falling tree, and there were no thunderheads in the sky, just a small speck as something—someone—flew above the canopy.

Briar swore under his breath.

Vatii said, "He's using the siphons."

Linden, astride his broomstick, tossed another siphon into the forest below. Another slap of thunder like an explosion. A shower of timber and foliage spat into the air then disintegrated, a chthonic spray of snaking tendrils surging above the canopy before they, too, crumbled to ash. The forest, weakened, couldn't reach Linden. The wards, destroyed, couldn't expel him. He chucked siphons into the densest parts of the forest, destroying its centers of power, leeching magic out of the very ground and using the surplus to continue his path of destruction.

The forest only had one source of power to draw from. Down the line of Coill Darraghns, several voices screamed.

If Briar's plan worked, the wards would be renewed, and Linden would perish in them just like his family had. There weren't any tourists in Coil Darragh now; most had left after the forest's attacks, and those remaining had wardstone bracelets.

As the forest let out another snarl of anguish, and someone cried out as a part of their body was consumed by tree roots, Briar decided he didn't have time to consider the consequences of murder on his mortal soul.

Niamh appeared at his elbow and wrapped a hand around it. "I'll help," she said.

Briar nodded. It would take a lot of magic, and he had so little. He didn't know if he had it in him to tithe so much for a single enchantment, but he had to try.

Closing his eyes, gripping Rowan's hand tight, he let the parched wellspring of magic spread from within. Niamh's power bolstered his own. Not only hers, but the wills of all around him. It felt unlike any spell he'd ever cast. At first familiar, the mark burned its way up his throat to take his tithe, then spread. Echoes of that flame flared and caught from one person to the other, growing into a blaze. It expanded, a scorching swell. When all the tithes were collected, the power held within was so large Briar thought he'd burn up like a sun gone supernova. Niamh and he were the dam holding it at bay, and together they released the flood.

Magic rushed into the ground, finding the roots of the trees, the interconnected web of the forest. The tide of it swept through the woods and filled in all the rotting holes, mending what Linden had broken. A noise of growth replaced the explosions of Linden's siphons. Saplings, sprouted from acorns, matured with miraculous speed.

The power filling Briar fled him, replaced with the agony of his curse like a pike through his chest. Dizzy vertigo. Wetness on his upper lip. It tasted coppery. His body trembled. Rowan had an arm all the way around his middle now. Someone caught Niamh before she fell.

Briar thought, *Was that enough?*

A thunderclap of a siphon, this time, was followed by a brooding silence. Not the crack and groan of trees, but an eerie quiet of preparation. Briar couldn't see anymore, closing his eyes and trying not to scream at the encroaching pain. Rowan kept him from pitching over. He squinted up into the sky, where Linden's figure still darted. He threw siphons into the forest only for it to immediately repair itself. The countless gifted tithes from the town had strengthened it. Now it watched, waited, and brewed its vengeance.

"I have to warn him." Briar's voice came out hoarse. He coughed into his hand. It came away speckled with blood.

"No." Rowan held him tighter. "He'll kill you."

"Right now, the curse might beat him to the punch."

"Don't—" Rowan's voice broke. "Don't say things like that."

"It's true."

"A cure—"

"Is out of our reach," Briar finished.

He pulled Éibhear's journal from within his vest. Beneath their feet, the ground pulsed a warning. Briar showed Rowan the page the journal fell open to naturally from its broken spine.

An Ambrosial Panacea—this brew revitalizes the sick and fatally ill. It reduces or outright erases the effects of curses. The red carnella is a key ingredient that has no substitute.

A flash of hope shone in Rowan's eyes. Yes, they'd found the dried carnellas Gretchen had hid, but . . . Briar pointed to a single line. On the ingredients list, it read:

Three red carnella blooms. Written in parentheses beside it was *(Fresh.)*

Rowan's face fell.

It was wretchedly, painfully unfair. The brewing instructions were otherwise simple. Steep everything in boiling water for two minutes, strain, and drink once temperate. Just a herbal tea. They were in the one place known to grow the plant, but it had long since gone extinct.

All the people of Coill Darragh still crowded the field. Rowan spoke so low that none could hear.

"But I only just got you back."

There were tears in his eyes, and Briar couldn't stand it. Rising on tiptoes, he swiped them away with his thumbs and kissed Rowan. It was meant as a comfort, or maybe a goodbye, but it only made Rowan hold him more tightly.

The ground gave a violent pulse again, and a cold voice broke them apart.

"How touching." Linden hovered on his broom out of reach of anyone below. "It's as though you're wed already. You couldn't even wait until the media circus around my humiliation was over?"

A burning fury kindled in Briar's chest. He wanted to say, *You used me. My mother died because of you. I'll die because of you.* All the guilt he'd felt for loving Rowan instead seemed insignificant by comparison. He could almost laugh. So much heartache over a man who couldn't summon a single ounce of compassion for anything aside from his status.

Briar had already said his piece, and it was on camera.

Rowan's embrace became protective. Once, Briar might have put his hands against Rowan's chest and pushed. He might have thought he had to stand alone.

A dervish of foliage rose in eddies around Linden. His hair whipped in inky strings around him. Still poised, still impassive, like the cameras were watching. But his eyes . . . there was something empty about them now. His parents, gone. Everything he'd worked for, gone. It was his turn to be afraid. Magic seethed within the woods, underground, throbbing through the roots like blood through veins.

Briar didn't want his last act to be just like Éibhear's.

"Linden." Briar's voice was so hoarse, he didn't know if it could be heard. "You need to leave here."

"Do not presume to give me orders after—"

"You'll die!" Briar shouted, his throat raw. "The wards are going to return, and if you're caught in them, nothing will save you."

"Don't be foolish! You think your tiny tithes amount to anything approaching the grand sacrifice Éibhear made?"

"Ours was greater."

"You know nothing of magic. You, who scraped for tithes and struggled through each spell."

Briar didn't let the petty jabs sink deep. "You need to go *now*."

Linden opened his mouth with a rebuttal but paused. Something in the air changed. Murmurs from the crowd of people. The wind ceased to blow. The trees no longer groaned. Even the pulse beneath their feet faded.

Everyone looked at the forest. In the dark of it, something moved.

It seeped from the trees and out of the ground. Its music started low like a drone, then undulated high like cicada song. From every pore of the forest, magic leaked out in a viscous violet tide, until it grew too large for the confines of the wood and, with frightening speed, rushed toward them.

Linden beheld the magic coming for them, getting faster, closer. It rose like a foggy wave, smelling like fungus and soil.

The people of Coill Darragh started to step back, but Briar said, "It won't hurt anyone Coill Darraghn, but it will kill you, Linden! Portal out, now!"

Finally, Linden reached for the pouch at his belt. He worked open the ties, but in his haste he fumbled the bag. The fine dust poured out, spreading in the wind. Linden's face went ashen, watching his only escape slip between his fingers. Normally he could cast spells without touching the tithes, but perhaps even the great Linden Fairchild had his limits. Perhaps, after everything, even he was tired. No portal opened.

Briar lurched forward and tried to snatch some of the powder from the air, but only caught a few granules. He tried using them to open a portal, but the window now shining in the air was too small to use.

The magic swept closer, only meters away. Linden could fly straight out to the border, but his broom wouldn't outstrip what came for him. Briar took the vial of bone powder he'd pinched from Linden's stores. Only a tiny increment remained in the bottom. He tossed what was left at the small portal he'd made, and hoped like mad it would expand.

He hated Linden. He wished to never see him again. But he couldn't bring himself to wish him dead.

The powder evaporated, and the portal grew just wide enough.

"Go!" Briar screamed, and Linden did. There was only the briefest pause. A look of stricken disbelief. Gratitude clouded by mutual loathing.

Then Linden streaked through the portal, low to his broom to make himself small enough to pass. Briar spat, and the portal closed seconds before the magic tide collided with them.

It washed over him in pins and needles. Rowan shuddered. A few of the townsfolk gasped. The wards swept through like a cold current, picking up speed. They flooded the town and rose in walls of light that arced and came together in a dome, protective and bright, before fading into invisibility.

Briar let out a breath. He took a step and crumpled. Brightness invaded his vision, narrowing it into a tunnel. Grass beneath his head. Rowan fumbling through his vest in search of a potion vial. Under his cheek, the earth throbbed with the healthy, beating heart of the forest.

Rowan propped him up. A glass rim touched his lips. He nearly choked. Weakness made it difficult to swallow, but he managed. A second vial followed the first. His vision came back, spotty to begin with, until he could see Rowan's blurry, worried face. He used his sleeve to dab under Briar's nose, which bled again.

Something about Rowan felt different. Briar reached, squinting, touching a hand to his face.

"Rowan, your scar." The filigree white lines still furled up his cheek, but the uneasy aura had vanished. All that remained was the campfire of Rowan's personal aura, the scent of cedar. "It's gone. The curse is gone."

Held in Rowan's arms, Briar could feel his relief. It was short-lived.

"But yours . . ."

Rowan didn't finish. One look at Briar was enough to see that he had one foot in the grave. Vatii crowded into their embrace. Rowan buried his face in Briar's shoulder beside her, his cheeks damp. Briar's vision rippled, and a cold crept through his limbs that Rowan's aura couldn't chase out.

It wasn't fair. They'd lost and found one another. Wounded men whose jagged edges matched up so perfectly that, fit together, the cracks ceased to be there at all. Only to be ripped apart again. Briar felt cold, but the tears in his eyes burned hot.

Small gasps and whispers from the crowd. A ripple of shock. Rowan lifted his head. It took effort, but Briar turned to follow everyone's gazes.

At first, he didn't understand what he saw. The forest bled. A blanket of scarlet seeped out from the trees' edge. Yet it looked . . . dappled and soft. Not liquid, not light, not magic.

Rowan supported him the few yards it took to investigate. As they got closer, hope that felt more like a knot in his throat threatened Briar with tears.

It was a carpet of blooms.

He kneeled to pick one of the red flowers, shaped like a bell.

CHAPTER 31

They returned to Rowan's cottage to brew the potion that would save Briar's life.

Rowan eased him onto the sofa. It required no magic to steep a few herbs, and he insisted on Briar resting. Left to sink into the cushions, it was the first moment Briar had to take stock of his body's various aches, and there were many. His joints protested. His blood pumped like poison through his veins. Grit coated his throat like sandpaper.

But he was alive, and safe, and home.

It might not be the last they heard of Linden. No doubt, he'd go to great lengths to defame Briar and restore his own reputation. There would be an investigation. Whatever proof Briar could provide, he would. Otherwise, he had every intention of sitting here for as long as he wanted.

Which was not long. He cast a look toward the kitchen. Aches and pains aside, the sofa was not his ideal source of comfort. Bracing a hand on the arm, he got to his feet and shuffled down the hall. He found Rowan, back turned as he poured steaming water into a mug. Briar came up behind him and looped both arms around his ribs. With a hand over Rowan's chest, he felt the steady beat of his heart. With his forehead nestled in the valley of his spine, the aura that had drawn him in from the start soothed the ache in his head. He took a deep breath.

One of Rowan's hands covered his. "You should be resting."

"Mm-hm."

"Are you all right?"

"I just . . ." Briar said, "needed this."

"This?"

"You."

Rowan turned and bundled him close, kissing the top of his head. "I never left."

Briar pressed his forehead into Rowan's chest instead. "I have to make the test thing. The test to see if I'm still cursed."

"What does it need?"

"Honeysuckle pollen."

"I'll get it."

Rowan went outside to fetch some from the garden while the potion steeped. After, they returned to the living room and sat on the sofa. The potion, smelling sweet and floral, was too hot to drink. Briar snuck under Rowan's arm while they waited for it to cool. They needed a shower, a change of clothes, a long night's sleep. His mind trailed along these thoughts and landed on the next morning, waking to Rowan's breath rising and falling under his ear. He choked on things unsaid. Rowan had asked if he was all right, but . . .

"Are *we* all right?" Briar said.

Rowan didn't answer. Briar's heart thudded, and he looked up to see Rowan looking back. The crease of pained worry on his brow yielded to a softer expression. "We will be," he said.

"I've put us through hell."

His smile was almost mocking now. "You can't take the whole of the credit."

"Um," Briar deadpanned, "I think I can."

Rowan shook his head. "I knew how I felt about you from the start. I was too much a coward to tell you. Maybe if I'd told you sooner . . . well."

Briar reached up to touch the edge of Rowan's jaw, now fuzzy after several days without shaving. He didn't think words could mend everything, but he wanted to be open. "I said what I did because I really thought I could save us both on my own." He swallowed the lump in his throat and pressed on. "The best thing for me was coming to Coill Darragh and finding you. I can't—I can't imagine going back to the way things were before we met. Ever since Mum died, I've felt . . . I don't know. Like I had to prove I mattered to the whole world before I got snuffed out of it. But you always made me feel like I mattered." A pause to get his voice under control. "I just feel stronger—everything's just *better* with you. I was such an idiot. I don't want you to ever doubt how much I love you."

Rowan listened. Then he gently tipped Briar's chin and kissed him. It was comforting, languorous after the long day they'd had. He pulled back to tuck Briar's hair behind his ear.

"Briar." Still, the way Rowan said his name was a spell all its own. "I'm not the best with words, but I'll say this. No hurt you caused is one I'll hold on to. I was more scared of losing you than getting my heart broke." He regarded the steaming mug on the coffee table. "I'd not waste a stolen minute I have with you ruminating."

"I don't want to just sweep it under the rug. I wish there was a spell to undo it. Something I could do."

"You can drink this for a start." Rowan picked up the mug, now cooled enough to drink.

Briar cupped it in his hands, bringing it to his lips. He sipped, chamomile, honey, and the carnella blooms—with their earthy taste—smooth on his tongue. Warmth spread gradually through him like liquid sunlight. He took another drink, this one easier to swallow than the first. Though his aches and tight muscles remained, a balm of comfort worked its way through him.

He set the mug down and picked away one of the scabs left by the forest's thorns. He let his blood drop into the glass of water and honeysuckle pollen. They waited. Briar pressed a hand to his chest and felt something subtly shift. Like a stake between his ribs had eroded enough to slip free. It had been there so long that the relief at its removal almost hurt. The glass, however, remained clear.

"It didn't—?" Rowan's voice snagged. He was still watching the glass. It hadn't turned color.

Briar frowned. His breath came easier. Shadows no longer crept into his vision. So why . . .

It started as a speck of sky in the clear liquid. A spiral of blue ink gradually swirling outward until the whole glass was the color of a robin's egg.

Rowan's jaw slackened with a huffed breath of disbelief and elation. Briar broke out in a grin. He flexed his fingers and, to test his strength, stood. Trembling and precarious, but he stood and knew he wasn't about to fall.

"Rowan . . . Rowan, I think it—"

Rowan leapt up and seized him around the middle, spinning him, nearly kicking over the coffee table, hugging him so tightly that unhealed injuries twinged in reminder. Briar laughed. Then burst into tears. The happy sort, which was new. He buried his hands in Rowan's hair and kissed him in a senseless euphoria. It was a special kind of gift to kiss and not wonder if this one would be the last.

All the trouble he'd caused, the whole tangled mess, Briar could handle it now. He had the time. Rowan pulled back and looked at him with fathomless hope.

"Now we have our lives back, what should we do?"

Briar drew him close and said, "Do you still have that ring?"

EPILOGUE

SEVEN WEEKS LATER

One last loop of red thread, and the string of bell-shaped flowers was done. Briar tied it off and set the embroidery hoop on his lap to admire his work. Along the chalky blue of the ribbon, he'd stitched runes for love and courage, delicate berries, white baby's breath, the leaves of rowan and briar trees, and lastly, strings of carnellas. Symbols that were woven into the fabric of his life.

It was the third he'd decorated. Another in white, the second cornflower blue.

Vatii hopped along the arm of the lounge, eyeing it sideways. Her feathers, returned to their iridescent glory, gleamed in the early dawn light.

A creak of the ladder from the loft, and Rowan leaned over the back of the chair to see Briar's work. "It's early for you to be up yet."

"I'm down to the wire finishing this," Briar said. "But it's done." He loosened the screw of the embroidery hoop and spread the ribbon across his hands.

"It's perfect." Rowan took Briar's hand, the one wearing two rings nested atop each other, and kissed his knuckles. "I should get ready. Sorcha will be here soon."

Briar tilted his head back, looking at Rowan upside down. "Hey." Rowan turned around. "After today, you'll be my husband."

Rowan returned to him, this time to kiss him full on the mouth.

A flurry of preparations followed once Sorcha arrived, Ciara in tow. Briar found himself shoving a croissant in his mouth while Sorcha plaited a ribbon into his hair, teasing the rest. Ciara showed Briar a dance she'd made up, twirling around in her dress of white tulle.

Past noon, the carriage arrived, driven by Diarmuid with his Clydesdale at the yoke. Sorcha helped pile Briar into it. Only then did he begin to feel nervous. Vatii sat on his shoulder, and they watched the town pass them. The forest canopy crowning the rooftops was protective instead of looming. Speckles of red dotted the fields.

It would be some time before Coill Darragh accepted tourists again. For now, Briar harvested carnellas in small amounts to ship to people suffering from Bowen's Wane. He and Rowan ventured into the woods sometimes. They were careful, listening and wondering when it would ask for something in return. So far, it hadn't, content with the hundreds of tithes given. These days, their postbox was often stuffed with letters and parcels from people cured of their curses. Some expressed gratitude, others included small tithes or gifts, despite any insistence that they weren't necessary.

Linden himself had been tried and convicted for his crimes. He'd denied them all the way to his prison cell, where he would remain until he found a means to leverage himself free. Perhaps he would not own up to his mistakes, but it brought Briar satisfaction to know the suffering wouldn't pass through generations any longer.

Briar endeavored to forget him, which for men like Linden, was perhaps the worst fate of all.

Briar's magic still took an effort to summon. He got headaches. Sometimes, his muscles seized. But death no longer dogged him, and when the long-term effects of his curse made him tire, Rowan was there. His family. The people of Coill Darragh, too.

As they got closer to the town square, people stopped to wave or take photos of the carriage. Briar waved back, basking in the attention. Ciara bounced in Sorcha's lap, blowing kisses out the window. Some of the townsfolk had their party dresses on. Some of those dresses Briar had made himself. Everyone had the same mark on their throats, one Briar shared.

Sorcha gave Briar's arm a jab, her cane between her knees. She'd crafted a cane for Briar, too, to use on his bad days. Her leg was mostly healed, but some damage was permanent. "Are you nervous?"

"A bit," Briar admitted. "I'll feel better when I see him."

"*He's* not about to leave you waiting at the altar."

"It's not that." Sorcha still teased him about the tumultuous beginning of his relationship with Rowan, though now it was in good humor. He bit down on a smile. "I just always feel better when I see him."

"I was harder on you than I should have been, back then."

"You were looking out for him."

"Just let me apologize, won't you? He's my baby brother, and I was fairly pissed with you for hurting him, but if I'm being honest, I was angrier with myself. I was the eldest. I abdicated responsibility as Keeper. All the worst things that happened to him happened because of that. So I saw you made him happy, and when you stopped, I felt guilty. I took it out on you. All right?"

Briar smirked. "All right. But you've made it up to me by doing my hair this morning."

"Ah, sure."

They arrived at the church, its big oak doors open. Briar waited at the bottom of the steps while Ciara skipped ahead with her basket of petals. Sorcha made her way down the aisle in her daughter's wake.

It was a small wedding party, made smaller by the fact Briar didn't have his mother there.

At his cue, he started up the steps. The bright sun outside meant his eyes took time to adjust inside, to the pews on either side filled with friends and family. Vatii swooped overhead, distributing more flower petals. The turn of everyone's cheek to look at him made Briar glow, but not as much as Rowan awaiting him. The crisp charcoal of his suit, the blue flowers in his pocket, the close cut of his beard—every inch the rugged man Briar loved.

The dress Briar wore had taken him the better part of a month to design. It was a satin gown with a simple front of lace and a neckline that dipped low enough to see the tithe on his chest made to keep Rowan safe. Pearl drop earrings and heels Briar would be kicking off very soon completed his look. He'd done it all thinking about that moment when Rowan had walked into a tent, looked at Briar, and couldn't stop looking.

Rowan looked at him now with unrestrained joy, better than that look from the tent. He wiped hastily at his eyes with the back of a hand, and Briar couldn't stand the long, slow walk down the aisle anymore. He picked up his train and ran.

It wasn't very traditional, leaping into his groom's arms and kissing him while the priest threw up his hands in exasperation, but Briar wore a dress so he obviously didn't care much for traditions when they didn't suit him.

Rowan didn't look away from his groom during the ceremony. Nor did Briar, captivated and protected by Rowan's gaze. At the edge of their shared gaze were three empty spots in the front pew, reserved with chalkboards for three people who couldn't be there. Éibhear. Eira, Briar's mother. And Gretchen.

Maebh and Sorcha joined them for the hand fasting. With the embroidered ribbons, they braided Briar's and Rowan's linked hands. The priest recited a poem about two trees grown side by side whose roots were entangled in the same way.

The short, sweet ceremony was followed by an extravagant amount of food, drink, and revelry. Maebh gave a speech that started with sarcastic rebukes of Briar's character then ended with a tearful confession that "Anyone who makes my son so blisteringly happy can't be all bad, even if you are an absolute cabbage and a diva." Briar fed Rowan from his plate, and vice versa. They danced to open the floor, walking slow circles to a tune played by one of Rowan's many cousins. Vatii gorged herself on appetizers and swooped among the dancers. Little Ciara dragged Rowan out of his shell to spin her around the floor.

No one shied away from him. No one cast him wary looks. They linked arms with him and didn't flinch.

Finola was there, looking stunning in buttercup yellow. She insisted Briar should create a line all his own for next year's runway. That she'd count upon it.

The evening seemed to span a decade and only a minute, the entirety of it focused on this singular feeling that Briar had sorely missed since his mother passed: a sense that he belonged, and he could rest his head over Rowan's heart that night and find himself at home.

The revelry went late, but it was latest for Rowan and Briar, who, after finally thanking and saying goodbye to everyone, returned to the cottage. Briar picked his way down the path with his shoes in one hand and his train in the other. Tired enough to trip, but Rowan swept him up and carried him the rest of the way.

At the reception, they'd stolen moments to whisper private jokes about how they'd be too dead on their feet by night's end to bother with removing their clothes, much less anything else, but in unbuttoning Rowan's shirt and pulling loose his tie, Briar found a reserve of energy he hadn't known he possessed. Months ago, he wouldn't have been able to stand long enough at the altar to say "I do."

He said with conspiratorial delight, "You're my husband now."

And Rowan breathed "husband" into his ear.

Sunrise threaded golden fingers through the curtains by the time they lay still with sweat cooling on their skin. Briar lay in the cradle of Rowan's arm and traced the scar that no longer pained him. He kissed it, then kissed Rowan. Then his stomach growled and ruined the moment.

Rowan said, "Should I make breakfast?"

"We haven't even slept."

"Ah, sure, but who needs it?"

Which was how they ended up at the breakfast bar, Rowan frying eggs and Briar wearing one of his shirts just like that first night he stayed over.

"Could you get the bread from the box?" Rowan said.

Briar had been looking at some of the photos people had taken of them from the wedding. He opened the breadbox and froze. Inside was a golden envelope. He pulled it out, looking at Rowan accusingly. "What is this?"

"A wedding gift."

"We promised we wouldn't! We have enough gifts from everyone anyway—"

He shrugged. "I cheated. It's for the both of us."

Briar glared.

"Open it."

He relented, sliding a finger through the seal. Inside were two tickets. He fanned them in his hands, a firework of bliss in his chest.

"A honeymoon in Pentawynn?"

Rowan was watching him, his brows raised in uncertainty. "Is it . . . too soon?"

Briar had told Rowan of what little he'd seen. He'd talked about the beauty of the skyline from the water, the mix of people thronging through the streets, the lights and crystal spires, all the things he'd only seen for a single carriage ride spent feeling sorry for himself and wishing Rowan were there.

"Marry me," he blurted.

Rowan's uncertainty melted. "But we're already married."

Briar flung his arms around Rowan's neck, kissing every inch of his face. "Again," he said. "Marry me *again*."

Warm brown eyes shone and fluttered closed.

"As many times as you like."

ACKNOWLEDGMENTS

My family name, McGonegal, is Irish, but I wouldn't visit Ireland myself until 2016. Cait, Sinead, and Ger introduced me to the food. (And I quote, "It's like English food, but good.") They taught me about Irish superstitions and slang. They took me to Tato Park. While walking around Dublin, Ger pointed to the walls and columns of the General Post Office, where there were chunks gouged out of the stone. He said, "Those are bullet holes from the Easter Rising."

It struck me in the moment how close the past felt to the present, like they were layered thinly over each other. It sparked an idea about a small Irish town wearing the scars of its magical history, auras of the past bleeding into the present, and the witch who could read them. That idea became the book you're holding.

It's my first published book, so it has the longest list of helpers. If I had the time and a better memory, I'd go as far back as the schoolteachers who encouraged my writing when I didn't know if I was any good at it. As is, I've been really blessed to find such amazing friends and critique partners, and I will die of shame if I forget anyone, so here we go.

I want to start by thanking Cait. We joke that without you I'd have gotten the fish pie recipe wrong, but we both know you're responsible for far more than that. You're truly the Wonderbra of support. Likewise, Sinead, Ger, and the beasties: thank you for being my Irish adopted family.

There are many friends without whom I would not be the writer I am today. I want to thank Sam for the hours and hours of role-playing our deranged, morally gray idiots, and for lending me your encyclopedic knowledge when I needed someone to consult on science things. Natalie and Manuela, thank you for all those evenings spent camping in Grand Bend plotting our new ideas together and getting hunted for sport by raccoons. Becca, thank you for all the brainstorming sessions spent laughing while we workshopped a ridiculous joke we wanted to include in our books and comics. Monica Bacatelo Guerra, thank you for reading the first draft, which was the literary equivalent of raw chicken, and telling me how to cook it rather than binning it. Sio, thank you for the hours of untangling plot holes created by annoying magical prophecies. Cameron Montague Taylor and August, thank you for listening to me ramble like the Pepe Silvia meme when I realized Briar's mom should be dead from the start. I also want to thank Avrah C Baren, Steve Westenra, Erin, and Keiron for all the chats, cheerleading, and generally just being awesome people.

Special thanks to my Pitch Wars mentors, Mary Ann Marlowe and Laura Elizabeth, for their invaluable advice about writing, the publishing industry, and life in general.

The majority of this book was written during lockdown, when I needed friends outside my writer-life more than ever. Thank you to Steph, Kat, Elliot, and Alexis for always giving me a reprieve and reminding me what's most important (watching indie lesbian films and being a human jungle gym for children). To Helen, Jonny, Ghost, and Nantoka: thanks for the D&D obsession. Aidan, thank you for sharing your own wonderful D&D stories with me and for always checking in.

So many people helped transform this book from a Google doc into a real thing. I want to thank my incredible agent, Ellen Goff, for being the best advocate and never giving up on this book over our long submission period. Thanks to my editor, Melissa Frain, for your thoughtful, enthusiastic editing eye. I also want to thank my copy editor, Crystal Wang, and my proofreader, Felix Chau Bradley, for their attention to detail. Thanks to Annie Stone for being the first person to pick up the book up and say, "This is the one." To Leah Zink and Ryan Willwerscheid: thank you for giving me the opportunity to illustrate my own cover. Thanks also to Cass Dolan, Nicole Antos, Stephanie Beard, Taylor Bryon, and my entire team at Podium for everything you did to take this from my hard drive to bookshelves. Lastly, to James Joseph: thank you for your brilliant narration, bringing Briar to life in the audiobook.

Finally, a huge thank you to my family. Mum, Dad, Shannon, Jenna, Marney and Dunc, thanks for supporting me both through transition and my extended hermit-writer-life. I love you.

ABOUT THE AUTHOR

Alistair Reeves is a romantasy author whose stories feature messy queers and morally gray characters. His influences range from video games to Chinese danmei, and when he's not writing, he can be found playing *Dungeons & Dragons* or tending to his frankly absurd collection of succulents. Born in Canada, Reeves now lives in England, indulging his addictions to hot beverages and rainy weather.

DISCOVER
STORIES UNBOUND

PodiumAudio.com

Printed in the USA
CPSIA information can be obtained
at www.ICGtesting.com
JSHW021545171024
71842JS00001B/1